BILLY BUDD
& Other Stories

BILLY BUDD
& Other Stories

———————— ◆ ————————

Herman Melville

WORDSWORTH CLASSICS

For my husband
ANTHONY JOHN RANSON
with love from your wife, the publisher.
Eternally grateful for your unconditional love.

Readers who are interested in other titles from
Wordsworth Editions are invited to visit our website at
www.wordsworth-editions.com

For our latest list and a full mail-order service, contact
Bibliophile Books, 5 Datapoint, South Crescent, London E16 4TL
TEL: +44 (0)20 7474 2474 FAX: +44 (0)20 7474 8589
ORDERS: orders@bibliophilebooks.com
WEBSITE: www.bibliophilebooks.com

This edition first published 1998 by Wordsworth Editions Limited
8B East Street, Ware, Hertfordshire SG12 9HJ

ISBN   978 1 85326 749 9

Text © Wordsworth Editions Limited 1998

Wordsworth® is a registered trade mark of
Wordsworth Editions Limited

Wordsworth Editions
is the company founded in 1987 by
MICHAEL TRAYLER

Typeset in Great Britain by Antony Gray
Printed and bound by Clays Ltd, St Ives plc

CONTENTS

INTRODUCTION

Though now celebrated as one of the giants of American literature, Herman Melville was the victim of contemporary misunderstanding. His early works, such as Typee of 1846 and Omoo of 1847, had provoked controversy even as they won him popular acclaim. Loosely based on Melville's own exotic experiences abroad and at sea, the novels reflected a sympathy with pagan tribes that went beyond the Romantic concept of the 'noble savage', and was perceived to imply a certain contempt for Western attitudes and practices. In 1851 Moby Dick, which is now regarded as possibly the greatest work of American fiction, was not well received. Its many complexities and metaphysical concerns were largely unappreciated, and perhaps fuelled the view of Melville as an eccentric. Pierre, the psychological and moral study based on his own childhood and published the following year, was virtually reviled. His reputation fast fading, Melville turned his hand to the short story. With the exception of Billy Budd, he wrote all the stories reproduced here during the mid 1850s for magazines such as Putnam's Monthly, Harper's and the English periodical Bentley's Miscellany.

Despite the indifference of nineteenth-century critics, posthumous reassessment of Melville's work brought long overdue recognition, and his stories are now esteemed as classics of the first order. He writes of adventures at sea, of other countries and cultures, of homely incidents and extraordinary events, all acutely observed and recounted with singular imagery in vivid, poetic language. All Melville's best work functions on more than one level, and the tales presented here are rich with symbolism and mystical depth that is always felt, if not always open to easy explanation.

Disguise is a deliberate part of Melville's art. Writing mostly of his personal concerns (though public fear is a factor that charges many of his tales, particularly that fear of anarchy that had been engendered by the French Revolution), he adopts a variety of personae when writing in the first person. And just as he blurs his identity, he uses allegory consciously as a means of masking his true intentions, subject matter and opinions. Allegory is the perfect vehicle for the artistic expression of Melville's preoccupation with the conflict between appearance and reality that underlies so much of human intercourse.

Melville's subjects are diverse, but his fundamental concern is with human nature and human relationships, and his insight is unerring. In Bartleby the Scrivener he combines pathos and humour to create an unforgettable fable where the curious stubbornness of an apparently inconsequential individual is seen as both a manipulative force and an existential act. 'Poor Man's Pudding and Rich Man's Crumbs' are companion pieces that show Melville most effectively coupling a pair of sharply contrasting images to illuminate contradictions of human behaviour and ambivalence in the human lot. 'The Paradise of Bachelors and The Tartarus of Maids' is another such pair, where in the second piece, allegory is very specifically used to treat a subject which demanded camouflage. Generally, the clues to allegorical significance in Melville's work are well hidden, and scholars have written fascinating articles detecting and analysing his symbolism. Yet there are pointers for the astute reader who would do well to take note of any quotations, book titles, echoes or allusions to other authors found in the narratives, as these are often vital clues to the real interest beneath the surface of a story.

'The Lightning Rod Man', 'I and My Chimney', 'The Apple-Tree Table' and 'The Piazza' (written as the title piece for a collection of some of the Putnam's stories published in 1856 as Piazza Tales) are all stories where ambiguous symbols create subtexts that are open to a variety of interpretations. The much longer tale 'Benito Cereno' is a sinister drama set at sea just off the coast of Peru, where concealment is central to the story on every plane, and again, symbols are multi-faceted. A sense of imminent danger pervades in the highly charged atmosphere that Melville so brilliantly establishes through the eyes of the naïve, amiably racist Yankee captain, Amasa Delano. Throughout an intricately constructed story where nothing is what it seems, there are clear indications that Melville is using symbolism to obscure the many contradictions and the probing questions that seethe within his presentation of intransigent white revenge. This is one of Melville's most haunting works.

The novella Billy Budd, Foretopman was not written until some twenty years after the other stories included here and remained unpublished until 1924, thirty-three years after Melville's death in 1891. It is a small masterpiece, composed with unexpected economy. Setting his story in 1797, Melville exploits the tension of this period following the mutinies in the English fleet during the war with France. With three central characters of symbolic significance, he creates a tale of satanic treachery, tragedy and great pathos that explores human relationships, the meaning of life and destiny, and the inherently ambiguous nature of man-made justice. Enriched with metaphysical implications, Billy Budd achieves a heroic grandeur that has inspired the making of a film and the writing of an acclaimed opera of the same title by Benjamin Britten.

Melville's admiration for his friend Nathaniel Hawthorne had a profound influence on the subtleties of his writing. Yet he has other qualities that are quite unique. Many of his stories share themes that derive from his own peculiar experience, and have the same penetration, vivid pictorial quality and poetic force. He writes with an energy that is always compelling, and shows a humanity and genuine egalitarianism that was remarkable in his time and has an enduring resonance.

BARTLEBY THE SCRIVENER

I AM A RATHER elderly man. The nature of my avocations, for the last thirty years, has brought me into more than ordinary contact with what would seem an interesting and somewhat singular set of men, of whom, as yet, nothing, that I know of, has ever been written – I mean, the law-copyists, or scriveners. I have known very many of them, professionally and privately, and, if I pleased, could relate divers histories, at which good-natured gentlemen might smile and sentimental souls might weep. But I waive the biographies of all other scriveners, for a few passages in the life of Bartleby, who was a scrivener, the strangest I ever saw, or heard of. While of other law-copyists I might write the complete life, of Bartleby nothing of that sort can be done. I believe that no materials exist for a full and satisfactory biography of this man. It is an irreparable loss to literature. Bartleby was one of those beings of whom nothing is ascertainable, except from the original sources, and, in his case, those are very small. What my own astonished eyes saw of Bartleby, *that* is all I know of him, except, indeed, one vague report, which will appear in the sequel.

Ere introducing the scrivener, as he first appeared to me, it is fit I make some mention of myself, my *employés*, my business, my chambers and general surroundings, because some such description is indispensable to an adequate understanding of the chief character about to be presented. Imprimis: I am a man who, from his youth upwards, has been filled with a profound conviction that the easiest way of life is the best. Hence, though I belong to a profession proverbially energetic and nervous, even to turbulence, at times, yet nothing of that sort have I ever suffered to invade my peace. I am one of those unambitious lawyers who never address a jury, or in any way draw down public applause; but, in the cool tranquillity of a snug retreat, do a snug business among rich men's bonds, and mortgages, and title-deeds. All who know me, consider me an eminently *safe* man. The late John Jacob Astor, a personage little given to poetic enthusiasm, had no hesitation in pronouncing my first grand point to be prudence; my next, method. I do not speak it in vanity, but simply record the fact, that I was not unemployed in my profession by the late John Jacob Astor; a name which, I admit, I love to repeat; for it hath a rounded and orbicular sound to it, and rings like unto bullion. I will freely add, that I was not insensible to the late John Jacob Astor's good opinion.

Some time prior to the period at which this little history begins, my avocations had been largely increased. The good old office, now extinct in the State of New York, of a Master in Chancery, had been conferred upon me. It was not a very arduous office, but very pleasantly remunerative. I seldom lose my temper; much more seldom indulge in dangerous indignation at wrongs and outrages; but I must be permitted to be rash here and declare that I consider the sudden and violent abrogation of the office of Master in Chancery, by the new constitution, as a premature act; inasmuch as I had counted upon a life-lease of the profits, whereas I only received those of a few short years. But this is by the way.

My chambers were upstairs, at No. — Wall Street. At one end, they looked upon the white wall of the interior of a spacious sky-light shaft, penetrating the building from top to bottom. This view might have been considered rather tame than otherwise, deficient in what landscape painters call 'life'. But, if so, the view from the other end of my chambers offered, at least, a contrast, if nothing more. In that direction, my windows commanded an unobstructed view of a lofty brick wall, black by age and everlasting shade; which wall required no spy-glass to bring out its lurking beauties, but, for the benefit of all near-sighted spectators, was pushed up to within ten feet of my window-panes. Owing to the great height of the surrounding buildings, and my chambers being on the second floor, the interval between this wall and mine not a little resembled a huge square cistern.

At the period just preceding the advent of Bartleby, I had two persons as copyists in my employment, and a promising lad as an office-boy. First, Turkey; second, Nippers; third, Ginger Nut. These may seem names the like of which are not usually found in the Directory. In truth, they were nicknames, mutually conferred upon each other by my three clerks, and were deemed expressive of their respective persons or characters. Turkey was a short, pursy Englishman, of about my own age – that is, somewhere not far from sixty. In the morning, one might say, his face was of a fine florid hue, but after twelve o'clock, meridian – his dinner hour – it blazed like a grate full of Christmas coals; and continued blazing – but, as it were, with a gradual wane – till six o'clock, p.m., or thereabouts; after which, I saw no more of the proprietor of the face, which, gaining its meridian with the sun, seemed to set with it, to rise, culminate, and decline the following day, with the like regularity and undiminished glory. There are many singular coincidences I have known in the course of my life, not the least among which was the fact that exactly when Turkey displayed his fullest beams from his red and radiant countenance, just then, too, at that critical moment, began the daily period when I considered his business capacities as seriously disturbed for the remainder of the twenty-four hours. Not that he was absolutely idle, or averse to business then; far from it. The difficulty was, he was apt to be altogether too energetic. There was a strange, inflamed, flurried, flighty recklessness of activity about him. He would be incautious in dipping his pen into his inkstand. All his blots upon my documents were dropped there after twelve o'clock, meridian. Indeed, not only would he be reckless, and sadly given to making blots in the afternoon, but, some days, he went further, and was rather noisy. At such times too, his face flamed with augmented blazonry, as if cannel coal had been heaped on anthracite. He made an unpleasant racket with his chair; spilled his sand-box; in mending his pens, impatiently split them all to pieces, and threw them on the floor in a sudden passion; stood up and leaned over his table, boxing his papers about in a most indecorous manner, very sad to behold in an elderly man like him. Nevertheless, as he was in many ways a most valuable person to me, and all the time before twelve o'clock, meridian, was the quickest, steadiest creature, too, accomplishing a great deal of work in a style not easily to be matched – for these reasons, I was willing to overlook his eccentricities, though, indeed, occasionally, I remonstrated with him. I did this very gently, however, because, though the civilest, nay, the blandest and most reverential of men in the morning, yet, in the afternoon, he was disposed, upon provocation, to be slightly rash with his tongue – in fact, insolent. Now, valuing his morning services as I did, and resolved not to lose them – yet, at the same time, made uncomfortable by his inflamed ways after twelve o'clock – and being a man of peace, unwilling by my admonitions to call forth unseemly retorts from him, I took upon me, one Saturday noon (he was always worse on Saturdays), to hint to him, very kindly, that, perhaps, now that he was growing old, it might be well to abridge his labours; in short, he need not come to my chambers after twelve o'clock, but, dinner over, had best go home to his lodgings, and rest himself till teatime. But no; he insisted upon his afternoon devotions. His countenance became intolerably fervid as he oratorically assured me – gesticulating with a long ruler at the other end of the room – that if his services in the morning were useful, how indispensable, then, in the afternoon?'

'With submission, sir,' said Turkey, on this occasion, 'I consider myself your right-hand man. In the morning I but marshal and deploy my columns; but in the afternoon I put myself at their head, and gallantly charge the foe, thus' – and he made a violent thrust with the ruler.

'But the blots, Turkey,' intimated I.

'True; but, with submission, sir, behold these hairs! I am getting old. Surely, sir, a blot or two of a warm afternoon is not to be severely urged against grey hairs. Old age – even if it blot the page – is honourable. With submission, sir, we *both* are getting old.'

This appeal to my fellow-feeling was hardly to be resisted. At all events, I saw that go he would not. So, I made up my mind to let him stay, resolving, nevertheless, to see to it that during the afternoon he had to do with my less important papers.

Nippers, the second on my list, was a whiskered, sallow and, upon the whole, rather piratical-looking young man, of about five-and-twenty. I always deemed him the victim of two evil powers – ambition and indigestion. The ambition was evinced by a certain impatience of the duties of a mere copyist, an unwarrantable usurpation of strictly professional affairs, such as the original drawing up of legal documents. The indigestion seemed betokened in an occasional nervous testiness and grinning irritability, causing the teeth to audibly grind together over mistakes committed in copying; unnecessary maledictions, hissed, rather than spoken, in the heat of business; and especially by a continual discontent with the height of the table where he worked. Though of a very ingenious mechanical turn, Nippers could never get this table to suit him. He put chips under it, blocks of various sorts, bits of pasteboard, and at last went so far as to attempt an exquisite adjustment, by final pieces of folded blotting-paper. But no invention would answer. If, for the sake of easing his back, he brought the table-lid at a sharp angle well up towards his chin, and wrote there like a man using the steep roof of a Dutch house for his desk, then he declared that it stopped the circulation in his arms. If now he lowered the table to his waistbands, and stooped over it in writing, then there was a sore aching in his back. In short, the truth of the matter was, Nippers knew not what he wanted. Or, if he wanted anything, it was to be rid of a scrivener's table altogether. Among the manifestations of his diseased ambition was a fondness he had for receiving visits from certain ambiguous-looking fellows in seedy coats, whom he called his clients. Indeed, I was aware that not only was he, at times, considerable of a ward-politician, but he occasionally did a little business at the Justices' courts, and was not unknown on the steps of the Tombs. I have good reason to believe, however, that one individual who called upon him at my chambers, and who, with a grand air, he insisted was his client, was no other than a dun, and the alleged title-deed, a bill. But, with all his failings, and the annoyances he caused me, Nippers, like his compatriot Turkey, was a very useful man to me; wrote a neat, swift hand; and, when he chose, was not deficient in a gentlemanly sort of deportment. Added to this, he always dressed in a gentlemanly sort of way; and so, incidentally, reflected credit upon my chambers. Whereas, with respect to Turkey, I had much ado to keep him from being a reproach to me. His clothes were apt to look oily and smell of eating-houses. He wore his pantaloons very loose and baggy in summer. His coats were execrable; his hat not to be handled. But while the hat was a thing of indifference to me, inasmuch as his natural civility and deference, as a dependent Englishman, always led him to doff it the moment he entered the room, yet his coat was another matter. Concerning his coats, I reasoned with him; but with no effect. The truth was, I suppose, that a man with so small an income could not afford to sport such a lustrous face and a lustrous coat at one and the same time. As Nippers once observed, Turkey's money went chiefly for red ink. One winter day, I presented Turkey with a highly respectable looking coat of my own – a padded grey coat, of a most comfortable warmth, and which buttoned straight up from the knee to the neck. I thought Turkey would appreciate the favour, and abate his rashness and obstreperousness of afternoons. But no; I verily believe that buttoning himself up in so downy and blanket-like a coat had a pernicious effect upon him – upon the same principle that too much oats are bad for horses. In fact, precisely as a rash, restive horse is said to feel his oats, so Turkey felt his coat. It made him insolent. He was a man whom prosperity harmed.

Though, concerning the self-indulgent habits of Turkey, I had my own private surmises, yet, touching Nippers, I was well persuaded that, whatever might be his faults in other respects, he was, at least, a temperate young man. But, indeed, nature herself seemed to have been his vintner, and, at his birth, charged him so thoroughly with an irritable, brandy-like disposition, that all subsequent potations were needless. When I consider how, amid the stillness of my chambers, Nippers would sometimes impatiently rise from his seat, and stooping over his table, spread his arms wide apart, seize the whole desk and move it and jerk it with a grim, grinding motion on the floor, as if the table were a perverse voluntary agent, intent on thwarting and vexing him, I plainly perceive that, for Nippers, brandy-and-water were altogether superfluous.

It was fortunate for me that, owing to its peculiar cause – indigestion – the irritability and consequent nervousness of Nippers were mainly observable in the morning, while in the afternoon he was comparatively mild. So that, Turkey's paroxysms only coming on about twelve o'clock, I never had to do with their eccentricities at one time. Their fits relieved each others like guards. When Nippers's was on, Turkey's was off; and vice versa. This was a good natural arrangement, under the circumstances.

Ginger Nut, the third on my list, was a lad, some twelve years old. His father was a carman, ambitious of seeing his son on the bench instead of a cart, before he died. So he sent him to my office, as student at law, errand-boy, cleaner and sweeper, at the rate of one dollar a week. He had a little desk to himself, but he did not use it much. Upon inspection, the drawer exhibited a great array of the shells of various sorts of nuts. Indeed, to this quick-witted youth, the whole noble science of the law was contained in a nutshell. Not the least among the employments of Ginger Nut, as well as one which he discharged with the most alacrity, was his duty as cake and apple purveyor for Turkey and Nippers. Copying law-papers being proverbially a dry, husky sort of business, my two scriveners were fain to moisten their mouths very often with Spitzenbergs, to be had at the numerous stalls nigh the custom house and post-office. Also, they sent Ginger Nut very frequently for that peculiar cake – small, flat, round, and very spicy – after which he had been named by them. Of a cold morning, when business was but dull, Turkey would gobble up scores of these cakes, as if they were mere wafers – indeed, they sell them at the rate of six or eight for a penny – the scrape of his pen blending with the crunching of the crisp particles in his mouth. Of all the fiery afternoon blunders and flurried rashnesses of Turkey was his once moistening a ginger-cake between his lips and clapping it on to a mortgage, for a seal. I came within an ace of dismissing him then. But he mollified me by making an oriental bow, and saying – 'With submission, sir, it was generous of me to find you in stationery on my own account.'

Now my original business – that of a conveyancer and title hunter, and drawer-up of recondite documents of all sorts – was considerably increased by receiving the Master's office. There was now great work for scriveners. Not only must I push the clerks already with me, but I must have additional help.

In answer to my advertisement, a motionless young man one morning stood upon my office threshold, the door being open, for it was summer. I can see that figure now – pallidly neat, pitiably respectable, incurably forlorn! It was Bartleby.

After a few words touching his qualifications, I engaged him, glad to have among my corps of copyists a man of so singularly sedate an aspect, which I thought might operate beneficially upon the flighty temper of Turkey, and the fiery one of Nippers.

I should have stated before that ground-glass folding-doors divided my premises into two parts, one of which was occupied by my scriveners, the other by myself. According to my humour, I threw open these doors or closed them. I resolved to assign Bartleby a corner by the folding-doors, but on my side of them so as to have this quiet man within easy call in case any trifling thing was to be done. I placed his desk close up to a small side-window in that part of the room, a window which originally had afforded a lateral view of certain grimy backyards and bricks but which, owing to subsequent erections, commanded at present no view at all, though it gave some light. Within three feet of the panes was a wall, and the light came down from far above, between two lofty buildings, as from a very small opening in a dome. Still further to a satisfactory arrangement, I procured a high green folding screen, which might entirely isolate Bartleby from my sight, though not remove him from my voice. And thus, in a manner, privacy and society were conjoined.

At first, Bartleby did an extraordinary quantity of writing. As if long famishing for something to copy, he seemed to gorge himself on my documents. There was no pause for digestion. He ran a day and night line, copying by sunlight and by candlelight. I should have been quite delighted with his application, had he been cheerfully industrious. But he wrote on silently, palely, mechanically.

It is, of course, an indispensable part of a scrivener's business to verify the accuracy of his copy, word by word. Where there are two or more scriveners in an office, they assist each other in this examination, one reading from the copy, the other holding the original. It is a very dull, wearisome and lethargic affair. I can readily imagine that, to some sanguine temperaments, it would be altogether intolerable. For example, I cannot credit that the mettle-some poet Byron would have contentedly sat down with Bartleby to examine a law document of, say five hundred pages, closely written in a crimpy hand.

Now and then, in the haste of business, it had been my habit to assist in comparing some brief document myself, calling Turkey or Nippers for this purpose. One object I had in placing Bartleby so handy to me behind the screen was to avail myself of his services on such trivial occasions. It was on the third day, I think, of his being with me, and before any necessity had arisen for having his own writing examined, that, being much hurried to complete a small affair I had in hand, I abruptly called to Bartleby. In my haste and natural expectancy of instant compliance, I sat with my head bent over the original on my desk and my right hand sideways, and somewhat nervously, extended with the copy, so that, immediately upon emerging from his retreat, Bartleby might snatch it and proceed to business without the least delay.

In this very attitude did I sit when I called to him, rapidly stating what it was I wanted him to do – namely, to examine a small paper with me. Imagine my surprise, nay, my consternation, when, without moving from his privacy, Bartleby, in a singularly mild, firm voice, replied, 'I would prefer not to.'

I sat awhile in perfect silence, rallying my stunned faculties. Immediately it occurred to me that my ears had deceived me, or Bartleby had entirely misunderstood my meaning. I repeated my request in the clearest tone I could assume; but in quite as clear a one came the previous reply, 'I would prefer not to.'

'Prefer not to,' echoed I, rising in high excitement, and crossing the room with a stride. 'What do you mean? Are you moon-struck? I want you to help me compare this sheet here – take it,' and I thrust it towards him.

'I would prefer not to,' he said.

I looked at him steadfastly. His face was leanly composed; his grey eye dimly calm. Not a wrinkle of agitation rippled him. Had there been the least uneasiness, anger, impatience or impertinence in his manner; in other words, had there been anything ordinarily human about him, doubtless I should have violently dismissed him from the premises. But as it was, I should have as soon thought of turning my pale plaster-of-paris bust of Cicero out of doors. I stood gazing at him awhile, as he went on with his own writing, and then reseated myself at my desk. This is very strange, thought I. What had one best do? But my business hurried me. I concluded to forget the matter for the present, reserving it for my future leisure. So, calling Nippers from the other room, the paper was speedily examined.

A few days after this, Bartleby concluded four lengthy documents, being quadruplicates of a week's testimony taken before me in my

High Court of Chancery. It became necessary to examine them. It was an important suit and great accuracy was imperative. Having all things arranged, I called Turkey, Nippers and Ginger Nut from the next room, meaning to place the four copies in the hands of my four clerks, while I should read from the original. Accordingly, Turkey, Nippers and Ginger Nut had taken their seats in a row, each with his document in his hand, when I called to Bartleby to join this interesting group.

'Bartleby! quick, I am waiting.'

I heard a slow scrape of his chair legs on the uncarpeted floor and soon he appeared standing at the entrance of his hermitage.

'What is wanted?' said he, mildly.

'The copies, the copies,' said I, hurriedly. 'We are going to examine them. There – ' and I held towards him the fourth quadruplicate.

'I would prefer not to,' he said, and gently disappeared behind the screen.

For a few moments I was turned into a pillar of salt, standing at the head of my seated column of clerks. Recovering myself, I advanced towards the screen, and demanded the reason for such extraordinary conduct.

'Why do you refuse?'

'I would prefer not to.'

With any other man I should have flown outright into a dreadful passion, scorned all further words, and thrust him ignominiously from my presence. But there was something about Bartleby that not only strangely disarmed me, but, in a wonderful manner, touched and disconcerted me. I began to reason with him.

'These are your own copies we are about to examine. It is labour saving to you, because one examination will answer for your four papers. It is common usage. Every copyist is bound to help examine his copy. Is it not so? Will you not speak? Answer!'

'I prefer not to,' he replied in a flute-like tone. It seemed to me that, while I had been addressing him, he had carefully revolved every statement that I made; fully comprehended the meaning; could not gainsay the irresistible conclusion; but, at the same time, some paramount consideration prevailed with him to reply as he did.

'You are decided, then, not to comply with my request – a request made according to common usage and common sense?'

He briefly gave me to understand that on that point my judgement was sound. Yes: his decision was irreversible.

It is not seldom the case that, when a man is browbeaten in some unprecedented and violently unreasonable way, he begins to stagger in his own plainest faith. He begins, as it were, vaguely to surmise that, wonderful as it may be, all the justice and all the reason is on the other side. Accordingly, if any disinterested persons are present, he turns to them for some reinforcement for his own faltering mind.

'Turkey,' said I, 'what do you think of this? Am I not right?'

'With submission, sir,' said Turkey, in his blandest tone, 'I think that you are.'

'Nippers,' said I, 'what do you think of it?'

'I think I should kick him out of the office.'

(The reader of nice perceptions will here perceive that, it being morning, Turkey's answer is couched in polite and tranquil terms, but Nippers replies in ill-tempered ones. Or, to repeat a previous sentence, Nippers's ugly mood was on duty, and Turkey's off.)

'Ginger Nut,' said I, willing to enlist the smallest suffrage in behalf, 'what do *you* think of it?'

'I think, sir, he's a little loony,' replied Ginger Nut, with a grin.

'You hear what they say,' said I, turning towards the screen, 'come forth and do your duty.'

But he vouchsafed no reply. I pondered a moment in sore perplexity. But once more business hurried me. I determined again to postpone the consideration of this dilemma to my future leisure. With a little trouble we made out to examine the papers without Bartleby, though at every page or two Turkey deferentially dropped his opinion that this proceeding was quite out of the common; while Nippers, twitching in his chair with a dyspeptic nervousness, ground out, between his set teeth, occasional hissing maledictions against the stubborn oaf behind the screen. And for his (Nippers's) part, this was the first and the last time he would do another man's business without pay.

Meanwhile Bartleby sat in his hermitage, oblivious to everything but his own peculiar business there.

Some days passed, the scrivener being employed upon another lengthy work. His late remarkable conduct led me to regard his ways narrowly. I observed that he never went to dinner; indeed, that he never went anywhere. As yet I had never, of my personal knowledge, known him to be outside of my office. He was a perpetual sentry in the corner. At about eleven o'clock though, in the morning, I noticed that Ginger Nut would advance towards the opening in Bartleby's screen, as if silently beckoned thither by a gesture invisible to me where I sat. The boy would then leave the office, jingling a few pence, and reappear with a handful of ginger-nuts, which he delivered in the hermitage, receiving two of the cakes for his trouble.

He lives, then, on ginger-nuts, thought I; never eats a dinner, properly speaking; he must be a vegetarian, then; but no, he never eats even vegetables, he eats nothing but ginger-nuts. My mind then ran on in reveries concerning the probable effects upon the human constitution of living entirely on ginger-nuts. Ginger-nuts are so called, because they contain ginger as one of their peculiar constituents, and the final flavouring one. Now, what was ginger? A hot, spicy thing. Was Bartleby hot and spicy? Not at all. Ginger, then, had no effect upon Bartleby. Probably he preferred it should have none.

Nothing so aggravates an earnest person as a passive resistance. If the individual so resisted be of a not inhumane temper, and the resisting one perfectly harmless in his passivity, then, in the better moods of the former, he will endeavour charitably to construe to his imagination what proves impossible to be solved by his judgement. Even so, for the most part, I regarded Bartleby and his ways. Poor fellow! thought I, he means no mischief; it is plain he intends no insolence; his aspect sufficiently evinces that his eccentricities are involuntary. He is useful to me. I can get along with him. If I turn him away, the chances are he will fall in with some less indulgent employer, and then he will be rudely treated, and perhaps driven forth miserably to starve. Yes. Here I can cheaply purchase a delicious self-approval. To befriend Bartleby; to humour him in his strange wilfulness, will cost me little or nothing, while I lay up in my soul what will eventually prove a sweet morsel for my conscience. But this mood was not invariable with me. The passiveness of Bartleby sometimes irritated me. I felt strangely goaded on to encounter him in new opposition – to elicit some angry spark from him answerable to my own. But, indeed, I might as well have essayed to strike fire with my knuckles against a bit of Windsor soap. But one afternoon the evil impulse in me mastered me, and the following little scene ensued:

'Bartleby,' said I, 'when those papers are all copied, I will compare them with you.'

'I would prefer not to.'

'How? Surely you do not mean to persist in that mulish vagary?'

No answer.

I threw open the folding-doors near by, and turning upon Turkey and Nippers, exclaimed: 'Bartleby a second time says he won't examine his papers. What do you think of it, Turkey?'

It was afternoon, be it remembered. Turkey sat glowing like a brass boiler; his bald head steaming; his hands reeling among his blotted papers.

'Think of it?' roared Turkey. 'I'll just step behind his screen, and black his eyes for him!'

So saying, Turkey rose to his feet and threw his arms into a pugilistic position. He was hurrying away to make good his promise, when I detained him, alarmed at the effect of incautiously rousing Turkey's combativeness after dinner.

'Sit down, Turkey,' said I, 'and hear what Nippers has to say. What do you think of it, Nippers? Would I not be justified in immediately dismissing Bartleby?'

'Excuse me, that is for you to decide, sir. I think his conduct quite unusual, and, indeed, unjust, as regards Turkey and myself. But it may only be a passing whim.'

'Ah,' exclaimed I, 'you have strangely changed your mind, then – you speak very gently of him now.'

'All beer,' cried Turkey; 'gentleness is effects of beer – Nippers and I dined together today. You see how gentle *I* am, sir. Shall I go and black his eyes?'

'You refer to Bartleby, I suppose. No, not today, Turkey,' I replied; 'pray, put up your fists.'

I closed the doors, and again advanced towards Bartleby. I felt additional incentives tempting me to my fate. I burned to be rebelled against again. I remembered that Bartleby never left the office.

'Bartleby,' said I, 'Ginger Nut is away; just step around to the post-office, won't you?' (it was but a three minutes' walk) 'and see if there is anything for me.'

'I would prefer not to.'

'You *will* not?'

'*I prefer* not.'

I staggered to my desk, and sat there in a deep study. My blind inveteracy returned. Was there any other thing in which I could procure myself to be ignominiously repulsed by this lean, penniless wight? – my hired clerk? What added thing is there, perfectly reasonable, that he will be sure to refuse to do?

'Bartleby!'

No answer.

'Bartleby,' in a louder tone.

No answer.

'Bartleby,' I roared.

Like a very ghost, agreeably to the laws of magical invocation at
the third summons, he appeared at the entrance of his hermitage.

'Go to the next room, and tell Nippers to come to me.'

'I prefer not to,' he respectfully and slowly said, and mildly
disappeared.

'Very good, Bartleby,' said I, in a quiet sort of serenely-severe,
self-possessed tone, intimating the unalterable purpose of some
terrible retribution very close at hand. At the moment I half
intended something of the kind. But upon the whole, as it was
drawing towards my dinner-hour, I thought it best to put on my hat
and walk home for the day, suffering much from perplexity and
distress of mind.

Shall I acknowledge it? The conclusion of this whole business was
that it soon became a fixed fact of my chambers that a pale young
scrivener, by the name of Bartleby, had a desk there; that he copied
for me at the usual rate of four cents a folio (one hundred words);
but he was permanently exempt from examining the work done by
him, that duty being transferred to Turkey and Nippers, out of
compliment, doubtless, to their superior acuteness; moreover, said
Bartleby was never, on any account, to be dispatched on the most
trivial errand of any sort; and that even if entreated to take upon
him such a matter, it was generally understood that he would 'prefer
me to' – in other words, that he would refuse point-blank.

As days passed on, I became considerably reconciled to Bartleby.
His steadiness, his freedom from all dissipation, his incessant industry (except when he chose to throw himself into a standing reverie
behind his screen), his great stillness, his unalterableness of demeanour under all circumstances, made him a valuable acquisition. One
prime thing was this – he was always there – first in the morning,
continually through the day, and the last at night. I had a singular
confidence in his honesty. I felt my most precious papers perfectly
safe in his hands. Sometimes, to be sure, I could not, for the very soul
of me, avoid falling into sudden spasmodic passions with him. For it
was exceeding difficult to bear in mind all the time those strange
peculiarities, privileges and unheard-of exemptions forming the tacit
stipulations on Bartleby's part under which he remained in my office.
Now and then, in the eagerness of dispatching pressing business, I
would inadvertently summon Bartleby, in a short, rapid tone, to put
his finger, say, on the incipient tie of a bit of red tape with which I
was about compressing some papers. Of course, from behind the
screen the usual answer, 'I prefer not to,' was sure to come, and then
how could a human creature, with the common infirmities of our

nature, refrain from bitterly exclaiming upon such perverseness – such unreasonableness? However, every added repulse of this sort which I received only tended to lessen the probability of my repeating the inadvertence.

Here it must be said that, according to the custom of most legal gentlemen occupying chambers in densely populated law buildings, there were several keys to my door. One was kept by a woman residing in the attic, which person weekly scrubbed and daily swept and dusted my apartments. Another was kept by Turkey for convenience sake. The third I sometimes carried in my own pocket. The fourth I knew not who had.

Now, one Sunday morning I happened to go to Trinity Church, to hear a celebrated preacher, and finding myself rather early on the ground I thought I would walk round to my chambers for a while. Luckily I had my key with me, but upon applying it to the lock, I found it resisted by something inserted from the inside. Quite surprised, I called out; when to my consternation a key was turned from within; and thrusting his lean visage at me, and holding the door ajar, the apparition of Bartleby appeared, in his shirt-sleeves, and otherwise in a strangely tattered deshabille, saying quietly that he was sorry, but he was deeply engaged just then, and – preferred not admitting me at present. In a brief word or two, he moreover added that perhaps I had better walk round the block two or three times, and by that time he would probably have concluded his affairs.

Now, the utterly unsurmised appearance of Bartleby, tenanting my law-chambers of a Sunday morning, with his cadaverously gentlemanly nonchalance, yet withal firm and self-possessed, had such a strange effect upon me that incontinently I slunk away from my own door, and did as desired. But not without sundry twinges of impotent rebellion against the mild effrontery of this unaccountable scrivener. Indeed, it was his wonderful mildness, chiefly, which not only disarmed me but unmanned me, as it were. For I consider that one, for the time, is a sort of unmanned when he tranquilly permits his hired clerk to dictate to him, and order him away from his own premises. Furthermore, I was full of uneasiness as to what Bartleby could possibly be doing in my office in his shirt-sleeves, and in an otherwise dismantled condition, of a Sunday morning. Was anything amiss going on? Nay, that was out of the question. It was not to be thought of for a moment that Bartleby was an immoral person. But what could he be doing there? – copying? Nay again, whatever might be his eccentricities, Bartleby was an eminently decorous person. He would be the last man to sit down to his desk in any state approaching to nudity. Besides, it was Sunday; and there was something about Bartleby that forbade the supposition that he would by any secular occupation violate the proprieties of the day.

Nevertheless, my mind was not pacified; and, full of a restless curiosity, at last I returned to the door. Without hindrance I inserted my key, opened it and entered. Bartleby was not to be seen. I looked round anxiously, peeped behind his screen; but it was very plain that he was gone. Upon more closely examining the place, I surmised that for an indefinite period Bartleby must have ate, dressed and slept in my office, and that too without plate, mirror or bed. The cushioned seat of a rickety old sofa in one corner bore the faint impress of a lean, reclining form. Rolled away under his desk, I found a blanket; under the empty grate, a blacking box and brush; on a chair, a tin basin, with soap and a ragged towel; in a newspaper a few crumbs of ginger-nuts and a morsel of cheese. Yes, thought I, it is evident enough that Bartleby has been making his home here, keeping bachelor's hall all by himself. Immediately then the thought came sweeping across me, what miserable friendlessness and loneliness are here revealed! His poverty is great; but his solitude, how horrible! Think of it. Of a Sunday, Wall Street is deserted as Petra; and every night of every day it is an emptiness. This building, too, which of weekdays hums with industry and life, at nightfall echoes with sheer vacancy, and all through Sunday is forlorn. And here Bartleby makes his home; sole spectator of a solitude which he has seen all populous – a sort of innocent and transformed Marius brooding among the ruins of Carthage!

For the first time in my life a feeling of overpowering stinging melancholy seized me. Before, I had never experienced aught but a not unpleasing sadness. The bond of a common humanity now drew me irresistibly to gloom. A fraternal melancholy! For both I and Bartleby were sons of Adam. I remembered the bright silks and sparkling faces I had seen that day, in gala trim, swan-like sailing down the Mississippi of Broadway; and I contrasted them with the pallid copyist, and thought to myself, Ah, happiness courts the light, so we deem the world is gay; but misery hides aloof, so we deem that misery there is none. These sad fancyings – chimeras, doubtless, of a sick and silly brain – led on to other and more special thoughts, concerning the eccentricities of Bartleby. Presentiments of strange discoveries hovered round me. The scrivener's pale form appeared to me laid out, among uncaring strangers, in its shivering winding-sheet.

Suddenly I was attracted by Bartleby's closed desk, the key in open sight left in the lock.

I mean no mischief, seek the gratification of no heartless curiosity, thought I; besides, the desk is mine, and its contents, too, so I will make bold to look within. Everything was methodically arranged, the papers smoothly placed. The pigeon-holes were deep, and removing the files of documents, I groped into their recesses. Presently I felt something there, and dragged it out. It was an old bandanna handkerchief, heavy and knotted. I opened it, and saw it was a savings bank.

I now recalled all the quiet mysteries which I had noted in the man. I remembered that he never spoke but to answer; that, though at intervals he had considerable time to himself, yet I had never seen him reading – no, not even a newspaper, that for long periods he would stand looking out, at his pale window behind the screen, upon the dead brick wall; I was quite sure he never visited any refectory or eating-house; while his pale face clearly indicated that he never drank beer like Turkey, or tea and coffee even, like other men; that he never went anywhere in particular that I could learn; never went out for a walk, unless, indeed, that was the case at present; that he had declined telling who he was, or whence he came, or whether he had any relatives in the world; that though so thin and pale, he never complained of ill-health. And more than all, I remembered a certain unconscious air of pallid – how shall I call it? – of pallid haughtiness, say, or rather an austere reserve about him, which had positively awed me into my tame compliance with his eccentricities, when I had feared to ask him to do the slightest incidental thing for me, even though I might know, from his long-continued motionlessness, that behind his screen he must be standing in one of those dead-wall reveries of his.

Revolving all these things, and coupling them with the recently discovered fact that he made my office his constant abiding place and home, and not forgetful of his morbid moodiness; revolving all these things, a prudential feeling began to steal over me. My first emotions had been those of pure melancholy and sincerest pity; but just in proportion as the forlornness of Bartleby grew and grew to my imagination did that same melancholy merge into fear, that pity into repulsion. So true it is, and so terrible, too, that up to a certain point the thought or sight of misery enlists our best affections; but, in certain special cases, beyond that point it does not. They err who would assert that invariably this is owing to the inherent selfishness of the human heart. It rather proceeds from a certain hopelessness of remedying excessive and organic ill. To a sensitive being, pity is not seldom pain. And when at last it is perceived that such pity cannot lead to effectual succour, common sense bids the soul be rid of it. What I saw that morning persuaded me that the scrivener was the victim of innate and incurable disorder. I might give alms to his body; but his body did not pain him; it was his soul that suffered, and his soul I could not reach.

I did not accomplish the purpose of going to Trinity Church that morning. Somehow, the things I had seen disqualified me for the time from church-going. I walked homeward, thinking what I would do with Bartleby. Finally, I resolved upon this – I would put certain calm questions to him the next morning, touching his history, etc., and if he declined to answer them openly and un-reservedly (and I supposed he would prefer not), then to give him a twenty-dollar bill over and above whatever I might owe him and tell him his services were no longer required; but that if in any other way I could assist him, I would be happy to do so; especially if he desired to return to his native place, wherever that might be, I would willingly help to defray the expenses. Moreover, if, after reaching home, he found himself at any time in want of aid, a letter from him would be sure of a reply.

The next morning came.

'Bartleby,' said I, gently calling to him behind his screen.

No reply.

'Bartleby,' said I, in a still gentler tone, 'come here; I am not going to ask you to do anything you would prefer not to do – I simply wish to speak to you.'

Upon this he noiselessly slid into view.

'Will you tell me, Bartleby, where you were born?'

'I would prefer not to.'

'Will you tell me *anything* about yourself?'

'I would prefer not to.'

'But what reasonable objection can you have to speak to me? I feel friendly towards you.'

He did not look at me while I spoke, but kept his glance fixed upon my bust of Cicero, which, as I then sat, was directly behind me, some six inches above my head.

'What is your answer, Bartleby?' said I, after waiting a con-siderable time for a reply, during which his countenance remained immovable; there was only the faintest conceivable tremor of the white attenuated mouth.

'At present I prefer to give no answer,' he said, and retired into his hermitage.

It was rather weak in me I confess, but his manner, on this occasion, nettled me. Not only did there seem to lurk in it a certain calm disdain, but his perverseness seemed ungrateful, considering the undeniable good usage and indulgence he had received from me.

Again I sat ruminating what I should do. Mortified as I was at his behaviour, and resolved as I had been to dismiss him when I entered my office, nevertheless I strangely felt something superstitious knocking at my heart, and forbidding me to carry out my purpose, and denouncing me for a villain if I dared to breathe one bitter word against this forlornest of mankind. At last, familiarly drawing my chair behind his screen, I sat down and said: 'Bartleby, never mind, then, about revealing your history; but let me entreat you, as a friend, to comply as far as may be with the usages of this office. Say now you will help to examine papers tomorrow or next day: in short, say now that in a day or two you will begin to be a little reasonable – say so, Bartleby.'

'At present I would prefer not to be a little reasonable,' was his mildly cadaverous reply.

Just then the folding-doors opened and Nippers approached. He seemed suffering from an unusually bad night's rest, induced by severer indigestion than common. He overheard those final words of Bartleby.

'*Prefer not*, eh?' gritted Nippers – 'I'd *prefer* him, if I were you, sir,' addressing me – 'I'd *prefer* him; I'd give him preferences, the stubborn mule! What is it, sir, pray, that he *prefers* not to do now?'

Bartleby moved not a limb.

'Mr Nippers,' said I, 'I'd prefer that you would withdraw for the present.'

Somehow, of late, I had got into the way of involuntarily using this word 'prefer' upon all sorts of not exactly suitable occasions. And I trembled to think that my contact with the scrivener had already and seriously affected me in a mental way. And what further and deeper aberration might it not yet produce? This apprehension had not been without efficacy in determining me to summary measures.

As Nippers, looking very sour and sulky, was departing, Turkey blandly and deferentially approached.

'With submission, sir,' said he, 'yesterday I was thinking about Bartleby here, and I think that if he would but prefer to take a quart of good ale every day, it would do much towards mending him and enabling him to assist in examining his papers.'

'So you have got the word, too,' said I, slightly excited.

'With submission, what word, sir?' asked Turkey, respectfully crowding himself into the contracted space behind the screen, and by so doing, making me jostle the scrivener. 'What word, sir?'

'I would prefer to be left alone here,' said Bartleby, as if offended at being mobbed in his privacy.

'*That's* the word, Turkey,' said I – '*that's* it.'

'Oh, *prefer*? oh yes – queer word. I never use it myself. But, sir, as I was saying, if he would but prefer – '

'Turkey,' interrupted I, 'you will please withdraw.'

'Oh, certainly, sir, if you prefer that I should.'

As he opened the folding-doors to retire, Nippers at his desk caught a glimpse of me, and asked whether I would prefer to have a certain paper copied on blue paper or white. He did not in the least roguishly accent the word 'prefer'. It was plain that it involuntarily rolled from his tongue. I thought to myself, surely I must get rid of a demented man, who already has in some degree turned the tongues if not the heads of myself and my clerks. But I thought it prudent not to break the dismission at once.

The next day I noticed that Bartleby did nothing but stand at his window in his dead-wall reverie. Upon asking him why he did not write, he said that he had decided upon doing no more writing.

'Why, how now? what next?' exclaimed I, 'do no more writing?'

'No more.'

'And what is the reason?'

'Do you not see the reason for yourself?' he indifferently replied.

I looked steadfastly at him, and perceived that his eyes looked dull and glazed. Instantly it occurred to me that his unexampled diligence in copying by his dim window for the first few weeks of his stay with me might have temporarily impaired his vision.

I was touched. I said something in condolence with him. I hinted that of course he did wisely in abstaining from writing for a while; and urged him to embrace that opportunity of taking wholesome exercise in the open air. This, however, he did not do. A few days after this, my other clerks being absent, and being in a great hurry to dispatch certain letters by the mail, I thought that, having nothing else earthly to do, Bartleby would surely be less inflexible than usual and carry these letters to the post-office. But he blankly declined. So, much to my inconvenience, I went myself.

Still added days went by. Whether Bartleby's eyes improved or not, I could not say. To all appearance, I thought they did. But when I asked him if they did, he vouchsafed no answer. At all events, he would do no copying. At last, in reply to my urgings, he informed me that he had permanently given up copying.

'What!' exclaimed I; 'suppose your eyes should get entirely well – better than ever before – would you not copy then?'

'I have given up copying,' he answered, and slid aside.

He remained as ever, a fixture in my chamber. Nay – if that were possible – he became still more of a fixture than before. What was to be done? He would do nothing in the office; why should he stay there? In plain fact, he had now become a millstone to me, not only useless as a necklace, but afflictive to bear. Yet I was sorry for him. I speak less than truth when I say that, on his own account, he occasioned me uneasiness. If he would but have named a single relative or friend, I would instantly have written and urged their taking the poor fellow away to some convenient retreat. But he seemed alone, absolutely alone in the universe. A bit of wreck in the mid-Atlantic. At length, necessities connected with my business tyrannised over all other considerations. Decently as I could, I told Bartleby that in six days' time he must unconditionally leave the office. I warned him to take measures, in the interval, for procuring some other abode. I offered to assist him in this endeavour, if he himself would but take the first step towards a removal. 'And when you finally quit me, Bartleby,' added I, 'I shall see that you go not away entirely unprovided. Six days from this hour, remember.'

At the expiration of that period, I peeped behind the screen, and lo! Bartleby was there.

I buttoned up my coat, balanced myself; advanced slowly towards him, touched his shoulder, and said, 'The time has come; you must quit this place; I am sorry for you; here is money; but you must go.'

'I would prefer not,' he replied, with his back still towards me.

'You must.'

He remained silent.

Now I had an unbounded confidence in this man's common honesty. He had frequently restored to me sixpences and shillings carelessly dropped upon the floor, for I am apt to be very reckless in such shirt-button affairs. The proceeding, then, which followed will not be deemed extraordinary.

'Bartleby,' said I, 'I owe you twelve dollars on account; here are thirty-two; the odd twenty are yours – Will you take it?' and I handed the bills towards him.

But he made no motion.

'I will leave them here, then,' putting them under a weight on the table. Then taking my hat and cane and going to the door, I tranquilly turned and added – 'After you have removed your things from these offices, Bartleby, you will of course lock the door – since everyone is now gone for the day but you – and if you please, slip your key underneath the mat, so that I may have it in the morning. I shall not see you again; so goodbye to you. If, hereafter, in your new place of abode, I can be of any service to you, do not fail to advise me by letter. Goodbye, Bartleby, and fare you well.'

But he answered not a word; like the last column of some ruined temple, he remained standing mute and solitary in the middle of the otherwise deserted room.

As I walked home in a pensive mood, my vanity got the better of my pity. I could not but highly plume myself on my masterly management in getting rid of Bartleby. Masterly I call it, and such it must appear to any dispassionate thinker. The beauty of my procedure seemed to consist in its perfect quietness. There was no vulgar bullying, no bravado of any sort, no choleric hectoring and striding to and fro across the apartment, jerking out vehement commands for Bartleby to bundle himself off with his beggarly traps. Nothing of the kind. Without loudly bidding Bartleby depart – as an inferior genius might have done – I *assumed* the ground that depart he must; and upon that assumption built all I had to say. The more I thought over my procedure, the more I was charmed with it. Nevertheless, next morning, upon awakening, I had my doubts – I had somehow slept off the fumes of vanity. One of the coolest and wisest hours a man has is just after he awakes in the morning. My procedure seemed as sagacious as ever – but only in theory. How it would prove in practice – there was the rub. It was truly a beautiful thought to have assumed Bartleby's departure; but, after all, that assumption was simply my own, and none of Bartleby's. The great point was not whether I had assumed that he would quit me, but whether he would prefer so to do. He was more a man of preferences than assumptions.

After breakfast, I walked downtown, arguing the probabilities *pro* and *con*. One moment I thought it would prove a miserable failure, and Bartleby would be found all alive at my office as usual; the next moment it seemed certain that I should find his chair empty. And so I kept veering about. At the corner of Broadway and Canal Street, I saw quite an excited group of people standing in earnest conversation.

'I'll take odds he doesn't,' said a voice I passed.

'Doesn't go? – done!' said, 'Put up your money.'

I was instinctively putting my hand in my pocket to produce my own, when I remembered that this was an election day. The words I had overheard bore no reference to Bartleby, but to the success or non-success of some candidate for the mayoralty. In my intent frame of mind, I had, as it were, imagined that all Broadway shared in my excitement, and were debating the same question with me. I passed on, very thankful that the uproar of the street screened my momentary absent-mindedness.

As I had intended, I was earlier than usual at my office door. I stood listening for a moment. All was still. He must be gone. I tried the knob. The door was locked. Yes, my procedure had worked to a charm; he indeed must be vanished. Yet a certain melancholy mixed with this: I was almost sorry for my brilliant success. I was fumbling under the doormat for the key, which Bartleby was to have left there for me, when accidentally my knee knocked against a panel, producing a summoning sound, and in response a voice came to me from within – 'Not yet; I am occupied.'

It was Bartleby.

I was thunderstruck. For an instant I stood like the man who, pipe in mouth, was killed one cloudless afternoon long ago in Virginia, by summer lightning; at his own warm open window he was killed, and remained leaning out there upon the dreamy afternoon, till someone touched him, when he fell.

'Not gone!' I murmured at last. But again obeying that wondrous ascendancy which the inscrutable scrivener had over me, and from which ascendancy, for all my chafing, I could not completely escape, I slowly went downstairs and out into the street, and while walking round the block, considered what I should next do in this unheard-of perplexity. Turn the man out by an actual thrusting I could not; to drive him away by calling him hard names would not do; calling in the police was an unpleasant idea; and yet, permit him to enjoy his cadaverous triumph over me – this, too, I could not think of. What was to be done? or, if nothing could be done, was there anything further that I could *assume* in the matter? Yes, as before I had prospectively assumed that Bartleby would depart, so now I might retrospectively assume that departed he was. In the legitimate carrying out of this assumption, I might enter my office in a great hurry, and pretending not to see Bartleby at all, walk straight against him as if he were air. Such a proceeding would in a singular degree have the appearance of a home-thrust. It was hardly possible that Bartleby could withstand such an application of the doctrine of assumptions. But upon second thoughts the success of the plan seemed rather dubious. I resolved to argue the matter over with him again.

'Bartleby,' said I, entering the office, with a quietly severe expression, 'I am seriously displeased. I am pained, Bartleby. I thought better of you. I had imagined you of such a gentlemanly organisation, that in any delicate dilemma a slight hint would suffice – in short, an assumption. But it appears I am deceived. Why,' I added, unaffectedly starting, 'you have not even touched that money yet,' pointing to it, just where I had left it the evening previous.

He answered nothing.

'Will you, or will you not, quit me?' I now demanded in a sudden passion, advancing close to him.

'I would prefer *not* to quit you,' he replied, gently emphasising the *not*.

'What earthly right have you to stay here? Do you pay any rent? Do you pay my taxes? Or is this property yours?'

He answered nothing.

'Are you ready to go on and write now? Are your eyes recovered? Could you copy a small paper for me this morning? Or help examine a few lines? or step round to the post-office? In a word, will you do anything at all to give a colouring to your refusal to depart the premises?'

He silently retired into his hermitage.

I was now in such a state of nervous resentment that I thought it but prudent to check myself at present from further demonstrations. Bartleby and I were alone. I remembered the tragedy of the unfortunate Adams and the still more unfortunate Colt in the solitary office of the latter; and how poor Colt, being dreadfully incensed by Adams, and imprudently permitting himself to get wildly excited, was at unawares hurried into his fatal act – an act which certainly no man could possibly deplore more than the actor himself. Often it had occurred to me in my ponderings upon the subject that had that altercation taken place in the public street, or at a private residence, it would not have terminated as it did. It was the circumstance of being alone in a solitary office, upstairs, of a building entirely unhallowed by humanising domestic associations – an uncarpeted office, doubtless, of a dusty, haggard sort of appearance – this it must have been which greatly helped to enhance the irritable desperation of the hapless Colt.

But when this old Adam of resentment rose in me and tempted me concerning Bartleby, I grappled him and threw him. How? Why, simply by recalling the divine injunction: 'A new commandment give I unto you, that ye love one another.' Yes, this it was that saved me. Aside from higher considerations, charity often operates as a vastly wise and prudent principle – a great safeguard to its possessor. Men have committed murder for jealousy's sake, and anger's sake, and hatred's sake, and selfishness's sake, and spiritual pride's sake; but no man, that ever I heard of, ever committed a diabolical murder for sweet charity's sake. Mere self-interest, then, if no better motive can be enlisted, should, especially with high-tempered men, prompt all beings to charity and philanthropy. At any rate, upon the occasion in question, I strove to drown my exasperated feelings towards the scrivener by benevolently construing his conduct. Poor fellow, poor fellow! thought I, he don't mean anything; and besides, he has seen hard times, and ought to be indulged.

I endeavoured, also, immediately to occupy myself, and at the same time to comfort my despondency. I tried to fancy that in the course of the morning, at such time as might prove agreeable to him, Bartleby, of his own free accord, would emerge from his hermitage and take up some decided line of march in the direction of the door. But no. Half-past twelve o'clock came; Turkey began to glow in the face, overturn his inkstand, and become generally obstreperous; Nippers abated down into quietude and courtesy: Ginger Nut munched his noon apple; and Bartleby remained standing at his window in one of his profoundest dead-wall reveries. Will it be credited? Ought I to acknowledge it? That afternoon I left the office without saying one further word to him.

Some days now passed, during which, at leisure intervals, I looked a little into *Edwards on the Will* and *Priestley on Necessity*. Under the circumstances, those books induced a salutary feeling. Gradually I slid into the persuasion that these troubles of mine, touching the scrivener, had been all predestinated from eternity, and Bartleby was billeted upon me for some mysterious purpose of an all-wise providence, which it was not for a mere mortal like me to fathom. Yes, Bartleby, stay there behind your screen, thought I; I shall persecute you no more; you are harmless and noiseless as any of these old chairs; in short, I never feel so private as when I know you are here. At last I see it, I feel it; I penetrate to the predestinated purpose of my life. I am content. Others may have loftier parts to enact; but my mission in this world, Bartleby, is to furnish you with office-room for such period as you may see fit to remain.

I believe that this wise and blessed frame of mind would have continued with me, had it not been for the unsolicited and uncharitable remarks obtruded upon me by my professional friends who visited the rooms. But thus it often is, that the constant friction of illiberal minds wears out at last the best resolves of the more generous. Though, to be sure, when I reflected upon it, it was not strange that people entering my office should be struck by the peculiar aspect of the unaccountable Bartleby and so be tempted to throw out some sinister observations concerning him. Sometimes an attorney, having business with me, and calling at my office, and finding no one but the scrivener there, would undertake to obtain some sort of precise information from him touching my whereabouts; but without heeding his idle talk, Bartleby would remain standing immovable in the middle of the room. So, after contemplating him in that position for a time, the attorney would depart, no wiser than he came.

Also, when a reference was going on, and the room full of lawyers and witnesses, and business driving fast, some deeply occupied legal gentleman present, seeing Bartleby wholly unemployed, would request him to run round to his (the legal gentleman's) office and fetch some papers for him. Thereupon, Bartleby would tranquilly decline, and yet remain idle as before. Then the lawyer would give a great stare, and turn to me. And what could I say? At last I was made aware that all through the circle of my professional acquaintance a whisper of wonder was running round, having reference to the strange creature I kept at my office. This worried me very much. And as the idea came upon me of his possibly turning out a long-lived man, and keep occupying my chambers, and denying my authority; and perplexing my visitors; and scandalising my professional reputation; and casting a general gloom over the premises; keeping soul and body together to the last upon his savings (for doubtless he spent but half a dime a day), and in the end perhaps outlive me, and claim possession of my office by right of his perpetual occupancy: as all these dark anticipations crowded upon me more and more, and my friends continually intruded their relentless remarks upon the apparition in my room, a great change was wrought in me. I resolved to gather all my faculties together, and forever rid me of this intolerable incubus.

Ere revolving any complicated project, however, adapted to this end, I first simply suggested to Bartleby the propriety of his permanent departure. In a calm and serious tone, I commended the idea to his careful and mature consideration. But, having taken three days to meditate upon it, he apprised me, that his original determination remained the same; in short, that he still preferred to abide with me.

What shall I do? I now said to myself, buttoning up my coat to the last button. What shall I do? what ought I to do? what does conscience say I *should* do with this man, or, rather, ghost. Rid myself of him, I must; go, he shall. But how? You will not thrust him, the poor, pale, passive mortal – you will not thrust such a helpless creature out of your door? you will not dishonour yourself by such cruelty? No, I will not, I cannot do that. Rather would I let him live and die here, and then mason up his remains in the wall. What, then, will you do? For all your coaxing, he will not budge. Bribes he leaves under your own paper-weight on your table; in short, it is quite plain that he prefers to cling to you.

Then something severe, something unusual must be done. What! surely you will not have him collared by a constable and commit his innocent pallor to the common jail? And upon what ground could you procure such a thing to be done? – a vagrant, is he? What! he a vagrant, a wanderer, who refuses to budge? It is because he will *not* be a vagrant, then, that you seek to count him *as* a vagrant. That is too absurd. No visible means of support: there I have him. Wrong again: for indubitably he *does* support himself, and that is the only unanswerable proof that any man can show of his possessing the means so to do. No more, then. Since he will not quit me, I must quit him. I will change my offices; I will move elsewhere, and give him fair notice that if I find him on my new premises I will then proceed against him as a common trespasser.

Acting accordingly, next day I thus addressed him: 'I find these chambers too far from the City Hall; the air is unwholesome. In a word, I propose to remove my offices next week, and shall no longer require your services. I tell you this now, in order that you may seek another place.'

He made no reply, and nothing more was said.

On the appointed day I engaged carts and men, proceeded to my chambers, and, having but little furniture, everything was removed in a few hours. Throughout, the scrivener remained standing behind the screen, which I directed to be removed the last thing. It was withdrawn; and, being folded up like a huge folio, left him the motionless occupant of a naked room. I stood in the entry watching him a moment, while something from within me upbraided me.

I re-entered, with my hand in my pocket – and – and my heart in my mouth.

'Goodbye, Bartleby; I am going – goodbye, and God some way

bless you; and take that,' slipping something in his hand. But it dropped upon the floor, and then – strange to say – I tore myself from him whom I had so longed to be rid of.

Established in my new quarters, for a day or two I kept the door locked, and started at every footfall in the passages. When I returned to my rooms, after any little absence, I would pause at the threshold for an instant, and attentively listen, ere applying my key. But these fears were needless. Bartleby never came nigh me.

I thought all was going well, when a perturbed-looking stranger visited me, enquiring whether I was the person who had recently occupied rooms at No. — Wall Street.

Full of forebodings, I replied that I was.

'Then, sir,' said the stranger, who proved a lawyer, 'you are responsible for the man you left there. He refuses to do any copying; he refuses to do anything; he says he prefers not to: and he refuses to quit the premises.'

'I am very sorry, sir,' said I, with assumed tranquillity, but an inward tremor, 'but, really, the man you allude to is nothing to me – he is no relation or apprentice of mine, that you should hold me responsible for him.'

'In mercy's name, who is he?'

'I certainly cannot inform you. I know nothing about him. Formerly I employed him as a copyist; but he has done nothing for me now for some time past.'

'I shall settle him, then – good morning, sir.'

Several days passed, and I heard nothing more; and, though I often felt charitable promptings to call at the place and see poor Bartleby, yet a certain squeamishness, of I know not what, withheld me.

All is over with him, by this time, thought I, at last, when, through another week, no further intelligence reached me. But, coming to my room the day after, I found several persons waiting at my door in a high state of nervous excitement.

'That's the man – here he comes,' cried the foremost one, whom I recognised as the lawyer who had previously called upon me alone.

'You must take him away, sir, at once,' cried a portly person among them, advancing upon me, and whom I knew to be the landlord of No. — Wall Street. 'These gentlemen, my tenants, cannot stand it any longer; Mr B—,' pointing to the lawyer, 'has turned him out of his room, and he now persists in haunting the building generally, sitting upon the banisters of the stairs by day, and sleeping in the entry by night. Everybody is concerned; clients are leaving the offices; some fears are entertained of a mob; something you must do, and that without delay.'

Aghast at this torrent, I fell back before it, and would fain have locked myself in my new quarters. In vain I persisted that Bartleby was nothing to me – no more than to anyone else. In vain – I was the last person known to have had anything to do with him, and they held me to the terrible account. Fearful, then, of being exposed in the papers (as one person present obscurely threatened), I considered the matter, and, at length, said that if the lawyer would give me a confidential interview with the scrivener, in his (the lawyer's) own room, I would, that afternoon, strive my best to rid them of the nuisance they complained of.

Going upstairs to my old haunt, there was Bartleby silently sitting upon the banister at the landing.

'What are you doing here, Bartleby?' said I.

'Sitting upon the banister,' he mildly replied.

I motioned him into the lawyer's room, who then left us.

'Bartleby,' said I, 'are you aware that you are the cause of great tribulation to me, by persisting in occupying the entry after being dismissed from the office?'

No answer.

'Now one of two things must take place. Either you must do something, or something must be done to you. Now what sort of business would you like to engage in? Would you like to re-engage in copying for someone?'

'No; I would prefer not to make any change.'

'Would you like a clerkship in a dry-goods store?'

'There is too much confinement about that. No, I would not like a clerkship; but I am not particular.'

'Too much confinement,' I cried, 'why, you keep yourself confined all the time!'

'I would prefer not to take a clerkship,' he rejoined, as if to settle that little item at once.

'How would a bartender's business suit you? There is no trying of the eyesight in that.'

'I would not like it at all; though, as I said before, I am not particular.'

His unwonted wordiness inspirited me. I returned to the charge.

'Well, then, would you like to travel through the country collecting bills for the merchants? That would improve your health.'

'No, I would prefer to be doing something else.'

'How, then, would going as a companion to Europe, to entertain some young gentleman with your conversation – how would that suit you?'

'Not at all. It does not strike me that there is anything definite about that. I like to be stationary. But I am not particular.'

'Stationary you shall be, then,' I cried, now losing all patience, and, for the first time in all my exasperating connection with him, fairly flying into a passion. 'If you do not go away from these premises before night, I shall feel bound – indeed, I am bound – to – to – to quit the premises myself!' I rather absurdly concluded, knowing not with what possible threat to try to frighten his immobility into compliance. Despairing of all further efforts, I was precipitately leaving him, when a final thought occurred to me – one which had not been wholly unindulged before.

'Bartleby,' said I, in the kindest tone I could assume under such exciting circumstances, 'will you go home with me now – not to my office, but my dwelling – and remain there till we can conclude upon some convenient arrangement for you at our leisure? Come, let us start now, right away.'

'No: at present I would prefer not to make any change at all.'

I answered nothing; but, effectually dodging everyone by the suddenness and rapidity of my flight, rushed from the building, ran up Wall Street towards Broadway, and, jumping into the first omnibus, was soon removed from pursuit. As soon as tranquillity returned, I distinctly perceived that I had now done all that I possibly could, both in respect to the demands of the landlord and his tenants, and with regard to my own desire and sense of duty, to benefit Bartleby and shield him from rude persecution. I now strove to be entirely carefree and quiescent; and my conscience justified me in the attempt; though, indeed, it was not so successful as I could have wished. So fearful was I of being again hunted out by the incensed landlord and his exasperated tenants, that, surrendering my business to Nippers for a few days, I drove about the upper part of the town and through the suburbs, in my rockaway; crossed over to Jersey City and Hoboken, and paid fugitive visits to Manhattanville and Astoria. In fact, I almost lived in my rockaway for the time.

When again I entered my office, lo, a note from the landlord lay upon the desk. I opened it with trembling hands. It informed me that the writer had sent to the police, and had Bartleby removed to the Tombs as a vagrant. Moreover, since I knew more about him than anyone else, he wished me to appear at that place, and make a suitable statement of the facts. These tidings had a conflicting effect upon me. At first I was indignant; but, at last, almost approved. The landlord's energetic, summary disposition, had led him to adopt a procedure which I do not think I would have decided upon myself; and yet, as a last resort, under such peculiar circumstances, it seemed the only plan.

As I afterwards learned, the poor scrivener, when told that he must be conducted to the Tombs, offered not the slightest obstacle, but, in his pale, unmoving way, silently acquiesced.

Some of the compassionate and curious bystanders joined the party; and headed by one of the constables arm in arm with Bartleby, the silent procession filed its way through all the noise, and heat, and joy of the roaring thoroughfares at noon.

The same day I received the note, I went to the Tombs, or, to speak more properly, the Halls of Justice. Seeking the right officer, I stated the purpose of my call, and was informed that the individual I described was, indeed, within. I then assured the functionary that Bartleby was a perfectly honest man, and greatly to be compassioned, however unaccountably eccentric. I narrated all I knew, and closed by suggesting the idea of letting him remain in as indulgent confinement as possible, till something less harsh might be done – though, indeed, I hardly knew what. At all events, if nothing else could be decided upon, the almshouse must receive him. I then begged to have an interview.

Being under no disgraceful charge, and quite serene and harmless in all his ways, they had permitted him freely to wander about the prison, and, especially, in the enclosed grass-plotted yards thereof. And so I found him there, standing all alone in the quietest of the yards, his face towards a high wall, while all around, from the narrow slits of the jail windows, I thought I saw peering out upon him the eyes of murderers and thieves.

'Bartleby!'

'I know you,' he said, without looking round – 'and I want nothing to say to you.'

'It was not I that brought you here, Bartleby,' said I, keenly pained at his implied suspicion. 'And to you, this should not be so vile a place. Nothing reproachful attaches to you by being here. And see, it is not so sad a place as one might think. Look, there is the sky, and here is the grass.'

'I know where I am,' he replied, but would say nothing more, and so I left him.

As I entered the corridor again, a broad meat-like man in an apron accosted me and, jerking his thumb over his shoulder, said – 'Is that your friend?'

'Yes.'

'Does he want to starve? If he does, let him live on the prison fare, that's all.'

'Who are you?' asked I, not knowing what to make of such an unofficially speaking person in such a place.

'I am the grub-man. Such gentlemen as have friends here, hire me to provide them with something good to eat.'

'Is this so?' said I, turning to the turnkey.

He said it was.

'Well, then,' said I, slipping some silver into the grub-man's hands (for so they called him), 'I want you to give particular attention to my friend there; let him have the best dinner you can get. And you must be as polite to him as possible.'

'Introduce me, will you?' said the grub-man, looking at me with an expression which seemed to say he was all impatience for an opportunity to give a specimen of his breeding.

Thinking it would prove of benefit to the scrivener, I acquiesced; and, asking the grub-man his name, went up with him to Bartleby.

'Bartleby, this is a friend; you will find him very useful to you.'

'Your sarvant, sir, your sarvant,' said the grub-man, making a low salutation behind his apron. 'Hope you find it pleasant here, sir; nice grounds – cool apartments – hope you'll stay with us some time try to make it agreeable. What will you have for dinner today?'

'I prefer not to dine today,' said Bartleby, turning away. 'It would disagree with me; I am unused to dinners.' So saying, he slowly moved to the other side of the enclosure, and took up a position fronting the dead-wall.

'How's this?' said the grub-man, addressing me with a stare of astonishment. 'He's odd, ain't he?'

'I think he is a little deranged,' said I, sadly.

'Deranged? deranged is it? Well, now, upon my word, I thought that friend of yourn was a gentleman forger; they are always pale and genteel-like, them forgers. I can't help pity 'em – can't help it, sir. Did you know Monroe Edwards?' he added, touchingly, and paused. Then, laying his hand piteously on my shoulder, sighed, 'He died of consumption at Sing-Sing. So you weren't acquainted with Monroe?'

'No, I was never socially acquainted with any forgers. But I cannot stop longer. Look to my friend yonder. You will not lose by it. I will see you again.'

Some few days after this, I again obtained admission to the Tombs, and went through the corridors in quest of Bartleby; but without finding him.

'I saw him coming from his cell not long ago,' said a turnkey, 'maybe he's gone to loiter in the yards.'

So I went in that direction.

'Are you looking for the silent man?' said another turnkey, passing me. 'Yonder he lies – sleeping in the yard there. 'Tis not twenty minutes since I saw him lie down.'

The yard was entirely quiet. It was not accessible to the common prisoners. The surrounding walls, of amazing thickness, kept off all sounds behind them. The Egyptian character of the masonry weighed upon me with its gloom. But a soft imprisoned turf grew under foot. The heart of the eternal pyramids, it seemed, wherein, by some strange magic, through the clefts, grass-seed, dropped by birds, had sprung.

Strangely huddled at the base of the wall, his knees drawn up, and lying on his side, his head touching the cold stones, I saw the wasted Bartleby. But nothing stirred. I paused; then went close up to him, stooped over, and saw that his dim eyes were open; otherwise he seemed profoundly sleeping. Something prompted me to touch him. I felt his hand, when a tingling shiver ran up my arm and down my spine to my feet.

The round face of the grub-man peered upon me now. 'His dinner is ready. Won't he dine today, either? Or does he live without dining?'

'Lives without dining,' said I, and closed the eyes.

'Eh! – He's asleep, ain't he?'

'With kings and counsellors,' murmured I.

There would seem little need for proceeding further in this history. Imagination will readily supply the meagre recital of poor Bartleby's interment. But, ere parting with the reader, let me say that if this little narrative has sufficiently interested him to awaken curiosity as to who Bartleby was and what manner of life he led prior to the present narrator's making his acquaintance, I can only reply that in such curiosity I fully share, but am wholly unable to gratify it. Yet here I hardly know whether I should divulge one little item of rumour, which came to my ear a few months after the scrivener's decease. Upon what basis it rested, I could never ascertain; and hence, how true it is I cannot now tell. But, inasmuch as this vague report has not been without a certain suggestive interest to me, however sad, it may prove the same with some others; and so I will briefly mention it. The report was this: that Bartleby had been a subordinate clerk in the dead-letter office at Washington, from which post he had been suddenly removed by a change in the administration. When I think over this rumour, hardly can I express the emotions which seize me. Dead letters! does it not sound like dead men? Conceive a man by nature and misfortune prone to a pallid hopelessness, can any business seem more fitted to heighten it than that of continually handling these dead letters, and assorting them for the flames? For by the cartload they are annually burned. Sometimes from out the folded paper the pale clerk takes a ring – the finger it was meant for, perhaps, moulders in the grave; a bank-note sent in swiftest charity – he whom it would relieve, nor eats nor hungers any more; pardon for those who died despairing; hope for those who died unhoping; good tidings for those who died stifled by unrelieved calamities. On errands of life, these letters speed to death.

Ah, Bartleby! Ah, humanity!

POOR MAN'S PUDDING AND
RICH MAN'S CRUMBS

Poor Man's Pudding

'You see,' said poet Blandmour, enthusiastically – as some forty years ago we walked along the road in a soft, moist snowfall, towards the end of March – 'you see, my friend, that the blessed almoner, nature, is in all things beneficent; and not only so, but considerate in her charities, as any discreet human philanthropist might be. This snow, now, which seems so unseasonable, is in fact just what a poor husbandman needs. Rightly is this soft March snow, falling just before seed-time, rightly is it called poor man's manure. Distilling from kind heaven upon the soil, by a gentle penetration it nourishes every clod, ridge and furrow. To the poor farmer it is as good as the rich farmer's farmyard enrichments. And the poor man has no trouble to spread it, while the rich man has to spread his.'

'Perhaps so,' said I, without equal enthusiasm, brushing some of the damp flakes from my chest. 'It may be as you say, dear Blandmour. But tell me, how is it that the wind drives yonder drifts of poor man's manure off poor Coulter's two-acre patch here, and piles it up yonder on rich Squire Teamster's twenty-acre field?'

'Ah! to be sure – yes – well; Coulter's field, I suppose, is sufficiently moist without further moistenings. Enough is as good as a feast, you know.'

'Yes,' replied I, 'of this sort of damp fare,' shaking another shower of the damp flakes from my person. 'But tell me, this warm spring-snow may answer very well, as you say; but how is it with the cold snows of the long, long winters here?'

'Why, do you not remember the words of the psalmist? – "The Lord giveth snow like wool" – meaning not only that snow is white as wool, but warm, too, as wool. For the only reason, as I take it, that wool is comfortable, is because air is entangled, and therefore warmed, among its fibres. Just so, then, take the temperature of a

December field when covered with this snow-fleece, and you will no doubt find it several degrees above that of the air. So, you see, the winter's snow *itself* is beneficent; under the pretence of frost – a sort of gruff philanthropist – actually warming the earth, which afterwards is to be fertilisingly moistened by these gentle flakes of March.'

'I like to hear you talk, dear Blandmour; and, guided by your benevolent heart, can only wish to poor Coulter plenty of this poor man's manure.'

'But that is not all,' said Blandmour, eagerly. 'Did you never hear of the poor man's eye-water? '

'Never.'

'Take this soft March snow, melt it, and bottle it. It keeps pure as alcohol. The very best thing in the world for weak eyes. I have a whole demijohn of it myself. But the poorest man, afflicted in his eyes, can freely help himself to this same all-bountiful remedy. Now, what a kind provision is that!'

'Then poor man's manure is poor man's eye-water too?'

'Exactly. And what could be more economically contrived? One thing answering two ends – ends so very distinct.'

'Very distinct, indeed.'

'Ah! that is your way. Making sport of earnest. But never mind. We have been talking of snow; but common rainwater – such as falls all the year round – is still more kindly. Not to speak of its known fertilising quality as to fields, consider it in one of its minor lights. Pray, did you ever hear of a poor man's egg?'

'Never. What is that, now?'

'Why, in making some culinary preparations of meal and flour, where eggs are recommended in the receipt-book, a substitute for the eggs may be had in a cup of cold rainwater, which acts as leaven. And so a cup of cold rainwater thus used is called by housewives a poor man's egg. And many rich men's housekeepers sometimes use it.'

'But only when they are out of hen's eggs, I presume, dear Blandmour. But your talk is – I sincerely say it – most agreeable to me. Talk on.'

'Then there's poor man's plaster, for wounds and other bodily harms: an alleviative and curative, compounded of simple, natural things; and so, being very cheap, accessible to the poorest of sufferers. Rich men often use poor man's plaster.'

'But not without the judicious advice of a fee'd physician, dear Blandmour.'

'Doubtless, they first consult the physician; but that may be an unnecessary precaution.'

'Perhaps so. I do not gainsay it. Go on.'

'Well, then, did you ever eat of a poor man's pudding?'

'I never so much as heard of it before.'

'Indeed! Well, now you shall eat of one; and you shall eat it, too, as made, unprompted, by a poor man's wife, and you shall eat it at a poor man's table and in a poor man's house. Come now, and if after this eating, you do not say that a poor man's pudding is as relishable as a rich man's, I will give up the point altogether; which briefly is that, through kind nature, the poor, out of their very poverty, extract comfort.'

Not to narrate any more of our conversations upon this subject (for we had several – I being at that time the guest of Blandmour in the country, for the benefit of my health), suffice it that, acting upon Blandmour's hint, I introduced myself into Coulter's house on a wet Monday noon (for the snow had thawed), under the innocent pretence of craving a pedestrian's rest and refreshment for an hour or two.

I was greeted, not without much embarrassment – owing I suppose, to my dress – but still with unaffected and honest kindness. Dame Coulter was just leaving the wash-tub to get ready her one o'clock meal against her good man's return from a deep wood about a mile distant among the hills, where he was chopping by day's-work – seventy-five cents per day – and found himself. The washing being done outside the main building, under an infirm-looking old shed, the dame stood upon a half-rotten, soaked board to protect her feet, as well as might be, from the penetrating damp of the bare ground; hence she looked pale and chill. But her paleness had still another and more secret cause – the paleness of a mother-to-be. A quiet, fathomless heart-trouble, too, couched beneath the mild, resigned blue of her soft and wife-like eye. But she smiled upon me, as apologising for the unavoidable disorder of a Monday and a washing day, and, conducting me into the kitchen, set me down in the best seat it had – an old-fashioned chair of an enfeebled constitution.

I thanked her; and sat rubbing my hands before the ineffectual low fire and – unobservantly as I could – glancing now and then about the room, while the good woman, throwing on more sticks, said she was sorry the room was no warmer. Something more she said, too – not repiningly, however – of the fuel, as old and damp; picked-up sticks from Squire Teamster's forest, where her husband was chopping the sappy logs of the living tree for the squire's fires.

It needed not her remark, whatever it was, to convince me of the inferior quality of the sticks, some being quite mossy and toadstooled with long lying bedded among the accumulated dead leaves of many autumns. They made a sad hissing and vain spluttering enough.

'You must rest yourself here till dinner-time, at least,' said the dame; 'what I have you are heartily welcome to.'

I thanked her again, and begged her not to heed my presence in the least, but go on with her usual affairs.

I was struck by the aspect of the room. The house was old, and constitutionally damp. The window-sills had beads of exuded dampness upon them. The shrivelled sashes shook in their frames, and the green panes of glass were clouded with the long thaw. On some little errand the dame passed into an adjoining chamber, leaving the door partly open. The floor of that room was carpetless, as the kitchen's was. Nothing but bare necessaries were about me; and those not of the best sort. Not a print on the wall; but an old volume of Doddridge lay on the smoked chimney-shelf.

'You must have walked a long way, sir; you sigh so with weariness.'

'No, I am not nigh so weary as yourself, I dare say.'

'Oh, but I am accustomed to that; you are not, I should think,' and her soft, sad blue eye ran over my dress. 'But I must sweep these shavings away; husband made him a new axe-helve this morning before sunrise, and I have been so busy washing, that I have had no time to clear up. But now they are just the thing I want for the fire. They'd be much better though, were they not so green.'

Now if Blandmour were here, thought I to myself, he would call those green shavings poor man's matches, or poor man's tinder, or some pleasant name of that sort.

'I do not know,' said the good woman, turning round to me again – as she stirred among her pots on the smoky fire – 'I do not know how you will like our pudding. It is only rice, milk and salt boiled together.'

'Ah, what they call poor man's pudding, I suppose you mean.'

A quick flush, half resentful, passed over her face.

'*We* do not call it so, sir,' she said, and was silent.

Upbraiding myself for my inadvertence, I could not but again think to myself what Blandmour would have said, had he heard those words and seen that flush.

At last a slow, heavy footfall was heard; then a scraping at the door, and another voice said, 'Come, wife; come, come – I must be back again in a jiff – if you say I *must* take all my meals at home, you must be speedy; because the squire – Good-day, sir,' he exclaimed, now first catching sight of me as he entered the room. He turned towards his wife, enquiringly, and stood stock-still, while the moisture oozed from his patched boots to the floor.

'This gentleman stops here awhile to rest and refresh: he will take dinner with us, too. All will be ready now in a trice; so sit down on the bench, husband, and be patient, I pray. You see, sir,' she continued, turning to me, 'William there wants, of mornings, to carry a cold meal into the woods with him, to save the long one-o'clock walk across the fields to and fro. But I won't let him. A warm dinner is more than pay for the long walk.'

'I don't know about that,' said William, shaking his head. 'I have often debated in my mind whether it really paid. There's not much odds, either way, between a wet walk after hard work and a wet dinner before it. But I like to oblige a good wife like Martha. And you know, sir, that women will have their whimsies.'

'I wish they all had as kind whimsies as your wife has,' said I.

'Well, I've heard that some women ain't all maple-sugar; but, content with dear Martha, I don't know much about others.'

'You find rare wisdom in the woods,' mused I.

'Now, husband, if you ain't too tired, just lend a hand to draw the table out.'

'Nay,' said I, 'let him rest, and let me help.'

'No,' said William, rising.

'Sit still,' said his wife to me.

The table set, in due time we all found ourselves with plates before us.

'You see what we have,' said Coulter – 'salt pork, ryebread, and pudding. Let me help you. I got this pork of the squire, some of his last year's pork, which he let me have on account. It isn't quite so sweet as this year's would be; but I find it hearty enough to work on, and that's all I eat for. Only let the rheumatiz and other sicknesses keep clear of me, and I ask no flavours or favours from any. But you don't eat of the pork!'

'I see,' said the wife, gently and gravely, 'that the gentleman knows the difference between this year's and last year's pork. But perhaps he will like the pudding.'

I summoned up all my self-control, and smilingly assented to the proposition of the pudding, without by my looks casting any reflections upon the pork. But, to tell the truth, it was quite impossible for me (not being ravenous, but only a little hungry at the time) to eat of the latter. It had a yellowish crust all round it, and was rather rankish, I thought, to the taste. I observed, too, that the dame did not eat of it, though she suffered some to be put on her plate, and pretended to be busy with it when Coulter looked that way. But she ate of the rye-bread, and so did I.

'Now, then, for the pudding,' said Coulter. 'Quick, wife; the squire sits in his sitting-room window, looking far out across the fields. His timepiece is true.'

'He don't play the spy on you, does he?' said I.

'Oh, no! – I don't say that. He's a good enough man. He gives me work. But he's particular. Wife, help the gentleman. You see, sir, if I lose the squire's work, what will become of – ' and, with a look for which I honoured humanity, with sly significance he glanced towards his wife; then, a little changing his voice, instantly continued – 'that fine horse I am going to buy.'

'I guess,' said the dame, with a strange, subdued sort of inefficient pleasantry – 'I guess that fine horse you sometimes so merrily dream of will long stay in the squire's stall. But sometimes his man gives me a Sunday ride.'

'A Sunday ride!' said I.

'You see,' resumed Coulter, 'wife loves to go to church; but the nighest is four miles off, over yon snowy hills. So she can't walk it; and I can't carry her in my arms, though I have carried her upstairs before now. But, as she says, the squire's man sometimes gives her a lift on the road and for this cause it is that I speak of a horse I am going to have one of these fine sunny days. And already, before having it, I have christened it "Martha". But what am I about? Come, come, wife! the pudding! Help the gentleman, do! The squire! the squire! – think of the squire! and help round the pudding. There, one – two – three mouthfuls must do me. Goodbye, wife. Goodbye, sir. I'm off.'

And, snatching his soaked hat, the noble poor man hurriedly went out into the soak and the mire.

I suppose now, thinks I to myself, that Blandmour would poetically say he goes to take a poor man's saunter.

'You have a fine husband,' said I to the woman, as we were now left together.

'William loves me this day as on the wedding-day, sir. Some hasty words, but never a harsh one. I wish I were better and stronger for his sake. And, oh! sir, both for his sake and mine' (and the soft, blue, beautiful eyes turned into two well-springs), 'how I wish little William and Martha lived – it is so lonely-like now. William named after him, and Martha for me.'

When a companion's heart of itself overflows, the best one can do is to do nothing. I sat looking down on my as yet untasted pudding.

'You should have seen little William, sir. Such a bright, manly boy, only six years old – cold, cold now!'

Plunging my spoon into the pudding, I forced some into my mouth to stop it.

'And little Martha – oh! sir, she was the beauty! Bitter, bitter! but needs must be borne.'

The mouthful of pudding now touched my palate, and touched it with a mouldy, briny taste. The rice, I knew, was of that damaged sort sold cheap; and the salt from the last year's pork barrel.

'Ah, sir, if those little ones yet to enter the world were the same little ones which so sadly have left it; returning friends, not strangers, strangers, always strangers! Yet does a mother soon learn to love them; for certain, sir, they come from where the others have gone. Don't you believe that, sir? Yes, I know all good people must. But, still, still – and I fear it is wicked, and very black-hearted, too – still, strive how I may to cheer me with thinking of little William and Martha in heaven, and with reading Dr Doddridge there – still, still does dark grief leak in, just like the rain through our roof. I am left so lonesome now, day after day; all the day long, dear William is gone; and all the damp day long grief drizzles and drizzles down on my soul. But I pray to God to forgive me for this; and for the rest, manage it as well as I may.

Bitter and mouldy is the poor man's pudding, groaned I to myself, half choked with but one little mouthful of it, which would hardly go down.

I could stay no longer to hear of sorrows for which the sincerest sympathies could give no adequate relief; of a fond persuasion, to which there could be furnished no further proof than already was had – a persuasion, too, of that sort which much speaking is sure more or less to mar; of causeless self-upbraidings, which no expostulations could have dispelled. I offered no pay for hospitalities gratuitous and honorable as those of a prince. I knew that such offerings would have been more than declined; charity resented.

The native American poor never lose their delicacy or pride; hence, though unreduced to the physical degradation of the European pauper, they yet suffer more in mind than the poor of any other people in the world. Those peculiar social sensibilities nourished by our own peculiar political principles, while they enhance the true dignity of a prosperous American, do but minister to the added wretchedness of the unfortunate: first, by prohibiting their acceptance of what little random relief charity may offer; and, second, by furnishing them with the keenest appreciation of the smarting distinction between their ideal of universal equality and their grindstone experience of the practical misery and infamy of poverty – a misery and infamy which is, ever has been and ever will be precisely the same in India, England and America.

Under pretence that my journey called me forthwith, I bade the dame goodbye; shook her cold hand; looked my last into her blue, resigned eye, and went out into the wet. But cheerless as it was, and damp, damp, damp – the heavy atmosphere charged with all sorts of incipiencies – I yet became conscious, by the suddenness of the contrast, that the house air I had quitted was laden down with that peculiar deleterious quality, the height of which – insufferable to some visitants – will be found in a poor-house ward.

This ill-ventilation in winter of the rooms of the poor – a thing, too, so stubbornly persisted in – is usually charged upon them as their disgraceful neglect of the most simple means to health. But the instinct of the poor is wiser than we think. The air which ventilates, likewise *cools*. And to any shiverer, ill-ventilated warmth is better than well-ventilated cold. Of all the preposterous assumptions of humanity over humanity, nothing exceeds most of the criticisms made on the habits of the poor by the well housed, well warmed and well fed.

'Blandmour,' said I that evening, as after tea I sat on his comfortable sofa, before a blazing fire, with one of his two ruddy little children on my knee, 'you are not what may rightly be called a rich man; you have a fair competence; no more. Is it not so? Well, then, I do not include you when I say that if ever a rich man speaks prosperously to me of a poor man, I shall set it down as – I won't mention the word.'

PICTURE SECOND

Rich Man's Crumbs

IN THE YEAR 1814, during the summer following my first taste of
the poor man's pudding, a sea-voyage was recommended to me by
my physician. The Battle of Waterloo having closed the long
drama of Napoleon's wars, many strangers were visiting Europe. I
arrived in London at the time the victorious princes were there
assembled enjoying the *Arabian Nights'* hospitalities of a grateful
and gorgeous aristocracy, and the courtliest of gentlemen and
kings – George the Prince Regent.

I had declined all letters but one to my banker. I wandered about
for the best reception an adventurous traveller can have – the
reception, I mean, which unsolicited chance and accident throw in
his venturous way.

But I omit all else to recount one hour's hap under the lead of a
very friendly man, whose acquaintance I made in the open street of
Cheapside. He wore a uniform, and was some sort of a civic
subordinate; I forget exactly what. He was off duty that day. His
discourse was chiefly of the noble charities of London. He took me
to two or three, and made admiring mention of many more.

'But,' said he, as we turned into Cheapside again, 'if you are at all
curious about such things, let me take you – if it be not too late – to
one of the most interesting of all – our Lord Mayor's Charities, sir;
nay, the charities not only of a lord mayor, but, I may truly say, in
this one instance, of emperors, regents and kings. You remember
the event of yesterday?'

'That sad fire on the riverside, you mean, unhousing so many of
the poor?'

'No. The grand Guildhall banquet to the princes. Who can forget
it? Sir, the dinner was served on nothing but solid silver and gold
plate, worth at the least £200,000 – that is, 1,000,000 of your
dollars; while the mere expenditure on meats, wines, attendance and

upholstery, etc., cannot be footed under £25,000 – 125,000 dollars of your hard cash.'

'But, surely, my friend, you do not call that charity – feeding kings at that rate?'

'No. The feast came first – yesterday; and the charity after – today. How else would you have it, where princes are concerned? But I think we shall be quite in time – come; here we are at King Street, and down there is Guildhall. Will you go?'

'Gladly, my good friend. Take me where you will. I came but to roam and see.'

Avoiding the main entrance of the hall, which was barred, he took me through some private way, and we found ourselves in a rear blind-walled place in the open air. I looked round amazed. The spot was grimy as a backyard in the Five Points. It was packed with a mass of lean, famished, ferocious creatures, struggling and fighting for some mysterious precedency, and all holding soiled blue tickets in their hands.

'There is no other way,' said my guide; 'we can only get in with the crowd. Will you try it? I hope you have not on your drawing-room suit? What do you say? It will be well worth your sight. So noble a charity does not often offer. The one following the annual banquet of Lord Mayor's day – fine a charity as that certainly is – is not to be mentioned with what will be seen today. Is it, aye?'

As he spoke, a basement door in the distance was thrown open, and the squalid mass made a rush for the dark vault beyond.

I nodded to my guide, and sideways we joined in with the rest. Ere long we found our retreat cut off by the yelping crowd behind, and I could not but congratulate myself on having a civic, as well as civil guide; one, too, whose uniform made evident his authority.

It was just the same as if I were pressed by a mob of cannibals on some pagan beach. The beings round me roared with famine. For in this mighty London misery but maddens. In the country it softens. As I gazed on the meagre, murderous pack, I thought of the blue eye of the gentle wife of poor Coulter. Some sort of curved, glittering steel thing (not a sword; I know not what it was), before worn in his belt, was now flourished overhead by my guide, menacing the creatures to forbear offering the stranger violence.

As we drove, slow and wedge-like, into the gloomy vault, the howls of the mass reverberated. I seemed seething in the Pit with the Lost. On and on, through the dark and the damp, and then up a stone stairway to a wide portal; when, diffusing, the pestiferous mob poured in bright day between painted walls and beneath a painted dome. I thought of the anarchic sack of Versailles.

A few moments more and I stood bewildered among the beggars in the famous Guildhall.

Where I stood – where the thronged rabble stood – less than twelve hours before sat His Imperial Majesty, Alexander of Russia; His Royal Majesty, Frederick William, King of Prussia; His Royal Highness, George, Prince Regent of England; His world-renowned Grace, the Duke of Wellington; with a mob of magnificoes, made up of conquering field marshals, earls, counts, and innumerable other nobles of mark.

The walls swept to and fro, like the foliage of a forest, with blazonings of conquerors' flags. Naught outside the hall was visible. No windows were within four-and-twenty feet of the floor. Cut off from all other sights, I was hemmed in by one splendid spectacle – splendid, I mean, everywhere but as the eye fell towards the floor. *That* was foul as a hovel's – as a kennel's – the naked boards being strewed with the smaller and more wasteful fragments of the feast, while the two long parallel lines, up and down the hall, of now unrobed, shabby, dirty pine tables were piled with less trampled wrecks. The dyed banners were in keeping with the last night's kings; the floor suited the beggars of today. The banners looked down upon the floor as from his balcony Dives upon Lazarus. A line of liveried men kept back with their staves the impatient jam of the mob, who, otherwise, might have instantaneously converted the charity into a pillage. Another body of gowned and gilded officials distributed the broken meats – the cold victuals and crumbs of kings. One after another the beggars held up their dirty blue tickets and were served with the plundered wreck of a pheasant or the rim of a pasty – like the detached crown of an old hat – the solids and meats stolen out.

'What a noble charity!' whispered my guide. 'See that pasty now, snatched by that pale girl; I dare say the Emperor of Russia ate of that last night.'

'Very probably,' murmured I; 'it looks as though some omnivorous emperor or other had had a finger in that pie.'

'And see yon pheasant, too – there – *that* one – the boy in the torn shirt has it now – look! The Prince Regent might have dined off that.' The two breasts were gouged ruthlessly out, exposing the bare bones, embellished with the untouched pinions and legs. 'Yes, who knows!' said my guide, 'his Royal Highness the Prince Regent might have eaten of that identical pheasant.'

'I don't doubt it,' murmured I, 'he is said to be uncommonly fond of the breast. But where is Napoleon's head in a charger? I should fancy *that* ought to have been the principal dish.'

'You are merry. Sir, even Cossacks are charitable here in Guildhall. Look! the famous Platoff, the Hetman himself – he was here last night with the rest – no doubt he thrust a lance into yon fat pork-pie there. Look! the old shirtless man has it now. How he licks his chops over it, little thinking of or thanking the good, kind Cossack that left it him! Ah! another – a stouter – has grabbed it. It falls; bless my soul! – the dish is quite empty – only a bit of the hacked crust.'

'The Cossacks, my friend, are said to be immoderately fond of fat,' observed I. 'The Hetman was hardly so charitable as you thought.'

'A noble charity, upon the whole, for all that. See, even Gog and Magog yonder, at the other end of the hall, fairly laugh out their delight at the scene.'

'But don't you think, though,' hinted I, 'that the sculptor, whoever he was, carved the laugh too much into a grin – a sort of sardonical grin?'

'Well, that's as you take it, sir. But see – now I'd wager a guinea the Lord Mayor's lady dipped her golden spoon into yonder golden-hued jelly. See, the jelly-eyed old body has slipped it, in one broad gulp, down his throat!'

'Peace to that jelly!' breathed I.

'What a generous, noble, magnanimous charity this is! Unheard of in any country but England, which feeds her very beggars with golden-hued jellies.'

'But not three times every day, my friend. And do you really think that jellies are the best sort of relief you can furnish to beggars? Would not plain beef and bread, with something to do and be paid for, be better?'

'But plain beef and bread were not eaten here. Emperors, and prince regents, and kings, and field marshals don't often dine on plain beef and bread. So the leavings are according. Tell me, can you expect that the crumbs of kings can be like the crumbs of squirrels?'

'*You!* I mean *you*! stand aside, or else be served and away! Here, take this pasty, and be thankful that you taste of the same dish with Her Grace the Duchess of Devonshire. Graceless ragamuffin, do you hear?'

These words were bellowed at me through the din by a red-gowned official nigh the board.

'Surely he does not mean *me*,' said I to my guide; 'he has not confounded *me* with the rest.'

'One is known by the company one keeps,' smiled my guide. 'See! not only stands your hat awry and bunged on your head, but your coat is fouled and torn. Nay,' he cried to the red-gown, 'this is an unfortunate friend; a simple spectator, I assure you.'

'Ah! is that you, old lad?' responded the red-gown, in familiar recognition of my guide – a personal friend, as it seemed. 'Well, convey your friend out forthwith. Mind the grand crash; it will soon be coming; hark! now! away with him!'

Too late. The last dish had been seized. The yet unglutted mob raised a fierce yell, which wafted the banners like a strong gust, and filled the air with a reek as from sewers. They surged against the tables, broke through all barriers and billowed over the hall – their bare tossed arms like the dashed ribs of a wreck. It seemed to me as if a sudden impotent fury of fell envy possessed them. That one half-hour's peep at the mere remnants of the glories of the banquets of kings, the unsatisfying mouthfuls of disembowelled pasties, plundered pheasants and half-sacked jellies, served to remind them of the intrinsic contempt of the alms. In this sudden mood, or whatever mysterious thing it was that now seized them, these Lazaruses seemed ready to spew up in repentant scorn the contumelious crumbs of Dives.

'This way, this way! stick like a bee to my back,' intensely whispered my guide. 'My friend there has answered my beck, and thrown open yon private door for us two. Wedge – wedge in – quick – there goes your bunged hat – never stop for your coat-tail – hit that man – strike him down! hold! jam! now! now! wrench along for your life! ha! here we breathe freely; thank God! You faint. Ho!'

'Never mind. This fresh air revives me.'

I inhaled a few more breaths of it, and felt ready to proceed.

'And now conduct me, my good friend, by some front passage into Cheapside, forthwith. I must home.'

'Not by the sidewalk though. Look at your dress. I must get a hack for you.'

'Yes, I suppose so,' said I, ruefully eying my tatters, and then glancing in envy at the close-bodied coat and flat cap of my guide, which defied all tumblings and tearings.

'There, now, sir,' said the honest fellow, as he put me into the hack, and tucked in me and my rags, 'when you get back to your own country, you can say you have witnessed the greatest of all England's noble charities. Of course, you will make reasonable allowances for the unavoidable jam. Goodbye. Mind, Jehu' –

addressing the driver on the box – 'this is a *gentleman* you carry. He is just from the Guildhall Charity, which accounts for his appearance. Go on now. London Tavern, Fleet Street, remember, is the place.'

'Now, heaven in its kind mercy save me from the noble charities of London,' sighed I, as that night I lay bruised and battered on my bed; 'and heaven save me equally from the poor man's pudding and the rich man's crumbs.'

THE PARADISE OF BACHELORS AND THE TARTARUS OF MAIDS

The Paradise of Bachelors

IT LIES NOT FAR FROM TEMPLE BAR.

Going to it, by the usual way, is like stealing from a heated plain into some cool, deep glen, shady among harbouring hills.

Sick with the din and soiled with the mud of Fleet Street – where the Benedick tradesmen are hurrying by, with ledger-lines ruled along their brows, thinking upon rise of bread and fall of babies – you adroitly turn a mystic corner – not a street – glide down a dim, monastic way, flanked by dark, sedate and solemn piles, and still wending on, give the whole care-worn world the slip and, disentangled, stand beneath the quiet cloisters of the Paradise of Bachelors.

Sweet are the oases in Sahara; charming the isle-groves of August prairies; delectable pure faith amidst a thousand perfidies; but sweeter, still more charming, most delectable, the dreamy Paradise of Bachelors, found in the stony heart of stunning London.

In mild meditation pace the cloisters; take your pleasure, sip your leisure, in the garden waterward; go linger in the ancient library; go worship in the sculptured chapel; but little have you seen, just nothing do you know, not the sweet kernel have you tasted, till you dine among the banded Bachelors, and see their convivial eyes and glasses sparkle. Not dine in bustling commons, during term-time, in the hall; but tranquilly, by private hint, at a private table; some fine Templar's hospitably invited guest.

Templar? That's a romantic name. Let me see. Brian de Bois-Guilbert was a Templar, I believe. Do we understand you to insinuate that those famous Templars still survive in modern London? May the ring of their armed heels be heard, and the rattle of their shields, as in mailed prayer the monk-knights kneel before the consecrated Host? Surely a monk-knight were a curious sight picking his way along the Strand, his gleaming corselet and snowy surcoat spattered by an omnibus. Long-bearded, too, according to his order's rule; his face fuzzy as a pard's; how would the grim ghost look among the crop-haired, close-shaven citizens? We know indeed – sad history recounts it – that a moral blight tainted at last this sacred brotherhood. Though no sworded foe might outskill them in the fence, yet the worm of luxury crawled beneath their guard, gnawing the core of knightly troth, nibbling the monastic vow, till at last the monk's austerity relaxed to wassailing and the sworn knights-bachelors grew to be but hypocrites and rakes.

But for all this, quite unprepared were we to learn that Knights Templars (if at all in being) were so entirely secularised as to be reduced from carving out immortal fame in glorious battling for the Holy Land to the carving of roast-mutton at a dinner-board. Like Anacreon, do these degenerate Templars now think it sweeter far to fall in banquet than in war? Or, indeed, how can there be any survival of that famous order? Templars in modern London! Templars in their red-cross mantles smoking cigars at the Divan! Templars crowded in a railway train, till, stacked with steel helmet, spear and shield, the whole train looks like one elongated locomotive!

No. The genuine Templar is long since departed. Go view the wondrous tombs in the Temple Church; see there the rigidly haughty forms stretched out, with crossed arms upon their stilly hearts, in everlasting and undreaming rest. Like the years before the flood, the bold Knights-Templars are no more. Nevertheless, the name remains, and the nominal society, and the ancient grounds, and some of the ancient edifices. But the iron heel is changed to a boot of patent-leather; the long two-handed sword to a one-handed quill; the monk-giver of gratuitous ghostly counsel now counsels for a fee; the defender of the sarcophagus (if in good practice with his weapon) now has more than one case to defend; the vowed opener and clearer of all highways leading to the Holy Sepulchre, now has it in particular charge to check, to clog, to hinder and embarrass all the courts and avenues of law; the knight-combatant of the Saracen, breasting spear-points at Acre, now fights law-points in Westminster Hall. The helmet is a wig. Struck by time's enchanter's wand, the Templar is today a lawyer.

But, like many others tumbled from proud glory's height – like the apple, hard on the bough but mellow on the ground – the Templar's fall has but made him all the finer fellow.

I dare say those old warrior-priests were but gruff and grouty at the best; cased in Birmingham hardware, how could the crimped arms give yours or mine a hearty shake? Their proud, ambitious, monkish souls clasped shut, like horn-book missals; their very faces clapped in bomb-shells; what sort of genial men were these? But best of comrades, most affable of hosts, capital diner is the modern Templar. His wit and wine are both of sparkling brands.

The church and cloisters, courts and vaults, lanes and passages banquet-halls, refectories, libraries, terraces, gardens, broad walks, domiciles and dessert-rooms, covering a very large space of ground, and all grouped in central neighbourhood, and quite sequestered from the old city's surrounding din; and everything about the place being kept in most bachelor-like particularity, no part of London offers to a quiet wight so agreeable a refuge.

The Temple is, indeed, a city by itself. A city with all the best appurtenances, as the above enumeration shows. A city with a park to it, and flower-beds, and a riverside – the Thames flowing by as openly, in one part, as by Eden's primal garden flowed the mild Euphrates. In what is now the Temple Garden, the old Crusaders used to exercise their steeds and lances; the modern Templars now lounge on the benches beneath the trees, and, switching their patent-leather boots, in gay discourse exercise at repartee.

Long lines of stately portraits in the banquet-halls, show what great men of mark – famous nobles, judges and Lord Chancellors have in their time been Templars. But all Templars are not known to universal fame; though, if the having warm hearts and warmer welcomes, full minds and fuller cellars, and giving good advice and glorious dinners, spiced with rare divertissements of fun and fancy, merit immortal mention, set down, ye muses, the names of R. F. C. and his imperial brother.

Though to be a Templar, in the one true sense, you must needs be a lawyer, or a student at the law, and be ceremoniously enrolled as member of the order, yet as many such, though Templars, do not reside within the Temple's precincts, though they may have their offices there, just so, on the other hand, there are many residents of the hoary old domiciles who are not admitted Templars. If being, say, a lounging gentleman and bachelor, or a quiet, unmarried, literary man, charmed with the soft seclusion of the spot, you much desire to pitch your shady tent among the rest in this serene encampment, then you must make some special friend among the order, and procure him to rent, in his name but at your charge, whatever vacant chamber you may find to suit.

Thus, I suppose, did Dr Johnson, that nominal Benedick and widower but virtual bachelor, when for a space he resided here. So, too, did that undoubted bachelor and rare good soul, Charles Lamb. And hundreds more, of sterling spirits, Brethren of the Order of Celibacy, from time to time have dined, and slept, and tabernacled here. Indeed, the place is all a honeycomb of offices and domiciles. Like any cheese, it is quite perforated through and through in all directions with the snug cells of bachelors. Dear, delightful spot! Ah! when I bethink me of the sweet hours there passed, enjoying such genial hospitalities beneath those time-honoured roofs, my heart only finds due utterance through poetry; and, with a sigh, I softly sing, 'Carry me back to old Virginny!'

Such then, at large, is the Paradise of Bachelors. And such I found it one pleasant afternoon in the smiling month of May, when, sallying from my hotel in Trafalgar Square, I went to keep my dinner appointment with that fine barrister, bachelor and bencher, R. F. C. (he *is* the first and second, and *should be* the third; I hereby nominate him), whose card I kept fast pinched between my gloved forefinger and thumb, and every now and then snatched still another look at the pleasant address inscribed beneath the name, 'No. — , Elm Court, Temple'.

At the core he was a right bluff, carefree, right comfortable and most companionable Englishman. If on a first acquaintance he seemed reserved, quite icy in his air – patience; this champagne will thaw. And if it never do, better frozen champagne than liquid vinegar.

There were nine gentlemen, all bachelors, at the dinner. One was from 'No. — , King's Bench Walk, Temple'; a second, third and fourth and fifth from various courts or passages christened with some similarly rich resounding syllables. It was, indeed, a sort of senate of the bachelors, sent to this dinner from widely scattered districts, to represent the general celibacy of the Temple. Nay, it was, by representation, a grand parliament of the best bachelors in universal London; several of those present being from distant quarters of the town, noted immemorial seats of lawyers and unmarried men – Lincoln's Inn, Furnival's Inn; and one gentleman, upon whom I looked with a sort of collateral awe, hailed from the spot where Lord Verulam once abode a bachelor – Gray's Inn.

The apartment was well up towards heaven. I know not how many strange old stairs I climbed to get to it. But a good dinner with famous company should be well earned. No doubt our host had his dining-room so high with a view to secure the prior exercise necessary to the due relishing and digesting of it.

The furniture was wonderfully unpretending, old and snug. No new shining mahogany, sticky with undried varnish; no uncomfortably luxurious ottomans and sofas too fine to use vexed you in this sedate apartment. It is a thing which every sensible American should learn from every sensible Englishman, that glare and glitter, gimcracks and gewgaws, are not indispensable to domestic solacement. The American Benedick snatches, downtown, a tough chop in a gilded showbox; the English bachelor leisurely dines at home on that incomparable South Down of his, off a plain deal board.

The ceiling of the room was low. Who wants to dine under the dome of St. Peter's? High ceilings! If that is your demand, and the higher the better, and you be so very tall, then go dine out with the topping giraffe in the open air.

In good time the nine gentlemen sat down to nine covers, and soon were fairly underway.

If I remember right, ox-tail soup inaugurated the affair. Of a rich russet hue, its agreeable flavour dissipated my first confounding of its main ingredient with teamsters' gads and the raw hides of ushers. (By way of interlude, we here drank a little claret.) Neptune's was the next tribute rendered – turbot coming second; snow-white, flaky, and just gelatinous enough, not too turtleish in its unctuousness. (At this point we refreshed ourselves with a glass of sherry.) After these light skirmishes had vanished, the heavy artillery of the feast marched in, led by that well-known English generalissimo, roast beef. For aides-de-camp we had a saddle of mutton, a fat turkey, a chicken-pie, and endless other savoury things; while for *avant couriers* came nine silver flagons of humming ale. This heavy ordnance having departed on the track of the light skirmishers, a picked brigade of game-fowl encamped upon the board, their camp-fires lit by the ruddiest of decanters.

Tarts and puddings followed, with innumerable niceties; then cheese and crackers. (By way of ceremony, simply, only to keep up good old fashions, we here each drank a glass of good old port.)

The cloth was now removed; and, like Blücher's army coming in at the death on the field of Waterloo, in marched a fresh detachment of bottles, dusty with their hurried march.

All these manoeuvrings of the forces were superintended by a surprising old field marshal (I cannot school myself to call him by the inglorious name of waiter), with snowy hair and napkin, and a head like Socrates. Amidst all the hilarity of the feast, intent on important business, he disdained to smile. Venerable man!

I have above endeavoured to give some slight schedule of the general plan of operations. But anyone knows that a good, genial dinner is a sort of pell-mell, indiscriminate affair, quite baffling to detail in all particulars. Thus, I spoke of taking a glass of claret, and a glass of sherry, and a glass of port, and a mug of ale – all at certain specific periods and times. But those were merely the state bumpers, so to speak. Innumerable impromptu glasses were drained between the periods of those grand imposing ones.

The nine bachelors seemed to have the most tender concern for each other's health. All the time, in flowing wine, they most earnestly expressed their sincerest wishes for the entire wellbeing and lasting hygiene of the gentleman on the right and on the left. I noticed that when one of these kind bachelors desired a little more wine (just for his stomach's sake, like Timothy), he would not help himself to it unless some other bachelor would join him. It seemed held something indelicate, selfish and unfraternal to be seen taking a lonely, unparticipated glass. Meantime, as the wine ran apace, the spirits of the company grew more and more to perfect genialness and unconstraint. They related all sorts of pleasant stories. Choice experiences in their private lives were now brought out, like choice brands of Moselle or Rhenish, only kept for particular company. One told us how mellowly he lived when a student at Oxford; with various spicy anecdotes of most frank-hearted noble lords, his liberal companions. Another bachelor, a grey-headed man with a sunny face, who, by his own account, embraced every opportunity of leisure to cross over into the Low Countries on sudden tours of inspection of the fine old Flemish architecture there – this learned, white-haired, sunny-faced old bachelor excelled in his descriptions of the elaborate splendours of those old guildhalls, town-halls and stadthold-houses to be seen in the land of the ancient Flemings. A third was a great frequenter of the British Museum, and knew all about scores of wonderful antiquities, of Oriental manuscripts and costly books without a duplicate. A fourth had lately returned from a trip to Old Granada, and, of course, was full of Saracenic scenery. A fifth had a funny case in law to tell. A sixth was erudite in wines. A seventh had a strange characteristic anecdote of the private life of the Iron Duke, never printed, and never before announced in any public or private company. An eighth had lately been amusing his evenings, now and then, with translating a comic poem of Pulci's. He quoted for us the more amusing passages.

And so the evening slipped along, the hours told, not by a water-clock, like King Alfred's, but a wine-chronometer. Meantime the table seemed a sort of Epsom Heath; a regular ring, where the decanters galloped round. For fear one decanter should not with sufficient speed reach his destination, another was sent express after him to hurry him; and then a third to hurry the second; and so on with a fourth and fifth. And throughout all this nothing loud, nothing unmannerly, nothing turbulent. I am quite sure, from the scrupulous gravity and austerity of his air, that had Socrates, the field marshal, perceived aught of indecorum in the company he served, he would have forthwith departed without giving warning. I afterwards learned that, during the repast, an invalid bachelor in an adjoining chamber enjoyed his first sound refreshing slumber in three long, weary weeks.

It was the very perfection of quiet absorption of good living, good drinking, good feeling and good talk. We were a band of brothers. Comfort – fraternal, household comfort, was the grand trait of the affair. Also, you could plainly see that these easy hearted men had no wives or children to give an anxious thought. Almost all of them were travellers, too; for bachelors alone can travel freely, and without any twinges of their consciences touching desertion of the fireside.

The thing called pain, the bugbear styled trouble – those two legends seemed preposterous to their bachelor imaginations. How could men of liberal sense, ripe scholarship in the world and capacious philosophical and convivial understandings – how could they suffer themselves to be imposed upon by such monkish fables? Pain! Trouble! As well talk of Catholic miracles. No such thing! – Pass the sherry, sir. Pooh, pooh! Can't be! – The port, sir, if you please. Nonsense; don't tell me so! The decanter stops with you, sir, I believe.

And so it went.

Not long after the cloth was drawn, our host glanced significantly upon Socrates, who, solemnly stepping to a stand, returned with an immense convolved horn, a regular Jericho horn, mounted with polished silver, and otherwise chased and curiously enriched; not omitting two life-like goats' heads, with four more horns of solid silver, projecting from opposite sides of the mouth of the noble main horn.

Not having heard that our host was a performer on the bugle, I was surprised to see him lift this horn from the table, as if he were about to blow an inspiring blast. But I was relieved from this, and set quite right as touching the purposes of the horn, by his now inserting his thumb and forefinger into its mouth; whereupon a slight aroma was stirred up, and my nostrils were greeted with the smell of some choice Rappee. It was a mull of snuff. It went the rounds. Capital idea this, thought I, of taking snuff about this juncture. This goodly fashion must be introduced among my countrymen at home, further ruminated I.

The remarkable decorum of the nine bachelors – a decorum not to be affected by any quantity of wine – a decorum unassailable by any degree of mirthfulness – this was again set in a forcible light to me by now observing that though they took snuff very freely, yet not a man so far violated the proprieties, or so far molested the invalid bachelor in the adjoining room, as to indulge himself in a sneeze. The snuff was snuffed silently, as if it had been some fine innoxious powder brushed off the wings of butterflies.

But fine though they be, bachelors' dinners, like bachelors' lives, cannot endure forever. The time came for breaking up. One by one the bachelors took their hats, and two by two and arm in arm they descended, still conversing, to the flagging of the court; some going to their neighbouring chambers to turn over the *Decameron* ere retiring for the night; some to smoke a cigar, promenading in the garden on the cool riverside; some to make for the street, call a hack, and be driven snugly to their distant lodgings.

I was the last lingerer.

'Well,' said my smiling host, 'what do you think of the Temple here, and the sort of life we bachelors make out to live in it?'

'Sir,' said I, with a burst of admiring candour – 'Sir, this is the very Paradise of Bachelors!'

The Tartarus of Maids

IT LIES NOT FAR from Woedolor Mountain in New England. Turning to the east, right out from among bright farms and sunny meadows, nodding in early June with odorous grasses, you enter ascendingly among bleak hills. These gradually close in upon a dusky pass, which, from the violent Gulf Stream of air unceasingly driving between its cloven walls of haggard rock, as well as from the tradition of a crazy spinster's hut having long ago stood somewhere hereabouts, is called the Mad Maid's Bellows-Pipe.

Winding along at the bottom of the gorge is a dangerously narrow wheel-road, occupying the bed of a former torrent. Following this road to its highest point, you stand as within a Dantean gateway. From the steepness of the walls here, their strangely ebon hue, and the sudden contraction of the gorge, this particular point is called the Black Notch. The ravine now expandingly descends into a great, purple, hopper-shaped hollow, far sunk among many Plutonian, shaggy-wooded mountains. By the country people this hollow is called the Devil's Dungeon. Sounds of torrents fall on all sides upon the ear. These rapid waters unite at last in one turbid brick-coloured stream, boiling through a flume among enormous boulders. They call this strange coloured torrent Blood River. Gaining a dark precipice it wheels suddenly to the west, and makes one maniac spring of sixty feet into the arms of a stunted wood of grey-haired pines, between which it thence eddies on its further way down to the invisible lowlands.

Conspicuously crowning a rocky bluff high to one side, at the cataract's verge, is the ruin of an old saw-mill, built in those primitive times when vast pines and hemlocks superabounded throughout the neighbouring region. The black-mossed bulk of those immense, rough-hewn and spike-knotted logs, here and there tumbled all together, in long abandonment and decay, or left in solitary, perilous projection over the cataract's gloomy brink, impart to this rude wooden ruin not only much of the aspect of one of rough-quarried stone, but also a sort of feudal, Rhineland and

Thurmberg look, derived from the pinnacled wildness of the neighbouring scenery.

Not far from the bottom of the Dungeon stands a large white-washed building, relieved, like some great whited sepulchre, against the sullen background of mountainside firs and other hardy ever-greens, inaccessibly rising in grim terraces for some two thousand feet.

The building is a paper-mill.

Having embarked on a large scale in the seedsman's business (so extensively and broadcast, indeed, that at length my seeds were distributed through all the Eastern and Northern States, and even fell into the far soil of Missouri and the Carolinas), the demand for paper at my place became so great that the expenditure soon amounted to a most important item in the general account. It need hardly be hinted how paper comes into use with seedsmen as envelopes. These are mostly made of yellowish paper folded square; and when filled, are all but flat, and being stamped and superscribed with the nature of the seeds contained, assume not a little the appearance of business letters ready for the mail. Of these small envelopes I used an incredible quantity – several hundreds of thousands in a year. For a time I had purchased my paper from the wholesale dealers in a neighbouring town. For economy's sake, and partly for the adventure of the trip, I now resolved to cross the mountains, some sixty miles, and order my future paper at the Devil's Dungeon paper-mill.

The sleighing being uncommonly fine towards the end of January, and promising to hold so for no small period, in spite of the bitter cold I started one grey Friday noon in my pung, well fitted with buffalo and wolf robes; and, spending one night on the road, next noon came in sight of Woedolor Mountain.

The far summit fairly smoked with frost; white vapours curled up from its white-wooded top, as from a chimney. The intense congelation made the whole country look like one petrifaction. The steel shoes of my pung crunched and gritted over the vitreous, chippy snow as if it had been broken glass. The forests here and there skirting the route, feeling the same all-stiffening influence, their inmost fibres penetrated with the cold, strangely groaned – not in the swaying branches merely, but likewise in the vertical trunk – as the fitful gusts remorselessly swept through them. Brittle with excessive frost, many colossal tough-grained maples, snapped in twain like pipestems, cumbered the unfeeling earth.

Flaked all over with frozen sweat, white as a milky ram, his nostrils at each breath sending forth two horn-shaped shoots of heated respiration, Black, my good horse, but six years old, started at a sudden turn, where, right across the track – not ten minutes fallen – an old distorted hemlock lay, darkly undulatory as an anaconda.

Gaining the Bellows-Pipe, the violent blast, dead from behind, all but shoved my high-backed pung uphill. The gust shrieked through the shivered pass, as if laden with lost spirits bound to the unhappy world. Ere gaining the summit, Black, my horse, as if exasperated by the cutting wind, slung out with his strong hindlegs, tore the light pung straight uphill, and sweeping grazingly through the narrow notch, sped downward madly past the ruined sawmill. Into the Devil's Dungeon horse and cataract rushed together.

With might and main, quitting my seat and robes, and standing backward, with one foot braced against the dashboard, I rasped and churned the bit, and stopped him just in time to avoid collision, at a turn, with the bleak nozzle of a rock, couchant like a lion in the way – a roadside rock.

At first I could not discover the paper-mill.

The whole hollow gleamed with the white, except, here and there, where a pinnacle of granite showed one windswept angle bare. The mountains stood pinned in shrouds – a pass of Alpine corpses. Where stands the mill? Suddenly a whirring, humming sound broke upon my ear. I looked, and there, like an arrested avalanche, lay the large whitewashed factory. It was subordinately surrounded by a cluster of other and smaller buildings, some of which, from their cheap, blank air, great length, gregarious windows and comfortless expression, no doubt were boarding-houses of the operatives. A snow-white hamlet amidst the snows. Various rude, irregular squares and courts resulted from the somewhat picturesque clusterings of these buildings, owing to the broken, rocky nature of the ground, which forbade all method in their relative arrangement. Several narrow lanes and alleys, too, partly blocked with snow fallen from the roof, cut up the hamlet in all directions.

When, turning from the travelled highway, jingling with bells of numerous farmers – who, availing themselves of the fine sleighing, were dragging their wood to market – and frequently diversified with swift cutters dashing from inn to inn of the scattered villages – when, I say, turning from that bustling main road, I by degrees wound into the Mad Maid's Bellows-Pipe, and saw the grim Black Notch beyond, then something latent, as well as something obvious in the time and scene, strangely brought back to my mind my first sight of dark and grimy Temple Bar. And when Black, my horse, went darting through the Notch, perilously grazing its rocky wall, I remembered being in a runaway London omnibus, which in much the same sort of style, though by no means at an equal rate, dashed through the ancient arch of Wren. Though the two objects did by no means completely correspond, yet this partial inadequacy but served to tinge the similitude not less with the vividness than the disorder of a dream. So that when, upon reining up at the protruding rock, I at last caught sight of the quaint groupings of the factory-buildings, and with the travelled highway and the Notch behind, found myself all alone, silently and privily stealing through deep-cloven passages into this sequestered spot, and saw the long, high-gabled main factory edifice, with a rude tower – for hoisting heavy boxes – at one end, standing among its crowded outbuildings and boarding-houses, as the Temple Church amidst the surrounding offices and dormitories, and when the marvellous retirement of this mysterious mountain nook fastened its whole spell upon me, then, what memory lacked, all tributary imagination furnished, and I said to myself, 'This is the very counterpart of the Paradise of Bachelors, but snowed upon, and frost-painted to a sepulchre.'

Dismounting and warily picking my way down the dangerous declivity – horse and man both sliding now and then upon the icy ledges – at length I drove, or the blast drove me, into the largest square, before one side of the main edifice. Piercingly and shrilly the shotted blast blew by the corner; and redly and demoniacally boiled Blood River at one side. A long wood-pile, of many scores of cords, all glittering in mail of crusted ice, stood crosswise in the square. A row of horse-posts, their north sides plastered with adhesive snow, flanked the factory wall. The bleak frost packed and paved the square as with some ringing metal.

The inverted similitude recurred – 'The sweet, tranquil Temple garden, with the Thames bordering its green beds,' strangely meditated I.

But where are the gay bachelors?

Then, as I and my horse stood shivering in the wind-spray, a girl ran from a neighbouring dormitory door, and throwing her thin apron over her bare head, made for the opposite building.

'One moment, my girl; is there no shed hereabouts which I may drive into?'

Pausing, she turned upon me a face pale with work and blue with cold; an eye supernatural with unrelated misery.

'Nay,' faltered I, 'I mistook you. Go on; I want nothing.'

Leading my horse close to the door from which she had come, I knocked. Another pale, blue girl appeared, shivering in the doorway as, to prevent the blast, she jealously held the door ajar.

'Nay, I mistake again. In God's name shut the door. But hold, is there no man about?'

That moment a dark-complexioned, well-wrapped personage passed, making for the factory door, and spying him coming, the girl rapidly closed the other one.

'Is there no horse-shed here, sir?'

'Yonder, to the wood-shed,' he replied, and disappeared inside the factory.

With much ado I managed to wedge in horse and pung between the scattered piles of wood all sawn and split. Then, blanketing my horse, and piling my buffalo on the blanket's top, and tucking in its edges well around the breast-band and breeching, so that the wind might not strip him bare, I tied him fast, and ran lamely for the factory door, stiff with frost, and cumbered with my driver's dread-naught.

Immediately I found myself standing in a spacious place, intolerably lighted by long rows of windows, focusing inward the snowy scene without.

At rows of blank-looking counters sat rows of blank-looking girls, with blank, white folders in their blank hands, all blankly folding blank paper.

In one corner stood some huge frame of ponderous iron, with a vertical thing like a piston periodically rising and falling upon a heavy wooden block. Before it – its tame minister – stood a tall girl, feeding the iron animal with half-quires of rose-hued notepaper which, at every downward dab of the piston-like machine, received in the corner the impress of a wreath of roses. I looked from the rosy paper to the pallid cheek, but said nothing.

Seated before a long apparatus, strung with long, slender strings like any harp, another girl was feeding it with foolscap sheets which, so soon as they curiously travelled from her on the cords, were withdrawn at the opposite end of the machine by a second girl. They came to the first girl blank; they went to the second girl ruled.

I looked upon the first girl's brow, and saw it was young and fair; I looked upon the second girl's brow, and saw it was ruled and wrinkled. Then, as I still looked, the two – for some small variety to the monotony – changed places; and where had stood the young, fair brow, now stood the ruled and wrinkled one.

Perched high upon a narrow platform, and still higher upon a high stool crowning it, sat another figure serving some other iron animal; while below the platform sat her mate in some sort of reciprocal attendance.

Not a syllable was breathed. Nothing was heard but the low, steady overruling hum of the iron animals. The human voice was banished from the spot. Machinery – that vaunted slave of humanity – here stood menially served by human beings, who served mutely and cringingly as the slave serves the Sultan. The girls did not so much seem accessory wheels to the general machinery as mere cogs to the wheels.

All this scene around me was instantaneously taken in at one sweeping glance – even before I had proceeded to unwind the heavy tippet from around my neck. But as soon as this fell from me, the dark-complexioned man, standing close by, raised a sudden cry, and seizing my arm, dragged me out into the open air, and without pausing for a word instantly caught up some congealed snow and began rubbing both my cheeks.

'Two white spots like the whites of your eyes,' he said; 'man, your cheeks are frozen.'

'That may well be,' muttered I; ' 'tis some wonder the frost of the Devil's Dungeon strikes in no deeper. Rub away.'

Soon a horrible, tearing pain caught at my reviving cheeks. Two gaunt bloodhounds, one on each side, seemed mumbling them. I seemed Actaeon.

Presently, when all was over, I re-entered the factory, made known my business, concluded it satisfactorily, and then begged to be conducted throughout the place to view it.

'Cupid is the boy for that,' said the dark-complexioned man. 'Cupid!' and by this odd fancy-name calling a dimpled, red-cheeked, spirited-looking, forward little fellow, who was rather impudently, I thought, gliding about among the passive-looking girls – like a gold-fish through hueless waves – yet doing nothing in particular that I could see, the man bade him lead the stranger through the edifice.

'Come first and see the water-wheel,' said this lively lad, with the air of boyishly-brisk importance.

Quitting the folding-room, we crossed some damp, cold boards, and stood beneath a great wet shed, incessantly showering with foam, like the green barnacled bow of some East Indiaman in a gale. Round and round here went the enormous revolutions of the dark colossal water-wheel, grim with its one immutable purpose.

'This sets our whole machinery a-going, sir; in every part of all these buildings; where the girls work and all.'

I looked, and saw that the turbid waters of Blood River had not changed their hue by coming under the use of man.

'You make only blank paper; no printing of any sort, I suppose? All blank paper, don't you?'

'Certainly; what else should a paper-factory make?'

The lad here looked at me as if suspicious of my common-sense.

'Oh, to be sure!' said I, confused and stammering; 'it only struck me as so strange that red waters should turn out pale chee – paper, I mean.'

He took me up a wet and rickety stair to a great light room, furnished with no visible thing but rude, manger-like receptacles running all round its sides; and up to these mangers, like so many mares haltered to the rack, stood rows of girls. Before each was vertically thrust up a long, glittering scythe, immovably fixed at bottom to the manger-edge. The curve of the scythe, and its having no snath to it, made it look exactly like a sword. To and fro, across the sharp edge, the girls forever dragged long strips of rags, washed white, picked from baskets at one side, thus ripping asunder every seam, and converting the tatters almost into lint. The air swam with the fine, poisonous particles, which from all sides darted, subtly, as motes in sunbeams, into the lungs.

'This is the rag-room,' coughed the boy.

'You find it rather stifling here,' coughed I, in answer; 'but the girls don't cough.'

'Oh, they are used to it.'

'Where do you get such hosts of rags?' picking up a handful from a basket.

'Some from the country round about; some from far over sea – Leghorn and London.'

' 'Tis not unlikely, then,' murmured I, 'that among these heaps of rags there may be some old shirts, gathered from the dormitories of the Paradise of Bachelors. But the buttons are all dropped off. Pray, my lad, do you ever find any bachelors' buttons hereabouts?'

'None grow in this part of the country. The Devil's Dungeon is no place for flowers.'

'Oh! you mean the *flowers* so called – the Bachelor's Buttons?'

'And was not that what you asked about? Or did you mean the gold bosom-buttons of our boss, Old Bach, as our whispering girls all call him?'

'The man, then, I saw below is a bachelor, is he?'

'Oh, yes, he's a Bach.'

'The edges of those swords, they are turned outward from the girls, if I see right; but their rags and fingers fly so, I cannot distinctly see.'

'Turned outward.'

Yes, murmured I to myself; I see it now; turned outward; and each erected sword is so borne, edge-outward, before each girl. If my reading fails me not, just so, of old, condemned state-prisoners went from the hall of judgment to their doom; an officer before, bearing a sword, its edge turned outward, in significance of their fatal sentence. So, through consumptive pallors of this blank, raggy life, go these white girls to death.

'Those scythes look very sharp,' again turning towards the boy.

'Yes; they have to keep them so. Look!'

That moment two of the girls, dropping their rags, plied each a whetstone up and down the sword-blade. My unaccustomed blood curdled at the sharp shriek of the tormented steel.

Their own executioners; themselves whetting the very swords that slay them, meditated I.

'What makes those girls so sheet-white, my lad?'

'Why' – with a roguish twinkle, pure ignorant drollery, not knowing heartlessness – 'I suppose the handling of such white bits of sheets all the time makes them so sheety.'

'Let us leave the rag-room now, my lad.'

More tragical and more inscrutably mysterious than any mystic sight, human or machine, throughout the factory, was the strange innocence of cruel-heartedness in this usage-hardened boy.

'And now,' said he, cheerily, 'I suppose you want to see our great machine, which cost us twelve thousand dollars only last autumn. That's the machine that makes the paper, too. This way, sir.'

Following him, I crossed a large, bespattered place, with two great round vats in it, full of a white, wet, woolly-looking stuff, not unlike the albuminous part of an egg, soft-boiled.

'There,' said Cupid, tapping the vats carelessly, 'these are the first beginnings of the paper, this white pulp you see. Look how it swims bubbling round and round, moved by the paddle here. From hence it pours from both vats into that one common channel yonder, and so goes, mixed up and leisurely, to the great machine. And now for that.'

He led me into a room, stifling with a strange, blood-like, abdominal heat, as if here, true enough, were being finally developed the germinous particles lately seen.

Before me, rolled out like some long Eastern manuscript, lay stretched one continuous length of iron framework – multitudinous and mystical, with all sorts of rollers, wheels and cylinders in slowly measured and unceasing motion.

'Here first comes the pulp now,' said Cupid, pointing to the nighest end of the machine. 'See; first it pours out and spreads itself upon this wide, sloping board; and then – look – slides, thin and quivering, beneath the first roller there. Follow on now, and see it as it slides from under that to the next cylinder. There; see how it has become just a very little less pulpy now. One step more, and it grows still more to some slight consistence. Still another cylinder, and it is so knitted – though as yet mere dragonfly wing – that it forms an air-bridge here, like a suspended cobweb, between two more separated rollers; and flowing over the last one, and under again, and doubling about there out of sight for a minute among all those mixed cylinders you indistinctly see, it reappears here, looking now at last a little less like pulp and more like paper, but still quite delicate and defective yet awhile. But – a little further onward, sir, if you please – here now, at this further point, it puts on something of a real look, as if it might turn out to be something you might possibly handle in the end. But it's not yet done, sir. Good way to travel yet, and plenty more cylinders must roll it.'

'Bless my soul!' said I, amazed at the elongation, interminable convolutions and deliberate slowness of the machine, 'it must take a long time for the pulp to pass from end to end, and come out paper.'

'Oh! not so long,' smiled the precocious lad, with a superior and patronising air; 'only nine minutes. But look; you may try it for yourself. Have you a bit of paper? Ah! here's a bit on the floor. Now mark that with any word you please, and let me dab it on here, and we'll see how long before it comes out at the other end.'

'Well, let me see,' said I, taking out my pencil; 'come, I'll mark it with your name.'

Bidding me take out my watch, Cupid adroitly dropped the inscribed slip on an exposed part of the incipient mass.

Instantly my eye marked the second-hand on my dial-plate.

Slowly I followed the slip, inch by inch, sometimes pausing for full half a minute as it disappeared beneath inscrutable groups of the lower cylinders, but only gradually to emerge again; and so, on and on and on – inch by inch; now in open sight, sliding along like a freckle on the quivering sheet; and then again wholly vanished; and so, on and on and on – inch by inch; all the time the main sheet growing more and more to final firmness – when, suddenly, I saw a sort of paperfall, not wholly unlike a waterfall; a scissory sound smote my ear, as of some cord being snapped; and down dropped an unfolded sheet of perfect foolscap, with my 'Cupid' half faded out of it, and still moist and warm.

My travels were at an end, for here was the end of the machine.

'Well, how long was it?' said Cupid.

'Nine minutes to a second,' replied I, watch in hand.

'I told you so.'

For a moment a curious emotion filled me, not wholly unlike that which one might experience at the fulfilment of some mysterious prophecy. But how absurd, thought I again; the thing is a mere machine, the essence of which is unvarying punctuality and precision.

Previously absorbed by the wheels and cylinders, my attention was now directed to a sad-looking woman standing by.

'That is rather an elderly person so silently tending the machine-end here. She would not seem wholly used to it either.'

'Oh,' knowingly whispered Cupid, through the din, 'she only came last week. She was a nurse formerly. But the business is poor in these parts, and she's left it. But look at the paper she is piling there.'

'Aye, foolscap,' handling the piles of moist, warm sheets, which continually were being delivered into the woman's waiting hands. 'Don't you turn out anything but foolscap at this machine?'

'Oh, sometimes, but not often, we turn out finer work – cream-laid and royal sheets, we call them. But foolscap being in chief demand, we turn out foolscap most.'

It was very curious. Looking at that blank paper continually dropping, dropping, dropping, my mind ran on in wonderings of those strange uses to which those thousand sheets eventually would be put. All sorts of writings would be writ on those now vacant things – sermons, lawyers' briefs, physicians' prescriptions, love-letters, marriage certificates, bills of divorce, registers of births, death-warrants, and so on, without end. Then, recurring back to them as they here lay all blank, I could not but bethink me of that celebrated comparison of John Locke, who, in demonstration of his theory that man had no innate ideas, compared the human mind at birth to a sheet of blank paper; something destined to be scribbled on, but what sort of characters no soul might tell.

Pacing slowly to and fro along the involved machine, still humming with its play, I was struck as well by the inevitability of the evolvement-power in all its motions.

'Does that thin cobweb there,' said I, pointing to the sheet in its more imperfect stage, 'does that never tear or break? It is marvellous fragile, and yet this machine it passes through is so mighty.'

'It never is known to tear a hair's point.'

'Does it never stop – get clogged?'

'No. It *must* go. The machinery makes it go just *so*; just that very way, and at that very pace you there plainly *see* it go. The pulp can't help going.'

Something of awe now stole over me as I gazed upon this inflexible iron animal. Always, more or less, machinery of this ponderous, elaborate sort strikes, in some moods, strange dread into the human heart, as some living, panting Behemoth might. But what made the thing I saw so specially terrible to me was the metallic necessity, the unbudging fatality which governed it. Though, here and there, I could not follow the thin, gauzy veil of pulp in the course of its more mysterious or entirely invisible advance, yet it was indubitable that, at those points where it eluded me, it still marched on in unvarying docility to the autocratic cunning of the machine. A fascination fastened on me. I stood spellbound and wandering in my soul. Before my eyes – there, passing in slow procession along the wheeling cylinders – I seemed to see, glued to the pallid incipience of the pulp, the yet more pallid faces of all the pallid girls I had eyed that heavy day. Slowly, mournfully, beseechingly, yet unresistingly, they gleamed along, their agony dimly outlined on the imperfect paper, like the print of the tormented face on the handkerchief of St Veronica.

'Halloa! the heat of the room is too much for you,' cried Cupid, staring at me.

'No – I am rather chill, if anything.'

'Come out, sir – out – out,' and, with the protecting air of a careful father, the precocious lad hurried me outside.

In a few moments, feeling revived a little, I went into the folding-room – the first room I had entered, and where the desk for transacting business stood, surrounded by the blank counters and blank girls engaged at them.

'Cupid here has led me a strange tour,' said I to the dark-complexioned man before mentioned, whom I had ere this discovered not only to be an old bachelor, but also the principal proprietor. 'Yours is a most wonderful factory. Your great machine is a miracle of inscrutable intricacy.'

'Yes, all our visitors think it so. But we don't have many. We are in a very out-of-the-way corner here. Few inhabitants, too. Most of our girls come from far-off villages.'

'The girls,' echoed I, glancing round at their silent forms. 'Why is it, sir, that in most factories, female operatives, of whatever age, are indiscriminately called girls, never women?'

'Oh! as to that – why, I suppose, the fact of their being generally unmarried – that's the reason, I should think. But it never struck me before. For our factory here we will not have married women; they are apt to be off-and-on too much. We want none but steady workers: twelve hours to the day, day after day, through the three hundred and sixty-five days, excepting Sundays, Thanksgiving and fast-days. That's our rule. And so, having no married women, what females we have are rightly enough called girls.'

'Then these are all maids,' said I, while some pained homage to their pale virginity made me involuntarily bow.

'All maids.'

Again the strange emotion filled me.

'Your cheeks look whitish yet, sir,' said the man, gazing at me narrowly. 'You must be careful going home. Do they pain you at all now? It's a bad sign, if they do.'

'No doubt, sir,' answered I, 'when once I have got out of the Devil's Dungeon, I shall feel them mending.'

'Ah, yes; the winter air in valleys, or gorges, or any sunken place, is far colder and more bitter than elsewhere. You would hardly believe it now, but it is colder here than at the top of Woedolor Mountain.'

'I dare say it is, sir. But time presses me; I must depart.'

With that, remuffling myself in dreadnaught and tippet, thrusting my hands into my huge sealskin mittens, I sallied out into the nipping air, and found poor Black, my horse, all cringing and doubled up with the cold.

Soon, wrapped in furs and meditations, I ascended from the Devil's Dungeon.

At the Black Notch I paused, and once more bethought me of Temple Bar. Then, shooting through the pass, all alone with inscrutable nature, I exclaimed – Oh! Paradise of Bachelors! and oh! Tartarus of Maids!

THE LIGHTNING-ROD MAN

WHAT GRAND IRREGULAR THUNDER, thought I, standing on my hearthstone among the Acroceraunian hills as the scattered bolts boomed overhead and crashed down among the valleys, every bolt followed by zigzag irradiations and swift slants of sharp rain, which audibly rang, like a charge of spear points, on my low shingled roof. I suppose, though, that the mountains hereabouts break and churn up the thunder, so that it is far more glorious here than on the plain. Hark! – someone at the door. Who is this that chooses a time of thunder for making calls? And why don't he, man-fashion, use the knocker, instead of making that doleful undertaker's clatter with his fist against the hollow panel? But let him in. Ah, here he comes. 'Good-day, sir:' an entire stranger. 'Pray be seated.' What is that strange-looking walking-stick he carries? 'A fine thunderstorm, sir.'

'Fine? – Awful!'

'You are wet. Stand here on the hearth before the fire.'

'Not for worlds!'

The stranger still stood in the exact middle of the cottage, where he had first planted himself. His singularity impelled a closer scrutiny. A lean, gloomy figure. Hair dark and lank, mattedly streaked over his brow. His sunken pitfalls of eyes were ringed by indigo halos and played with an innocuous sort of lightning: the gleam without the bolt. The whole man was dripping. He stood in a puddle on the bare oak floor, his strange walking-stick vertically resting at his side.

It was a polished copper rod, four feet long, lengthwise attached to a neat wooden staff by insertion into two balls of greenish glass, ringed with copper bands. The metal rod terminated at the top tripodwise, in three keen tines, brightly gilt. He held the thing by the wooden part alone.

'Sir,' said I, bowing politely, 'have I the honour of a visit from that illustrious god, Jupiter Tonans? So stood he in the Greek statue of old, grasping the lightning-bolt. If you be he, or his viceroy, I have to thank you for this noble storm you have brewed among our mountains. Listen: that was a glorious peal. Ah, to a lover of the majestic, it is a good thing to have the Thunderer himself in one's cottage. The thunder grows finer for that. But pray be seated. This old rush-bottomed armchair, I grant, is a poor substitute for your evergreen throne on Olympus; but condescend to be seated.'

While I thus pleasantly spoke, the stranger eyed me, half in wonder and half in a strange sort of horror; but did not move a foot.

'Do, sir, be seated; you need to be dried ere going forth again.'

I planted the chair invitingly on the broad hearth, where a little fire had been kindled that afternoon to dissipate the dampness, not the cold; for it was early in the month of September.

But without heeding my solicitation, and still standing in the middle of the floor, the stranger gazed at me portentously and spoke.

'Sir,' said he, 'excuse me; but instead of my accepting your invitation to be seated on the hearth there, I solemnly warn *you* that you had best accept *mine*, and stand with me in the middle of the room. Good heavens!' he cried, starting – 'there is another of those awful crashes. I warn you, sir, quit the hearth.'

'Mr Jupiter Tonans,' said I, quietly rolling my body on the stone, 'I stand very well here.'

'Are you so horridly ignorant, then,' he cried, 'as not to know that by far the most dangerous part of a house, during such a terrific tempest as this, is the fireplace?'

'Nay, I did not know that,' involuntarily stepping upon the first board next to the stone.

The stranger now assumed such an unpleasant air of successful admonition, that – quite involuntarily again – I stepped back upon the hearth, and threw myself into the erectest, proudest posture I could command. But I said nothing.

'For heaven's sake,' he cried, with a strange mixture of alarm and intimidation – 'for heaven's sake, get off the hearth! Know you not, that the heated air and soot are conductors; – to say nothing of those immense iron fire-dogs? Quit the spot – I conjure – I command you.'

'Mr Jupiter Tonans, I am not accustomed to be commanded in my own house.'

'Call me not by that pagan name. You are profane in this time of terror.'

'Sir, will you be so good as to tell me your business? If you seek shelter from the storm, you are welcome, so long as you be civil; but if you come on business, open it forthwith. Who are you?'

'I am a dealer in lightning-rods,' said the stranger, softening his tone; 'my special business is – Merciful heaven! what a crash! – Have you ever been struck – your premises, I mean? No? It's best to be provided' – significantly rattling his metallic staff on the floor –

'by nature, there are no castles in thunderstorms; yet, say but the word, and of this cottage I can make a Gibraltar by a few waves of this wand. Hark, what Himalayas of concussions!'

'You interrupted yourself; your special business you were about to speak of.'

'My special business is to travel the country for orders for lightning-rods. This is my specimen rod,' tapping his staff; 'I have the best of references' – fumbling in his pockets. 'In Criggan last month, I put up three-and-twenty rods on only five buildings.'

'Let me see. Was it not at Criggan last week, about midnight on Saturday, that the steeple, the big elm and the assembly-room cupola were struck? Any of your rods there?'

'Not on the tree and cupola, but the steeple.'

'Of what use is your rod, then?'

'Of life-and-death use. But my workman was heedless. In fitting the rod at top to the steeple, he allowed a part of the metal to graze the tin sheeting. Hence the accident. Not my fault, but his. Hark!'

'Never mind. That clap burst quite loud enough to be heard without finger-pointing. Did you hear of the event at Montreal last year? A servant girl struck at her bedside with a rosary in her hand; the beads being metal. Does your beat extend into the Canadas?'

'No. And I hear that there, iron rods only are in use. They should have *mine*, which are copper. Iron is easily fused. Then they draw out the rod so slender that it has not body enough to conduct the full electric current. The metal melts; the building is destroyed. My copper rods never act so. Those Canadians are fools. Some of them knob the rod at the top, which risks a deadly explosion, instead of imperceptibly carrying down the current into the earth, as this sort of rod does. *Mine* is the only true rod. Look at it. Only one dollar a foot.'

'This abuse of your own calling in another might make one distrustful with respect to yourself.'

'Hark! The thunder becomes less muttering. It is nearing us, and nearing the earth, too. Hark! One crammed crash! All the vibrations made one by nearness. Another flash. Hold.'

'What do you do?' I said, seeing him now instantaneously relinquishing his staff, lean intently forward towards the window, with his right fore and middle fingers on his left wrist.

But ere the words had well escaped me, another exclamation escaped him.

'Crash! only three pulses – less than a third of a mile off – yonder, somewhere in that wood. I passed three stricken oaks there, ripped out new and glittering. The oak draws lightning more than other timber, having iron in solution in its sap. Your floor here seems oak.'

'Heart-of-oak. From the peculiar time of your call upon me, I suppose you purposely select stormy weather for your journeys. When the thunder is roaring, you deem it an hour peculiarly favourable for producing impressions favourable to your trade.'

'Hark! – Awful!'

'For one who would arm others with fearlessness, you seem unbeseemingly timorous yourself. Common men choose fair weather for their travels: you choose thunderstorms; and yet – '

'That I travel in thunderstorms, I grant; but not without particular precautions, such as only a lightning-rod man may know. Hark! Quick – look at my specimen rod. Only one dollar a foot.'

'A very fine rod, I dare say. But what are these particular precautions of yours? Yet first let me close yonder shutters; the slanting rain is beating through the sash. I will bar up.'

'Are you mad? Know you not that yon iron bar is a swift conductor? Desist.'

'I will simply close the shutters, then, and call my boy to bring me a wooden bar. Pray, touch the bell-pull there.'

'Are you frantic? That bell-wire might blast you. Never touch bell-wire in a thunderstorm, nor ring a bell of any sort.'

'Nor those in belfries? Pray, will you tell me where and how one may be safe in a time like this? Is there any part of my house I may touch with hopes of my life?'

'There is; but not where you now stand. Come away from the wall. The current will sometimes run down a wall, and – a man being a better conductor than a wall – it would leave the wall and run into him. Swoop! *that* must have fallen very nigh. That must have been globular lightning.'

'Very probably. Tell me at once which is, in your opinion, the safest part of this house?'

'This room, and this one spot in it where I stand. Come hither.'

'The reasons first.'

'Hark! – after the flash, the gust – the sashes shiver – the house, the house! – Come hither to me!'

'The reasons, if you please.'

'Come hither to me!'

'Thank you again, I think I will try my old stand – the hearth. And now, Mr Lightning-Rod-Man, in the pauses of the thunder, be so good as to tell me your reasons for esteeming this one room of the house the safest, and your own one standpoint there the safest spot in it.'

There was now a little cessation of the storm for a while. The lightning-rod man seemed relieved, and replied: 'Your house is a one-storeyed house, with an attic and a cellar; this room is between. Hence its comparative safety. Because lightning sometimes passes from the clouds to the earth, and sometimes from the earth to the clouds. Do you comprehend? – and I choose the middle of the room, because, if the lightning should strike the house at all, it would come down the chimney or walls; so obviously, the further you are from them, the better. Come hither to me, now.'

'Presently. Something you just said, instead of alarming me, has strangely inspired confidence.'

'What have I said?'

'You said that sometimes lightning flashes from the earth to the clouds.'

'Aye, the returning-stroke, as it is called; when the earth, being overcharged with the fluid, flashes its surplus upward.'

'The returning-stroke; that is, from earth to sky? Better and better. But come here on the hearth and dry yourself.'

'I am better here, and better wet.'

'How?'

'It is the safest thing you can do – Hark, again! – to get yourself thoroughly drenched in a thunderstorm. Wet clothes are better conductors than the body; and so, if the lightning strike, it might pass down the wet clothes without touching the body. The storm deepens again. Have you a rug in the house? Rugs are non-conductors. Get one, that I may stand on it here, and you, too. The skies blacken – it is dusk at noon. Hark! – the rug, the rug!'

I gave him one; while the hooded mountains seemed closing and tumbling into the cottage.

'And now, since our being dumb will not help us,' said I, resuming my place, 'let me hear your precautions in travelling during thunderstorms.'

'Wait till this one is passed.'

'Nay, proceed with the precautions. You stand in the safest possible place according to your own account. Go on.'

'Briefly, then. I avoid pine trees, high houses, lonely barns, upland pastures, running water, flocks of cattle and sheep, a crowd of men. If I travel on foot – as today – I do not walk fast; if in my buggy, I touch not its back or sides; if on horseback, I dismount and lead the horse. But of all things, I avoid tall men.'

'Do I dream? Man avoid man? and in danger-time, too.'

'Tall men in a thunderstorm I avoid. Are you so grossly ignorant as not to know that the height of a six-footer is sufficient to discharge an electric cloud upon him? Are not lonely Kentuckians, ploughing, smit in the unfinished furrow? Nay, if the six-footer stand by running water, the cloud will sometimes *select* him as its conductor to that running water. Hark! Sure, yon black pinnacle is split. Yes, a man is a good conductor. The lightning goes through and through a man, but only peels a tree. But sir, you have kept me so long answering your questions that I have not yet come to business. Will you order one of my rods? Look at this specimen one. See: it is of the best of copper. Copper's the best conductor. Your house is low; but being upon the mountains, that lowness does not one whit depress it. You mountaineers are most exposed. In mountainous countries the lightning-rod man should have most business. Look at the specimen, sir. One rod will answer for a house so small as this. Look over these recommendations. Only one rod, sir; cost, only twenty dollars. Hark! There go all the granite Taconics and Hoosics dashed together like pebbles. By the sound, that must have struck something. An elevation of five feet above the house will protect twenty feet radius all about the rod. Only twenty dollars, sir – dollar a foot. Hark! – Dreadful! – Will you order? Will you buy? Shall I put down your name? Think of being a heap of charred offal, like a haltered horse burnt in his stall; and all in one flash!'

'You pretended envoy extraordinary and minister plenipotentiary to and from Jupiter Tonans,' laughed I; 'you mere man who come here to put you and your pipestem between clay and sky, do you think that because you can strike a bit of green light from the Leyden jar, you can thoroughly avert the supernal bolt? Your rod rusts, or breaks, and where are you? Who has empowered you, you Tetzel, to peddle round your indulgences from divine ordinations? The hairs of our heads are numbered and the days of our lives. In thunder as in sunshine, I stand at ease in the hands of my God. False negotiator, away! See, the scroll of the storm is rolled back; the house is unharmed; and in the blue heavens I read in the rainbow, that the Deity will not, of purpose, make war on man's earth.'

'Impious wretch!' foamed the stranger, blackening in the face as the rainbow beamed, 'I will publish your infidel notions.'

'Begone! move quickly! if quickly you can, you that shine forth into sight in moist times like the worm.'

The scowl grew blacker on his face; the indigo-circles enlarged round his eyes as the storm-rings round the midnight moon. He sprang upon me, his tri-forked thing at my heart.

I seized it; I snapped it; I dashed it; I trod it; and dragging the dark lightning-king out of my door, flung his elbowed, copper sceptre after him.

But spite of my treatment, and spite of my dissuasive talk of him to my neighbours, the lightning-rod man still dwells in the land; still travels in storm-time and drives a brave trade with the fears of man.

BENITO CERENO

IN THE YEAR 1799, Captain Amasa Delano, of Duxbury, in Massachusetts, commanding a large sealer and general trader, lay at anchor with a valuable cargo, in the harbour of Santa Maria – a small, desert, uninhabited island towards the southern extremity of the long coast of Chile. There he had touched for water.

On the second day, not long after dawn, while lying in his berth, his mate came below, informing him that a strange sail was coming into the bay. Ships were then not so plenty in those waters as now. He rose, dressed, and went on deck.

The morning was one peculiar to that coast. Everything was mute and calm; everything grey. The sea, though undulated into long roods of swells, seemed fixed, and was sleeked at the surface like waved lead that has cooled and set in the smelter's mould. The sky seemed a grey surtout. Flights of troubled grey fowl, kith and kin with flights of troubled grey vapours among which they were mixed, skimmed low and fitfully over the waters, as swallows over meadows before storms. Shadows present, foreshadowing deeper shadows to come.

To Captain Delano's surprise, the stranger, viewed through the glass, showed no colours; though to do so upon entering a haven, however uninhabited in its shores, where but a single other ship might be lying, was the custom among peaceful seamen of all nations. Considering the lawlessness and loneliness of the spot, and the sort of stories, at that day, associated with those seas, Captain Delano's surprise might have deepened into some uneasiness had he not been a person of a singularly undistrustful good nature, not liable, except on extraordinary and repeated incentives and hardly then, to indulge in personal alarms any way involving the imputation of malign evil in man. Whether, in view of what humanity is capable, such a trait implies, along with a benevolent heart, more than ordinary quickness and accuracy of intellectual perception, may be left to the wise to determine.

But whatever misgivings might have obtruded on first seeing the stranger, would almost, in any seaman's mind, have been dissipated by observing that the ship, in navigating into the harbour, was drawing too near the land; a sunken reef making out off her bow. This seemed to prove her a stranger, indeed, not only to the sealer, but the island; consequently, she could be no wonted freebooter on that ocean. With no small interest, Captain Delano continued to watch her – a proceeding not much facilitated by the vapours partly mantling the hull, through which the far matin light from her cabin streamed equivocally enough; much like the sun – by this time hemisphered on the rim of the horizon, and, apparently, in company with the strange ship entering the harbour – which, wimpled by the same low, creeping clouds, showed not unlike a Lima intriguante's one sinister eye peering across the plaza from the Indian loop-hole of her dusk *saya-y-manto*.

It might have been but a deception of the vapours, but the longer the stranger was watched the more singular appeared her manoeuvres. Ere long it seemed hard to decide whether she meant to come in or no – what she wanted or what she was about. The wind, which had breezed up a little during the night, was now extremely light and baffling, which the more increased the apparent uncertainty of her movements.

Surmising, at last, that it might be a ship in distress, Captain Delano ordered his whale-boat to be dropped, and, much to the wary opposition of his mate, prepared to board her, and, at the least, pilot her in. On the night previous, a fishing party of the seamen had gone a long distance to some detached rocks out of sight from the sealer, and, an hour or two before daybreak, had returned, having met with no small success. Presuming that the stranger might have been long off soundings, the good captain put several baskets of the fish, for presents, into his boat, and so pulled away. From her continuing too near the sunken reef, deeming her in danger, calling to his men, he made all haste to apprise those on board of their situation. But, some time ere the boat came up, the wind, light though it was, having shifted, had headed the vessel off, as well as partly broken the vapours from about her.

Upon gaining a less remote view, the ship, when made signally visible on the verge of the leaden-hued swells, with the shreds of fog here and there raggedly furring her, appeared like a whitewashed monastery after a thunderstorm, seen perched upon some dun cliff among the Pyrenees. But it was no purely fanciful resemblance which now, for a moment, almost led Captain Delano to think that nothing less than a ship-load of monks was before him. Peering over the bulwarks were what really seemed, in the hazy distance, throngs of dark cowls; while, fitfully revealed through the open port-holes, other dark moving figures were dimly descried, as of Black Friars pacing the cloisters.

Upon a still nigher approach, this appearance was modified, and the true character of the vessel was plain – a Spanish merchantman of the first class, carrying negro slaves, amongst other valuable freight, from one colonial port to another. A very large, and, in its time, a very fine vessel, such as in those days were at intervals encountered along that main; sometimes superseded Acapulco treasure-ships or retired frigates of the Spanish king's navy, which, like superannuated Italian palaces, still, under a decline of masters, preserved signs of former state.

As the whale-boat drew more and more nigh, the cause of the peculiar pipe-clayed aspect of the stranger was seen in the slovenly neglect pervading her. The spars, ropes and great part of the bulwarks looked woolly, from long unacquaintance with the scraper, tar and the brush. Her keel seemed laid, her ribs put together and she launched from Ezekiel's Valley of Dry Bones.

In the present business in which she was engaged, the ship's general model and rig appeared to have undergone no material change from their original warlike and Froissart pattern. However, no guns were seen.

The tops were large, and were railed about with what had once been octagonal net-work, all now in sad disrepair. These tops hung overhead like three ruinous aviaries, in one of which was seen perched, on a ratlin, a white noddy, a strange fowl, so called from its lethargic, somnambulistic character, being frequently caught by hand at sea. Battered and mouldy, the castellated forecastle seemed some ancient turret, long ago taken by assault, and then left to decay. Towards the stern, two high-raised quarter-galleries – the balustrades here and there covered with dry, tindery sea-moss – opening out from the unoccupied state-cabin, whose dead-lights, for all the mild weather, were hermetically closed and calked – these tenantless balconies hung over the sea as if it were the grand Venetian canal. But the principal relic of faded grandeur was the ample oval of the shield-like stern-piece, intricately carved with the arms of Castile and Leon, medallioned about by groups of mythological or symbolical devices; uppermost and central of which was a dark satyr in a mask, holding his foot on the prostrate neck of a writhing figure, likewise masked.

Whether the ship had a figure-head, or only a plain beak, was not quite certain, owing to canvas wrapped about that part, either to protect it while undergoing a refurbishing, or else decently to hide its decay. Rudely painted or chalked, as in a sailor freak, along the forward side of a sort of pedestal below the canvas, was the sentence, *Seguid vuestro jefe* (Follow your leader); while upon the tarnished headboards, near by, appeared, in stately capitals, once gilt, the ship's name, *SAN DOMINICK*, each letter streakingly corroded with tricklings of copper-spike rust; while, like mourning weeds, dark festoons of sea-grass slimily swept to and fro over the name, with every hearse-like roll of the hull.

As, at last, the boat was hooked from the bow along towards the gangway amidship, its keel, while yet some inches separated from the hull, harshly grated as on a sunken coral reef. It proved a huge bunch of conglobated barnacles adhering below the water to the side like a wen – a token of baffling airs and long calms passed somewhere in those seas.

Climbing the side, the visitor was at once surrounded by a clamorous throng of whites and blacks, but the latter outnumbering the former more than could have been expected, negro transportation-ship as the stranger in port was. But, in one language, and as with one voice, all poured out a common tale of suffering; in which the negresses, of whom there were not a few, exceeded the others in their dolorous vehemence. The scurvy, together with the fever, had swept off a great part of their number, more especially the Spaniards. Off Cape Horn they had narrowly escaped shipwreck; then, for days together, they had lain tranced without wind; their provisions were low; their water next to none; their lips that moment were baked.

While Captain Delano was thus made the mark of all eager tongues, his one eager glance took in all faces, with every other object about him.

Always upon first boarding a large and populous ship at sea, especially a foreign one with a nondescript crew such as Lascars or Manila men, the impression varies in a peculiar way from that produced by first entering a strange house with strange inmates in a strange land. Both house and ship – the one by its walls and blinds, the other by its high bulwarks like ramparts – hoard from view their interiors till the last moment; but in the case of the ship there is this addition: that the living spectacle it contains, upon its sudden and complete disclosure, has, in contrast with the blank ocean which zones it, something of the effect of enchantment. The ship seems unreal, these strange costumes, gestures and faces but a shadowy tableau just emerged from the deep, which directly must receive back what it gave.

Perhaps it was some such influence, as above is attempted to be described, which, in Captain Delano's mind, heightened whatever, upon a staid scrutiny, might have seemed unusual; especially the conspicuous figures of four elderly grizzled negroes, their heads like black, doddered willow tops, who, in venerable contrast to the tumult below them, were couched, sphinx-like, one on the starboard cat-head, another on the larboard, and the remaining pair face to face on the opposite bulwarks above the main-chains. They each had bits of unstranded old junk in their hands, and, with a sort of stoical self-content, were picking the junk into oakum, a small heap of which lay by their sides. They accompanied the task with a continuous, low, monotonous chant, droning and drooling away like so many grey-headed bagpipers playing a funeral march.

The quarter-deck rose into an ample elevated poop, upon the forward verge of which, lifted, like the oakum-pickers, some eight feet above the general throng, sat along in a row, separated by regular spaces, the cross-legged figures of six other blacks; each with a rusty hatchet in his hand, which, with a bit of brick and a rag, he was engaged like a scullion in scouring; while between each two was a small stack of hatchets, their rusted edges turned forward awaiting a like operation. Though occasionally the four oakum-pickers would briefly address some person or persons in the crowd below, yet the six hatchet-polishers neither spoke to others, nor breathed a whisper among themselves, but sat intent upon their task, except at intervals, when, with the peculiar love in negroes of uniting industry with pastime, two and two they sideways clashed their hatchets together, like cymbals, with a barbarous din. All six, unlike the generality, had the raw aspect of unsophisticated Africans.

But that first comprehensive glance which took in those ten figures, with scores less conspicuous, rested but an instant upon them, as, impatient of the hubbub of voices, the visitor turned in quest of whomsoever it might be that commanded the ship.

But as if not unwilling to let nature make known her own case among his suffering charge, or else in despair of restraining it for the time, the Spanish captain, a gentlemanly, reserved-looking, and rather young man to a stranger's eye, dressed with singular richness, but bearing plain traces of recent sleepless cares and disquietudes, stood passively by, leaning against the main-mast, at one moment casting a dreary, spiritless look upon his excited people, at the next an unhappy glance towards his visitor. By his side stood a black of small stature, in whose rude face, as occasionally, like a shepherd's dog, he mutely turned it up into the Spaniard's, sorrow and affection were equally blended. Struggling through the throng, the American advanced to the Spaniard, assuring him of his sympathies, and offering to render whatever assistance might be in his power. To which the Spaniard returned for the present but grave and ceremonious acknowledgements, his national formality dusked by the saturnine mood of ill-health.

But losing no time in mere compliments, Captain Delano, returning to the gangway, had his baskets of fish brought up; and as the wind still continued light, so that some hours at least must elapse ere the ship could be brought to the anchorage, he bade his men return to the sealer, and fetch back as much water as the whale-boat could carry, with whatever soft bread the steward might have, all the remaining pumpkins on board, with a box of sugar, and a dozen of his private bottles of cider.

Not many minutes after the boat's pushing off, to the vexation of all, the wind entirely died away, and the tide turning, began drifting back the ship helplessly seaward. But trusting this would not long last, Captain Delano sought, with good hopes, to cheer up the strangers, feeling no small satisfaction that, with persons in their condition, he could – thanks to his frequent voyages along the Spanish main – converse with some freedom in their native tongue.

While left alone with them, he was not long in observing some things tending to heighten his first impressions; but surprise was lost in pity, both for the Spaniards and blacks, alike evidently reduced from scarcity of water and provisions; while long-continued suffering seemed to have brought out the less good-natured qualities of the negroes, besides, at the same time, impairing the Spaniard's authority over them. But, under the circumstances, precisely this condition of things was to have been anticipated. In armies, navies, cities or families, in nature herself, nothing more relaxes good order than misery. Still, Captain Delano was not without the idea that had Benito Cereno been a man of greater energy, misrule would hardly have come to the present pass. But the debility, constitutional or induced by hardships, bodily and mental, of the Spanish captain was too obvious to be overlooked. A prey to settled dejection, as if long mocked with hope he would not now indulge it, even when it had ceased to be a mock, the prospect of that day, or evening at furthest, lying at anchor, with plenty of water for his people and a brother captain to counsel and befriend, seemed in no perceptible degree to encourage him. His mind appeared unstrung, if not still more seriously affected. Shut up in these oaken walls, chained to one dull round of command, whose unconditionality cloyed him, like some hypochondriac abbot he moved slowly about, at times suddenly pausing, starting or staring, biting his lip, biting his fingernail, flushing, paling, twitching his beard, with other symptoms of an absent or moody mind. This distempered spirit was lodged, as before hinted, in as distempered a frame. He was rather tall, but seemed never to have been robust, and now with nervous suffering was almost worn to a skeleton. A tendency to some pulmonary complaint appeared to have been lately confirmed. His voice was like that of one with lungs half gone – hoarsely suppressed, a husky whisper. No wonder that, as in this state he tottered about, his private servant apprehensively followed him. Sometimes the negro gave his master his arm, or took his handkerchief out of his pocket for him, performing these and similar offices with that affectionate zeal which transmutes into something filial or fraternal acts in themselves but menial, and which has gained for the negro the repute of making the most pleasing body-servant in the world; one too whom a master need be on no stiffly superior terms with, but may treat with familiar trust; less a servant than a devoted companion.

Marking the noisy indocility of the blacks in general, as well as what seemed the sullen inefficiency of the whites, it was not without humane satisfaction that Captain Delano witnessed the steady good conduct of Babo.

But the good conduct of Babo, hardly more than the ill-behaviour of others, seemed to withdraw the half-lunatic Don Benito from his cloudy languor. Not that such precisely was the impression made by the Spaniard on the mind of his visitor. The Spaniard's individual unrest was, for the present, but noted as a conspicuous feature in the ship's general affliction. Still, Captain Delano was not a little concerned at what he could not help taking for the time to be Don Benito's unfriendly indifference towards himself. The Spaniard's manner, too, conveyed a sort of sour and gloomy disdain, which he seemed at no pains to disguise. But this the American in charity ascribed to the harassing effects of sickness, since, in former instances, he had noted that there are peculiar natures on whom prolonged physical suffering seems to cancel every social instinct of kindness; as if, forced to black bread themselves, they deemed it but equity that each person coming nigh them should, indirectly, by some slight or affront, be made to partake of their fare.

But ere long Captain Delano bethought him that, indulgent as he was at the first in judging the Spaniard, he might not, after all, have exercised charity enough. At bottom it was Don Benito's reserve which displeased him; but the same reserve was shown towards all but his faithful personal attendant. Even the formal reports which, according to sea-usage, were, at stated times, made to him by some petty underling, either a white, mulatto or black, he hardly had patience enough to listen to without betraying contemptuous aversion. His manner upon such occasions was, in its degree, not unlike that which might be supposed to have been his imperial countryman's, Charles V, just previous to the anchoritish retirement of that monarch from the throne.

This splenetic disrelish of his place was evinced in almost every function pertaining to it. Proud as he was moody, he condescended to no personal mandate. Whatever special orders were necessary, their delivery was delegated to his body-servant, who in turn transferred them to their ultimate destination through runners, alert Spanish boys or slave boys, like pages or pilot-fish, within easy call, continually hovering round Don Benito. So that to have beheld this undemonstrative invalid gliding about, apathetic and mute, no landsman could have dreamed that in him was lodged a dictatorship beyond which, while at sea, there was no earthly appeal.

Thus, the Spaniard, regarded in his reserve, seemed the involuntary victim of mental disorder. But, in fact, his reserve might, in some degree, have proceeded from design. If so, then here was evinced the unhealthy climax of that icy though conscientious policy, more or less adopted by all commanders of large ships, which, except in signal emergencies, obliterates alike the manifestation of sway with every trace of sociality; transforming the man into a block, or rather into a loaded cannon, which, until there is call for thunder, has nothing to say.

Viewing him in this light, it seemed but a natural token of the perverse habit induced by a long course of such hard self-restraint, that, notwithstanding the present condition of his ship, the Spaniard should still persist in a demeanour, which, however harmless, or, it may be, appropriate, in a well-appointed vessel, such as the *San Dominick* might have been at the outset of the voyage, was anything but judicious now. But the Spaniard, perhaps, thought that it was with captains as with gods: reserve, under all events, must still be their cue. But probably this appearance of slumbering dominion might have been but an attempted disguise to conscious imbecility – not deep policy, but shallow device. But be all this as it might, whether Don Benito's manner was designed or not, the more Captain Delano noted its pervading reserve, the less he felt uneasiness at any particular manifestation of that reserve towards himself.

Neither were his thoughts taken up by the captain alone. Wonted to the quiet orderliness of the sealer's comfortable family of a crew, the noisy confusion of the *San Dominick*'s suffering host repeatedly challenged his eye. Some prominent breaches, not only of discipline but of decency, were observed. These Captain Delano could not but ascribe, in the main, to the absence of those subordinate deck-officers to whom, along with higher duties, is entrusted what may be styled the police department of a populous ship. True, the old oakum-pickers appeared at times to act the part of monitorial constables to their countrymen, the blacks; but though occasionally succeeding in allaying trifling outbreaks now and then between man and man, they could do little or nothing towards establishing general quiet. The *San Dominick* was in the condition of a transatlantic emigrant ship, among whose multitude of living freight are some individuals, doubtless, as little troublesome as crates and bales; but the friendly remonstrances of such with their ruder companions are of not so much avail as the unfriendly arm of the mate. What the *San Dominick* wanted was what the emigrant ship has, stern superior officers. But on these decks not so much as a fourth-mate was to be seen.

The visitor's curiosity was roused to learn the particulars of those mishaps which had brought about such absenteeism, with its consequences; because, though deriving some inkling of the voyage from the wails which at the first moment had greeted him, yet of the details no clear understanding had been had. The best account would, doubtless, be given by the captain. Yet at first the visitor was loth to ask it, unwilling to provoke some distant rebuff. But plucking up courage, he at last accosted Don Benito, renewing the expression of his benevolent interest, adding that did he (Captain Delano) but know the particulars of the ship's misfortunes, he would, perhaps, be better able in the end to relieve them. Would Don Benito favour him with the whole story?

Don Benito faltered; then, like some somnambulist suddenly interfered with, vacantly stared at his visitor, and ended by looking down on the deck. He maintained this posture so long that Captain Delano, almost equally disconcerted, and involuntarily almost as rude, turned suddenly from him, walking forward to accost one of the Spanish seamen for the desired information. But he had hardly gone five paces, when, with a sort of eagerness, Don Benito invited him back, regretting his momentary absence of mind and professing readiness to gratify him.

While most part of the story was being given, the two captains stood on the after part of the main-deck, a privileged spot, no one being near but the servant.

'It is now a hundred and ninety days,' began the Spaniard, in his husky whisper, 'that this ship, well officered and well manned, with several cabin passengers – some fifty Spaniards in all – sailed from Buenos Aires bound to Lima, with a general cargo – hardware, Paraguay tea and the like – and,' pointing forward, 'that parcel of negroes, now not more than a hundred and fifty, as you see, but then numbering over three hundred souls. Off Cape Horn we had heavy gales. In one moment, by night, three of my best officers, with fifteen sailors, were lost, with the main-yard; the spar snapping under them in the slings, as they sought, with heavers, to beat down the icy sail. To lighten the hull, the heavier sacks of maté were thrown into the sea, with most of the water-pipes lashed on deck at the time. And this last necessity it was, combined with the prolonged detentions afterwards experienced, which eventually brought about our chief causes of suffering. When – '

Here there was a sudden fainting attack of his cough, brought on, no doubt, by his mental distress. His servant sustained him, and drawing a cordial from his pocket placed it to his lips. He a little revived. But unwilling to leave him unsupported while yet imperfectly restored, the black with one arm still encircled his master, at the same time keeping his eye fixed on his face, as if to watch for the first sign of complete restoration, or relapse, as the event might prove.

The Spaniard proceeded, but brokenly and obscurely, as one in a dream. 'Oh, my God! rather than pass through what I have, with joy I would have hailed the most terrible gales; but – ' His cough returned and with increased violence; this subsiding, with reddened lips and closed eyes he fell heavily against his supporter.

'His mind wanders. He was thinking of the plague that followed the gales,' plaintively sighed the servant; 'my poor, poor master!' wringing one hand, and with the other wiping the mouth. 'But be patient, señor,' again turning to Captain Delano, 'these fits do not last long; master will soon be himself.'

Don Benito reviving, went on; but as this portion of the story was very brokenly delivered, the substance only will here be set down.

It appeared that after the ship had been many days tossed in storms off the Cape, the scurvy broke out, carrying off numbers of the whites and blacks. When at last they had worked round into the Pacific, their spars and sails were so damaged, and so inadequately handled by the surviving mariners, most of whom were become invalids, that, unable to lay her northerly course by the wind, which was powerful, the unmanageable ship, for successive

days and nights, was blown north-westward, where the breeze
suddenly deserted her, in unknown waters, to sultry calms. The
absence of the water-pipes now proved as fatal to life as before
their presence had menaced it. Induced, or at least aggravated, by
the more than scanty allowance of water, a malignant fever
followed the scurvy; with the excessive heat of the lengthened
calm, making such short work of it as to sweep away, as by billows,
whole families of the Africans, and a yet larger number,
proportionably, of the Spaniards, including, by a luckless fatality,
every remaining officer on board. Consequently, in the smart west
winds eventually following the calm, the already rent sails, having
to be simply dropped, not furled, at need, had been gradually
reduced to the beggars' rags they were now. To procure substi-
tutes for his lost sailors, as well as supplies of water and sails, the
captain, at the earliest opportunity, had made for Valdivia, the
southernmost civilised port of Chile and South America; but upon
nearing the coast the thick weather had prevented him from so
much as sighting that harbour. Since which period, almost without
a crew, and almost without canvas, and almost without water, and,
at intervals, giving its added dead to the sea, the *San Dominick* had
been battledored about by contrary winds, inveigled by currents or
grown weedy in calms. Like a man lost in woods, more than once
she had doubled upon her own track.

'But throughout these calamities,' huskily continued Don Benito,
painfully turning in the half embrace of his servant, 'I have to thank
those negroes you see, who, though to your inexperienced eyes
appearing unruly, have, indeed, conducted themselves with less of
restlessness than even their owner could have thought possible
under such circumstances.'

Here he again fell faintly back. Again his mind wandered; but he
rallied, and less obscurely proceeded.

'Yes, their owner was quite right in assuring me that no fetters
would be needed with his blacks; so that while, as is wont in this
transportation, those negroes have always remained upon deck –
not thrust below, as in the Guineamen – they have, also, from the
beginning, been freely permitted to range within given bounds at
their pleasure.'

Once more the faintness returned – his mind roved – but,
recovering, he resumed: 'But it is Babo here to whom, under God, I
owe not only my own preservation, but likewise to him, chiefly, the
merit is due of pacifying his more ignorant brethren, when at
intervals tempted to murmurings.'

'Ah, master,' sighed the black, bowing his face, 'don't speak of me; Babo is nothing; what Babo has done was but duty.'

'Faithful fellow!' cried Captain Delano. 'Don Benito, I envy you such a friend; slave I cannot call him.'

As master and man stood before him, the black upholding the white, Captain Delano could not but bethink him of the beauty of that relationship which could present such a spectacle of fidelity on the one hand and confidence on the other. The scene was heightened by the contrast in dress, denoting their relative positions. The Spaniard wore a loose Chile jacket of dark velvet; white small-clothes and stockings, with silver buckles at the knee and instep; a high-crowned sombrero, of fine grass; a slender sword, silver mounted, hung from a knot in his sash – the last being an almost invariable adjunct, more for utility than ornament, of a South American gentleman's dress to this hour. Excepting when his occasional nervous contortions brought about disarray, there was a certain precision in his attire curiously at variance with the unsightly disorder around; especially in the belittered ghetto, forward of the main-mast, wholly occupied by the blacks.

The servant wore nothing but wide trousers, apparently, from their coarseness and patches, made out of some old topsail; they were clean, and confined at the waist by a bit of unstranded rope, which, with his composed, deprecatory air at times, made him something like a begging friar of St Francis.

However unsuitable for the time and place, at least in the blunt-thinking American's eyes, and however strangely surviving in the midst of all his afflictions, the toilette of Don Benito might not, in fashion at least, have gone beyond the style of the day among South Americans of his class. Though on the present voyage sailing from Buenos Aires, he had avowed himself a native and resident of Chile, whose inhabitants had not so generally adopted the plain coat and once plebeian pantaloons but, with a becoming modification, adhered to their provincial costume, picturesque as any in the world. Still, relatively to the pale history of the voyage, and his own pale face, there seemed something so incongruous in the Spaniard's apparel as almost to suggest the image of an invalid courtier tottering about London streets in the time of the plague.

The portion of the narrative which, perhaps, most excited interest, as well as some surprise, considering the latitudes in question, was the long calms spoken of, and more particularly the ship's so long drifting about. Without communicating the opinion, of course, the American could not but impute at least part of the detentions both to clumsy seamanship and faulty navigation. Eyeing Don Benito's small, yellow hands, he easily inferred that the young captain had not got into command at the hawse-hole, but the cabin-window; and if so, why wonder at incompetence in youth, sickness and gentility united?

But drowning criticism in compassion, after a fresh repetition of his sympathies, Captain Delano, having heard out his story, not only engaged, as in the first place, to see Don Benito and his people supplied in their immediate bodily needs, but, also, now further promised to assist him in procuring a large permanent supply of water, as well as some sails and rigging; and, though it would involve no small embarrassment to himself, yet he would spare three of his best seamen for temporary deck-officers; so that without delay the ship might proceed to Concepción, there fully to refit for Lima, her destined port.

Such generosity was not without its effect, even upon the invalid. His face lighted up; eager and hectic, he met the honest glance of his visitor. With gratitude he seemed overcome.

'This excitement is bad for master,' whispered the servant, taking his arm, and with soothing words gently drawing him aside.

When Don Benito returned, the American was pained to observe that his hopefulness, like the sudden kindling in his cheek, was but febrile and transient.

Ere long, with a joyless mien, looking up towards the poop, the host invited his guest to accompany him there, for the benefit of what little breath of wind might be stirring

As during the telling of the story, Captain Delano had once or twice started at the occasional cymballing of the hatchet-polishers, wondering why such an interruption should be allowed, especially in that part of the ship, and in the ears of an invalid; and moreover, as the hatchets had anything but an attractive look, and the handlers of them still less so, it was, therefore, to tell the truth, not without some lurking reluctance, or even shrinking, it may be, that Captain Delano, with apparent complaisance, acquiesced in his host's invitation. The more so, since, with an untimely caprice of punctilio, rendered distressing by his cadaverous aspect, Don Benito, with Castilian bows, solemnly insisted upon his guest's preceding him up the ladder leading to the elevation where, one on each side of the last step, sat for armorial supporters and sentries two of the ominous file. Gingerly enough stepped good Captain Delano between them, and in the instant of leaving them behind, like one running the gauntlet, he felt an apprehensive twitch in the calves of his legs.

But when, facing about, he saw the whole file, like so many organ-grinders, still stupidly intent on their work, unmindful of everything beside, he could not but smile at his late fidgety panic.

Presently, while standing with his host, looking forward upon the decks below, he was struck by one of those instances of insubordination previously alluded to. Three black boys, with two Spanish boys, were sitting together on the hatches, scraping a rude wooden platter in which some scanty mess had recently been cooked. Suddenly, one of the black boys, enraged at a word dropped by one of his white companions, seized a knife, and though called to forbear by one of the oakum-pickers, struck the lad over the head, inflicting a gash from which blood flowed.

In amazement, Captain Delano enquired what this meant. To which the pale Don Benito dully muttered that it was merely the sport of the lad.

'Pretty serious sport, truly,' rejoined Captain Delano. 'Had such a thing happened on board the *Bachelor's Delight*, instant punishment would have followed.'

At these words the Spaniard turned upon the American one of his sudden, staring, half-lunatic looks; then, relapsing into his torpor, answered, 'Doubtless, doubtless, señor.'

Is it, thought Captain Delano, that this hapless man is one of those paper captains I've known, who by policy wink at what by power they cannot put down? I know no sadder sight than a commander who has little of command but the name.

'I should think, Don Benito,' he now said, glancing towards the oakum-picker who had sought to interfere with the boys, 'that you would find it advantageous to keep all your blacks employed, especially the younger ones, no matter at what useless task, and no matter what happens to the ship. Why, even with my little band, I find such a course indispensable. I once kept a crew on my quarter-deck thrumming mats for my cabin, when, for three days, I had given up my ship – mats, men and all – for a speedy loss, owing to the violence of a gale, in which we could do nothing but helplessly drive before it.'

'Doubtless, doubtless,' muttered Don Benito.

'But,' continued Captain Delano, again glancing upon the oakum-pickers and then at the hatchet-polishers, near by, 'I see you keep some, at least, of your host employed.'

'Yes,' was again the vacant response.

'Those old men there, shaking their pows from their pulpits,' continued Captain Delano, pointing to the oakum-pickers, 'seem to act the part of old dominies to the rest, little heeded as their admonitions are at times. Is this voluntary on their part, Don Benito, or have you appointed them shepherds to your flock of black sheep?'

'What posts they fill, I appointed them,' rejoined the Spaniard, in an acrid tone, as if resenting some supposed satiric reflection.

'And these others, these Ashantee conjurors here,' continued Captain Delano, rather uneasily eyeing the brandished steel of the hatchet-polishers, where, in spots, it had been brought to a shine, 'this seems a curious business they are at, Don Benito.

'In the gales we met,' answered the Spaniard, 'what of our general cargo was not thrown overboard was much damaged by the brine. Since coming into calm weather, I have had several cases of knives and hatchets daily brought up for overhauling and cleaning.'

'A prudent idea, Don Benito. You are part owner of ship and cargo, I presume; but none of the slaves, perhaps?'

'I am owner of all you see,' impatiently returned Don Benito, 'except the main company of blacks, who belonged to my late friend, Alexandro Aranda.'

As he mentioned this name, his air was heart-broken; his knees shook; his servant supported him.

Thinking he divined the cause of such unusual emotion, to confirm his surmise, Captain Delano, after a pause, said: 'And may I ask, Don Benito, whether – since a while ago you spoke of some cabin passengers – the friend, whose loss so afflicts you, at the outset of the voyage accompanied his blacks?'

'Yes.'

'But died of the fever?'

'Died of the fever. Oh, could I but – ' Again quivering, the Spaniard paused.

'Pardon me,' said Captain Delano, lowly, 'but I think that by a sympathetic experience, I conjecture, Don Benito, what it is that gives the keener edge to your grief. It was once my hard fortune to lose, at sea, a dear friend, my own brother, then supercargo. Assured of the welfare of his spirit, its departure I could have borne like a man; but that honest eye, that honest hand – both of which had so often met mine – and that warm heart; all, all – like scraps to the dogs – to throw all to the sharks! It was then I vowed never to have for fellow-voyager a man I loved, unless, unbeknown to him, I had provided every requisite, in case of a fatality, for embalming his mortal part for interment on shore. Were your friend's remains now on board this ship, Don Benito, not thus strangely would the mention of his name affect you.'

'On board this ship?' echoed the Spaniard. Then, with horrified gestures, as directed against some spectre, he unconsciously fell into the ready arms of his attendant, who, with a silent appeal towards Captain Delano, seemed beseeching him not again to broach a theme so unspeakably distressing to his master.

This poor fellow now, thought the pained American, is the victim of that sad superstition which associates goblins with the deserted body of man, as ghosts with an abandoned house. How unlike are we made! What to me, in like case, would have been a solemn satisfaction, the bare suggestion, even, terrifies the Spaniard into this trance. Poor Alexandro Aranda! what would you say could you here see your friend – who, on former voyages, when you, for months, were left behind, has, I dare say, often longed and longed for one peep at you – now transported with terror at the least thought of having you anyway nigh him.

At this moment, with a dreary graveyard toll betokening a flaw, the ship's forecastle bell, smote by one of the grizzled oakum-pickers, proclaimed ten o'clock, through the leaden calm; hereupon, Captain Delano's attention was caught by the moving figure of a gigantic black, emerging from the general crowd below, and slowly advancing towards the elevated poop. An iron collar was about his neck, from which depended a chain, thrice wound round his body; the terminating links padlocked together at a broad band of iron, his girdle.

'How like a mute Atufal moves,' murmured the servant.

The black mounted the steps of the poop, and, like a brave prisoner, brought up to receive sentence, stood in unquailing muteness before Don Benito, now recovered from his attack.

At the first glimpse of his approach, Don Benito had started; a resentful shadow swept over his face and, as with the sudden memory of bootless rage, his white lips glued together.

This is some mulish mutineer, thought Captain Delano, sur-veying, not without a mixture of admiration, the colossal form of the negro.

'See, he waits your question, master,' said the servant.

Thus reminded, Don Benito, nervously averting his glance, as if shunning, by anticipation, some rebellious response, in a discon-certed voice thus spoke: 'Atufal, will you ask my pardon, now?'

The black was silent.

'Again, master,' murmured the servant, with bitter upbraiding eyeing his countryman. 'Again, master; he will bend to master yet.'

'Answer,' said Don Benito, still averting his glance, 'say but the one word, *pardon*, and your chains shall be off.'

Upon this, the black, slowly raising both arms, let them lifelessly fall, his links clanking, his head bowed; as much as to say, 'No, I am content.'

'Go,' said Don Benito, with inkept and unknown emotion.

Deliberately as he had come, the black obeyed.

'Excuse me, Don Benito,' said Captain Delano, 'but this scene surprises me; what means it, pray?'

'It means that that negro alone, of all the band, has given me peculiar cause of offence. I have put him in chains; I – '

Here he paused, his hand to his head, as if there were a swimming there, or a sudden bewilderment of memory had come over him; but meeting his servant's kindly glance seemed reassured, and proceeded: 'I could not scourge such a form. But I told him he must ask my pardon. As yet he has not. At my command, every two hours he stands before me.'

'And how long has this been?'

'Some sixty days.'

'And obedient in all else? And respectful?'

'Yes.'

'Upon my conscience, then,' exclaimed Captain Delano impulsively, 'he has a royal spirit in him, this fellow.'

'He may have some right to it,' bitterly returned Don Benito; 'he says he was king in his own land.'

'Yes,' said the servant, entering a word, 'those slits in Atufal's ears once held wedges of gold; but poor Babo here, in his own land, was only a poor slave; a black man's slave was Babo, who now is the white's.'

Somewhat annoyed by these conversational familiarities, Captain Delano turned curiously upon the attendant, then glanced enquiringly at his master; but, as if long wonted to these little informalities, neither master nor man seemed to understand him.

'What, pray, was Atufal's offence, Don Benito?' asked Captain Delano; 'if it was not something very serious, take a fool's advice and, in view of his general docility, as well as in some natural respect for his spirit, remit him his penalty.'

'No, no, master never will do that,' here murmured the servant to himself, 'proud Atufal must first ask master's pardon. The slave there carries the padlock, but master here carries the key.'

His attention thus directed, Captain Delano now noticed for the first time that, suspended by a slender silken cord, from Don Benito's neck hung a key. At once, from the servant's muttered syllables, divining the key's purpose, he smiled and said: 'So, Don Benito – padlock and key – significant symbols, truly.'

Biting his lip, Don Benito faltered.

Though the remark of Captain Delano, a man of such native simplicity as to be incapable of satire or irony, had been dropped in playful allusion to the Spaniard's singularly evidenced lordship over the black; yet the hypochondriac seemed some way to have taken it as a malicious reflection upon his confessed inability thus far to break down, at least, on a verbal summons, the entrenched will of the slave. Deploring this supposed misconception, yet despairing of correcting it, Captain Delano shifted the subject; but finding his companion more than ever withdrawn, as if still sourly digesting the lees of the presumed affront above-mentioned, by and by Captain Delano likewise became less talkative, oppressed, against his own will, by what seemed the secret vindictiveness of the morbidly sensitive Spaniard. But the good sailor, himself of a quite contrary disposition, refrained, on his part, alike from the appearance as from the feeling of resentment, and if silent, was only so from contagion.

Presently the Spaniard, assisted by his servant, somewhat discourteously crossed over from his guest; a procedure which sensibly enough, might have been allowed to pass for idle caprice of ill-humour, had not master and man, lingering round the corner of the elevated skylight, begun whispering together in low voices. This was unpleasing. And more: the moody air of the Spaniard, which at times had not been without a sort of valetudinarian stateliness, now seemed anything but dignified; while the menial familiarity of the servant lost its original charm of simple-hearted attachment.

In his embarrassment, the visitor turned his face to the other side of the ship. By so doing, his glance accidentally fell on a young Spanish sailor, a coil of rope in his hand, just stepped from the deck to the first round of the mizzen-rigging. Perhaps the man would not have been particularly noticed were it not that, during his ascent to one of the yards, he, with a sort of covert intentness, kept his eye fixed on Captain Delano, from whom, presently, it passed, as if by a natural sequence, to the two whisperers.

His own attention thus redirected to that quarter, Captain Delano gave a slight start. From something in Don Benitos manner just then, it seemed as if the visitor had, at least partly, been the subject of the withdrawn consultation going on – a conjecture as little agreeable to the guest as it was little flattering to the host.

The singular alternations of courtesy and ill-breeding in the Spanish captain were unaccountable, except on one of two suppositions – innocent lunacy or wicked imposture.

But the first idea, though it might naturally have occurred to an indifferent observer, and, in some respect, had not hitherto been wholly a stranger to Captain Delano's mind, yet, now that in an incipient way he began to regard the stranger's conduct something in the light of an intentional affront, of course the idea of lunacy was virtually vacated. But if not a lunatic, what then. Under the circumstances, would a gentleman, nay, any honest boor, act the part now acted by his host? The man was an impostor. Some low-born adventurer, masquerading as an oceanic grandee; yet so ignorant of the first requisites of mere gentlemanhood as to be betrayed into the present remarkable indecorum. That strange ceremoniousness, too, at other times evinced, seemed not uncharacteristic of one playing a part above his real level. Benito Cereno – Don Benito Cereno – a sounding name. One, too, at that period, not unknown, in the surname, to supercargoes and sea captains trading along the Spanish Main, as belonging to one of the most enterprising and extensive mercantile families in all those provinces; several members of it having titles; a sort of Castilian Rothschild, with a noble brother, or cousin, in every great trading town of South America. The alleged Don Benito was in early manhood, about twenty-nine or thirty. To assume a sort of roving cadetship in the maritime affairs of such a house, what more likely scheme for a young knave of talent and spirit? But the Spaniard was a pale invalid. Never mind. For even to the degree of simulating mortal disease, the craft of some tricksters had been known to attain. To think that, under the aspect of infantile weakness, the most savage energies might be couched – those velvets of the Spaniard but the silky paw to his fangs.

From no train of thought did these fancies come; not from within, but from without; suddenly, too, and in one throng, like hoar frost; yet as soon to vanish as the mild sun of Captain Delano's good nature regained its meridian.

Glancing over once more towards his host – whose side-face, revealed above the skylight, was now turned towards him – he was struck by the profile, whose clearness of cut was refined by the thinness, incident to ill-health, as well as ennobled about the chin by the beard. Away with suspicion. He was a true off-shoot of a true hidalgo Cereno.

Relieved by these and other better thoughts, the visitor, lightly humming a tune, now began indifferently pacing the poop, so as not to betray to Don Benito that he had at all mistrusted incivility, much less duplicity; for such mistrust would yet be proved illusory, and by the event; though, for the present, the circumstance which had provoked that distrust remained unexplained. But when that little mystery should have been cleared up, Captain Delano thought he might extremely regret it, did he allow Don Benito to become aware that he had indulged in ungenerous surmises. In short, to the Spaniard's black-letter text, it was best, for a while, to leave open margin.

Presently, his pale face twitching and overcast, the Spaniard, still supported by his attendant, moved over towards his guest, when, with even more than his usual embarrassment, and a strange sort of intriguing intonation in his husky whisper, the following conversation began: 'Señor, may I ask how long you have lain at this isle?'

'Oh, but a day or two, Don Benito.'

'And from what port are you last?'

'Canton.'

'And there, señor, you exchanged your sealskins for teas and silks, I think you said?'

'Yes. Silks, mostly.'

'And the balance you took in specie, perhaps?'

Captain Delano, fidgeting a little, answered, 'Yes; some silver; not a very great deal, though.'

'Ah – well. May I ask how many men have you, señor?'

Captain Delano slightly started, but answered, 'About five-and-twenty, all told.'

'And at present, señor, all on board, I suppose?'

'All on board, Don Benito,' replied the captain, now with satisfaction.

'And will be tonight, señor?'

At this last question, following so many pertinacious ones, for the soul of him Captain Delano could not but look very earnestly at the questioner, who, instead of meeting the glance, with every token of craven discomposure dropped his eyes to the deck – presenting an unworthy contrast to his servant, who, just then, was kneeling at his feet, adjusting a loose shoe-buckle; his disengaged face meantime, with humble curiosity, turned openly up into his master's downcast one.

The Spaniard, still with a guilty shuffle, repeated his question: 'And – and will be tonight, señor?'

'Yes, for aught I know,' returned Captain Delano – 'but nay,' rallying himself into fearless truth, 'some of them talked of going off on another fishing party about midnight.'

'Your ships generally go – go more or less armed, I believe, señor.'

'Oh, a six-pounder or two, in case of emergency,' was the intrepidly indifferent reply, 'with a small stock of muskets, sealing-spears and cutlasses, you know.'

As he thus responded, Captain Delano again glanced at Don Benito, but the latter's eyes were averted; while abruptly and awkwardly shifting the subject, he made some peevish allusion to the calm, and then, without apology, once more, with his attendant, withdrew to the opposite bulwarks, where the whispering was resumed.

At this moment, and ere Captain Delano could cast a cool thought upon what had just passed, the young Spanish sailor, before mentioned, was seen descending from the rigging. In act of stooping over to spring inboard to the deck, his voluminous, unconfined frock, or shirt, of coarse woollen, much spotted with tar, opened out far down the chest, revealing a soiled undergarment of what seemed the finest linen, edged, about the neck, with a narrow blue ribbon, sadly faded and worn. At this moment the young sailor's eye was again fixed on the whisperers and Captain Delano thought he observed a lurking significance in it, as if silent signs, of some Freemason sort, had that instant been interchanged.

This once more impelled his own glance in the direction of Don Benito, and, as before, he could not but infer that he himself formed the subject of the conference. He paused. The sound of the hatchet-polishing fell on his ears. He cast another swift side-look at the two. They had the air of conspirators. In connection with the late questionings, and the incident of the young sailor, these things now begat such return of involuntary suspicion that the singular guile-lessness of the American could not endure it. Plucking up a gay and humorous expression, he crossed over to the two rapidly, saying – 'Ha, Don Benito, your black here seems high in your trust; a sort of privy-counsellor, in fact.'

Upon this, the servant looked up with a good-natured grin but the master started as from a venomous bite. It was a moment or two before the Spaniard sufficiently recovered himself to reply; which he did, at last, with cold constraint – 'Yes, señor, I have trust in Babo.'

Here Babo, changing his previous grin of mere animal humour into an intelligent smile, not ungratefully eyed his master.

Finding that the Spaniard now stood silent and reserved, as if involuntarily, or purposely, giving hint that his guest's proximity was inconvenient just then, Captain Delano, unwilling to appear uncivil even to incivility itself, made some trivial remark and moved off; again and again turning over in his mind the mysterious demeanour of Don Benito Cereno.

He had descended from the poop, and, wrapped in thought, was passing near a dark hatchway leading down into the steerage, when, perceiving motion there, he looked to see what moved. The same instant there was a sparkle in the shadowy hatchway, and he saw one of the Spanish sailors, prowling there, hurriedly placing his hand in the bosom of his frock, as if hiding something. Before the man could have been certain who it was that was passing, he slunk below out of sight. But enough was seen of him to make it sure that he was the same young sailor before noticed in the rigging.

What was that which so sparkled? thought Captain Delano. It was no lamp – no match – no live coal. Could it have been a jewel? But how come sailors with jewels? – or with silk-trimmed under-shirts either? Has he been robbing the trunks of the dead cabin-passengers? But if so, he would hardly wear one of the stolen articles on board ship here. Ah, ah – if, now, that was, indeed, a secret sign I saw passing between this suspicious fellow and his captain awhile since; if I could only be certain that, in my uneasiness, my senses did not deceive me, then –

Here, passing from one suspicious thing to another, his mind revolved the strange questions put to him concerning his ship.

By a curious coincidence, as each point was recalled, the black wizards of Ashantee would strike up with their hatchets, as in ominous comment on the white stranger's thoughts. Pressed by such enigmas and portents, it would have been almost against nature, had not, even into the least distrustful heart, some ugly misgivings obtruded.

Observing the ship, now helplessly fallen into a current, with enchanted sails, drifting with increased rapidity seaward; and noting that, from a lately intercepted projection of the land, the sealer was hidden, the stout mariner began to quake at thoughts which he barely durst confess to himself. Above all, he began to feel a ghostly dread of Don Benito. And yet, when he roused himself, dilated his chest, felt himself strong on his legs, and coolly considered it – what did all these phantoms amount to?

Had the Spaniard any sinister scheme, it must have reference not so much to him (Captain Delano) as to his ship (the *Bachelor's*

Delight). Hence the present drifting away of the one ship from the other, instead of favouring any such possible scheme, was, for the time, at least, opposed to it. Clearly any suspicion, combining such contradictions, must need be delusive. Besides, was it not absurd to think of a vessel in distress – a vessel by sickness almost dismanned of her crew – a vessel whose inmates were parched for water – was it not a thousand times absurd that such a craft should, at present, be of a piratical character; or her commander, either for himself or those under him, cherish any desire but for speedy relief and refreshment? But then, might not general distress, and thirst in particular, be affected? And might not that same undiminished Spanish crew, alleged to have perished off to a remnant, be at that very moment lurking in the hold? On heart-broken pretence of entreating a cup of cold water, fiends in human form had got into lonely dwellings, nor retired until a dark deed had been done. And among the Malay pirates, it was no unusual thing to lure ships after them into their treacherous harbours, or entice boarders from a declared enemy at sea by the spectacle of thinly manned or vacant decks, beneath which prowled a hundred spears with yellow arms ready to upthrust them through the mats. Not that Captain Delano had entirely credited such things. He had heard of them – and now, as stories, they recurred. The present destination of the ship was the anchorage. There she would be near his own vessel. Upon gaining that vicinity, might not the *San Dominick*, like a slumbering volcano, suddenly let loose energies now hid?

He recalled the Spaniard's manner while telling his story. There was a gloomy hesitancy and subterfuge about it. It was just the manner of one making up his tale for evil purposes, as he goes. But if that story was not true, what was the truth? That the ship had unlawfully come into the Spaniard's possession? But in many of its details, especially in reference to the more calamitous parts, such as the fatalities among the seamen, the consequent prolonged beating about, the past sufferings from obstinate calms, and still continued suffering from thirst; in all these points, as well as others, Don Benito's story had been corroborated by not only the wailing ejaculations of the indiscriminate multitude, white and black, but likewise – what seemed impossible to be counterfeit – by the very expression and play of every human feature which Captain Delano saw. If Don Benito's story was, throughout, an invention, then every soul on board, down to the youngest negress, was his carefully drilled recruit in the plot: an incredible inference. And yet, if there was ground for mistrusting his veracity, that inference was a legitimate one.

But those questions of the Spaniard. There, indeed, one might pause. Did they not seem put with much the same object with which the burglar or assassin, by daytime, reconnoitres the walls of a house? But, with ill purposes, to solicit such information openly of the chief person endangered, and so, in effect, setting him on his guard; how unlikely a procedure was that? Absurd, then, to suppose that those questions had been prompted by evil designs. Thus, the same conduct, which, in this instance, had raised the alarm, served to dispel it. In short, there was scarce any suspicion or uneasiness, however apparently reasonable at the time, which was not now, with equally apparent reason, dismissed.

At last he began to laugh at his former forebodings; and laugh at the strange ship for, in its aspect, someway siding with them, as it were; and laugh, too, at the odd-looking blacks! particularly those old scissors-grinders, the Ashantees; and those bedridden old knitting women, the oakum-pickers; and almost at the dark Spaniard himself, the central hobgoblin of all.

For the rest, whatever in a serious way seemed enigmatical, was now good-naturedly explained away by the thought that, for the most part, the poor invalid scarcely knew what he was about, either sulking in black vapours, or putting idle questions without sense of object. Evidently, for the present, the man was not fit to be entrusted with the ship. On some benevolent plea withdrawing the command from him, Captain Delano would yet have to send her to Concepción in charge of his second mate, a worthy person and good navigator – a plan not more convenient for the *San Dominick* than for Don Benito; for, relieved from all anxiety, keeping wholly to his cabin, the sick man, under the good nursing of his servant, would, probably, by the end of the passage, be in a measure restored to health, and with that he should also be restored to authority.

Such were the American's thoughts. They were tranquillising. There was a difference between the idea of Don Benito's darkly preordaining Captain Delano's fate, and Captain Delano's lightly arranging Don Benito's. Nevertheless, it was not without something of relief that the good seaman presently perceived his whale-boat in the distance. Its absence had been prolonged by unexpected detention at the sealer's side, as well as its returning trip lengthened by the continual recession of the goal.

The advancing speck was observed by the blacks. Their shouts attracted the attention of Don Benito, who, with a return of courtesy, approaching Captain Delano, expressed satisfaction at the coming of some supplies, slight and temporary as they must necessarily prove.

Captain Delano responded; but while doing so, his attention was drawn to something passing on the deck below: among the crowd climbing the landward bulwarks, anxiously watching the coming boat, two blacks, to all appearances accidentally incommoded by one of the sailors, violently pushed him aside, which the sailor someway resenting, they dashed him to the deck, despite the earnest cries of the oakum-pickers.

'Don Benito,' said Captain Delano quickly, 'do you see what is going on there? Look!'

But, seized by his cough, the Spaniard staggered, with both hands to his face, on the point of falling. Captain Delano would have supported him, but the servant was more alert, and with one hand sustaining his master, with the other applied the cordial. Don Benito restored, the black withdrew his support, slipping aside a little, but dutifully remaining within call of a whisper. Such discretion was here evinced as quite wiped away, in the visitor's eyes, any blemish of impropriety which might have attached to the attendant from the indecorous conferences before mentioned, showing, too, that if the servant were to blame, it might be more the master's fault than his own, since when left to himself, he could conduct thus well.

His glance called away from the spectacle of disorder to the more pleasing one before him, Captain Delano could not avoid again congratulating his host upon possessing such a servant who, though perhaps a little too forward now and then, must upon the whole be invaluable to one in the invalid's situation.

'Tell me, Don Benito,' he added, with a smile – 'I should like to have your man here, myself – what will you take for him? Would fifty doubloons be any object?'

'Master wouldn't part with Babo for a thousand doubloons,' murmured the black, overhearing the offer, and taking it in earnest, and, with the strange vanity of a faithful slave, appreciated by his master, scorning to hear so paltry a valuation put upon him by a stranger. But Don Benito, apparently hardly yet completely restored, and again interrupted by his cough, made but some broken reply.

Soon his physical distress became so great, affecting his mind, too, apparently, that, as if to screen the sad spectacle, the servant gently conducted his master below.

Left to himself, the American, to while away the time till his boat should arrive, would have pleasantly accosted some one of the few Spanish seamen he saw; but recalling something that Don Benito had said touching their ill conduct, he refrained, as a shipmaster indisposed to countenance cowardice or unfaithfulness in seamen.

While, with these thoughts, standing with eye directed forward towards that handful of sailors, suddenly he thought that one or two of them returned the glance and with a sort of meaning. He rubbed his eyes, and looked again; but again seemed to see the same thing. Under a new form, but more obscure than any previous one, the old suspicions recurred, but, in the absence of Don Benito, with less of panic than before. Despite the bad account given of the sailors, Captain Delano resolved forthwith to accost one of them. Descending the poop, he made his way through the blacks, his movement drawing a queer cry from the oakum-pickers, prompted by whom, the negroes, twitching each other aside, divided before him – but, as if curious to see what was the object of this deliberate visit to their ghetto, closing in behind, in tolerable order, followed the white stranger up. His progress thus proclaimed as by mounted kings-at-arms, and escorted as by a Kaffir guard of honour, Captain Delano, assuming a good-humoured, off-handed air, continued to advance; now and then saying a blithe word to the negroes, and his eye curiously surveying the white faces, here and there sparsely mixed in with the blacks, like stray white pawns venturously involved in the ranks of the chessmen opposed.

While thinking which of them to select for his purpose, he chanced to observe a sailor seated on the deck engaged in tarring the strap of a large block, a circle of blacks squatted round him inquisitively eyeing the process.

The mean employment of the man was in contrast with something superior in his figure. His hand, black with continually thrusting it into the tar-pot held for him by a negro, seemed not naturally allied to his face, a face which would have been a very fine one but for its haggardness. Whether this haggardness had aught to do with criminality, could not be determined since, as intense heat and cold, though unlike, produce like sensations, so innocence and guilt, when, through casual association with mental pain, stamping any visible impress, use one seal – a hacked one.

Not again that this reflection occurred to Captain Delano at the time, charitable man as he was. Rather another idea. Because observing so singular a haggardness combined with a dark eye, averted as in trouble and shame, and then again recalling Don Benito's confessed ill opinion of his crew, insensibly he was operated upon by certain general notions which, while disconnecting pain and abashment from virtue, invariably link them with vice.

If, indeed, there be any wickedness on board this ship, thought Captain Delano, be sure that man there has fouled his hand in it, even as now he fouls it in the pitch. I don't like to accost him. I will speak to this other, this old Jack here on the windlass.

He advanced to an old Barcelona tar, in ragged red breeches and dirty nightcap, cheeks trenched and bronzed, whiskers dense as thorn hedges. Seated between two sleepy-looking Africans, this mariner, like his younger shipmate, was employed upon some rigging – splicing a cable – the sleepy-looking blacks performing the inferior function of holding the outer parts of the ropes for him.

Upon Captain Delano's approach, the man at once hung his head below its previous level; the one necessary for business. It appeared as if he desired to be thought absorbed, with more than common fidelity, in his task. Being addressed, he glanced up but with what seemed a furtive, diffident air, which sat strangely enough on his weather-beaten visage, much as if a grizzly bear instead of growling and biting, should simper and cast sheep's eyes. He was asked several questions concerning the voyage   questions purposely referring to several particulars in Don Benito's narrative, not previously corroborated by those impulsive cries greeting the visitor on first coming on board. The questions were briefly answered, confirming all that remained to be confirmed of the story. The negroes about the windlass joined in with the old sailor; but, as they became talkative, he by degrees became mute, and at length quite glum, seemed morosely unwilling to answer more questions, and yet, all the while, this ursine air was somehow mixed with his sheepish one.

Despairing of getting into unembarrassed talk with such a centaur, Captain Delano, after glancing round for a more promising countenance, but seeing none, spoke pleasantly to the blacks to make way for him; and so, amid various grins and grimaces, returned to the poop, feeling a little strange at first, he could hardly tell why, but upon the whole with regained confidence in Benito Cereno.

How plainly, thought he, did that old whiskerando yonder betray a consciousness of ill desert. No doubt, when he saw me coming, he dreaded lest I, apprised by his captain of the crew's general misbehaviour, came with sharp words for him, and so down with his head. And yet – and yet, now that I think of it, that very fellow, if I err not, was one of those who seemed so earnestly eyeing me here awhile since. Ah, these currents spin one's head round almost as much as they do the ship. Ha, there now's a pleasant sort of sunny sight; quite sociable, too.

His attention had been drawn back to a slumbering negress, partly disclosed through the lacework of some rigging, lying, with youthful limbs carelessly disposed, under the lee of the bulwarks, like a doe in the shade of a woodland rock. Sprawling at her lapped breasts was her wide-awake fawn, stark naked, its black little body half lifted from the deck, crosswise with its dam's; its hands, like two paws, clambering upon her; its mouth and nose ineffectually rooting to get at the mark; and meantime giving a vexatious half-grunt, blending with the composed snore of the negress.

The uncommon vigour of the child at length roused the mother. She started up, at a distance facing Captain Delano. But as if not at all concerned at the attitude in which she had been caught, delightedly she caught the child up, with maternal transports, covering it with kisses.

There's naked nature, now; pure tenderness and love, thought Captain Delano, well pleased.

This incident prompted him to remark the other negresses more particularly than before. He was gratified with their manners: like most uncivilised women, they seemed at once tender of heart and tough of constitution; equally ready to die for their infants or fight for them. Unsophisticated as leopardesses; loving as doves. Ah! thought Captain Delano, these, perhaps, are some of the very women whom Ledyard saw in Africa, and gave such a noble account of.

These natural sights somehow insensibly deepened his confidence and ease. At last he looked to see how his boat was getting on; but it was still pretty remote. He turned to see if Don Benito had returned; but he had not.

To change the scene, as well as to please himself with a leisurely observation of the coming boat, stepping over into the mizzen-chains, he clambered his way into the starboard quarter-gallery – one of those abandoned Venetian-looking water-balconies previously mentioned – retreats cut off from the deck. As his foot pressed the half-damp, half-dry sea-mosses matting the place, and a chance phantom cat's-paw – an islet of breeze, unheralded, unfollowed – as this ghostly cat's-paw came fanning his cheek; as his glance fell upon the row of small, round deadlights – all closed like coppered eyes of the coffined – and the state-cabin door, once connecting with the gallery, even as the dead-lights had once looked out upon it, but now calked fast like a sarcophagus lid; and to a purple-black, tarred-over panel, threshold and post; and he bethought him of the time when that state-cabin and this state-balcony had heard the voices of the Spanish king's officers and the forms of the Lima viceroy's daughters had perhaps leaned where he stood – as these and other images flitted through his mind, as the cat's-paw through the calm, gradually he felt rising a dreamy inquietude, like that of one who alone on the prairie feels unrest from the repose of the noon.

He leaned against the carved balustrade, again looking off towards his boat; but found his eye falling upon the ribbon grass, trailing along the ship's water-line, straight as a border of green box; and parterres of sea-weed, broad ovals and crescents, floating nigh and far, with what seemed long formal alleys between, crossing the terraces of swells, and sweeping round as if leading to the grottoes below. And overhanging all was the balustrade by his arm, which, partly stained with pitch and partly embossed with moss, seemed the charred ruin of some summer-house in a grand garden long running to waste.

Trying to break one charm, he was but becharmed anew. Though upon the wide sea, he seemed in some far inland country; prisoner in some deserted château, left to stare at empty grounds, and peer out at vague roads, where never wagon or wayfarer passed.

But these enchantments were a little disenchanted as his eye fell on the corroded main-chains. Of an ancient style, massy and rusty in link, shackle and bolt, they seemed even more fit for the ship's present business than the one for which she had been built.

Presently he thought something moved nigh the chains. He rubbed his eyes, and looked hard. Groves of rigging were about the chains; and there, peering from behind a great stay, like an Indian from behind a hemlock, a Spanish sailor, a marlingspike in his hand, was seen, who made what seemed an imperfect gesture towards the balcony, but immediately, as if alarmed by some advancing step along the deck within, vanished into the recesses of the hempen forest, like a poacher.

What meant this? Something the man had sought to communicate, unbeknown to anyone, even to his captain. Did the secret involve aught unfavourable to his captain? Were those previous misgivings of Captain Delano's about to be verified? Or, in his haunted mood at the moment, had some random, unintentional motion of the man, while busy with the stay, as if repairing it, been mistaken for a significant beckoning?

Not unbewildered, again he gazed off for his boat. But it was temporarily hidden by a rocky spur of the isle. As with some eagerness he bent forward, watching for the first shooting view of its beak, the balustrade gave way before him like charcoal. Had he not clutched an outreaching rope he would have fallen into the sea. The crash, though feeble, and the fall, though hollow, of the rotten fragments, must have been overheard. He glanced up. With sober curiosity peering down upon him was one of the old oakum-pickers, slipped from his perch to an outside boom; while below the old negro, and, invisible to him, reconnoitring from a port-hole like a fox from the mouth of its den, crouched the Spanish sailor again. From something suddenly suggested by the man's air, the mad idea now darted into Captain Delano's mind that Don Benito's plea of indisposition, in withdrawing below, was but a pretence: that he was engaged there maturing his plot, of which the sailor, by some means gaining an inkling, had a mind to warn the stranger against; incited, it may be, by gratitude for a kind word on first boarding the ship. Was it from foreseeing some possible interference like this that Don Benito had, beforehand, given such a bad character of his sailors, while praising the negroes; though, indeed, the former seemed as docile as the latter the contrary? The whites, too, by nature, were the shrewder race. A man with some evil design, would he not be likely to speak well of that stupidity which was blind to his depravity, and malign that intelligence from which it might not be hidden? Not unlikely, perhaps. But if the whites had dark secrets concerning Don Benito, could then Don Benito be any way in complicity with the blacks? But they were too stupid. Besides, who ever heard of a white so far a renegade as to apostatise from his very species almost by leaguing in against it with negroes? These difficulties recalled former ones. Lost in their mazes, Captain Delano, who had now regained the deck, was uneasily advancing along it, when he observed a new face; an aged sailor seated cross-legged near the main hatchway. His skin was shrunk up with wrinkles like a pelican's empty pouch; his hair frosted; his countenance grave and composed. His hands were full of ropes, which he was working into a large knot. Some blacks were about him obligingly dipping the strands for him, here and there, as the exigencies of the operation demanded.

Captain Delano crossed over to him, and stood in silence surveying the knot; his mind, by a not uncongenial transition, passing from its own entanglements to those of the hemp. For intricacy, such a knot he had never seen in an American ship, nor indeed in any other. The old man looked like an Egyptian priest, making Gordian knots for the temple of Ammon. The knot seemed a combination of double-bowline-knot, treble-crown-knot, back-handed-well-knot, knot-in-and-out-knot and jamming-knot.

At last, puzzled to comprehend the meaning of such a knot, Captain Delano addressed the knotter: 'What are you knotting there, my man?'

'The knot,' was the brief reply, without looking up.

'So it seems; but what is it for?'

'For someone else to undo,' muttered back the old man, plying his fingers harder than ever, the knot being now nearly completed.

While Captain Delano stood watching him, suddenly the old man threw the knot towards him, saying in broken English – the first heard in the ship – something to this effect: 'Undo it, cut it, quick.' It was said lowly, but with such condensation of rapidity, that the long, slow words in Spanish, which had preceded and followed, almost operated as covers to the brief English between.

For a moment, knot in hand, and knot in head, Captain Delano stood mute; while, without further heeding him, the old man was now intent upon other ropes. Presently there was a slight stir behind Captain Delano. Turning, he saw the chained negro, Atufal, standing quietly there. The next moment the old sailor rose, muttering, and, followed by his subordinate negroes, removed to the forward part of the ship, where in the crowd he disappeared.

An elderly negro, in a clout like an infant's, and with a pepper-and-salt head and a kind of attorney air, now approached Captain Delano. In tolerable Spanish, and with a good-natured, knowing wink, he informed him that the old knotter was simple-witted, but harmless; often playing his odd tricks. The negro concluded by begging the knot, for of course the stranger would not care to be troubled with it. Unconsciously, it was handed to him. With a sort of *congé*, the negro received it, and, turning his back, ferreted into it, like a detective custom-house officer after smuggled laces. Soon, with some African word, equivalent to pshaw, he tossed the knot overboard.

All this is very queer now, thought Captain Delano, with a qualmish sort of emotion; but, as one feeling incipient sea-sickness, he strove, by ignoring the symptoms, to get rid of the malady. Once more he looked off for his boat. To his delight, it was now again in view, leaving the rocky spur astern.

The sensation here experienced, after at first relieving his uneasiness with unforeseen efficacy soon began to remove it. The less distant sight of that well-known boat – showing it, not as before, half blended with the haze, but with outline defined, so that its individuality, like a man's, was manifest; that boat, *Rover* by name, which, though now in strange seas, had often pressed the beach of Captain Delano's home, and, brought to its threshold for repairs, had familiarly lain there, as a Newfoundland dog; the sight of that household boat evoked a thousand trustful associations, which, contrasted with previous suspicions, filled him not only with lightsome confidence, but somehow with half-humorous self-reproaches at his former lack of it.

'What, I, Amasa Delano – Jack of the Beach, as they called me when a lad – I, Amasa; the same that, duck-satchel in hand, used to paddle along the waterside to the schoolhouse made from the old hulk – I, little Jack of the Beach, that used to go berrying with cousin Nat and the rest; I to be murdered here at the ends of the earth, on board a haunted pirate-ship by a horrible Spaniard? Too nonsensical to think of! Who would murder Amasa Delano? His conscience is clean. There is Someone above. Fie, fie, Jack of the Beach! you are a child indeed: a child of the second childhood, old boy; you are beginning to dote and drool, I'm afraid.'

Light of heart and foot, he stepped aft, and there was met by Don Benito's servant, who, with a pleasing expression, responsive to his own present feelings, informed him that his master had recovered from the effects of his coughing fit, and had just ordered him to go present his compliments to his good guest, Don Amasa, and say that he (Don Benito) would soon have the happiness to rejoin him.

There now, do you mark that? again thought Captain Delano, walking the poop. What a donkey I was. This kind gentleman who here sends me his kind compliments, he, but ten minutes ago, dark-lantern in hand, was dodging round some old grindstone in the hold, sharpening a hatchet for me, I thought. Well, well; these long calms have a morbid effect on the mind, I've often heard, though I never believed it before. Ha! glancing towards the boat; there's *Rover*; good dog; a white bone in her mouth. A pretty big bone though, seems to me. – What? Yes she has fallen afoul of the bubbling tide-rip there. It sets her the other way, too, for the time. Patience.

It was now about noon, though, from the greyness of everything, it seemed to be getting towards dusk.

The calm was confirmed. In the far distance, away from the influence of land, the leaden ocean seemed laid out and leaded up, its course finished, soul gone, defunct. But the current from landward, where the ship was, increased; silently sweeping her further and further towards the tranced waters beyond.

Still, from his knowledge of those latitudes, cherishing hopes of a breeze, and a fair and fresh one, at any moment, Captain Delano, despite present prospects, buoyantly counted upon bringing the *San Dominick* safely to anchor ere night. The distance swept over was nothing; since, with a good wind, ten minutes' sailing would retrace more than sixty minutes' drifting. Meantime, one moment turning to mark *Rover* fighting the tide-rip, and the next to see Don Benito approaching, he continued walking the poop.

Gradually he felt a vexation arising from the delay of his boat; this soon merged into uneasiness; and at last – his eye falling continually, as from a stage-box into the pit, upon the strange crowd before and below him, and, by and by, recognising there the face – now composed to indifference – of the Spanish sailor who had seemed to beckon from the main-chains – something of his old trepidations returned.

Ah, thought he – gravely enough – this is like the ague: because it went off, it follows not that it won't come back.

Though ashamed of the relapse, he could not altogether subdue it; and so, exerting his good nature to the utmost, insensibly he came to a compromise.

Yes, this is a strange craft; a strange history, too, and strange folks on board. But – nothing more.

By way of keeping his mind out of mischief till the boat should arrive, he tried to occupy it with turning over and over, in a purely speculative sort of way, some lesser peculiarities of the captain and crew. Among others, four curious points recurred:

First, the affair of the Spanish lad assailed with a knife by the slave boy; an act winked at by Don Benito. Second, the tyranny in Don Benito's treatment of Atufal, the black: as if a child should lead a bull of the Nile by the ring in his nose. Third, the trampling of the sailor by the two negroes; a piece of insolence passed over without so much as a reprimand. Fourth, the cringing submission to their master, of all the ship's underlings, mostly blacks; as if by the least inadvertence they feared to draw down his despotic displeasure.

Coupling these points, they seemed somewhat contradictory. But what then, thought Captain Delano, glancing towards his now nearing boat – what then? Why, Don Benito is a very capricious commander. But he is not the first of the sort I have seen; though it's true he rather exceeds any other. But as a nation – continued he in his reveries – these Spaniards are all an odd set; the very word Spaniard has a curious, conspirator, Guy Fawkish twang to it. And yet, I dare say, Spaniards in the main are as good folks as any in Duxbury, Massachusetts. Ah good! At last *Rover* has come.

As, with its welcome freight, the boat touched the side, the oakum-pickers, with venerable gestures, sought to restrain the blacks, who, at the sight of three gurried water-casks in its bottom and a pile of wilted pumpkins in its bow, hung over the bulwarks in disorderly raptures.

Don Benito, with his servant, now appeared; his coming, perhaps, hastened by hearing the noise. Of him Captain Delano sought permission to serve out the water, so that all might share alike, and none injure themselves by unfair excess. But sensible, and, on Don Benito's account, kind as this offer was, it was received with what seemed impatience; as if aware that he lacked energy as a commander, Don Benito, with the true jealousy of weakness, resented as an affront any interference. So, at least, Captain Delano inferred.

In another moment the casks were being hoisted in, when some of the eager negroes accidentally jostled Captain Delano, where he stood by the gangway; so that, unmindful of Don Benito, yielding to the impulse of the moment, with good-natured authority he bade the blacks stand back; to enforce his words making use of a half-mirthful, half-menacing gesture. Instantly the blacks paused, just where they were, each negro and negress suspended in his or her posture, exactly as the word had found them – for a few seconds continuing so – while, as between the responsive posts of a telegraph, an unknown syllable ran from man to man among the perched oakum-pickers. While the visitor's attention was fixed by this scene, suddenly the hatchet-polishers half rose, and a rapid cry came from Don Benito.

Thinking that at the signal of the Spaniard he was about to be massacred, Captain Delano would have sprung for his boat, but paused, as the oakum-pickers, dropping down into the crowd with earnest exclamations, forced every white and every negro back, at the same moment, with gestures friendly and familiar, almost jocose, bidding him, in substance, not be a fool. Simultaneously, the hatchet-polishers resumed their seats, quietly as so many tailors, and at once, as if nothing had happened, the work of hoisting in the casks was resumed, whites and blacks singing at the tackle.

Captain Delano glanced towards Don Benito. As he saw his meagre form in the act of recovering itself from reclining in the servant's arms, into which the agitated invalid had fallen, he could not but marvel at the panic by which himself had been surprised, on the darting supposition that such a commander, who, upon a legitimate occasion, so trivial, too, as it now appeared, could lose all self-command, was, with energetic iniquity, going to bring about his murder.

The casks being on deck, Captain Delano was handed a number of jars and cups by one of the steward's aids, who, in the name of his captain, entreated him to do as he had proposed – dole out the water. He complied, with republican impartiality as to this republican element, which always seeks one level, serving the oldest white no better than the youngest black; excepting, indeed, poor Don Benito, whose condition, if not rank, demanded an extra allowance. To him, in the first place, Captain Delano presented a fair pitcher of the fluid; but, thirsting as he was for it, the Spaniard quaffed not a drop until after several grave bows and salutes. A reciprocation of courtesies which the sight-loving Africans hailed with clapping of hands.

Two of the less wilted pumpkins being reserved for the cabin table, the residue were minced up on the spot for the general regalement. But the soft bread, sugar and bottled cider, Captain Delano would have given the whites alone, and in chief Don Benito; but the latter objected; which disinterestedness not a little pleased the American; and so mouthfuls all around were given alike to whites and blacks; excepting one bottle of cider, which Babo insisted upon setting aside for his master.

Here it may be observed that as, on the first visit of the boat, the American had not permitted his men to board the ship, neither did he now; being unwilling to add to the confusion of the decks.

Not uninfluenced by the peculiar good-humour at present prevailing, and for the time oblivious of any but benevolent thoughts, Captain Delano, who, from recent indications, counted upon a breeze within an hour or two at furthest, dispatched the boat back to the sealer, with orders for all the hands that could be spared immediately to set about rafting casks to the watering-place and filling them. Likewise he bade word be carried to his chief officer, that if, against present expectation, the ship was not brought to anchor by sunset, he need be under no concern; for as there was to be a full moon that night, he (Captain Delano) would remain on board ready to play the pilot, come the wind soon or late.

As the two captains stood together, observing the departing boat – the servant, as it happened, having just spied a spot on his master's velvet sleeve and being silently engaged in rubbing it out – the American expressed his regrets that the *San Dominick* had no boats; none, at least, but the unseaworthy old hulk of the longboat, which, warped as a camel's skeleton in the desert, and almost as bleached, lay pot-wise inverted amidships, one side a little tipped, furnishing a subterraneous sort of den for family groups of the blacks, mostly women and small children; who, squatting on old mats below, or perched above in the dark dome, on the elevated seats, were descried, some distance within, like a social circle of bats, sheltering in some friendly cave; at intervals, ebon flights of naked boys and girls, three or four years old, darting in and out of the den's mouth.

'Had you three or four boats now, Don Benito,' said Captain Delano, 'I think that, by tugging at the oars, your negroes here might help along matters some. Did you sail from port without boats, Don Benito?'

'They were stove in the gales, señor.'

'That was bad. Many men, too, you lost then. Boats and men Those must have been hard gales, Don Benito.'

'Past all speech,' cringed the Spaniard.

'Tell me, Don Benito,' continued his companion with increased interest, 'tell me, were these gales immediately off the pitch of Cape Horn?'

'Cape Horn? – who spoke of Cape Horn?'

'Yourself did, when giving me an account of your voyage,' answered Captain Delano, with almost equal astonishment at this eating of his own words, even as he ever seemed eating his own heart, on the part of the Spaniard. 'You yourself, Don Benito, spoke of Cape Horn,' he emphatically repeated.

The Spaniard turned, in a sort of stooping posture, pausing an instant, as one about to make a plunging exchange of elements, as from air to water.

At this moment a messenger-boy, a white, hurried by, in the regular performance of his function carrying the last expired half-hour forward to the forecastle from the cabin time piece, to have it struck at the ship's large bell.

'Master,' said the servant, discontinuing his work on the coat sleeve, and addressing the rapt Spaniard with a sort of timid apprehensiveness, as one charged with a duty, the discharge of which, it was foreseen, would prove irksome to the very person who had imposed it, and for whose benefit it was intended, 'master told me never mind where he was, or how engaged, always to remind him, to a minute, when shaving-time comes. Miguel has gone to strike the half-hour afternoon. It is *now*, master. Will master go into the cuddy?'

'Ah – yes,' answered the Spaniard, starting, as from dreams into realities; then, turning upon Captain Delano, he said that ere long he would resume the conversation.

'Then if master means to talk more to Don Amasa,' said the servant, 'why not let Don Amasa sit by master in the cuddy, and master can talk, and Don Amasa can listen, while Babo here lathers and strops.'

'Yes,' said Captain Delano, not unpleased with this sociable plan, 'yes, Don Benito, unless you had rather not, I will go with you.'

'Be it so, señor.'

As the three passed aft, the American could not but think it another strange instance of his host's capriciousness, this being shaved with such uncommon punctuality in the middle of the day. But he deemed it more than likely that the servant's anxious fidelity had something to do with the matter; inasmuch as the timely interruption served to rally his master from the mood which had evidently been coming upon him.

The place called the cuddy was a light deck-cabin formed by the poop, a sort of attic to the large cabin below. Part of it had formerly been the quarters of the officers; but since their death all the partitionings had been thrown down, and the whole interior converted into one spacious and airy marine hall; for absence of fine furniture and picturesque disarray of odd appurtenances, somewhat answering to the wide, cluttered hall of some eccentric bachelor-squire in the country, who hangs his shooting-jacket and tobacco-pouch on deer antlers and keeps his fishing-rod, tongs and walking-stick in the same corner.

The similitude was heightened, if not originally suggested, by glimpses of the surrounding sea; since, in one aspect, the country and the ocean seem cousins-german.

The floor of the cuddy was matted. Overhead, four or five old muskets were stuck into horizontal holes along the beams. On one side was a claw-footed old table lashed to the deck; a thumbed missal on it, and over it a small, meagre crucifix attached to the bulkhead. Under the table lay a dented cutlass or two, with a hacked harpoon, among some melancholy old rigging, like a heap of poor friars' girdles. There were also two long, sharp, ribbed settees of malacca cane, black with age, and uncomfortable to look at as inquisitors' racks, with a large, misshapen armchair, which, furnished with a rude barber's crotch at the back, working with a screw, seemed some grotesque engine of torment. A flag-locker was in one corner, open, exposing various coloured bunting, some rolled up, others half unrolled, still others tumbled. Opposite was a cumbrous washstand, of black mahogany, all of one block, with a pedestal, like a font, and over it a railed shelf, containing combs, brushes and other implements of the toilet. A torn hammock of stained grass swung near, the sheets tossed, and the pillow wrinkled up like a brow, as if whoever slept here slept but illy, with alternate visitations of sad thoughts and bad dreams.

The further extremity of the cuddy, overhanging the ship's stern, was pierced with three openings, windows or port-holes according as men or cannon might peer, socially or unsocially, out of them. At present neither men nor cannon were seen, though huge ring-bolts and other rusty iron fixtures of the woodwork hinted of twenty-four-pounders.

Glancing towards the hammock as he entered, Captain Delano said, 'You sleep here, Don Benito?'

'Yes, señor, since we got into mild weather.'

'This seems a sort of dormitory, sitting-room, sail-loft, chapel, armoury and private closet all together, Don Benito,' added Captain Delano, looking round.

'Yes, señor; events have not been favourable to much order in my arrangements.'

Here the servant, napkin on arm, made a motion as if waiting his master's good pleasure. Don Benito signified his readiness, whereupon, seating him in the malacca armchair, and for the guest's convenience drawing opposite one of the settees, the servant commenced operations by throwing back his master's collar and loosening his cravat.

There is something in the negro which, in a peculiar way, fits him for avocations about one's person. Most negroes are natural valets and hairdressers; taking to the comb and brush congenially as to the castanets, and flourishing them apparently with almost equal satisfaction. There is, too, a smooth tact about them in this employment, with a marvellous, noiseless, gliding briskness, not ungraceful in its way, singularly pleasing to behold, and still more so to be the manipulated subject of. And above all is the great gift of good-humour. Not the mere grin or laugh is here meant. Those were unsuitable. But a certain easy cheerfulness, harmonious in every glance and gesture; as though God had set the whole negro to some pleasant tune.

When to this is added the docility arising from the unaspiring contentment of a limited mind, and that susceptibility of blind attachment sometimes inhering in indisputable inferiors, one readily perceives why those hypochondriacs, Johnson and Byron – it may be, something like the hypochondriac Benito Cereno – took to their hearts, almost to the exclusion of the entire white race, their serving men, the negroes, Barber and Fletcher. But if there be that in the negro which exempts him from the inflicted sourness of the morbid or cynical mind, how, in his most prepossessing aspects, must he appear to a benevolent one? When at ease with respect to exterior things, Captain Delano's nature was not only benign, but familiarly and humorously so. At home, he had often taken rare satisfaction in sitting in his door, watching some free man of colour at his work or play. If on a voyage he chanced to have a black sailor, invariably he was on chatty and half-gamesome terms with him. In fact, like most men of a good, blithe heart, Captain Delano took to negroes, not philanthropically, but genially, just as other men to Newfoundland dogs.

Hitherto, the circumstances in which he found the *San Dominick* had repressed the tendency. But in the cuddy, relieved from his former uneasiness, and, for various reasons, more sociably inclined than at any previous period of the day, and seeing the coloured servant, napkin on arm, so debonair about his master, in a business so familiar as that of shaving, too, all his old weakness for negroes returned.

Among other things, he was amused with an odd instance of the African love of bright colours and fine shows, in the black's informally taking from the flag-locker a great piece of bunting of all hues and lavishly tucking it under his master's chin for an apron.

The mode of shaving among the Spaniards is a little different from what it is with other nations. They have a basin, specifically called a barber's basin, which on one side is scooped out, so as accurately to receive the chin, against which it is closely held in lathering; which is done, not with a brush, but with soap dipped in the water of the basin and rubbed on the face.

In the present instance salt-water was used for lack of better; and the parts lathered were only the upper lip, and low down under the throat, all the rest being cultivated beard.

The preliminaries being somewhat novel to Captain Delano, he sat curiously eyeing them, so that no conversation took place, nor, for the present, did Don Benito appear disposed to renew any.

Setting down his basin, the negro searched among the razors, as for the sharpest, and having found it, gave it an additional edge by expertly stropping it on the firm, smooth, oily skin of his open palm; he then made a gesture as if to begin, but midway stood suspended for an instant, one hand elevating the razor, the other professionally dabbling among the bubbling suds on the Spaniard's lank neck. Not unaffected by the close sight of the gleaming steel, Don Benito nervously shuddered; his usual ghastliness was heightened by the lather, which lather, again, was intensified in its hue by the contrasting sootiness of the negro's body. Altogether the scene was somewhat peculiar, at least to Captain Delano, nor, as he saw the two thus postured, could he resist the vagary that in the black he saw a headsman and in the white a man at the block. But this was one of those antic conceits, appearing and vanishing in a breath, from which, perhaps, the best regulated mind is not always free.

Meantime the agitation of the Spaniard had a little loosened the bunting from around him, so that one broad fold swept curtain-like over the chair-arm to the floor, revealing, amid a profusion of armorial bars and ground-colours – black, blue and yellow – a closed castle in a blood-red field diagonal with a lion rampant in a white.

'The castle and the lion,' exclaimed Captain Delano – 'why, Don Benito, this is the flag of Spain you use here. It's well it's only I, and not the king, that sees this,' he added, with a smile, 'but' – turning towards the black – 'it's all one, I suppose, so the colours be gay,' which playful remark did not fail somewhat to tickle the negro.

'Now, master,' he said, readjusting the flag, and pressing the head gently further back into the crotch of the chair; 'now, master,' and the steel glanced nigh the throat.

Again Don Benito faintly shuddered.

'You must not shake so, master. See, Don Amasa, master always shakes when I shave him. And yet master knows I never yet have drawn blood, though it's true, if master will shake so, I may some of these times. Now, master,' he continued; 'and now, Don Amasa, please go on with your talk about the gale, and all that; master can hear, and, between times, master can answer.'

'Ah yes, these gales,' said Captain Delano; 'but the more I think of your voyage, Don Benito, the more I wonder, not at the gales, terrible as they must have been, but at the disastrous interval following them. For here, by your account, have you been these two months and more getting from Cape Horn to Santa Maria, a distance which I myself, with a good wind, have sailed in a few days. True, you had calms, and long ones, but to be becalmed for two months, that is, at least, unusual. Why, Don Benito, had almost any other gentleman told me such a story, I should have been half disposed to a little incredulity.'

Here an involuntary expression came over the Spaniard, similar to that just before on the deck, and whether it was the start he gave, or a sudden gawky roll of the hull in the calm, or a momentary unsteadiness of the servant's hand, however it was, just then the razor drew blood, spots of which stained the creamy lather under the throat: immediately the black barber drew back his steel, and, remaining in his professional attitude, back to Captain Delano and face to Don Benito, held up the trickling razor, saying, with a sort of half-humorous sorrow, 'See, master – you shook so – here's Babo's first blood.'

No sword drawn before James I of England, no assassination in that timid king's presence, could have produced a more terrified aspect than was now presented by Don Benito.

Poor fellow, thought Captain Delano, so nervous he can't even bear the sight of barber's blood; and this unstrung, sick man, is it credible that I should have imagined he meant to spill all my blood, who can't endure the sight of one little drop of his own? Surely, Amasa Delano, you have been beside yourself this day. Tell it not when you get home, sappy Amasa. Well, well, he looks like a murderer, doesn't he? More like as if himself were to be done for. Well, well, this day's experience shall be a good lesson.

Meantime, while these things were running through the honest seaman's mind, the servant had taken the napkin from his arm, and to Don Benito had said – 'But answer Don Amasa, please, master, while I wipe this ugly stuff off the razor, and strop it again.'

As he said the words, his face was turned half round, so as to be alike visible to the Spaniard and the American, and seemed, by its expression, to hint that he was desirous, by getting his master to go on with the conversation, considerately to withdraw his attention from the recent annoying accident. As if glad to snatch the offered relief, Don Benito resumed, rehearsing to Captain Delano that not only were the calms of unusual duration, but the ship had fallen in with obstinate currents; and other things he added, some of which were but repetitions of former statements, to explain how it came to pass that the passage from Cape Horn to Santa Maria had been so exceedingly long; now and then mingling with his words incidental praises, less qualified than before, to the blacks, for their general good conduct. These particulars were not given consecutively, the servant, at convenient times, using his razor, and so, between the intervals of shaving, the story and panegyric went on with more than usual huskiness.

To Captain Delano's imagination, now again not wholly at rest, there was something so hollow in the Spaniard's manner, with apparently some reciprocal hollowness in the servant's dusky comment of silence, that the idea flashed across him that possibly master and man, for some unknown purpose, were acting out, both in word and deed, nay, to the very tremor of Don Benito's limbs, some juggling play before him. Neither did the suspicion of collusion lack apparent support, from the fact of those whispered conferences before mentioned. But then, what could be the object of enacting this play of the barber before him? At last, regarding the notion as a whimsy, insensibly suggested, perhaps, by the theatrical aspect of Don Benito in his harlequin ensign, Captain Delano speedily banished it.

The shaving over, the servant bestirred himself with a small bottle of scented waters, pouring a few drops on the head, and then diligently rubbing; the vehemence of the exercise causing the muscles of his face to twitch rather strangely.

His next operation was with comb, scissors and brush; going round and round, smoothing a curl here, clipping an unruly whisker-hair there, giving a graceful sweep to the temple-lock, with other impromptu touches evincing the hand of a master; while, like any resigned gentleman in barber's hands, Don Benito bore all, much less uneasily, at least, than he had done the razoring; indeed, he sat so pale and rigid now that the negro seemed a Nubian sculptor finishing off a white statue-head.

All being over at last, the standard of Spain removed, tumbled up, and tossed back into the flag-locker, the negro's warm breath blowing away any stray hair which might have lodged down his master's neck; collar and cravat readjusted; a speck of lint whisked off the velvet lapel; all this being done, backing off a little space, and pausing with an expression of subdued self-complacency, the servant for a moment surveyed his master, as, in toilet at least, the creature of his own tasteful hands.

Captain Delano playfully complimented him upon his achievement, at the same time congratulating Don Benito.

But neither sweet waters, nor shampooing, nor fidelity, nor sociality, delighted the Spaniard. Seeing him relapsing into forbidding gloom, and still remaining seated, Captain Delano, thinking that his presence was undesired just then, withdrew, on pretence of seeing whether, as he had prophesied, any signs of a breeze were visible.

Walking forward to the main-mast, he stood awhile thinking over the scene, and not without some undefined misgivings, when he heard a noise near the cuddy, and turning, saw the negro, his hand to his cheek. Advancing, Captain Delano perceived that the cheek was bleeding. He was about to ask the cause, when the negro's wailing soliloquy enlightened him.

'Ah, when will master get better from his sickness; only the sour heart that sour sickness breeds made him serve Babo so; cutting Babo with the razor, because, only by accident, Babo had given master one little scratch; and for the first time in so many a day, too. Ah, ah, ah,' holding his hand to his face.

Is it possible? thought Captain Delano; was it to wreak in private his Spanish spite against this poor friend of his, that Don Benito, by his sullen manner, impelled me to withdraw? Ah, this slavery breeds ugly passions in man. Poor fellow!

He was about to speak in sympathy to the negro, but with a timid reluctance he now re-entered the cuddy.

Presently master and man came forth; Don Benito leaning on his servant as if nothing had happened.

But a sort of love-quarrel, after all, thought Captain Delano.

He accosted Don Benito, and they slowly walked together. They had gone but a few paces, when the steward – a tall, rajah-looking mulatto, orientally set off with a pagoda turban formed by three or four Madras handkerchiefs wound about his head, tier on tier – approaching with a salaam, announced lunch in the cabin.

On their way thither, the two captains were preceded by the mulatto, who, turning round as he advanced, with continual smiles and bows, ushered them on, a display of elegance which quite completed the insignificance of the small bare-headed Babo, who, as if not unconscious of inferiority, eyed askance the graceful steward. But in part, Captain Delano imputed his jealous watchfulness to that peculiar feeling which the full-blooded African entertains for the adulterated one. As for the steward, his manner, if not bespeaking much dignity of self-respect, yet evidenced his extreme desire to please; which is doubly meritorious, as at once Christian and Chesterfieldian.

Captain Delano observed with interest that while the complexion of the mulatto was hybrid, his physiognomy was European – classically so.

'Don Benito,' whispered he, 'I am glad to see this usher-of-the-golden-rod of yours; the sight refutes an ugly remark once made to me by a Barbados planter: that when a mulatto has a regular European face, look out for him; he is a devil. But see, your steward here has features more regular than King George's of England; and yet there he nods, and bows, and smiles; a king, indeed – the king of kind hearts and polite fellows. What a pleasant voice he has, too.'

'He has, señor.'

'But tell me, has he not, so far as you have known him, always proved a good, worthy fellow?' said Captain Delano, pausing, while with a final genuflexion the steward disappeared into the cabin; 'come, for the reason just mentioned, I am a curious to know.'

'Francesco is a good man,' a sort of sluggishly responded Don Benito, like a phlegmatic appreciator, who would neither find fault nor flatter.

'Ah, I thought so. For it were strange, indeed, and not very creditable to us whiteskins, if a little of our blood mixed with the African's, should, far from improving the latter's quality, have the sad effect of pouring vitriolic acid into black broth; improving the hue, perhaps, but not the wholesomeness.'

'Doubtless, doubtless, señor, but,' – glancing at Babo – 'not to speak of negroes, your planter's remark I have heard applied to the Spanish and Indian intermixtures in our provinces. But I know nothing about the matter,' he listlessly added.

And here they entered the cabin.

The lunch was a frugal one. Some of Captain Delano's fresh fish and pumpkins, biscuit and salt beef, the reserved bottle of cider, and the *San Dominick*'s last bottle of Canary.

As they entered, Francesco, with two or three coloured aids, was hovering over the table giving the last adjustments. Upon perceiving their master they withdrew, Francesco making a smiling *congé*, and the Spaniard, without condescending to notice it, fastidiously remarking to his companion that he relished not superfluous attendance.

Without companions, host and guest sat down, like a childless married couple, at opposite ends of the table, Don Benito waving Captain Delano to his place, and, weak as he was, insisting upon that gentleman being seated before himself.

The negro placed a rug under Don Benito's feet, and a cushion behind his back, and then stood behind, not his master's chair, but Captain Delano's. At first, this a little surprised the latter. But it was soon evident that, in taking his position, the black was still true to his master; since by facing him he could the more readily anticipate his slightest want.

'This is an uncommonly intelligent fellow of yours, Don Benito,' whispered Captain Delano across the table.

'You say true, señor.'

During the repast, the guest again reverted to parts of Don Benito's story, begging further particulars here and there. He enquired how it was that the scurvy and fever should have committed such wholesale havoc upon the whites, while destroying less than half the blacks. As if this question reproduced the whole scene of plague before the Spaniard's eyes, miserably reminding him of his solitude in a cabin where before he had had so many friends and officers round him, his hand shook, his face became hueless, broken words escaped; but directly the sane memory of the past seemed replaced by insane terrors of the present. With starting eyes he stared before him at vacancy. For nothing was to be seen but the hand of his servant pushing the Canary over towards him. At length a few sips served partially to restore him. He made random reference to the different constitution of races, enabling one to offer more resistance to certain maladies than another. The thought was new to his companion.

Presently Captain Delano, intending to say something to his host concerning the pecuniary part of the business he had undertaken for him, especially – since he was strictly accountable to his owners – with reference to the new suit of sails, and other things of that sort, and naturally preferring to conduct such affairs in private, was desirous that the servant should withdraw; imagining that Don Benito for a few minutes could dispense with his attendance. He, however, waited awhile, thinking that, as the conversation proceeded, Don Benito, without being prompted, would perceive the propriety of the step.

But it was otherwise. At last catching his host's eye, Captain Delano, with a slight backward gesture of his thumb, whispered, 'Don Benito, pardon me, but there is an interference with the full expression of what I have to say to you.'

Upon this the Spaniard changed countenance; which was imputed to his resenting the hint, as in some way a reflection upon his servant. After a moment's pause, he assured his guest that the black's remaining with them could be of no disservice; because since losing his officers he had made Babo (whose original office, it now appeared, had been captain of the slaves) not only his constant attendant and companion, but in all things his confidant.

After this, nothing more could be said; though, indeed, Captain Delano could hardly avoid some little tinge of irritation upon being left ungratified in so inconsiderable a wish, by one, too, for whom he intended such solid services. But it is only his querulousness, thought he; and so filling his glass he proceeded to business.

The price of the sails and other matters was fixed upon. But while this was being done, the American observed that, though his original offer of assistance had been hailed with hectic animation, yet now, when it was reduced to a business transaction, indifference and apathy were betrayed. Don Benito, in fact, appeared to submit to hearing the details more out of regard to common propriety than from any impression that weighty benefit to himself and his voyage was involved.

Soon, his manner became still more reserved. The effort was vain to seek to draw him into social talk. Gnawed by his splenetic mood, he sat twitching his beard, while to little purpose the hand of his servant, mute as that on the wall, slowly pushed over the Canary.

Lunch being over, they sat down on the cushioned transom; the servant placing a pillow behind his master. The long continuance of the calm had now affected the atmosphere. Don Benito sighed heavily, as if for breath.

'Why not adjourn to the cuddy?' said Captain Delano. 'There is more air there.' But the host sat silent and motionless.

Meantime his servant knelt before him, with a large fan of feathers. And Francesco, coming in on tiptoes, handed the negro a little cup of aromatic waters, with which at intervals he chafed his master's brow; smoothing the hair along the temples as a nurse does a child's. He spoke no word. He only rested his eye on his master's, as if, amid all Don Benito's distress, a little to refresh his spirit by the silent sight of fidelity.

Presently the ship's bell sounded two o'clock; and through the cabin windows a slight rippling of the sea was discerned; and from the desired direction.

'There,' exclaimed Captain Delano, 'I told you so, Don Benito, look!'

He had risen to his feet, speaking in a very animated tone, with a view the more to rouse his companion. But though the crimson curtain of the stern-window near him that moment fluttered against his pale cheek, Don Benito seemed to have even less welcome for the breeze than the calm.

Poor fellow, thought Captain Delano, bitter experience has taught him that one ripple does not make a wind, any more than one swallow a summer. But he is mistaken for once. I will get his ship in for him, and prove it.

Briefly alluding to his weak condition, he urged his host to remain quietly where he was, since he (Captain Delano) would with pleasure take upon himself the responsibility of making the best use of the wind.

Upon gaining the deck, Captain Delano started at the unexpected figure of Atufal, monumentally fixed at the threshold, like one of those sculptured porters of black marble guarding the porches of Egyptian tombs.

But this time the start was, perhaps, purely physical. Atufal's presence, singularly attesting docility even in sullenness, was contrasted with that of the hatchet-polishers, who in patience evinced their industry; while both spectacles showed that lax as Don Benito's general authority might be, still, whenever he chose to exert it, no man so savage or colossal but must, more or less, bow.

Snatching a trumpet which hung from the bulwarks, with a free step Captain Delano advanced to the forward edge of the poop, issuing his orders in his best Spanish. The few sailors and many negroes, all equally pleased, obediently set about heading the ship towards the harbour.

While giving some directions about setting a lower stu'n-sail, suddenly Captain Delano heard a voice faithfully repeating his orders. Turning, he saw Babo, now for the time acting, under the pilot, his original part of captain of the slaves. This assistance proved valuable. Tattered sails and warped yards were soon brought into some trim. And no brace or halyard was pulled but to the blithe songs of the inspirited negroes.

Good fellows, thought Captain Delano, a little training would make fine sailors of them. Why see, the very women pull and sing too. These must be some of those Ashantee negresses that make such capital soldiers, I've heard. But who's at the helm? I must have a good hand there.

He went to see.

The *San Dominick* steered with a cumbrous tiller, with large horizontal pulleys attached. At each pulley-end stood a subordinate black, and between them, at the tiller-head, the responsible post, a Spanish seaman, whose countenance evinced his due share in the general hopefulness and confidence at the coming of the breeze.

He proved the same man who had behaved with so shamefaced an air on the windlass.

'Ah – it is you, my man,' exclaimed Captain Delano – 'well, no more sheep's eyes now – look straight forward and keep the ship so. Good hand, I trust? And want to get into the harbour, don't you?'

The man assented with an inward chuckle, grasping the tiller-head firmly. Upon this, unperceived by the American, the two blacks eyed the sailor intently.

Finding all right at the helm, the pilot went forward to the forecastle, to see how matters stood there.

The ship now had way enough to breast the current. With the approach of evening, the breeze would be sure to freshen.

Having done all that was needed for the present, Captain Delano, giving his last orders to the sailors, turned aft to report affairs to Don Benito in the cabin; perhaps additionally incited to rejoin him by the hope of snatching a moment's private chat while the servant was engaged upon deck.

From opposite sides, there were, beneath the poop, two approaches to the cabin; one further forward than the other, and consequently communicating with a longer passage. Marking the servant still above, Captain Delano, taking the nighest entrance – the one last named, and at whose porch Atufal still stood – hurried on his way, till, arrived at the cabin threshold, he paused an instant, a little to recover from his eagerness. Then, with the words of his intended business upon his lips, he entered. As he advanced towards the seated Spaniard, he heard another footstep, keeping time with his. From the opposite door, a salver in hand, the servant was likewise advancing.

'Confound the faithful fellow,' thought Captain Delano; 'what a vexatious coincidence.'

Possibly, the vexation might have been something different, were it not for the brisk confidence inspired by the breeze. But even as it was, he felt a slight twinge, from a sudden indefinite association in his mind of Babo with Atufal.

'Don Benito,' said he, 'I give you joy; the breeze will hold, and will increase. By the way, your tall man and timepiece, Atufal, stands without. By your order, of course?'

Don Benito recoiled, as if at some bland satirical touch, delivered with such adroit garnish of apparent good breeding as to present no handle for retort.

He is like one flayed alive, thought Captain Delano; where may one touch him without causing a shrink?

The servant moved before his master, adjusting a cushion; recalled to civility, the Spaniard stiffly replied: 'You are right. The slave appears where you saw him, according to my command; which is, that if at the given hour I am below, he must take his stand and abide my coming.'

'Ah now, pardon me, but that is treating the poor fellow like an ex-king indeed. Ah, Don Benito,' smiling, 'for all the licence you permit in some things, I fear lest, at bottom, you are a bitter hard master.'

Again Don Benito shrank; and this time, as the good sailor thought, from a genuine twinge of his conscience.

Again conversation became constrained. In vain Captain Delano called attention to the now perceptible motion of the keel gently cleaving the sea; with lack-lustre eye, Don Benito returned words few and reserved.

By and by, the wind, having steadily risen and still blowing right into the harbour, bore the *San Dominick* swiftly on. Rounding a point of land, the sealer at distance came into open view.

Meantime Captain Delano had again repaired to the deck, remaining there some time. Having at last altered the ship's course, so as to give the reef a wide berth, he returned for a few moments below.

I will cheer up my poor friend, this time, thought he.

'Better and better, Don Benito,' he cried as he blithely re-entered: 'there will soon be an end to your cares, at least for a while. For when, after a long, sad voyage, you know, the anchor drops into the haven, all its vast weight seems lifted from the captain's heart. We are getting on famously, Don Benito. My ship is in sight. Look through this side-light here; there she is; all a-taunt-o! The *Bachelor's Delight*, my good friend. Ah, how this wind braces one up. Come, you must take a cup of coffee with me this evening. My old steward will give you as fine a cup as ever any sultan tasted. What say you, Don Benito, will you?'

At first, the Spaniard glanced feverishly up, casting a longing look towards the sealer, while with mute concern his servant gazed into his face. Suddenly the old ague of coldness returned and dropping back to his cushions he was silent.

'You do not answer. Come, all day you have been my host; would you have hospitality all on one side?'

'I cannot go,' was the response.

'What? It will not fatigue you. The ships will lie together as near as they can, without swinging foul. It will be little more than stepping from deck to deck; which is but as from room to room. Come, come, you must not refuse me.'

'I cannot go,' decisively and repulsively repeated Don Benito.

Renouncing all but the last appearance of courtesy, with a sort of cadaverous sullenness, and biting his thin nails to the quick, he glanced, almost glared, at his guest, as if impatient that a stranger's presence should interfere with the full indulgence of his morbid hour. Meantime the sound of the parted waters came more and more gurglingly and merrily in at the windows, as reproaching him for his dark spleen; as telling him that, sulk as he might, and go mad with it, nature cared not a jot; since, whose fault was it, pray?

But the foul mood was now at its depth, as the fair wind at its height.

There was something in the man so far beyond any mere unsociality or sourness previously evinced that even the forbearing good nature of his guest could no longer endure it. Wholly at a loss to account for such demeanour, and deeming sickness with eccentricity, however extreme, no adequate excuse, well satisfied, too, that nothing in his own conduct could justify it, Captain Delano's pride began to be roused. Himself became reserved. But all seemed one to the Spaniard. Quitting him, therefore, Captain Delano once more went to the deck.

The ship was now within less than two miles of the sealer. The whale-boat was seen darting over the interval.

To be brief, the two vessels, thanks to the pilot's skill, ere long in neighbourly style lay anchored together.

Before returning to his own vessel, Captain Delano had intended communicating to Don Benito the smaller details of the proposed services to be rendered. But, as it was, unwilling anew to subject himself to rebuffs, he resolved, now that he had seen the *San Dominick* safely moored, immediately to quit her, without further allusion to hospitality or business. Indefinitely postponing his ulterior plans, he would regulate his future actions according to future circumstances. His boat was ready to receive him; but his host still tarried below. Well, thought Captain Delano, if he has little breeding, the more need to show mine. He descended to the cabin to bid a ceremonious, and, it may be, tacitly rebukeful adieu. But to his great satisfaction, Don Benito, as if he began to feel the weight of that treatment with which his slighted guest had, not indecorously, retaliated upon him, now supported by his servant, rose to his feet, and grasping Captain Delano's hand, stood tremulous; too much agitated to speak. But the good augury hence drawn was suddenly dashed, by his resuming all his previous reserve, with augmented gloom, as, with half-averted eyes, he silently reseated himself on his cushions. With a corresponding return of his own chilled feelings, Captain Delano bowed and withdrew.

He was hardly midway in the narrow corridor, dim as a tunnel, leading from the cabin to the stairs, when a sound, as of the tolling for execution in some jail-yard, fell on his ears. It was the echo of the ship's flawed bell, striking the hour, drearily reverberated in this subterranean vault. Instantly, by a fatality not to be withstood, his mind, responsive to the portent, swarmed with superstitious suspicions. He paused. In images far swifter than these sentences, the minutest details of all his former distrusts swept through him.

Hitherto, credulous good nature had been too ready to furnish excuses for reasonable fears. Why was the Spaniard, so superfluously punctilious at times, now heedless of common propriety in not accompanying to the side his departing guest? Did indisposition forbid? Indisposition had not forbidden more irksome exertion that day. His last equivocal demeanour recurred. He had risen to his feet, grasped his guest's hand, motioned towards his hat; then, in an instant, all was eclipsed in sinister muteness and gloom. Did this imply one brief, repentant relenting, at the final moment, from some iniquitous plot, followed by remorseless return to it? His last glance seemed to express a calamitous yet acquiescent farewell to Captain Delano forever. Why decline the invitation to visit the sealer that evening? Or was the Spaniard less hardened than the Jew, who refrained not from supping at the board of him whom the same night he meant to betray? What imported all those day-long enigmas and contradictions, except they were intended to mystify, preliminary to some stealthy blow? Atufal, the pretended rebel, but punctual shadow, that moment lurked by the threshold without. He seemed a sentry, and more. Who, by his own confession, had stationed him there? Was the negro now lying in wait?

The Spaniard behind – his creature before: to rush from darkness to light was the involuntary choice.

The next moment, with clenched jaw and hand, he passed Atufal, and stood unharmed in the light. As he saw his trim ship lying peacefully at anchor, and almost within ordinary call; as he saw his household boat, with familiar faces in it, patiently rising and falling on the short waves by the *Sun Dominick*'s side; and then, glancing about the decks where he stood, saw the oakum-pickers still gravely plying their fingers; and heard the low, buzzing whistle and industrious hum of the hatchet-polishers, still bestirring themselves over their endless occupation; and more than all, as he saw the benign aspect of nature, taking her innocent repose in the evening; the screened sun in the quiet camp of the west shining out like the mild light from Abraham's tent; as charmed eye and ear took in all these, with the chained figure of the black, clenched jaw and hand relaxed. Once again he smiled at the phantoms which had mocked him, and felt something like a tinge of remorse that, by harbouring them even for a moment, he should, by implication, have betrayed an atheist doubt of the ever-watchful providence above.

There was a few minutes' delay, while, in obedience to his orders, the boat was being hooked along to the gangway. During this interval, a sort of saddened satisfaction stole over Captain Delano, at thinking of the kindly offices he had that day discharged for a stranger. Ah, thought he, after good actions one's conscience is never ungrateful, however much so the benefited party may be.

Presently, his foot, in the first act of descent into the boat, pressed the first round of the side-ladder, his face presented inward upon the deck. In the same moment, he heard his name courteously sounded; and, to his pleased surprise, saw Don Benito advancing – an unwonted energy in his air, as if, at the last moment, intent upon making amends for his recent discourtesy. With instinctive good feeling, Captain Delano, withdrawing his foot, turned and reciprocally advanced. As he did so, the Spaniard's nervous eagerness increased, but his vital energy failed; so that, the better to support him, the servant, placing his master's hand on his naked shoulder, and gently holding it there, formed himself into a sort of crutch.

When the two captains met, the Spaniard again fervently took the hand of the American, at the same time casting an earnest glance into his eyes, but, as before, too much overcome to speak.

I have done him wrong, self-reproachfully thought Captain Delano; his apparent coldness has deceived me; in no instance has he meant to offend.

Meantime, as if fearful that the continuance of the scene might too much unstring his master, the servant seemed anxious to terminate it. And so, still presenting himself as a crutch, and walking between the two captains, he advanced with them towards the gangway; while still, as if full of kindly contrition, Don Benito would not let go the hand of Captain Delano, but retained it in his, across the black's body.

Soon they were standing by the side, looking over into the boat, whose crew turned up their curious eyes. Waiting a moment for the Spaniard to relinquish his hold, the now embarrassed Captain Delano lifted his foot to overstep the threshold of the open gangway; but still Don Benito would not let go his hand. And yet, with an agitated tone, he said, 'I can go no further; here I must bid you adieu. Adieu, my dear, dear Don Amasa. Go – go!' suddenly tearing his hand loose, 'go and God guard you better than me, my best friend.'

Not unaffected, Captain Delano would now have lingered but catching the meekly admonitory eye of the servant, with hasty farewell he descended into his boat, followed by the continual adieus of Don Benito, standing rooted in the gangway.

Seating himself in the stern, Captain Delano, making a last salute, ordered the boat shoved off. The crew had their oars on end. The bowsman pushed the boat a sufficient distance for the oars to be lengthwise dropped. The instant that was done, Don Benito sprang over the bulwarks, falling at the feet of Captain Delano; at the same time calling towards his ship, but in tones so frenzied, that none in the boat could understand him. But, as if not equally obtuse, three sailors, from three different and distant parts of the ship, splashed into the sea, swimming after their captain, as if intent upon his rescue.

The dismayed officer of the boat eagerly asked what this meant. To which, Captain Delano, turning a disdainful smile upon the unaccountable Spaniard, answered that, for his part, he neither knew nor cared; but it seemed as if Don Benito had taken it into his head to produce the impression among his people that the boat wanted to kidnap him. 'Or else – give way for your lives,' he wildly added, starting at a clattering hubbub in the ship, above which rang the tocsin of the hatchet-polishers; and seizing Don Benito by the throat he added, 'this plotting pirate means murder!' Here, in apparent verification of the words, the servant, a dagger in his hand, was seen on the rail overhead, poised, in the act of leaping, as if with desperate fidelity to befriend his master to the last; while, seemingly to aid the black, the three white sailors were trying to clamber into the hampered bow. Meantime, the whole host of negroes, as if inflamed at the sight of their jeopardised captain, impended in one sooty avalanche over the bulwarks.

All this, with what preceded and what followed, occurred with such involutions of rapidity, that past, present and future seemed one.

Seeing the negro coming, Captain Delano had flung the Spaniard aside, almost in the very act of clutching him, and, by the unconscious recoil, shifting his place, with arms thrown up, so promptly grappled the servant in his descent that, with dagger presented at Captain Delano's heart, the black seemed of purpose to have leaped there as to his mark. But the weapon was wrenched away, and the assailant dashed down into the bottom of the boat, which now, with disentangled oars, began to speed through the sea.

At this juncture, the left hand of Captain Delano, on one side, again clutched the half-reclining Don Benito, heedless that he was in a speechless faint, while his right foot, on the other side, ground the prostrate negro; and his right arm pressed for added speed on the after oar, his eye bent forward, encouraging his men to their utmost.

But here, the officer of the boat, who had at last succeeded in beating off the towing sailors, and was now, with face turned aft, assisting the bowsman at his oar, suddenly called to Captain Delano to see what the black was about; while a Portuguese oarsman shouted to him to give heed to what the Spaniard was saying.

Glancing down at his feet, Captain Delano saw the freed hand of the servant aiming with a second dagger – a small one, before concealed in his wool; with this he was snakishly writhing up from the boat's bottom at the heart of his master, his countenance lividly vindictive, expressing the centred purpose of his soul; while the Spaniard, half-choked, was vainly shrinking away, with husky words, incoherent to all but the Portuguese.

That moment, across the long-benighted mind of Captain Delano, a flash of revelation swept, illuminating, in unanticipated clearness, his host's whole mysterious demeanour, with every enigmatic event of the day, as well as the entire past voyage of the *San Dominick*. He smote Babo's hand down, but his own heart smote him harder. With infinite pity he withdrew his hold from Don Benito. Not Captain Delano, but Don Benito, the black, in leaping into the boat, had intended to stab.

Both the black's hands were held as, glancing up towards the *San Dominick*, Captain Delano, now with scales dropped from his eyes, saw the negroes, not in misrule, not in tumult, not as if frantically concerned for Don Benito, but with mask torn away flourishing hatchets and knives, in ferocious piratical revolt. Like delirious black dervishes, the six Ashantees danced on the poop. Prevented by their foes from springing into the water, the Spanish boys were hurrying up to the topmost spars, while such of the few Spanish sailors not already in the sea, less alert, were descried, helplessly mixed in, on deck, with the blacks.

Meantime Captain Delano hailed his own vessel, ordering the ports up and the guns run out. But by this time the cable of the *San Dominick* had been cut; and the fag-end, in lashing out, whipped away the canvas shroud about the beak, suddenly revealing, as the bleached hull swung round towards the open ocean, death for the figure-head, in a human skeleton; chalky comment on the chalked words below, '*Follow your leader.*'

At the sight, Don Benito, covering his face, wailed out: ' 'Tis he, Aranda! my murdered, unburied friend!'

Upon reaching the sealer, calling for ropes, Captain Delano bound the negro, who made no resistance, and had him hoisted to the deck. He would then have assisted the now almost helpless Don

Benito up the side; but Don Benito, wan as he was, refused to move, or be moved, until the negro should have been first put below out of view. When, presently assured that it was done, he no more shrank from the ascent.

The boat was immediately dispatched back to pick up the three swimming sailors. Meantime, the guns were in readiness, though, owing to the *San Dominick* having glided somewhat astern of the sealer, only the aftermost one could be brought to bear. With this, they fired six times, thinking to cripple the fugitive ship by bringing down her spars. But only a few inconsiderable ropes were shot away. Soon the ship was beyond the gun's range, steering broad out of the bay; the blacks thickly clustering round the bowsprit, one moment with taunting cries towards the whites, the next with upthrown gestures hailing the new dusky moors of ocean – cawing crows escaped from the hand of the fowler.

The first impulse was to slip the cables and give chase. But, upon second thoughts, to pursue with whale-boat and yawl seemed more promising.

Upon enquiring of Don Benito what firearms they had on board the *San Dominick*, Captain Delano was answered that they had none that could be used; because, in the earlier stages of the mutiny, a cabin-passenger, since dead, had secretly put out of order the locks of what few muskets there were. But with all his remaining strength, Don Benito entreated the American not to give chase, either with ship or boat; for the negroes had already proved themselves such desperadoes that, in case of a present assault, nothing but a total massacre of the whites could be looked for. But, regarding this warning as coming from one whose spirit had been crushed by misery, the American did not give up his design.

The boats were got ready and armed. Captain Delano ordered his men into them. He was going himself when Don Benito grasped his arm. 'What! have you saved my life, señor, and are you now going to throw away your own?'

The officers also, for reasons connected with their interests and those of the voyage, and a duty owing to the owners, strongly objected against their commander's going. Weighing their remonstrances a moment, Captain Delano felt bound to remain and appointed his chief mate – an athletic and resolute man, who had been a privateer's-man – to head the party. The more to encourage the sailors, they were told that the Spanish captain considered his ship good as lost; that she and her cargo, including some gold and silver, were worth more than a thousand doubloons. Take her, and no small part should be theirs. The sailors replied with a shout.

The fugitives had now almost gained an offing. It was nearly night; but the moon was rising. After hard, prolonged pulling, the boats came up on the ship's quarters, at a suitable distance laying upon their oars to discharge their muskets. Having no bullets to return, the negroes sent their yells. But, upon the second volley, Indian-like, they hurled their hatchets. One took off a sailor's fingers. Another struck the whale-boat's bow, cutting off the rope there, and remaining stuck in the gunwale like a woodman's axe. Snatching it, quivering, from its lodgment, the mate hurled it back. The returned gauntlet now stuck in the ship's broken quarter-gallery, and so remained.

The negroes giving too hot a reception, the whites kept a more respectful distance. Hovering now just out of reach of the hurtling hatchets, they, with a view to the close encounter which must soon come, sought to decoy the blacks into entirely disarming themselves of their most murderous weapons in a hand-to-hand fight, by foolishly flinging them, as missiles, short of the mark, into the sea. But, ere long, perceiving the stratagem, the negroes desisted, though not before many of them had to replace their lost hatchets with handspikes; an exchange which, as counted upon, proved, in the end, favourable to the assailants.

Meantime, with a strong wind, the ship still clove the water the boats alternately falling behind, and pulling up, to discharge fresh volleys.

The fire was mostly directed towards the stern, since there chiefly, the negroes, at present, were clustering. But to kill or maim the negroes was not the object. To take them, with the ship, was the object. To do it, the ship must be boarded; which could not be done by boats while she was sailing so fast.

A thought now struck the mate. Observing the Spanish boys still aloft, high as they could get, he called to them to descend to the yards and cut adrift the sails. It was done. About this time owing to causes hereafter to be shown, two Spaniards, in the dress of sailors, and conspicuously showing themselves, were killed; not by volleys, but by deliberate marksman's shots; while, as it afterwards appeared, by one of the general discharges, Atufal, the black, and the Spaniard at the helm likewise were killed. What, now, with the loss of the sails, and loss of leaders, the ship became unmanageable to the negroes.

With creaking masts, she came heavily round to the wind; the prow slowly swinging into view of the boats, its skeleton gleaming in the horizontal moonlight, and casting a gigantic ribbed shadow upon the water. One extended arm of the ghost seemed beckoning the whites to avenge it.

'Follow your leader!'cried the mate; and, one on each bow, the boats boarded. Sealing-spears and cutlasses crossed hatchets and handspikes. Huddled upon the longboat amidships, the negresses raised a wailing chant, whose chorus was the clash of the steel.

For a time, the attack wavered; the negroes wedging themselves to beat it back; the half-repelled sailors, as yet unable to gain a footing, fighting as troopers in the saddle, one leg sideways flung over the bulwarks, and one without, plying their cutlasses like carters' whips. But in vain. They were almost overborne, when, rallying themselves into a squad as one man, with a huzza, they sprang inboard, where, entangled, they involuntarily separated again. For a few breaths' space, there was a vague, muffled, inner sound, as of submerged sword-fish rushing hither and thither through shoals of black-fish. Soon, in a reunited band, and joined by the Spanish seamen, the whites came to the surface, irresistibly driving the negroes towards the stern. But a barricade of casks and sacks, from side to side, had been thrown up by the main-mast. Here the negroes faced about, and though scorning peace or truce, yet fain would have had respite. But, without pause, overleaping the barrier, the unflagging sailors again closed. Exhausted, the blacks now fought in despair. Their red tongues lolled, wolf-like, from their black mouths. But the pale sailors' teeth were set; not a word was spoken; and in five minutes more, the ship was won.

Nearly a score of the negroes were killed. Exclusive of those by the balls, many were mangled, their wounds, mostly inflicted by the long-edged sealing-spears, resembling those shaven ones of the English at Preston Pans, made by the poled scythes of the High-landers. On the other side, none were killed, though several were wounded; some severely, including the mate. The surviving negroes were temporarily secured, and the ship, towed back into the harbour at midnight, once more lay anchored.

Omitting the incidents and arrangements ensuing, suffice it that, after two days spent in refitting, the ships sailed in company for Concepción, in Chile, and thence for Lima, in Peru; where, before the vice-regal courts, the whole affair, from the beginning, under-went investigation.

Though, midway on the passage, the ill-fated Spaniard, relaxed from constraint, showed some signs of regaining health with free-will; yet, agreeably to his own foreboding, shortly before arriving at Lima, he relapsed, finally becoming so reduced as to be carried ashore in arms. Hearing of his story and plight, one of the many religious institutions of the City of Kings opened an hospitable refuge to him, where both physician and priest were his nurses, and a member of the order volunteered to be his one special guardian and consoler, by night and by day.

The following extracts, translated from one of the official Spanish documents, will, it is hoped, shed light on the preceding narrative, as well as, in the first place, revealing the true port of departure and true history of the *San Dominick*'s voyage, down to the time of her touching at the island of Santa Maria.

But, ere the extracts come, it may be well to preface them with a remark.

The document selected, from among many others, for partial translation, contains the deposition of Benito Cereno; the first taken in the case. Some disclosures therein were, at the time, held dubious for both learned and natural reasons. The tribunal inclined to the opinion that the deponent, not undisturbed in his mind by recent events, raved of some things which could never have happened. But subsequent depositions of the surviving sailors, bearing out the revelations of their captain in several of the strangest particulars, gave credence to the rest. So that the tribunal, in its final decision, rested its capital sentences upon statements which, had they lacked confirmation, it would have deemed it but duty to reject.

I, Don José de Abos and Padila, His Majesty's Notary for the Royal Revenue, Register of this Province and Notary Public of the Holy Crusade of this Bishoprick, etc., do certify and declare, as much as is requisite in law, that, in the criminal cause commenced the twenty-fourth of the month of September in the year seventeen hundred and ninety-nine against the negroes of the ship *San Dominick*, the following declaration before me was made:

Declaration of the first witness, Don Benito Cereno

The same day and month and year, His Honour, Dr Juan Martinez de Rozas, Councillor of the Royal Audience of this Kingdom, and learned in the law of this Intendancy, ordered the captain of the ship *San Dominick*, Don Benito Cereno, to appear; which he did in his litter, attended by the monk Infelez; of whom he received the oath, which he took by God, our Lord and a Sign of the Cross; under which he promised to tell the truth of whatever he should know and should be asked; and being interrogated agreeably to the tenor of the act, commencing the process, he said, that on the twentieth of May last, he set sail with his ship from the port of Valparaiso, bound to that of Callao; loaded with the produce of the country, beside thirty cases of hardware and one hundred and sixty blacks, of both sexes, mostly belonging to Don Alexandro Aranda, gentleman, of the City of Mendoza; that the crew of the ship consisted of thirty-six men, beside the persons who went as passengers; that the negroes were in part as follows:

Here, in the original, follows a list of some fifty names, descriptions, and ages, compiled from certain recovered documents of Aranda's and also from recollections of the deponent, from which portions only are extracted.

One, from about eighteen to nineteen years, named José, and this was the man that waited upon his master, Don Alexandro, and who speaks well the Spanish, having served him four or five years . . . A mulatto, named Francesco, the cabin steward, of a good person and voice, having sung in the Valparaiso churches, native of the province of Buenos Aires, aged about thirty-five years . . . A smart negro, named Dago, who had been for many years a gravedigger among the Spaniards, aged forty-six years . . . Four old negroes, born in Africa, from sixty to seventy, but sound, calkers by trade, whose names are as follows: the first was named Mure, and he was killed (as was also his son named Diamelo); the second, Nacta; the third, Yola, likewise killed; the fourth, Ghofan . . . And six full-grown negroes, aged from thirty to forty-five, all raw, and born among the Ashantees – Matinqui, Yau, Lecbe, Mapenda, Yambaio, Akim, four of whom were killed . . . A powerful negro named Atufal, who being supposed to have been a chief in Africa, his owner set great store by him . . . And a small negro of Senegal, but some years among the Spaniards, aged about thirty, which negro's name was Babo . . . That he does not remember the names of the others, but that still expecting the residue of Don Alexandro's papers will be found, will then take due account of them all and remit to the court . . . And thirty-nine women and children of all ages.

The catalogue over, the deposition goes on:

. . . That all the negroes slept upon deck, as is customary in this navigation, and none wore fetters because the owner, his friend Aranda, told him that they were all tractable; . . . that on the seventh day after leaving port, at three o'clock in the morning, all the Spaniards being asleep except two officers of the watch, who were the boatswain, Juan Robles, and the carpenter, Juan Bautista Gayete, and the helmsman and his boy, the negroes revolted suddenly, wounded dangerously the boatswain and the carpenter, and successively killed eighteen men of those who were sleeping upon deck, some with handspikes and hatchets, and others by throwing them alive overboard, after tying them; that of the Spaniards upon deck, they left about seven, as he thinks, alive and tied, to manoeuvre the ship, and three or four more, who hid themselves, remained also alive. Although in the act of revolt the negroes made themselves masters of the hatchway, six or seven wounded went through it to the cockpit, without any hindrance on their part; that during the act of revolt, the mate and another person, whose name he does not recollect, attempted to come up through the hatchway, but being quickly wounded, were obliged to return to the cabin; that the deponent resolved at break of day to come up the companionway, where the negro Babo was, being the ringleader, and Atufal, who assisted him, and having spoken to them, exhorted them to cease committing such atrocities, asking them, at the same time, what they wanted and intended to do, offering, himself, to obey their commands; that notwithstanding this, they threw, in his presence, three men, alive and tied, overboard; that they told the deponent to come up and that they would not kill him; which having done, the negro Babo asked him whether there were in those seas any negro countries where they might be carried, and he answered them, No; that the negro Babo afterwards told him to carry them to Senegal, or to the neighbouring islands of St Nicholas; and he answered that this was impossible, on account of the great distance, the necessity involved of rounding Cape Horn, the bad condition of the vessel, the want of provisions, sails and water; but that the negro Babo replied to him he must carry them in any way; that they would do and conform themselves to anything the deponent should require as to eating and drinking; that after a long conference, being absolutely compelled to

please them, for they threatened to kill all the whites if they
were not, at all events, carried to Senegal, he told them that
what was most wanting for the voyage was water; that they
would go near the coast to take it, and thence they would
proceed on their course; that the negro Babo agreed to it; and
the deponent steered towards the intermediate ports, hoping to
meet some Spanish or foreign vessel that would save them; that
within ten or eleven days they saw the land, and continued their
course by it in the vicinity of Nasca; that the deponent observed
that the negroes were now restless and mutinous, because he
did not effect the taking in of water, the negro Babo having
required, with threats, that it should be done, without fail, the
following day; he told him he saw plainly that the coast was
steep, and the rivers designated in the maps were not to be
found, with other reasons suitable to the circumstances; that the
best way would be to go to the island of Santa Maria, where
they might water easily, it being a solitary island, as the
foreigners did; that the deponent did not go to Pisco, that was
near, nor make any other port of the coast, because the negro
Babo had intimated to him several times that he would kill all
the whites the very moment he should perceive any city, town
or settlement of any kind on the shores to which they should be
carried; that having determined to go to the island of Santa
Maria, as the deponent had planned, for the purpose of trying
whether, on the passage or near the island itself, they could
find any vessel that should favour them, or whether he could
escape from it in a boat to the neighbouring coast of Arauco, to
adopt the necessary means he immediately changed his course,
steering for the island; that the negroes Babo and Atufal held
daily conferences, in which they discussed what was necessary
for their design of returning to Senegal, whether they were to
kill all the Spaniards, and particularly the deponent; that eight
days after parting from the coast of Nasca, the deponent being
on the watch a little after daybreak, and soon after the negroes
had their meeting, the negro Babo came to the place where the
deponent was, and told him that he had determined to kill his
master, Don Alexandro Aranda, both because he and his companions could not otherwise be sure of their liberty, and
because, to keep the seamen in subjection, he wanted to prepare
a warning of what road they should be made to take did they or
any of them oppose him; and that, by means of the death of
Don Alexandro, that warning would best be given; but, that

what this last meant, the deponent did not at the time comprehend, nor could not, further than the death of Don Alexandro
was intended; and moreover the negro Babo proposed to the
deponent to call the mate Raneds, who was sleeping in the
cabin, before the thing was done, for fear, as the deponent
understood it, that the mate, who was a good navigator, should
not be killed with Don Alexandro and the rest; that the
deponent, who was the friend, from youth, of Don Alexandro,
prayed and conjured, but all was useless; for the negro Babo
answered him that the thing could not be prevented, and that
all the Spaniards risked their death if they should attempt to
frustrate his will in this matter, or any other; that, in this
conflict, the deponent called the mate, Raneds, who was forced
to go apart, and immediately the negro Babo commanded the
Ashantee Matinqui and the Ashantee Lecbe to go and commit
the murder; that those two went down with hatchets to the
berth of Don Alexandro; that, yet half alive and mangled, they
dragged him on deck; that they were going to throw him
overboard in that state, but the negro Babo stopped them,
bidding the murder be completed on the deck before him,
which was done, when, by his orders, the body was carried
below, forward; that nothing more was seen of it by the
deponent for three days; . . . that Don Alonzo Sidonia, an old
man, long resident at Valparaiso, and lately appointed to a civil
office in Peru, whither he had taken passage, was at the time
sleeping in the berth opposite Don Alexandro's; that awakening
at his cries, surprised by them, and at the sight of the negroes
with their bloody hatchets in their hands, he threw himself into
the sea through a window which was near him, and was
drowned, without it being in the power of the deponent to
assist or take him up . . . that a short time after killing Aranda,
they brought upon deck his cousin-german, of middle-age, Don
Francisco Masa, of Mendoza, and the young Don Joaquin,
Marques de Aramboalaza, then lately from Spain, with his
Spanish servant Ponce, and the three young clerks of Aranda,
Jose Morairi, Lorenzo Bargas and Hermenegildo Gandix, all of
Cadiz; that Don Joaquin and Hermenegildo Gandix, the negro
Babo, for purposes hereafter to appear, preserved alive; but
Don Francisco Masa, Jose Morairi and Lorenzo Bargas, with
Ponce the servant, beside the boatswain, Juan Robles, the
boatswain's mates, Manuel Viscaya and Roderigo Hurta, and
four of the sailors, the negro Babo ordered to be thrown alive

into the sea, although they made no resistance, nor begged for anything else but mercy; that the boatswain Juan Robles, who knew how to swim, kept the longest above water, making acts of contrition, and, in the last words he uttered, charged this deponent to cause mass to be said for his soul to our Lady of Succour; . . . that, during the three days which followed, the deponent, uncertain what fate had befallen the remains of Don Alexandra, frequently asked the negro Babo where they were, and, if still on board, whether they were to be preserved for interment ashore, entreating him so to order it; that the negro Babo answered nothing till the fourth day, when, at sunrise, the deponent coming on deck, the negro Babo showed him a skeleton, which had been substituted for the ship's proper figure-head – the image of Cristobal Colon, the discoverer of the New World; that the negro Babo asked him whose skeleton that was, and whether, from its whiteness, he should not think it a white's; that, upon discovering his face, the negro Babo, coming close, said words to this effect: 'Keep faith with the blacks from here to Senegal, or you shall in spirit, as now in body, follow your leader,' pointing to the prow; . . . that the same morning the negro Babo took by succession each Spaniard forward, and asked him whose skeleton that was, and whether, from its whiteness, he should not think it a white's; that each Spaniard covered his face; that then to each the negro Babo repeated the words in the first place said to the deponent; . . . that they (the Spaniards), being then assembled aft, the negro Babo harangued them, saying that he had now done all; that the deponent (as navigator for the negroes) might pursue his course, warning him and all of them that they should, soul and body, go the way of Don Alexandro, if he saw them (the Spaniards) speak or plot anything against them (the negroes), a threat which was repeated every day; that, before the events last mentioned, they had tied the cook to throw him overboard, for it is not known what thing they heard him speak, but finally the negro Babo spared his life, at the request of the deponent; that a few days after, the deponent, endeavouring not to omit any means to preserve the lives of the remaining whites, spoke to the negroes peace and tranquillity, and agreed to draw up a paper, signed by the deponent and the sailors who could write, as also by the negro Babo, for himself and all the blacks, in which the deponent obliged himself to carry them to Senegal, and they not to kill any more, and he formally to make over to them the ship, with the cargo, with which they were for that time satisfied and quieted . . . But the next day, the more surely to guard against the sailors' escape, the negro Babo commanded all the boats to be destroyed but the longboat, which was unseaworthy, and another, a cutter in good condition, which, knowing it would yet be wanted for towing the water-casks, he had lowered down into the hold . . .

Various particulars of the prolonged and perplexed navigation ensuing here follow, with incidents of a calamitous calm, from which portion one passage is extracted, to wit:

That on the fifth day of the calm, all on board suffering much from the heat and want of water, and five having died in fits, and mad, the negroes became irritable, and for a chance gesture, which they deemed suspicious – though it was harmless – made by the mate, Raneds, to the deponent in the act of handing a quadrant, they killed him; but that for this they afterwards were sorry, the mate being the only remaining navigator on board, except the deponent.

*   *   *

That omitting other events, which daily happened, and which can only serve uselessly to recall past misfortunes and conflicts, after seventy-three days' navigation, reckoned from the time they sailed from Nasca, during which they navigated under a scanty allowance of water, and were afflicted with the calms before mentioned, they at last arrived at the island of Santa Maria, on the seventeenth of the month of August, at about six o'clock in the afternoon, at which hour they cast anchor very near the American ship *Bachelor's Delight*, which lay in the same bay, commanded by the generous Captain Amasa Delano; but at six o'clock in the morning, they had already descried the port, and the negroes became uneasy as soon as at distance they saw the ship, not having expected to see one there; that the negro Babo pacified them, assuring them that no fear need be had; that straightway he ordered the figure on the bow to be covered with canvas, as for repairs, and had the decks a little set in order; that for a time the negro Babo and the negro Atufal conferred; that the negro Atufal was for sailing away, but the negro Babo would not, and, by himself, cast about what to do; that at last he came to the deponent, proposing to him to say and do all that the deponent declares to have said and done to the American captain; . . . that the negro Babo warned him that if he varied in the least, or uttered any word, or gave any look that should give the least intimation of the past events or present state, he would instantly kill him, with all his companions, showing a dagger, which he carried hid, saying something which, as he understood it, meant that that dagger would be alert as his eye; that the negro Babo then announced the plan to all his companions, which pleased them; that he then, the better to disguise the truth, devised many expedients, in some of them uniting deceit and defence; that of this sort was the device of the six Ashantees before named, who were his bravoes; that them he stationed on the break of the poop, as if to clean certain hatchets (in cases, which were part of the cargo), but in reality to use them, and distribute them at need, and at a given word; that among other devices was the device of presenting Atufal, his right-hand man, as chained, though in a moment the chains could be dropped; that in every particular he informed the deponent what part he was expected to enact in every device, and what story he was to tell on every occasion, always threatening him with instant death if he varied in the least: that, conscious that many of the negroes would be turbulent, the negro Babo appointed the four aged negroes, who were calkers, to keep what domestic order they could on the decks; that again and again he harangued the Spaniards and his companions, informing them of his intent, and of his devices, and of the invented story that this deponent was to tell; charging them lest any of them varied from that story; that these arrangements were made and matured during the interval of two or three hours, between their first sighting the ship and the arrival on board of Captain Amasa Delano; that this happened about half-past seven o'clock in the morning, Captain Amasa Delano coming in his boat, and all gladly receiving him; that the deponent, as well as he could force himself, acting then the part of principal owner and a free captain of the ship, told Captain Amasa Delano, when called upon, that he came from Buenos Aires, bound to Lima, with three hundred negroes; that off Cape Horn, and in a subsequent fever, many negroes had died; that also, by similar casualties, all the sea-officers and the greatest part of the crew had died.

* * *

And so the deposition goes on, circumstantially recounting the fictitious story dictated to the deponent by Babo, and through the

deponent imposed upon Captain Delano; and also recounting the
friendly offers of Captain Delano, with other things, but all of
which is here omitted. After the fictitious story, etc., the deposition
proceeds:

. . . that the generous Captain Amasa Delano remained on
board all the day, till he left the ship anchored at six o'clock in
the evening, the deponent speaking to him always of his
pretended misfortunes, under the aforementioned principles,
without having had it in his power to tell a single word, or give
him the least hint, that he might know the truth and state of
things; because the negro Babo, performing the office of an
officious servant with all the appearance of submission of the
humble slave, did not leave the deponent one moment; that this
was in order to observe the deponent's actions and words, for
the negro Babo understands well the Spanish; and besides,
there were thereabout some others who were constantly on the
watch, and likewise understood the Spanish; . . . that upon one
occasion, while the deponent was standing on the deck conversing with Amasa Delano, by a secret sign the negro Babo drew
him (the deponent) aside, the act appearing as if originating
with the deponent; that then, he being drawn aside, the negro
Babo proposed to him to gain from Amasa Delano full particulars about his ship, and crew, and arms; that the deponent
asked, 'For what?'; that the negro Babo answered he might
conceive; that, grieved at the prospect of what might overtake
the generous Captain Amasa Delano, the deponent at first
refused to ask the desired questions, and used every argument
to induce the negro Babo to give up this new design; that the
negro Babo showed the point of his dagger; that, after the
information had been obtained, the negro Babo again drew him
aside, telling him that that very night he (the deponent) would
be captain of two ships, instead of one, for that, the great part of
the American's ship's crew being absent fishing, the six Ashantees,
without anyone else, would easily take it; that at this time he
said other things to the same purpose; that no entreaties
availed; that, before Amasa Delano's coming on board, no hint
had been given touching the capture of the American ship; that
to prevent this project the deponent was powerless; . . . that in
some things his memory is confused, he cannot distinctly recall
every event; . . . that as soon as they had cast anchor at six
o'clock in the evening, as has before been stated, the American

captain took leave, to return to his vessel; that upon a sudden impulse, which the deponent believes to have come from God and his angels, he, after the farewell had been said, followed the generous Captain Amasa Delano as far as the gunwale, where he stayed, under pretence of taking leave, until Amasa Delano should have been seated in his boat; that on its shoving off, the deponent sprang from the gunwale into the boat, and fell into it, he knows not how, God guarding him; that . . .

Here, in the original, follows the account of what further happened at the escape, and how the *San Dominick* was retaken, and of the passage to the coast; including in the recital many expressions of 'eternal gratitude' to the 'generous Captain Amasa Delano'. The deposition then proceeds with recapitulatory remarks, and a partial renumeration of the negroes, making record of their individual part in the past events, with a view to furnishing, according to command of the court, the data whereon to found the criminal sentences to be pronounced. From this portion is the following:

That he believes that all the negroes, though not in the first place knowing to the design of revolt, when it was accomplished, approved it . . . That the negro José, eighteen years old, and in the personal service of Don Alexandro, was the one who communicated the information to the negro Babo about the state of things in the cabin, before the revolt; that this is known, because, in the preceding nights, he used to come from his berth, which was under his master's, in the cabin, to the deck where the ringleader and his associates were, and had secret conversations with the negro Babo, in which he was several times seen by the mate; that one night, the mate drove him away twice; . . . that this same negro José was the one who, without being commanded to do so by the negro Babo, as Lecbe and Matinqui were, stabbed his master, Don Alexandro, after he had been dragged half-lifeless to the deck; . . . that the mulatto steward, Francesco, was of the first band of revolters; that he was, in all things, the creature and tool of the negro Babo; that, to make his court, he, just before a repast in the cabin, proposed, to the negro Babo, poisoning a dish for the generous Captain Amasa Delano; this is known and believed, because the negroes have said it; but that the negro Babo, having another design, forbade Francesco; . . . that the Ashantee Lecbe was one of the worst of them; for that, on the day the ship was retaken, he assisted in the defence of her, with a hatchet in each hand, with

one of which he wounded, in the breast, the chief mate of Amasa
Delano, in the first act of boarding; this all knew; that, in sight
of the deponent, Lecbe struck with a hatchet Don Francisco
Masa, when, by the negro Babo's orders, he was carrying him to
throw him overboard alive, beside participating in the murder,
before mentioned, of Don Alexandro Aranda, and others of the
cabin-passengers; that, in spite of the fury with which the
Ashantees fought in the engagement with the boats, Lecbe and
Yau survived; that Yau was bad as Lecbe; that Yau was the man
who, by Babo's command, willingly prepared the skeleton of
Don Alexandro, in a way the negroes afterwards told the
deponent, but which he, so long as reason is left him, can never
divulge; that Yau and Lecbe were the two who, in a calm by
night, riveted the skeleton to the bow; this also the negroes told
him; that the negro Babo was he who traced the inscription
below it; that the negro Babo was the plotter from first to last;
he ordered every murder, and was the helm and keel of the
revolt; that Atufal was his lieutenant in all; but Atufal, with his
own hand, committed no murder; nor did the negro Babo; . . .
that Atufal was shot, being killed in the fight with the boats, ere
boarding . . . that the negresses of age were knowing to the
revolt, and testified themselves satisfied at the death of their
master, Don Alexandro; that, had the negroes not restrained
them, they would have tortured to death, instead of simply
killing, the Spaniards slain by command of the negro Babo; that
the negresses used their utmost influence to have the deponent
made away with; that, in the various acts of murder, they sang
songs and danced – not gaily, but solemnly; and before the
engagement with the boats, as well as during the action, they
sang melancholy songs to the negroes, and that this melancholy
tone was more inflaming than a different one would have been,
and was so intended; that all this is believed, because the negroes
have said it; . . . that of the thirty-six men of the crew, exclusive
of the passengers (all of whom are now dead), which the
deponent had knowledge of, six only remained alive, with four
cabin-boys and ship-boys, not included with the crew; . . . that
the negroes broke an arm of one of the cabin-boys and gave him
strokes with hatchets.

Then follow various random disclosures referring to various
periods of time. The following are extracted:

That during the presence of Captain Amasa Delano on board,

some attempts were made by the sailors, and one by Hermenegildo Gandix, to convey hints to him of the true state of affairs; but that these attempts were ineffectual, owing to fear of incurring death, and furthermore, owing to the devices which offered contradictions to the true state of affairs, as well as owing to the generosity and piety of Amasa Delano incapable of sounding such wickedness; . . . that Luys Galgo, a sailor about sixty years of age, and formerly of the king's navy, was one of those who sought to convey tokens to Captain Amasa Delano; but his intent, though undiscovered, being suspected, he was, on a pretence, made to retire out of sight, and at last into the hold and there was made away with. This the negroes have since said; . . . that one of the ship-boys feeling, from Captain Amasa Delano's presence, some hopes of release, and not having enough prudence, dropped some chance word respecting his expectations, which being overheard and understood by a slave-boy with whom he was eating at the time, the latter struck him on the head with a knife, inflicting a bad wound, but of which the boy is now healing; that likewise, not long before the ship was brought to anchor, one of the seamen, steering at the time, endangered himself by letting the blacks remark some expression in his countenance arising from a similar cause to the above; but this sailor, by his heedful after conduct, escaped; . . . that these statements are made to show the court that from the beginning to the end of the revolt, it was impossible for the deponent and his men to act otherwise than they did; . . . that the third clerk, Hermenegildo Gandix, who before had been forced to live among the seamen, wearing a seaman's habit, and in all respects appearing to be one for the time, he, Gandix, was killed by a musket ball fired through mistake from the boats before boarding, having in his fright run up the mizzen-rigging, calling to the boats, 'Don't board' – lest upon their boarding the negroes should kill him; that this inducing the Americans to believe he some way favoured the cause of the negroes, they fired two balls at him, so that he fell wounded from the rigging, and was drowned in the sea; . . . that the young Don Joaquin, Marques de Aramboalaza, like Hermenegildo Gandix, the third clerk, was degraded to the office and appearance of a common seaman; that upon one occasion when Don Joaquin shrank, the negro Babo commanded the Ashantee Lecbe to take tar, and heat it, and pour it upon Don Joaquin's hands; . . . that Don Joaquin was killed owing to another mistake of the Americans, but one impossible to be avoided, as upon the approach of the boats, Don Joaquin, with a hatchet tied edge out and upright to his hand, was made by the negroes to appear on the bulwarks; whereupon, seen with arms in his hands, and in a questionable attitude, he was shot for a renegade seaman; . . . that on the person of Don Joaquin was found secreted a jewel, which, by papers that were discovered, proved to have been meant for the shrine of our Lady of Mercy in Lima; a votive offering, beforehand prepared and guarded, to attest his gratitude, when he should have landed in Peru, his last destination for the safe conclusion of his entire voyage from Spain; . . . that the jewel, with the other effects of the late Don Joaquin, is in the custody of the Hospital de Sacerdotes, awaiting the disposition of the honourable court; . . . that, owing to the condition of the deponent, as well as the haste in which the boats departed for the attack, the Americans were not forewarned that there were, among the apparent crew, a passenger and one of the clerks disguised by the negro Babo; . . . that, beside the negroes killed in the action, some were killed after the capture and re-anchoring at night, when shackled to the ring-bolts on deck; that these deaths were committed by the sailors, ere they could be prevented. That so soon as informed of it, Captain Amasa Delano used all his authority, and in particular, with his own hand, struck down Martinez Gola, who, having found a razor in the pocket of an old jacket of his, which one of the shackled negroes had on, was aiming it at the negro's throat; that the noble Captain Amasa Delano also wrenched from the hand of Bartholomew Barlo a dagger, secreted at the time of the massacre of the whites, with which he was in the act of stabbing a shackled negro, who, the same day, with another negro, had thrown him down and jumped upon him; . . . that, for all the events befalling through so long a time, during which the ship was in the hands of the negro Babo, he cannot here give account; but that, what he has said is the most substantial of what occurs to him at present, and is the truth under the oath which he has taken; which declaration he affirmed and ratified, after hearing it read to him.

He said that he is twenty-nine years of age, and broken in body and mind; that when finally dismissed by the court, he shall not return home to Chile, but betake himself to the monastery on Mount Agonia without; and signed with his honour, and crossed himself, and, for the time, departed as he came, in his litter, with the monk Infelez, to the Hospital de Sacerdotes.

BENITO CERENO
DR ROZAS

If the deposition have served as the key to fit into the lock of the complications which precede it, then, as a vault whose door has been flung back, the *San Dominick*'s hull lies open today.

Hitherto the nature of this narrative, besides rendering the intricacies in the beginning unavoidable, has more or less required that many things, instead of being set down in the order of occurrence, should be retrospectively or irregularly given; this last is the case with the following passages, which will conclude the account.

During the long, mild voyage to Lima, there was, as before hinted, a period during which the sufferer a little recovered his health, or, at least in some degree, his tranquillity. Ere the decided relapse which came, the two captains had many cordial conversations – their fraternal unreserve in singular contrast with former withdrawments.

Again and again it was repeated, how hard it had been to enact the part forced on the Spaniard by Babo.

'Ah, my dear friend,' Don Benito once said, 'at those very times when you thought me so morose and ungrateful, nay, when, as you now admit, you thought me plotting your murder, at those very times my heart was frozen; I could not look at you, thinking of what, both on board this ship and your own, hung, from other hands, over my kind benefactor. And as God lives, Don Amasa, I know not whether desire for my own safety alone could have nerved me to that leap into your boat, had it not been for the thought that, did you, unenlightened, return to your ship, you, my best friend, with all who might be with you, stolen upon, that night, in your hammocks, would never in this world have wakened again. Do but think how you walked this deck, how you sat in this cabin, every inch of ground mined into honeycombs under you. Had I dropped the least hint, made the least advance towards an understanding between us, death, explosive death – yours as mine – would have ended the scene.'

'True, true,' cried Captain Delano, starting, 'you have saved my life, Don Benito, more than I yours; saved it, too, against my knowledge and will.'

'Nay, my friend,' rejoined the Spaniard, courteous even to the point of religion, 'God charmed your life, but you saved mine. To think of some things you did – those smilings and chattings, rash pointings and gesturings. For less than these, they slew my mate, Raneds; but you had the Prince of Heaven's safe-conduct through all ambuscades.'

'Yes, all is owing to Providence, I know: but the temper of my mind that morning was more than commonly pleasant, while the sight of so much suffering, more apparent than real, added to my good-nature, compassion and charity, happily interweaving the three. Had it been otherwise, doubtless, as you hint, some of my interferences might have ended unhappily enough. Besides, those feelings I spoke of enabled me to get the better of momentary distrust, at times when acuteness might have cost me my life, without saving another's. Only at the end did my suspicions get the better of me, and you know how wide of the mark they then proved.'

'Wide, indeed,' said Don Benito, sadly; 'you were with me all day; stood with me, sat with me, talked with me, looked at me, ate with me, drank with me; and yet, your last act was to clutch for a monster not only an innocent man, but the most pitiable of all men. To such degree may malign machinations and deceptions impose. So far may even the best man err in judging the conduct of one with the recesses of whose condition he is not acquainted. But you were forced to it; and you were in time undeceived. Would that, in both respects, it was so ever, and with all men.'

'You generalise, Don Benito; and mournfully enough. But the past is passed; why moralise upon it? Forget it. See, yon bright sun has forgotten it all, and the blue sea, and the blue sky; these have turned over new leaves.'

'Because they have no memory,' he dejectedly replied; 'because they are not human.'

'But these mild trades that now fan your cheek, do they not come with a human-like healing to you? Warm friends, steadfast friends are the trades.'

'With their steadfastness they but waft me to my tomb, señor,' was the foreboding response.

'You are saved,' cried Captain Delano, more and more astonished and pained; 'you are saved; what has cast such a shadow upon you?'

'The negro.'

There was silence, while the moody man sat, slowly and unconsciously gathering his mantle about him, as if it were a pall.

There was no more conversation that day.

But if the Spaniard's melancholy sometimes ended in muteness upon topics like the above, there were others upon which he never spoke at all; on which, indeed, all his old reserves were piled. Pass over the worst, and, only to elucidate, let an item or two of these be cited. The dress, so precise and costly, worn by him on the day whose events have been narrated, had not willingly been put on. And that silver-mounted sword, apparent symbol of despotic command, was not, indeed, a sword, but the ghost of one. The scabbard, artificially stiffened, was empty.

As for the black – whose brain, not body, had schemed and led the revolt, with the plot – his slight frame, inadequate to that which it held, had at once yielded to the superior muscular strength of his captor, in the boat. Seeing all was over, he uttered no sound, and could not be forced to. His aspect seemed to say, since I cannot do deeds, I will not speak words. Put in irons in the hold, with the rest, he was carried to Lima. During the passage, Don Benito did not visit him. Nor then, nor at any time after, would he look at him. Before the tribunal he refused. When pressed by the judges he fainted. On the testimony of the sailors alone rested the legal identity of Babo.

Some months after, dragged to the gibbet at the tail of a mule, the black met his voiceless end. The body was burned to ashes; but for many days, the head, that hive of subtlety, fixed on a pole in the plaza, met, unabashed, the gaze of the whites; and across the plaza looked towards St Bartholomew's Church, in whose vaults slept then, as now, the recovered bones of Aranda; and across the Rimac Bridge looked towards the monastery, on Mount Agonia without, where, three months after being dismissed by the court, Benito Cereno, borne on the bier, did indeed, follow his leader.

I AND MY CHIMNEY

I AND MY CHIMNEY, two grey-headed old smokers, reside in the country. We are, I may say, old settlers here; particularly my old chimney, which settles more and more every day.

Though I always say, *I and my chimney*, as Cardinal Wolsey used to say, *I and my King*, yet this egotistic way of speaking, wherein I take precedence of my chimney, is hardly borne out by the facts; in everything, except the above phrase, my chimney taking precedence of me.

Within thirty feet of the turf-sided road, my chimney – a huge, corpulent old Harry VIII of a chimney – rises full in front of me and all my possessions. Standing well up a hillside, my chimney, like Lord Rosse's monster telescope, swung vertical to hit the meridian moon, is the first object to greet the approaching traveller's eye, nor is it the last which the sun salutes. My chimney, too, is before me in receiving the first-fruits of the seasons. The snow is on its head ere on my hat; and every spring, as in a hollow beech tree, the first swallows build their nests in it.

But it is within doors that the pre-eminence of my chimney is most manifest. When in the rear room, set apart for that object, I stand to receive my guests (who, by the way, call more, I suspect, to see my chimney than me), I then stand, not so much before, as, strictly speaking, behind my chimney, which is, indeed, the true host. Not that I demur. In the presence of my betters, I hope I know my place.

From this habitual precedence of my chimney over me, some even think that I have got into a sad rearward way altogether; in short, from standing behind my old-fashioned chimney so much, I have got to be quite behind the age, too, as well as running behind-hand in everything else. But to tell the truth, I never was a very forward old fellow, nor what my farming neighbours call a forehanded one. Indeed, those rumours about my behindhandedness are so far correct that I have an odd sauntering way with me sometimes of going about with my hands behind my back. As for my belonging to the rearguard in general, certain it is, I bring up the rear of my chimney – which, by the way, is this moment before me – and that, too, both in fancy and fact. In brief, my chimney is my superior; my superior by I know not how many heads and shoulders; my superior, too, in that humbly bowing over with shovel and tongs, I much minister to it; yet never does it minister, or incline over to me; but, if anything, in its settlings, rather leans the other way.

My chimney is grand seignior here – the one great domineering object, not more of the landscape, than of the house; all the rest of which house, in each architectural arrangement, as may shortly appear, is, in the most marked manner, accommodated, not to my wants, but to my chimney's, which, among other things, has the centre of the house to himself, leaving but the odd holes and corners to me.

But I and my chimney must explain; and, as we are both rather obese, we may have to expatiate.

In those houses which are strictly double houses – that is, where the hall is in the middle – the fireplaces usually are on opposite sides; so that while one member of the household is warming himself at a fire built into a recess of the north wall, say, another member, the former's own brother perhaps, may be holding his feet to the blaze before a hearth in the south wall – the two thus fairly sitting back to back. Is this well? Be it put to any man who has a proper fraternal feeling. Has it not a sort of sulky appearance? But very probably this style of chimney building originated with some architect afflicted with a quarrelsome family.

Then again, almost every modern fireplace has its separate flue – separate throughout, from hearth to chimney-top. At least such an arrangement is deemed desirable. Does not this look egotistical, selfish? But still more, all these separate flues, instead of having independent masonry establishments of their own, or instead of being grouped together in one federal stock in the middle of the house – instead of this, I say, each flue is surreptitiously honey-combed into the walls; so that these last are here and there, or indeed almost anywhere, treacherously hollow, and, in consequence, more or less weak. Of course, the main reason of this style of chimney building is to economise room. In cities, where lots are sold by the inch, small space is to spare for a chimney constructed on magnanimous principles; and, as with most thin men, who are generally tall, so with such houses, what is lacking in breadth must be made up in height. This remark holds true even with regard to many very stylish abodes, built by the most stylish of gentlemen. And yet, when that stylish gentleman, Louis le Grand of France, would build a palace for his lady friend, Madame de Maintenon, he built it but one storey high – in fact, in the cottage style. But then, how uncommonly quadrangular, spacious, and broad – horizontal acres, not vertical ones. Such is the palace which, in all its one-storeyed magnificence of Languedoc marble, in the garden of Versailles, still remains to this day. Any man can buy a square foot of land and plant a liberty-pole on it; but it takes a king to set apart whole acres for a grand Trianon.

But nowadays it is different; and furthermore, what originated in a necessity has been mounted into a vaunt. In towns there is large rivalry in building tall houses. If one gentleman builds his house four storeys high, and another gentleman comes next door and builds five storeys high, then the former, not to be looked down upon that way, immediately sends for his architect and claps a fifth and a sixth storey on top of his previous four. And, not till the gentleman has achieved his aspiration, not till he has stolen over the way by twilight and observed how his sixth storey soars beyond his neighbour's fifth – not till then does he retire to his rest with satisfaction.

Such folks, it seems to me, need mountains for neighbours, to take this emulous conceit of soaring out of them.

If, considering that mine is a very wide house, and by no means lofty, aught in the above may appear like interested pleading, as if I did but fold myself about in the cloak of a general proposition, cunningly to tickle my individual vanity beneath it, such misconception must vanish upon my frankly conceding that land adjoining my alder swamp was sold last month for ten dollars an acre, and thought a rash purchase at that; so that for wide houses hereabouts there is plenty of room, and cheap. Indeed, so cheap – dirt cheap – is the soil, that our elms thrust out their roots in it, and hang their great boughs over it, in the most lavish and reckless way. Almost all our crops, too, are sown broadcast, even peas and turnips. A farmer among us, who should go about his twenty-acre field, poking his finger into it here and there, and dropping down a mustard seed, would be thought a penurious, narrow-minded husbandman. The dandelions in the river-meadows, and the forget me-nots along the mountain roads, you see at once they are put to no economy in space. Some seasons, too, our rye comes up, here and there a spear, sole and single like a church-spire. It doesn't care to crowd itself where it knows there is such a deal of room. The world is wide, the world is all before us, says the rye. Weeds, too, it is amazing how they spread. No such thing as arresting them – some of our pastures being a sort of Alsatia for the weeds. As for the grass, every spring it is like Kossuth's rising of what he calls the peoples. Mountains, too, a regular camp-meeting of them. For the same reason, the same all-sufficiency of room, our shadows march and countermarch, going through their various drills and masterly evolutions, like the old imperial guard on the Champs de Mars. As for the hills, especially where the roads cross them, the supervisors of our various towns have given notice to all concerned, that they can come and dig them down and cart them off, and never a cent to pay, no more than for the privilege of picking blackberries. The stranger who is buried here, what liberal-hearted landed proprietor among us grudges him his six feet of rocky pasture?

Nevertheless, cheap, after all, as our land is, and much as it is trodden under foot, I, for one, am proud of it for what it bears; and chiefly for its three great lions – the Great Oak, Ogg Mountain and my chimney.

Most houses here are but one and a half storeys high; few exceed two. That in which I and my chimney dwell is in width nearly twice its height, from sill to eaves – which accounts for the magnitude of its main content – besides, showing that in this house, as in this country at large, there is abundance of space, and to spare, for both of us.

The frame of the old house is of wood – which but the more sets forth the solidity of the chimney, which is of brick. And as the great wrought nails, binding the clapboards, are unknown in these degenerate days, so are the huge bricks in the chimney walls. The architect of the chimney must have had the pyramid of Cheops before him, for after that famous structure it seems modelled, only its rate of decrease towards the summit is considerably less and it is truncated. From the exact middle of the mansion it soars from the cellar right up through each successive floor, till, four feet square, it breaks water from the ridge pole of the roof, like an anvil-headed whale, through the crest of a billow. Most people, though, liken it, in that part, to a razeed observatory, masoned up.

The reason for its peculiar appearance above the roof touches upon rather delicate ground. How shall I reveal that, forasmuch as many years ago the original gable roof of the old house had become very leaky, a temporary proprietor hired a band of woodmen, with their huge, cross-cut saws, and went to sawing the old gable roof clean off. Off it went, with all its birds' nests and dormer windows. It was replaced with a modern roof, more fit for a railway wood-house than an old country gentleman's abode. This operation – razeeing the structure some fifteen feet – was, in effect upon the chimney, something like the falling of the great spring tides. It left uncommon low water all about the chimney – to abate which appearance, the same person now proceeds to slice fifteen feet off the chimney itself, actually beheading my royal old chimney – a regicidal act which, were it not for the palliating fact that he was a poulterer by trade, and, therefore, hardened to such neck-wringings, should send that former proprietor down to posterity in the same cart with Cromwell.

Owing to its pyramidal shape, the reduction of the chimney inordinately widened its razeed summit. Inordinately, I say, but only in the estimation of such as have no eye to the picturesque. What care I, if, unaware that my chimney, as a free citizen of this free land, stands upon an independent basis of its own, people passing it wonder how such a brick-kiln, as they call it, is supported upon mere joists and rafters? What care I? I will give a traveller a cup of switchel, if he want it; but am I bound to supply him with a sweet taste? Men of cultivated minds see, in my old house and chimney, a goodly old elephant-and-castle.

All feeling hearts will sympathise with me in what I am now about to add. The surgical operation above referred to necessarily brought into the open air a part of the chimney previously under cover, and intended to remain so and, therefore, not built of what are called weather-bricks. In consequences the chimney, though of a vigorous constitution, suffered not a little from so naked an exposure; and, unable to acclimate itself, ere long began to fail – showing blotchy symptoms akin to those in measles. Whereupon travellers, passing my way, would wag their heads, laughing: 'See that wax nose – how it melts off!' But what cared I? The same travellers would travel across the sea to view Kenilworth peeling away, and for a very good reason: that of all artists of the picturesque, decay wears the palm – I would say, the ivy. In fact, I've often thought that the proper place for my old chimney is ivied old England.

In vain my wife – with what probable ulterior intent will, ere long, appear – solemnly warned me that unless something were done, and speedily, we should be burnt to the ground, owing to the holes crumbling through the aforesaid blotchy parts where the chimney joined the roof. 'Wife,' said I, 'far better that my house should burn down, than that my chimney should be pulled down, though but a few feet. They call it a wax nose; very good; not for me to tweak the nose of my superior.' But at last the man who has a mortgage on the house dropped me a note, reminding me that, if my chimney was allowed to stand in that invalid condition, my policy of insurance would be void. This was a sort of hint not to be neglected. All the world over, the picturesque yields to the pocketesque. The mortgagor cared not, but the mortgagee did.

So another operation was performed. The wax nose was taken off, and a new one fitted on. Unfortunately for the expression – being put up by a squint-eyed mason who, at the time, had a bad stitch in the same side – the new nose stands a little awry, in the same direction.

Of one thing, however, I am proud. The horizontal dimensions of the new part are unreduced.

Large as the chimney appears upon the roof, that is nothing to its spaciousness below. At its base in the cellar, it is precisely twelve feet square; and hence covers precisely one hundred and forty-four superficial feet. What an appropriation of terra firma for a chimney, and what a huge load for this earth! In fact, it was only because I and my chimney formed no part of his ancient burden, that that stout peddler, Atlas of old, was enabled to stand up so bravely under his pack. The dimensions given may, perhaps, seem fabulous. But, like those stones at Gilgal, which Joshua set up for a memorial of having passed over Jordan, does not my chimney remain, even unto this day?

Very often I go down into my cellar, and attentively survey that vast square of masonry. I stand long, and ponder over, and wonder at it. It has a druidical look, away down in the umbrageous cellar there, whose numerous vaulted passages, and far glens of gloom, resemble the dark, damp depths of primeval woods. So strongly did this conceit steal over me, so deeply was I penetrated with wonder at the chimney, that one day – when I was a little out of my mind, I now think – getting a spade from the garden, I set to work digging round the foundation, especially at the corners thereof, obscurely prompted by dreams of striking upon some old, earthen-worn memorial of that bygone day when, into all this gloom, the light of heaven entered, as the masons laid the foundation-stones, perad-venture sweltering under an August sun or pelted by a March storm. Plying my blunted spade, how vexed was I by that ungracious interruption of a neighbour who, calling to see me upon some business, and being informed that I was below, said I need not be troubled to come up but he would go down to me; and so, without ceremony, and without my having been forewarned, suddenly discovered me, digging in my cellar.

'Gold digging, sir?'

'Nay, sir,' answered I, starting, 'I was merely – ahem! – merely – I say I was merely digging – round my chimney.'

'Ah, loosening the soil, to make it grow. Your chimney, sir, you regard as too small, I suppose; needing further development, especially at the top?'

'Sir!' said I, throwing down the spade, 'do not be personal. I and my chimney – '

'Personal?'

'Sir, I look upon this chimney less as a pile of masonry than as a personage. It is the king of the house. I am but a suffered and inferior subject.'

In fact, I would permit no gibes to be cast at either myself or my chimney; and never again did my visitor refer to it in my hearing, without coupling some compliment with the mention. It well deserves a respectful consideration. There it stands, solitary and alone – not a council of ten flues, but, like his sacred majesty of Russia, a unit of an autocrat.

Even to me, its dimensions, at times, seem incredible. It does not look so big – no, not even in the cellar. By the mere eye, its magnitude can be but imperfectly comprehended, because only one side can be received at one time; and said side can only present twelve feet, linear measure. But then, each other side also is twelve feet long; and the whole obviously forms a square; and twelve times twelve is one hundred and forty-four. And so, an adequate conception of the magnitude of this chimney is only to be got at by a sort of process in the higher mathematics, by a method somewhat akin to those whereby the surprising distances of fixed stars are computed.

It need hardly be said, that the walls of my house are entirely free from fireplaces. These all congregate in the middle – in the one grand central chimney, upon all four sides of which are hearths – two tiers of hearths – so that when, in the various chambers, my family and guests are warming themselves of a cold winter's night, just before retiring, then, though at the time they may not be thinking so, all their faces mutually look towards each other, yea all their feet point to one centre; and, when they go to sleep in their beds, they all sleep round one warm chimney, like so many Iroquois Indians, in the woods, round their one heap of embers. And just as the Indians' fire serves, not only to keep them comfortable, but also to keep off wolves, and other savage monsters, so my chimney, by its obvious smoke at top, keeps off prowling burglars from the towns – for what burglar or murderer would dare break into an abode from whose chimney issues such a continual smoke – betokening that if the inmates are not stirring, at least fires are, and in case of an alarm, candles may readily be lighted, to say nothing of muskets.

But stately as is the chimney – yea, grand high altar as it is, right

worthy for the celebration of high mass before the Pope of Rome
and all his cardinals – yet what is there perfect in this world? Caius
Julius Caesar, had he not been so inordinately great, they say that
Brutus, Cassius, Antony, and the rest, had been greater. My
chimney, were it not so mighty in its magnitude, my chambers had
been larger. How often has my wife ruefully told me that my
chimney, like the English aristocracy, casts a contracting shade all
round it? She avers that endless domestic inconveniences arise –
more particularly from the chimney's stubborn central locality. The
grand objection with her is that it stands midway in the place where
a fine entrance-hall ought to be. In truth, there is no hall whatever
to the house – nothing but a sort of square landing-place, as you
enter from the wide front door. A roomy enough landing-place, I
admit, but not attaining to the dignity of a hall. Now, as the front
door is precisely in the middle of the front of the house, inwards it
faces the chimney. In fact, the opposite wall of the landing-place is
formed solely by the chimney; and hence – owing to the gradual
tapering of the chimney – is a little less than twelve feet in width.
Climbing the chimney in this part is the principal staircase – which,
by three abrupt turns, and three minor landing-places, mounts to
the second floor, where, over the front door, runs a sort of narrow
gallery, something less than twelve feet long, leading to chambers
on either hand. This gallery, of course, is railed; and so, looking
down upon the stairs, and all those landing-places together, with
the main one at bottom, resembles not a little a balcony for
musicians, in some jolly old abode, in times Elizabethan. Shall I tell
a weakness? I cherish the cobwebs there, and many a time arrest
Biddy in the act of brushing them with her broom, and have many a
quarrel with my wife and daughters about it.

Now the ceiling, so to speak, of the place where you enter the
house, that ceiling is, in fact, the ceiling of the second floor, not the
first. The two floors are made one here; so that ascending this
turning stairs, you seem going up into a kind of soaring tower, or
lighthouse. At the second landing, midway up the chimney, is a
mysterious door, entering to a mysterious closet; and here I keep
mysterious cordials, of a choice, mysterious flavour, made so by the
constant nurturing and subtle ripening of the chimney's gentle
heat, distilled through that warm mass of masonry. Better for wines
is it than voyages to the Indias; my chimney itself a tropic. A chair
by my chimney on a November day is as good for an invalid as a
long season spent in Cuba. Often I think how grapes might ripen
against my chimney. How my wife's geraniums bud there! Bud in

December. Her eggs, too – can't keep them near the chimney, on account of hatching. Ah, a warm heart has my chimney.

How often my wife was at me about that projected grand entrance-hall of hers, which was to be knocked clean through the chimney, from one end of the house to the other, and astonish all guests by its generous amplitude. 'But, wife,' said I, 'the chimney – consider the chimney: if you demolish the foundation, what is to support the superstructure?' 'Oh, that will rest on the second floor.' The truth is, women know next to nothing about the realities of architecture. However, my wife still talked of running her entries and partitions. She spent many long nights elaborating her plans; in imagination building her boasted hall through the chimney, as though its high mightiness were a mere spear of sorrel-top. At last, I gently reminded her that, little as she might fancy it, the chimney was a fact – a sober, substantial fact, which, in all her plannings, it would be well to take into full consideration. But this was not of much avail.

And here, respectfully craving her permission, I must say a few words about this enterprising wife of mine. Though in years nearly old as myself, in spirit she is young as my little sorrel mare, Trigger, that threw me last fall. What is extraordinary, though she comes of a rheumatic family, she is straight as a pine, never has any aches; while for me, with the sciatica, I am sometimes as crippled up as any old apple tree. But she has not so much as a toothache. As for her hearing – let me enter the house in my dusty boots, and she away up in the attic. And for her sight – Biddy, the housemaid, tells other people's housemaids, that her mistress will spy a spot on the dresser straight through the pewter platter put up on purpose to hide it. Her faculties are alert as her limbs and her senses. No danger of my spouse dying of torpor. The longest night in the year I've known her lie awake, planning her campaign for the morrow. She is a natural projector. The maxim, Whatever is, is right, is not hers. Her maxim is, Whatever is, is wrong; and what is more, must be altered; and what is still more, must be altered right away. Dreadful maxim for the wife of a dozy old dreamer like me, who dote on seventh days as days of rest, and, out of a sabbatical horror of industry, will, on a weekday, go out of my road a quarter of a mile, to avoid the sight of a man at work.

That matches are made in heaven, may be, but my wife would have been just the wife for Peter the Great, or Peter the Piper. How she would have set in order that huge littered empire of the one and with indefatigable painstaking picked the peck of pickled peppers for the other.

But the most wonderful thing is, my wife never thinks of her end. Her youthful incredulity, as to the plain theory, and still plainer fact of death, hardly seems Christian. Advanced in years, as she knows she must be, my wife seems to think that she is to teem on, and be inexhaustible forever. She doesn't believe in old age. At that strange promise in the plain of Mamre, my old wife, unlike old Abraham's, would not have jeeringly laughed within herself.

Judge how to me, who, sitting in the comfortable shadow of my chimney, smoking my comfortable pipe, with ashes not unwelcome at my feet, and ashes not unwelcome all but in my mouth; and who am thus in a comfortable sort of not unwelcome, though, indeed, ashy enough way, reminded of the ultimate exhaustion even of the most fiery life; judge how to me this unwarrantable vitality in my wife must come, sometimes, it is true, with a moral and a calm, but oftener with a breeze and a ruffle.

If the doctrine be true, that in wedlock contraries attract, by how cogent a fatality must I have been drawn to my wife! While spicily impatient of present and past, like a glass of ginger-beer she overflows with her schemes; and with like energy as she puts down her foot, puts down her preserves and her pickles, and lives with them in a continual future; or ever full of expectations both from time and space, is ever restless for newspapers and ravenous for letters. Content with the years that are gone, taking no thought for the morrow, and looking for no new thing from any person or quarter whatever, I have not a single scheme or expectation on earth, save in unequal resistance of the undue encroachment of hers.

Old myself, I take to oldness in things; for that cause mainly loving old Montaigne, and old cheese, and old wine; and eschewing young people, hot rolls, new books and early potatoes, and very fond of my old claw-footed chair, and old club-footed Deacon White, my neighbour, and that still nigher old neighbour, my betwisted old grape-vine, that of a summer evening leans in his elbow for cosy company at my window-sill, while I, within doors, lean over mine to meet his; and above all, high above all, am fond of my high-manteled old chimney. But she, out of that infatuate juvenility of hers, takes to nothing but newness; for that cause mainly, loving new cider in autumn and in spring, as if she were own daughter of Nebuchadnezzar, fairly raving after all sorts of salads and spinaches, and more particularly green cucumbers (though all the time nature rebukes such unsuitable young hankerings in so elderly a person by never permitting such things to agree with her), and has an itch after recently discovered fine prospects (so no graveyard be in the background), and also after Swedenborgianism, and the Spirit Rapping philosophy, with other new views, alike in things natural and unnatural; and immortally hopeful, is forever making new flowerbeds even on the north side of the house, where the bleak mountain wind would scarce allow the wiry weed called hard-hack to gain a thorough footing; and on the roadside sets out mere pipestems of young elms, though there is no hope of any shade from them, except over the ruins of her great-grand daughters' gravestones; and won't wear caps, but plaits her grey hair; and takes the *Ladies' Magazine* for the fashions; and always buys her new almanac a month before the new year; and rises at dawn; and to the warmest sunset turns a cold shoulder; and still goes on at odd hours with her new course of history, and her French, and her music; and likes young company; and offers to ride young colts; and sets out young suckers in the orchard; and has a spite against my elbowed old grape-vine, and my club-footed old neighbour, and my claw-footed old chair, and above all, high above all, would fain persecute, unto death, my high-manteled old chimney. By what perverse magic, I a thousand times think, does such a very autumnal old lady have such a very vernal young soul? When I would remonstrate at times, she spins round on me with, 'Oh, don't you grumble, old man' (she always calls me old man), 'it's I, young I, that keep you from stagnating.' Well, I suppose it is so. Yea, after all, these things are well ordered. My wife, as one of her poor relations, good soul, intimates, is the salt of the earth, and none the less the salt of my sea, which otherwise were unwholesome. She is its monsoon, too, blowing a brisk gale over it, in the one steady direction of my chimney.

Not insensible of her superior energies, my wife has frequently made me propositions to take upon herself all the responsibilities of my affairs. She is desirous that, domestically, I should abdicate; that, renouncing further rule, like the venerable Charles V, I should retire into some sort of monastery. But indeed, the chimney excepted, I have little authority to lay down. By my wife's ingenious application of the principle that certain things belong of right to female jurisdiction, I find myself, through my easy compliances, insensibly stripped by degrees of one masculine prerogative after another. In a dream I go about my fields, a sort of lazy, happy-go-lucky, good-for-nothing, loafing, old Lear. Only by some sudden revelation am I reminded who is over me; as, year before last, one day seeing in one corner of the premises fresh deposits of mysterious boards and timbers, the oddity of the incident at length begat serious meditation. 'Wife,' said I, 'whose boards and timbers are those I see near the orchard there? Do you know anything about them, wife? Who put them there? You know I do not like the neighbours to use my land that way; they should ask permission first.'

She regarded me with a pitying smile.

'Why, old man, don't you know I am building a new barn? Didn't you know that, old man?'

This is the poor old lady that was accusing me of tyrannising over her.

To return now to the chimney. Upon being assured of the futility of her proposed hall, so long as the obstacle remained, for a time my wife was for a modified project. But I could never exactly comprehend it. As far as I could see through it, it seemed to involve the general idea of a sort of irregular archway, or elbowed tunnel, which was to penetrate the chimney at some convenient point under the staircase, and carefully avoiding dangerous contact with the fireplaces, and particularly steering clear of the great interior flue, was to conduct the enterprising traveller from the front door all the way into the dining-room in the remote rear of the mansion. Doubtless it was a bold stroke of genius, that plan of hers, and so was Nero's when he schemed his grand canal through the Isthmus of Corinth. Nor will I take oath that, had her project been accomplished, then, by help of lights hung at judicious intervals through the tunnel, some Belzoni or other might have succeeded in future ages in penetrating through the masonry, and actually emerging into the dining-room, and once there, it would have been inhospitable treatment of such a traveller to have denied him a recruiting meal.

But my bustling wife did not restrict her objections, nor in the end confine her proposed alterations, to the first floor. Her ambition was of the mounting order. She ascended with her schemes to the second floor, and so to the attic. Perhaps there was some small ground for her discontent with things as they were. The truth is, there was no regular passage-way upstairs or down, unless we again except that little orchestra-gallery before mentioned. And all this was owing to the chimney, which my gamesome spouse seemed despitefully to regard as the bully of the house. On all its four sides, nearly all the chambers sidled up to the chimney for the benefit of a fireplace. The chimney would not go to them; they must needs go to it. The consequence was, almost every room, like a philosophical system, was in itself an entry, or passage-way to other rooms, and systems of rooms – a whole suite of entries, in fact. Going through the house, you seem to be forever going somewhere and getting nowhere. It is like losing oneself in the woods; round and round the chimney you go, and if you arrive at all, it is just where you started, and so you begin again, and again get nowhere. Indeed – though I say it not in the way of fault-finding at all – never was there so labyrinthine an abode. Guests will tarry with me several weeks, and every now and then be anew astonished at some unforeseen apartment.

The puzzling nature of the mansion, resulting from the chimney, is peculiarly noticeable in the dining-room, which has no less than nine doors, opening in all directions, and into all sorts of places. A stranger, for the first time entering this dining-room, and naturally taking no special heed at what door he entered, will, upon rising to depart, commit the strangest blunders. Such, for instance, as opening the first door that comes handy, and finding himself stealing upstairs by the back passage. Shutting that door, he will proceed to another, and be aghast at the cellar yawning at his feet. Trying a third, he surprises the housemaid at her work. In the end, no more relying on his own unaided efforts, he procures a trusty guide in some passing person and in good time successfully emerges. Perhaps as curious a blunder as any was that of a certain stylish young gentleman, a great exquisite, in whose judicious eyes my daughter Anna had found especial favour. He called upon the young lady one evening, and found her alone in the dining-room at her needlework. He stayed rather late; and after abundance of superfine discourse, all the while retaining his hat and cane, made his profuse adieus, and with repeated graceful bows proceeded to depart, after the fashion of courtiers from the queen, and by so doing, opening a door at random, with one hand placed behind, very effectually succeeded in backing himself into a dark pantry, where he carefully shut himself up, wondering there was no light in the entry. After several strange noises as of a cat among the crockery, he reappeared through the same door, looking uncommonly crestfallen, and, with a deeply embarrassed air, requested my daughter to designate at which of the nine he should find exit. When the mischievous Anna told me the story, she said it was surprising how unaffected and matter-of-fact the young gentleman's manner was after his reappearance. He was more candid than ever, to be sure, having inadvertently thrust his white kids into an open drawer of Havana sugar, under the impression, probably, that being what they call 'a sweet fellow', his route might possibly lie in that direction.

Another inconvenience resulting from the chimney is the bewilderment of a guest in gaining his chamber, many strange doors lying between him and it. To direct him by finger-posts would look rather queer; and just as queer in him to be knocking at every door on his route, like London's city guest, the king, at Temple Bar.

Now, of all these things and many, many more, my family continually complained. At last my wife came out with her sweeping proposition – *in toto* to abolish the chimney.

'What!' said I, 'abolish the chimney? To take out the backbone of anything, wife, is a hazardous affair. Spines out of backs, and chimneys out of houses, are not to be taken like frosted lead-pipes from the ground. Besides,' added I, 'the chimney is the one grand permanence of this abode. If undisturbed by innovators, then in future ages, when all the house shall have crumbled from it, this chimney will still survive – a Bunker Hill monument. No, no, wife, I can't abolish my backbone.'

So said I then. But who is sure of himself, especially an old man, with both wife and daughters ever at his elbow and ear? In time, I was persuaded to think a little better of it; in short, to take the matter into preliminary consideration. At length it came to pass that a master-mason – a rough sort of architect – one Mr Scribe, was summoned to a conference. I formally introduced him to my chimney. A previous introduction from my wife had introduced him to myself. He had been not a little employed by that lady in preparing plans and estimates for some of her extensive operations in drainage. Having, with much ado, extorted from my spouse the promise that she would leave us to an unmolested survey, I began by leading Mr Scribe down to the root of the matter, in the cellar. Lamp in hand, I descended; for though upstairs it was noon, below it was night.

We seemed in the pyramids; and I, with one hand holding my lamp overhead, and with the other pointing out, in the obscurity, the hoar mass of the chimney, seemed some Arab guide, showing the cobwebbed mausoleum of the great god Apis.

'This is a most remarkable structure, sir,' said the master mason, after long contemplating it in silence, 'a most remarkable structure, sir.'

'Yes,' said I, complacently, 'everyone says so.'

'But large as it appears above the roof, I would not have inferred the magnitude of this foundation, sir,' eying it critically.

Then taking out his rule, he measured it.

'Twelve feet square; one hundred and forty-four square feet! Sir, this house would appear to have been built simply for the accommodation of your chimney.'

'Yes, my chimney and me. Tell me candidly, now,' I added, 'would you have such a famous chimney abolished?'

'I wouldn't have it in a house of mine, sir, for a gift,' was the reply. 'It's a losing affair altogether, sir. Do you know, sir, that in retaining this chimney, you are losing, not only one hundred and forty-four square feet of good ground, but likewise a considerable interest upon a considerable principal?'

'How?'

'Look, sir,' said he, taking a bit of red chalk from his pocket, and figuring against a whitewashed wall, 'twenty times eight is so and so; then forty-two times thirty-nine is so and so – ain't it, sir? Well, add those together, and subtract this here, then that makes so and so,' still chalking away.

To be brief, after no small ciphering, Mr Scribe informed me that my chimney contained, I am ashamed to say how many thousand and odd valuable bricks.

'No more,' said I fidgeting. 'Pray now, let us have a look above.'

In that upper zone we made two more circumnavigations for the first and second floors. That done, we stood together at the foot of the stairway by the front door; my hand upon the knob, and Mr Scribe hat in hand.

'Well, sir,' said he, a sort of feeling his way, and, to help himself, fumbling with his hat, 'well, sir, I think it can be done.'

'What, pray, Mr Scribe; *what* can be done?'

'Your chimney, sir; it can without rashness be removed, I think.'

'I will think of it, too, Mr Scribe,' said I, turning the knob, and bowing him towards the open space without, 'I will *think* of it, sir; it demands consideration; much obliged to ye; good morning, Mr Scribe.'

'It is all arranged, then,' cried my wife with great glee, bursting from the nighest room.

'When will they begin?' demanded my daughter Julia.

'Tomorrow?' asked Anna.

'Patience, patience, my dears,' said I, 'such a big chimney is not to be abolished in a minute.'

Next morning it began again.

'You remember the chimney,' said my wife.

'Wife,' said I, 'it is never out of my house, and never out of my mind.'

'But when is Mr Scribe to begin to pull it down?' asked Anna.

'Not today, Anna,' said I.

'*When*, then?' demanded Julia, in alarm.

Now, if this chimney of mine was, for size, a sort of belfry, for ding-donging at me about it, my wife and daughters were a sort of bells, always chiming together, or taking up each other's melodies at every pause, my wife the key-clapper of all. A very sweet ringing, and pealing, and chiming, I confess; but then, the most silvery of bells may, sometimes, dismally toll as well as merrily play. And as touching the subject in question, it became so now. Perceiving a strange relapse of opposition in me, wife and daughters began a soft and dirge-like melancholy tolling over it.

At length my wife, getting much excited, declared to me, with pointed finger, that so long as that chimney stood, she should regard it as the monument of what she called my broken pledge. But finding this did not answer, the next day she gave me to understand that either she or the chimney must quit the house.

Finding matters coming to such a pass, I and my pipe philosophised over them awhile, and finally concluded between us, that little as our hearts went with the plan, yet for peace's sake, I might write out the chimney's death-warrant, and, while my hand was in, scratch a note to Mr Scribe.

Considering that I and my chimney and my pipe, from having been so much together, were three great cronies, the facility with which my pipe consented to a project so fatal to the goodliest of our trio – or rather, the way in which I and my pipe, in secret, conspired together, as it were, against our unsuspicious old comrade – this may seem rather strange, if not suggestive of sad reflections upon us two. But, indeed, we sons of clay, that is my pipe and I, are no whit better than the rest. Far from us, indeed, to have volunteered the betrayal of our crony. We are of a peaceable nature, too. But that love of peace it was which made us false to a mutual friend, as soon as his cause demanded a vigorous vindication. But I rejoice to add that better and braver thoughts soon returned, as will now briefly be set forth.

To my note, Mr Scribe replied in person.

Once more we made a survey, mainly now with a view to a pecuniary estimate.

'I will do it for five hundred dollars,' said Mr Scribe at last, again hat in hand.

'Very well, Mr Scribe, I will think of it,' replied I, again bowing him to the door.

Not unvexed by this, for the second time, unexpected response, again he withdrew, and from my wife and daughters again burst the old exclamations.

The truth is, resolve how I would, at the last pinch I and my chimney could not be parted.

'So Holofernes will have his way, never mind whose heart breaks for it,' said my wife next morning, at breakfast, in that half-didactic, half-reproachful way of hers, which is harder to bear than her most energetic assault. Holofernes, too, is with her a pet name for any fell domestic despot. So, whenever, against her most ambitious innovations, those which saw me quite across the grain, I, as in the present instance, stand with however little steadfastness on the defence, she is sure to call me Holofernes, and ten to one takes the first opportunity to read aloud, with a suppressed emphasis, of an evening, the first newspaper paragraph about some tyrannic day-labourer who, after being for many years the Caligula of his family, ends by beating his long-suffering spouse to death, with a garret door wrenched off its hinges, and then, pitching his little innocents out of the window, suicidally turns inward towards the broken wall scored with the butcher's and baker's bills, and so rushes headlong to his dreadful account.

Nevertheless, for a few days, not a little to my surprise, I heard no further reproaches. An intense calm pervaded my wife, but one beneath which, as in the sea, there was no knowing what portentous movements might be going on. She frequently went abroad, and in a direction which I thought not unsuspicious; namely, in the direction of New Petra, a griffin-like house of wood and stucco, in the highest style of ornamental art, graced with four chimneys in the form of erect dragons spouting smoke from their nostrils: the elegant modern residence of Mr Scribe, which he had built for the purpose of a standing advertisement, not more of his taste as an architect than of his solidity as a master mason.

At last, smoking my pipe one morning, I heard a rap at the door, and my wife, with an air unusually quiet for her, brought me a note. As I have no correspondents except Solomon, with whom, in his sentiments, at least, I entirely correspond, the note occasioned me some little surprise, which was not diminished upon reading the following:

New Petra, April 1st

SIR – During my last examination of your chimney, possibly you may have noted that I frequently applied my rule to it in a manner apparently unnecessary. Possibly also, at the same time, you might have observed in me more or less of perplexity, to which, however, I refrained from giving any verbal expression.

I now feel it obligatory upon me to inform you of what was then but a dim suspicion, and as such would have been unwise to give utterance to, but which now, from various subsequent calculations assuming no little probability, it may be important that you should not remain in further ignorance of.

It is my solemn duty to warn you, sir, that there is architectural cause to conjecture that somewhere concealed in your chimney is a reserved space, hermetically closed, in short, a secret chamber or, rather, closet. How long it has been there, it is for me impossible to say. What it contains is hid, with itself, in darkness. But probably a secret closet would not have been contrived except for some extraordinary object, whether for the concealment of treasure, or what other purpose, may be left to those better acquainted with the history of the house to guess.

But enough: in making this disclosure, sir, my conscience is eased. Whatever step you choose to take upon it is, of course, a matter of indifference to me; though, I confess, as respects the character of the closet, I cannot but share in a natural curiosity.

Trusting that you may be guided aright in determining whether it is Christian-like knowingly to reside in a house hidden in which is a secret closet,

I remain,

With much respect,

Yours very humbly,

HIRAM SCRIBE

My first thought upon reading this note was not of the alleged mystery of manner to which, at the outset, it alluded – for none such had I at all observed in the master-mason during his surveys – but of my late kinsman, Captain Julian Dacres, long a ship-master and merchant in the Indian trade, who, about thirty years ago, and at the ripe age of ninety, died a bachelor, and in this very house, which he had built. He was supposed to have retired into this country with a large fortune. But to the general surprise, after being at great cost in building himself this mansion, he settled down into a sedate, reserved and inexpensive old age, which by the neighbours was thought all the better for his heirs; but lo! upon opening the will, his property was found to consist but of the house and grounds, and some ten thousand dollars in stocks; but the place, being found heavily mortgaged, was in consequence sold. Gossip had its day, and left the grass quietly to creep over the captain's grave, where he still slumbers in a privacy as unmolested as if the billows of the Indian Ocean, instead of the billows of inland verdure, rolled over him. Still, I remembered, long ago hearing strange solutions whispered by the country people for the mystery involving his will, and, by reflex, himself; and that, too, as well in conscience as purse. But people who could circulate the report (which they did) that Captain Julian Dacres had, in his day, been a Borneo pirate, surely were not worthy of credence in their collateral notions. It is queer what wild whimsies of rumours will, like toadstools, spring up about any eccentric stranger who, settling down among a rustic population, keeps quietly to himself. With some, inoffensiveness would seem a prime cause of offence. But what chiefly had led me to scout at these rumours, particularly as referring to concealed treasure, was the circumstance that the stranger (the same who razeed the roof and the chimney) into whose hands the estate had passed on my kinsman's death, was of that sort of character that, had there been the least ground for those reports, he would speedily have tested them by tearing down and rummaging the walls.

Nevertheless, the note of Mr Scribe, so strangely recalling the memory of my kinsman, very naturally chimed in with what had been mysterious, or at least unexplained, about him; vague flashings of ingots united in my mind with vague gleamings of skulls. But the first cool thought soon dismissed such chimeras; and, with a calm smile, I turned towards my wife, who, meantime, had been sitting near by, impatient enough, I dare say, to know who could have taken it into his head to write me a letter.

'Well, old man,' said she, 'who is it from, and what is it about?'

'Read it, wife,' said I, handing it.

Read it she did, and then – such an explosion! I will not pretend to describe her emotions or repeat her expressions. Enough that my daughters were quickly called in to share the excitement. Although they had never before dreamed of such revelation as Mr Scribe's, yet upon the first suggestion they instinctively saw the extreme likelihood of it. In corroboration, they cited first my kinsman, and second my chimney; alleging that the profound mystery involving the former, and the equally profound masonry involving the latter, though both acknowledged facts, were alike preposterous on any other supposition than the secret closet.

But all this time I was quietly thinking to myself: Could it be hidden from me that my credulity in this instance would operate very favourably to a certain plan of theirs? How to get to the secret closet, or how to have any certainty about it at all, without making such fell work with the chimney as to render its set destruction superfluous? That my wife wished to get rid of the chimney, it needed no reflection to show; and that Mr Scribe, for all his pretended disinterestedness, was not opposed to pocketing five hundred dollars by the operation, seemed equally evident. That my wife had, in secret, laid heads together with Mr Scribe, I at present refrain from affirming. But when I consider her enmity against my chimney, and the steadiness with which at the last she is wont to carry out her schemes, if by hook or by crook she can, especially after having been once baffled, why, I scarcely knew at what step of hers to be surprised.

Of one thing only was I resolved, that I and my chimney should not budge.

In vain all protests. Next morning I went out into the road, where I had noticed a diabolical-looking old gander that, for its doughty exploits in the way of scratching into forbidden enclosures, had been rewarded by its master with a portentous, four-pronged, wooden decoration in the shape of a collar of the Order of the Garotte. This gander I cornered, and rummaging out its stiffest quill, plucked it, took it home and, making a stiff pen, inscribed the following stiff note:

> *Chimney Side, April 2nd*
>
> Mr Scribe: Sir – For your conjecture, we return you our joint thanks and compliments, and beg leave to assure you, that
>
> We shall remain,
> Very faithfully,
> The same,
>
> I and my Chimney

Of course, for this epistle we had to endure some pretty sharp raps. But having at last explicitly understood from me that Mr Scribe's note had not altered my mind one jot, my wife, to move me, among other things said that, if she remembered aright, there was a statute placing the keeping in private houses of secret closets on the same unlawful footing with the keeping of gunpowder. But it had no effect.

A few days after, my spouse changed her key.

It was nearly midnight, and all were in bed but ourselves, who sat up, one in each chimney-corner; she, needles in hand, indefatigably knitting a sock; I, pipe in mouth, indolently weaving my vapours.

It was one of the first of the chill nights in autumn. There was a fire on the hearth, burning low. The air without was torpid and heavy; the wood, by an oversight, of the sort called soggy.

'Do look at the chimney,' she began; 'can't you see that something must be in it?'

'Yes, wife. Truly there is smoke in the chimney, as in Mr Scribe's note.

'Smoke? Yes, indeed, and in my eyes, too. How you two wicked old sinners do smoke! – this wicked old chimney and you.'

'Wife,' said I, 'I and my chimney like to have a quiet smoke together, it is true, but we don't like to be called names.'

'Now, dear old man,' said she, softening down, and a little shifting the subject, 'when you think of that old kinsman of yours, you *know* there must be a secret closet in this chimney.'

'Secret ash-hole, wife, why don't you have it? Yes, I dare say there is a secret ash-hole in the chimney; for where do all the ashes go to that we drop down the queer hole yonder?'

'I know where they go to; I've been there almost as many times as the cat.'

'What devil, wife, prompted you to crawl into the ash-hole! Don't you know that St Dunstan's devil emerged from the ash-hole? You will get your death one of these days, exploring all about as you do. But supposing there be a secret closet, what then?'

'What, then? why what should be in a secret closet but – '

'Dry bones, wife,' broke in I with a puff, while the sociable old chimney broke in with another.

'There again! Oh, how this wretched old chimney smokes,' wiping her eyes with her handkerchief. 'I've no doubt the reason it smokes so is because that secret closet interferes with the flue. Do see, too, how the jambs here keep settling; and it's downhill all the way from the door to this hearth. This horrid old chimney will fall on our heads yet; depend upon it, old man.'

'Yes, wife, I do depend on it; yes, indeed, I place every dependence on my chimney. As for its settling, I like it. I, too, am settling, you know, in my gait. I and my chimney are settling together, and shall keep settling, too, till, as in a great feather-bed, we shall both have settled away clean out of sight. But this secret oven – I mean, secret closet of yours, wife; where exactly do you suppose that secret closet is?'

'That is for Mr Scribe to say.'

'But suppose he cannot say exactly; what, then?'

'Why, then he can prove, I am sure, that it must be somewhere or other in this horrid old chimney.'

'And if he can't prove that, what then?'

'Why, then, old man,' with a stately air, 'I shall say little more about it.'

'Agreed, wife,' returned I, knocking my pipe-bowl against the jamb, 'and now, tomorrow, I will a third time send for Mr Scribe. Wife, the sciatica takes me; be so good as to put this pipe on the mantel.'

'If you get the step-ladder for me, I will. This shocking old chimney, this abominable old-fashioned old chimney's mantels are so high I can't reach them.'

No opportunity, however trivial, was overlooked for a subordinate fling at the pile.

Here, by way of introduction, it should be mentioned that besides the fireplaces all round it, the chimney was, in the most haphazard way, excavated on each floor for certain curious out-of-the-way cupboards and closets, of all sorts and sizes, clinging here and there, like nests in the crotches of some old oak. On the second floor these closets were by far the most irregular and numerous. And yet this should hardly have been so, since the theory of the chimney was that it pyramidically diminished as it ascended. The abridgment of its square on the roof was obvious enough; and it was supposed that the reduction must be methodically graduated from bottom to top.

'Mr Scribe,' said I when, the next day, with an eager aspect, that individual again came, 'my object in sending for you this morning is not to arrange for the demolition of my chimney, nor to have any particular conversation about it, but simply to allow you every reasonable facility for verifying, if you can, the conjecture communicated in your note.'

Though in secret not a little crestfallen, it may be, by my phlegmatic reception, so different from what he had looked for, with much apparent alacrity he commenced the survey: throwing open the cupboards on the first floor, and peering into the closets on the second; measuring one within, and then comparing that measurement with the measurement without. Removing the fire-boards, he would gaze up the flues. But no sign of the hidden work yet.

Now, on the second floor the rooms were the most rambling conceivable. They, as it were, dovetailed into each other. They were of all shapes; not one mathematically square room among them all – a peculiarity which by the master-mason had not been unobserved. With a significant, not to say portentous expression, he took a circuit of the chimney, measuring the area of each room around it; then going downstairs, and out of doors, he measured the entire ground area; then compared the sum total of all the areas of all the rooms on the second floor with the ground area; then, returning to me in no small excitement, announced that there was a difference of no less than two hundred and odd square feet – room enough, in all conscience, for a secret closet.

'But, Mr Scribe,' said I, stroking my chin, 'have you allowed for the walls, both main and sectional? They take up some space, you know.'

'Ah, I had forgotten that,' tapping his forehead; 'but,' still ciphering on his paper, 'that will not make up the deficiency.'

'But, Mr Scribe, have you allowed for the recesses of so many fire-places on a floor, and for the fire-walls, and the flues; in short, Mr Scribe, have you allowed for the legitimate chimney itself – some one hundred and forty-four square feet or thereabouts, Mr Scribe?'

'How unaccountable. That slipped my mind, too.'

'Did it, indeed, Mr Scribe?'

He faltered a little, and burst forth with, 'But we must not allow one hundred and forty-four square feet for the legitimate chimney. My position is that within those undue limits the secret closet is contained.'

I eyed him in silence a moment; then spoke: 'Your survey is concluded, Mr Scribe; be so good now as to lay your finger upon the exact part of the chimney wall where you believe this secret closet to be; or would a witch hazel wand assist you, Mr Scribe?'

'No, sir, but a crow-bar would,' he, with temper, rejoined.

Here, now, thought I to myself, the cat leaps out of the bag. I looked at him with a calm glance, under which he seemed somewhat uneasy. More than ever now I suspected a plot. I remembered what my wife had said about abiding by the decision of Mr Scribe. In a bland way, I resolved to buy up the decision of Mr Scribe.

'Sir,' said I, 'really I am much obliged to you for this survey. It has quite set my mind at rest. And no doubt you, too, Mr Scribe, must feel much relieved. Sir,' I added, 'you have made three visits to the chimney. With a businessman, time is money. Here are fifty dollars, Mr Scribe. Nay, take it. You have earned it. Your opinion is worth it. And by the way,' as he modestly received the money, 'have you any objections to giving me a – a – little certificate – something, say, like a steamboat certificate, certifying that you, a competent surveyor, have surveyed my chimney and found no reason to believe any unsoundness; in short, any – any secret closet in it. Would you be so kind, Mr Scribe?'

'But, but, sir – ' stammered he with honest hesitation.

'Here, here are pen and paper,' said I, with entire assurance. Enough.

That evening I had the certificate framed and hung over the dining-room fireplace, trusting that the continual sight of it would forever put at rest at once the dreams and stratagems of my household.

But, no. Inveterately bent upon the extirpation of that noble old chimney, still to this day my wife goes about it, with my daughter Anna's geological hammer, tapping the wall all over, and then holding her ear against it, as I have seen the physicians of life insurance companies tap a man's chest, and then incline over for the echo. Sometimes of nights she almost frightens one, going about on this phantom errand, and still following the sepulchral response of the chimney, round and round, as if it were leading her to the threshold of the secret closet.

'How hollow it sounds,' she will hollowly cry. 'Yes, I declare,' with an emphatic tap, 'there is a secret closet here. Here, in this very spot. Hark! How hollow!'

'Pshaw! wife, of course it is hollow. Who ever heard of a solid chimney?'

But nothing avails. And my daughters take after, not me, but their mother.

Sometimes all three abandon the theory of the secret closet, and return to the genuine ground of attack – the unsightliness of so cumbrous a pile, with comments upon the great addition of room to be gained by its demolition, and the fine effect of the projected grand hall, and the convenience resulting from the collateral running in one direction and another of their various partitions. Not more ruthlessly did the Three Powers partition away poor Poland, than my wife and daughters would fain partition away my chimney.

But seeing that, despite all, I and my chimney still smoke our pipes, my wife reoccupies the ground of the secret closet, enlarging upon what wonders are there, and what a shame it is not to seek it out and explore it.

'Wife,' said I, upon one of these occasions, 'why speak more of that secret closet, when there before you hangs contrary testimony of a master-mason, elected by yourself to decide. Besides, even if there were a secret closet, secret it should remain, and secret it shall. Yes, wife, here for once I must say my say. Infinite sad mischief has resulted from the profane bursting open of secret recesses. Though standing in the heart of this house, though hitherto we have all nestled about it, unsuspicious of aught hidden within, this chimney may or may not have a secret closet. But if it have, it is my kinsman's. To break into that wall would be to break into his breast. And that wall-breaking wish of Momus I account the wish of a church-robbing gossip and knave. Yes, wife, a vile eaves-dropping varlet was Momus.'

'Moses? – Mumps? Stuff with your mumps and your Moses!'

The truth is, my wife, like all the rest of the world, cares not a fig for my philosophical jabber. In dearth of other philosophical companionship, I and my chimney have to smoke and philosophise together. And sitting up so late as we do at it, a mighty smoke it is that we two smoky old philosophers make.

But my spouse, who likes the smoke of my tobacco as little as she does that of the soot, carries on her war against both. I live in continual dread lest, like the golden bowl, the pipes of me and my chimney shall yet be broken. To stay that mad project of my wife's, naught answers. Or, rather, she herself is incessantly answering, incessantly besetting me with her terrible alacrity for improvement, which is a softer name for destruction. Scarce a day I do not find her with her tape-measure, measuring for her grand hall, while Anna holds a yardstick on one side, and Julia looks approvingly on from the other. Mysterious intimations appear in the nearest village paper, signed 'Claude', to the effect that a certain structure, standing on a certain hill, is a sad blemish to an otherwise lovely landscape. Anonymous letters arrive, threatening me with I know not what, unless I remove my chimney. Is it my wife, too, or who, that sets up the neighbours to badgering me on the same subject, and hinting to me that my chimney, like a huge elm, absorbs all moisture from my garden? At night, also, my wife will start as from sleep, professing to hear ghostly noises from the secret closet. Assailed on all sides, and in all ways, small peace have I and my chimney.

Were it not for the baggage, we would together pack up, and remove from the country.

What narrow escapes have been ours! Once I found in a drawer a whole portfolio of plans and estimates. Another time, upon return-ing after a day's absence, I discovered my wife standing before the chimney in earnest conversation with a person whom I at once recognised as a meddlesome architectural reformer, who, because he had no gift for putting up anything, was ever intent upon pulling down – in various parts of the country having prevailed upon half-witted old folks to destroy their old-fashioned houses, particularly the chimneys.

But worst of all was that time I unexpectedly returned at early morning from a visit to the city, and upon approaching the house, narrowly escaped three brickbats which fell, from high aloft, at my feet. Glancing up, what was my horror to see three savages, in blue-jean overalls, in the very act of commencing the long-threatened attack. Aye, indeed, thinking of those three brickbats, I and my chimney have had narrow escapes.

It is now some seven years since I have stirred from home. My city friends all wonder why I don't come to see them, as in former times. They think I am getting sour and unsocial. Some say that I have become a sort of mossy old misanthrope, while all the time, the fact is, I am simply standing guard over my mossy old chimney; for it is resolved between me and my chimney that I and my chimney will never surrender.

THE APPLE-TREE TABLE
or Original Spiritual Manifestations

WHEN I FIRST SAW THE TABLE, dingy and dusty, in the furthest corner of the old hopper-shaped garret, and set out with broken, be-crusted old purple vials and flasks, and a ghostly, dismantled old quarto, it seemed just such a necromantic little old table as might have belonged to Friar Bacon. Two plain features it had, significant of conjurations and charms – the circle and tripod – the slab being round, supported by a twisted little pillar, which, about a foot from the bottom, sprawled out into three crooked legs, terminating in three cloven feet. A very satanic-looking little old table, indeed.

In order to convey a better idea of it, some account may as well be given of the place it came from. A very old garret of a very old house in an old-fashioned quarter of one of the oldest towns in America. This garret had been closed for years. It was thought to be haunted – a rumour, I confess, which, however absurd (in my opinion), I did not, at the time of purchasing, very vehemently contradict; since, not improbably, it tended to place the property the more conveniently within my means.

It was, therefore, from no dread of the reputed goblins aloft that, for five years after first taking up my residence in the house, I never entered the garret. There was no special inducement The roof was well slated, and thoroughly tight. The company that insured the house waived all visitation of the garret; why, then, should the owner be over-anxious about it? – particularly as he had no use for it, the house having ample room below. Then the key of the stair-door leading to it was lost. The lock was a huge, old-fashioned one. To open it, a smith would have to be called; an unnecessary trouble, I thought. Besides, though I had taken some care to keep my two daughters in ignorance of the rumour above-mentioned, still they had, by some means, got an inkling of it, and were well enough pleased to see the entrance to the haunted ground closed. It might have remained so for a still longer time, had it not been for my accidentally discovering, in a corner of our old, glen-like, terraced garden, a large and curious key, very old and rusty, which I at once concluded must belong to the garret-door – a supposition which, upon trial, proved correct. Now, the possession of a key to anything at once provokes a desire to unlock and explore; and this, too, from a mere instinct of gratification, irrespective of any particular benefit to accrue.

Behold me, then, turning the rusty old key, and going up, alone, into the haunted garret.

It embraced the entire area of the mansion. Its ceiling was formed by the roof, showing the rafters and boards on which the slates were laid. The roof shedding the water four ways from a high point in the centre, the space beneath was much like that of a general's marquee – only midway broken by a labyrinth of timbers, for braces, from which waved innumerable cobwebs that, of a summer's noon, shone like Baghdad tissues and gauzes. On every hand, some strange insect was seen, flying or running or creeping on rafter and floor.

Under the apex of the roof was a rude, narrow, decrepit step-ladder, something like a Gothic pulpit-stairway, leading to a pulpit-like platform, from which a still narrower ladder – a sort of Jacob's ladder – led some ways higher to the lofty scuttle. The slide of this scuttle was about two feet square, all in one piece, furnishing a massive frame for a single small pane of glass, inserted into it like a bull's-eye. The light of the garret came from this sole source, filtrated through a dense curtain of cobwebs. Indeed, the whole stairs, and platform, and ladder, were festooned, and carpeted, and canopied with cobwebs; which, in funereal accumulations hung, too, from the groined, murky ceiling, like the Carolina moss in the cypress forest. In these cobwebs swung, as in aerial catacombs, myriads of all tribes of mummied insects.

Climbing the stairs to the platform, and pausing there to recover my breath, a curious scene was presented. The sun was about half-way up. Piercing the little skylight, it slopingly bored a rainbowed tunnel clear across the darkness of the garret. Here, millions of butterfly moles were swarming. Against the skylight itself, with a cymbal-like buzzing, thousands of insects clustered in a golden mob.

Wishing to shed a clearer light through the place, I sought to withdraw the scuttle-slide. But no sign of latch or hasp was visible. Only after long peering, did I discover a little padlock, embedded, like an oyster at the bottom of the sea, amid matted masses of weedy webs, chrysalides and insectivorous eggs. Brushing these away, I found it locked. With a crooked nail, I tried to pick the lock, when scores of small ants and flies, half-torpid, crawled forth from the key-hole and, feeling the warmth of the sun in the pane, began frisking around me. Others appeared. Presently, I was overrun by them. As if incensed at this invasion of their retreat, countless bands darted up from below, beating about my head like hornets. At last, with a sudden jerk, I burst open the scuttle. And ah! what a change. As from the gloom of the grave and the companionship of worms, man shall at last rapturously rise into the living greenness and glory immortal, so, from my cobwebbed old garret, I thrust forth my head into the balmy air, and found myself hailed by the verdant tops of great trees, growing in the little garden below – trees whose leaves soared high above my topmost slate.

Refreshed by this outlook, I turned inward to behold the garret, now unwontedly lit up. Such humped masses of obsolete furniture. An old escritoire, from whose pigeonholes sprang mice, and from whose secret drawers came subterranean squeakings, as from chipmunks' holes in the woods; and broken-down old chairs, with strange carvings which seemed fit to seat a conclave of conjurors. And a rusty, iron-bound chest, lidless, and packed full of mildewed old documents; one of which, with a faded red inkblot at the end, looked as if it might have been the original bond that Doctor Faust gave to Mephistopheles. And, finally, in the least lighted corner of all, where was a profuse litter of indescribable old rubbish – among which was a broken telescope, and a celestial globe staved in – stood the little old table, one hoofed foot, like that of the Evil One, dimly revealed through the cobwebs. What a thick dust, half paste, had settled upon the old vials and flasks; how their once liquid contents had caked, and how strangely looked the mouldy old book in the middle – Cotton Mather's *Magnalia*.

Table and book I removed below, and had the dislocations of the one and the tatters of the other repaired. I resolved to surround this sad little hermit of a table, so long banished from genial neighbourhood, with all the kindly influences of warm urns, warm fires and warm hearts; little dreaming what all this warm nursing would hatch.

I was pleased by the discovery that the table was not of the ordinary mahogany, but of apple-tree wood, which age had darkened nearly to walnut. It struck me as being quite an appropriate piece of furniture for our cedar-parlour – so called, from its being, after the old fashion, wainscoted with that wood. The table's round slab, or *orb*, was so contrived as to be readily changed from a horizontal to a perpendicular position, so that, when not in use, it could be placed snugly in a corner. For myself, wife and two daughters, I thought it would make a nice little breakfast and tea-table. It was just the thing for a whist table, too. And I also pleased myself with the idea that it would make a famous reading-table.

In these fancies, my wife, for one, took little interest. She disrelished the idea of so unfashionable and indigent-looking a stranger as the table intruding into the polished society of more prosperous furniture. But when, after seeking its fortune at the cabinet-maker's, the table came home, varnished over, bright as a guinea, no one exceeded my wife in a gracious reception of it. It was advanced to an honourable position in the cedar-parlour.

But, as for my daughter Julia, she never got over her strange emotions upon first accidentally encountering the table. Unfortunately, it was just as I was in the act of bringing it down from the garret. Holding it by the slab, I was carrying it before me, one cob-webbed hoof thrust out, which weird object, at a turn of the stairs, suddenly touched my girl as she was ascending; whereupon, turning, and seeing no living creature – for I was quite hidden behind my shield – seeing nothing, indeed, but the apparition of the Evil One's foot, as it seemed, she cried out, and there is no knowing what might have followed, had I not immediately spoken.

From the impression thus produced, my poor girl, of a very nervous temperament, was long recovering. Superstitiously grieved at my violating the forbidden solitude above, she associated in her mind the cloven-footed table with the reputed goblins there. She besought me to give up the idea of domesticating the table. Nor did her sister fail to add her entreaties. Between my girls there was a constitutional sympathy. But my matter-of-fact wife had now de-clared in the table's favour. She was not wanting in firmness and energy. To her, the prejudices of Julia and Anna were simply ridiculous. It was her maternal duty, she thought, to drive such weakness away. By degrees, the girls, at breakfast and tea, were induced to sit down with us at the table. Continual proximity was not without effect. By and by, they would sit pretty tranquilly, though Julia, as much as possible, avoided glancing at the hoofed feet, and, when at this I smiled, she would look at me seriously – as much as to say, Ah, papa, you, too, may yet do the same. She prophesied that, in connection with the table, something strange would yet happen. But I would only smile the more, while my wife indignantly chided.

Meantime, I took particular satisfaction in my table as a night reading-table. At a ladies' fair, I bought me a beautifully worked reading-cushion, and, with elbow leaning thereon, and hand shad-ing my eyes from the light, spent many a long hour – nobody by, but the queer old book I had brought down from the garret.

All went well, till the incident now about to be given – an incident, be it remembered, which, like every other in this narration, happened long before the time of the 'Fox Girls'.

It was late on a Saturday night in December. In the little old cedar-parlour, before the little old apple-tree table, I was sitting up, as usual, alone. I had made more than one effort to get up and go to bed; but I could not. I was, in fact, under a sort of fascination. Somehow, too, certain reasonable opinions of mine seemed not so reasonable as before. I felt nervous. The truth was that, though, in my previous night-readings, Cotton Mather had but amused me, upon this particular night he terrified me. A thousand times I had laughed at such stories. Old wives' fables, I thought, however entertaining. But now, how different. They began to put on the aspect of reality. Now, for the first time it struck me that this was no romantic Mrs Radcliffe who had written the *Magnalia*, but a practical, hardworking, earnest, upright man, a learned doctor, too, as well as a good Christian and orthodox clergyman. What possible motive could such a man have to deceive? His style had all the plainness and unpoetic boldness of truth. In the most straight-forward way, he laid before me detailed accounts of New England witchcraft, each important item corroborated by respectable townsfolk, and of which not a few of the most surprising he himself had been eyewitness. Cotton Mather testified whereof he had seen. But, is it possible, I asked myself. Then I remembered that Dr Johnson, the matter-of-fact compiler of a dictionary, had been a believer in ghosts, besides many other sound, worthy men. Yielding to the fascination, I read deeper and deeper into the night. At last, I found myself starting at the least chance sound, and yet wishing that it were not so very still.

A tumbler of warm punch stood by my side, with which beverage, in a moderate way, I was accustomed to treat myself every Saturday night; a habit, however, against which my good wife had long remonstrated; predicting that, unless I gave it up, I would yet die a miserable sot. Indeed, I may here mention that, on the Sunday mornings following my Saturday nights, I had to be exceedingly cautious how I gave way to the slightest impatience at any acciden-tal annoyance, because such impatience was sure to be quoted against me as evidence of the melancholy consequence of over-night indulgence. As for my wife, she, never sipping punch, could yield to any little passing peevishness as much as she pleased.

But, upon the night in question, I found myself wishing that, instead of my usual mild mixture, I had concocted some potent draught. I felt the need of stimulus. I wanted something to hearten me against Cotton Mather – doleful, ghostly, ghastly Cotton Mather. I grew more and more nervous. Nothing but fascination kept me from fleeing the room. The candles burnt low, with long snuffs and huge winding-sheets. But I durst not raise the snuffers to them. It would make too much noise. And yet, previously, I had been wishing for noise. I read on and on. My hair began to have a sensation. My eyes felt strained; they pained me. I was conscious of it. I knew I was injuring them. I knew I should rue this abuse of them next day; but I read on and on. I could not help it. The skinny hand was on me.

All at once – Hark!

My hair felt like growing grass.

A faint sort of inward rapping or rasping – a strange, inexplicable sound, mixed with a slight kind of woodpecking or ticking.

Tick! Tick!

Yes, it was a faint sort of ticking.

I looked up at my great Strasbourg clock in one corner. It was not that. The clock had stopped.

Tick! Tick!

Was it my watch?

According to her usual practice at night, my wife had, upon retiring, carried my watch off to our chamber to hang it up on its nail.

I listened with all my ears.

Tick! Tick!

Was it a death-tick in the wainscot?

With a tremulous step I went all round the room, holding my ear to the wainscot.

No; it came not from the wainscot.

Tick! Tick!

I shook myself. I was ashamed of my fright.

Tick! Tick!

It grew in precision and audibleness. I retreated from the wainscot. It seemed advancing to meet me.

I looked round and round, but saw nothing, only one cloven foot of the little apple-tree table.

Bless me, said I to myself, with a sudden revulsion, it must be very late; ain't that my wife calling me? Yes, yes; I must to bed. I suppose all is locked up. No need to go the rounds.

The fascination had departed, though the fear had increased. With trembling hands, putting Cotton Mather out of sight, I soon found myself, candlestick in hand, in my chamber, with a peculiar rearward feeling, such as some truant dog may feel. In my eagerness to get well into the chamber, I stumbled against a chair.

'Do try and make less noise, my dear,' said my wife from the bed. 'You have been taking too much of that punch, I fear. That sad habit grows on you. Ah, that I should ever see you thus staggering at night into your chamber.'

'Wife, wife,' hoarsely whispered I, 'there is – is something tick – ticking in the cedar-parlour.'

'Poor old man – quite out of his mind – I knew it would be so. Come to bed; come and sleep it off.'

'Wife, wife!'

'Do, do come to bed. I forgive you. I won't remind you of it tomorrow. But you must give up the punch-drinking, my dear. It quite gets the better of you.'

'Don't exasperate me,' I cried, now truly beside myself; 'I will quit the house!'

'No, no! not in that state. Come to bed, my dear. I won't say another word.'

The next morning, upon waking, my wife said nothing about the past night's affair, and, feeling no little embarrassment myself, especially at having been thrown into such a panic, I also was silent. Consequently, my wife must still have ascribed my singular conduct to a mind disordered, not by ghosts, but by punch. For my own part as I lay in bed watching the sun in the panes, I began to think that much midnight reading of Cotton Mather was not good for man; that it had a morbid influence upon the nerves, and gave rise to hallucinations. I resolved to put Cotton Mather permanently aside. That done, I had no fear of any return of the ticking. Indeed, I began to think that what seemed the ticking in the room, was nothing but a sort of buzzing in my ear.

As is her wont, my wife having preceded me in rising, I made a deliberate and agreeable toilet. Aware that most disorders of the mind have their origin in the state of the body, I made vigorous use of the flesh-brush, and bathed my head with New England rum, a specific once recommended to me as good for buzzing in the ear. Wrapped in my dressing-gown, with cravat nicely adjusted and fingernails neatly trimmed, I complacently descended to the little cedar-parlour to breakfast.

What was my amazement to find my wife on her knees, rummaging about the carpet nigh the little apple-tree table, on which the morning meal was laid, while my daughters, Julia and Anna, were running about the apartment distracted.

'Oh, papa, papa!' cried Julia, hurrying up to me, 'I knew it would be so. The table, the table!'

'Spirits! spirits!' cried Anna, standing far away from it, with pointed finger.

'Silence!' cried my wife. 'How can I hear it, if you make such a noise? Be still. Come here, husband, was this the ticking you spoke of? Why don't you move? Was this it? Here, kneel down and listen to it. Tick, tick, tick! – don't you hear it now?'

'I do, I do,' cried I, while my daughters besought us both to come away from the spot.

Tick, tick, tick!

Right from under the snowy cloth, and the cheerful urn, and the smoking milk-toast, the unaccountable ticking was heard.

'Ain't there a fire in the next room, Julia?' said I. 'Let us breakfast there, my dear,' turning to my wife – 'let us go – leave the table – tell Biddy to remove the things.'

And so saying, I was moving towards the door in high self-possession, when my wife interrupted me.

'Before I quit this room, I will see into this ticking,' she said with energy. 'It is something that can be found out, depend upon it. I don't believe in spirits, especially at breakfast-time. Biddy! Biddy! Here, carry these things back to the kitchen,' handing the urn. Then, sweeping off the cloth, the little table lay bare to the eye.

'It's the table, the table!' cried Julia.

'Nonsense,' said my wife. 'Who ever heard of a ticking table? It's on the floor. Biddy! Julia! Anna! move everything out of the room – table and all. Where are the tack-hammers?'

'Heavens, mamma – you are not going to take up the carpet?' screamed Julia.

'Here's the hammers, marm,' said Biddy, advancing tremblingly.

'Hand them to me, then,' cried my wife; for poor Biddy was, at long gun-distance, holding them out as if her mistress had the plague.

'Now, husband, do you take up that side of the carpet, and I will this.' Down on her knees she then dropped, while I followed suit.

The carpet being removed, and the ear applied to the naked floor, not the slightest ticking could be heard.

'The table – after all, it is the table,' cried my wife. 'Biddy, bring it back.'

'Oh no, marm, not I, please, marm,' sobbed Biddy.

'Foolish creature! – Husband, do you bring it.'

'My dear,' said I, 'we have plenty of other tables; why be so particular?'

'Where is that table?' cried my wife, contemptuously, regardless of my gentle remonstrance.

'In the wood-house, marm. I put it away as far as ever I could, marm,' sobbed Biddy.

'Shall I go to the wood-house for it, or will you?' said my wife, addressing me in a frightful, businesslike manner.

Immediately I darted out of the door, and found the little apple-tree table, upside down, in one of my chip-bins. I hurriedly returned with it, and once more my wife examined it attentively. Tick, tick, tick! Yes, it was the table.

'Please, marm,' said Biddy, now entering the room, with hat and shawl – 'please, marm, will you pay me my wages?'

'Take your hat and shawl off directly,' said my wife; 'set this table again.'

'Set it,' roared I, in a passion, 'set it, or I'll go for the police.'

'Heavens! heavens!' cried my daughters, in one breath. 'What will become of us! – Spirits! Spirits!'

'Will you set the table?' cried I, advancing upon Biddy.

'I will, I will – yes, marm – yes, master – I will, I will. Spirits! – Holy Vargin!'

'Now, husband,' said my wife, 'I am convinced that, whatever it is that causes this ticking, neither the ticking nor the table can hurt us, for we are all good Christians, I hope. I am determined to find out the cause of it, too, which time and patience will bring to light. I shall breakfast on no other table but this, so long as we live in this house. So, sit down, now that all things are ready again, and let us quietly breakfast. My dears,' turning to Julia and Anna, 'go to your room, and return composed. Let me have no more of this childishness.'

Upon occasion my wife was mistress in her house.

During the meal, in vain was conversation started again and again; in vain my wife said something brisk to infuse into others an animation akin to her own. Julia and Anna, with heads bowed over their tea-cups, were still listening for the tick. I confess, too, that their example was catching. But, for the time, nothing was heard. Either the ticking had died quite away, or else, slight as it was, the increasing uproar of the street, with the general hum of day, so contrasted with the repose of night and early morning, smothered the sound. At the lurking inquietude of her companions, my wife was indignant; the more so, as she seemed to glory in her own exemption from panic. When breakfast was cleared away she took my watch and, placing it on the table, addressed the supposed spirits in it, with a jocosely defiant air: 'There, tick away, let us see who can tick loudest!'

All that day, while abroad, I thought of the mysterious table.

Could Cotton Mather speak true? Were there spirits? And would spirits haunt a tea-table? Would the Evil One dare show his cloven hoof in the bosom of an innocent family? I shuddered when I thought that I myself, against the solemn warnings of my daughters, had wilfully introduced the cloven hoof there. Yea, three cloven feet. But, towards noon, this sort of feeling began to wear off. The continual rubbing against so many practical people in the street brushed such chimeras away from me. I remembered that I had not acquitted myself very intrepidly either on the previous night or in the morning. I resolved to regain the good opinion of my wife.

To evince my hardihood the more signally, when tea was dismissed, and the three rubbers of whist had been played, and no ticking had been heard – which the more encouraged me – I took my pipe and, saying that bedtime had arrived for the rest, drew my chair towards the fire, and, removing my slippers, placed my feet on the fender, looking as calm and composed as old Democritus in the tombs of Abdera, when one midnight the mischievous little boys of the town tried to frighten that sturdy philosopher with spurious ghosts.

And I thought to myself, that the worthy old gentleman had set a good example to all times in his conduct on that occasion. For, when at the dead hour, intent on his studies, he heard the strange sounds, he did not so much as move his eyes from his page, only simply said: 'Boys, little boys, go home. This is no place for you. You will catch cold here.' The philosophy of which words lies here: that they imply the foregone conclusion, that any possible investigation of any possible spiritual phenomena was absurd; that upon the first face of such things, the mind of a sane man instinctively affirmed them a humbug, unworthy the least attention; more especially if such phenomena appear in tombs, since tombs are peculiarly the place of silence, lifelessness and solitude; for which cause, by the way, the old man, as upon the occasion in question, made the tombs of Abdera his place of study.

Presently I was alone, and all was hushed. I laid down my pipe, not feeling exactly tranquil enough now thoroughly to enjoy it. Taking up one of the newspapers, I began, in a nervous, hurried sort of way, to read by the light of a candle placed on a small stand drawn close to the fire. As for the apple-tree table, having lately concluded that it was rather too low for a reading-table, I thought best not to use it as such that night. But it stood not very distant in the middle of the room.

Try as I would, I could not succeed much at reading. Somehow I seemed all ear and no eye; a condition of intense auricular suspense. But ere long it was broken.

Tick, tick, tick!

Though it was not the first time I had heard that sound, nay, though I had made it my particular business on this occasion to wait for that sound, nevertheless, when it came, it seemed unexpected, as if a cannon had boomed through the window.

Tick! tick! tick!

I sat stock-still for a time, thoroughly to master, if possible, my first discomposure. Then rising, I looked pretty steadily at the table; went up to it pretty steadily; took hold of it pretty steadily; but let it go pretty quickly; then paced up and down, stopping every moment or two, with ear pricked to listen. Meantime, within me, the contest between panic and philosophy remained not wholly decided.

Tick! tick! tick!

With appalling distinctness the ticking now rose on the night.

My pulse fluttered – my heart beat. I hardly know what might not have followed, had not Democritus just then come to the rescue. For shame, said I to myself, what is the use of so fine an example of philosophy, if it cannot be followed? Straightway I resolved to imitate it, even to the old sage's occupation and attitude.

Resuming my chair and paper, with back presented to the table, I remained thus for a time, as if buried in study; when, the ticking still continuing, I drawled out, in as indifferent and dryly jocose a way as I could: 'Come, come, Tick, my boy, fun enough for tonight.'

Tick! tick! tick!

There seemed a sort of jeering defiance in the ticking now. It seemed to exult over the poor affected part I was playing. But much as the taunt stung me, it only stung me into persistence. I resolved not to abate one whit in my mode of address.

'Come, come, you make more and more noise, Tick, my boy; too much of a joke – time to have done.'

No sooner said than the ticking ceased. Never was responsive obedience more exact. For the life of me, I could not help turning round upon the table, as one would upon some reasonable being, when – could I believe my senses? I saw something moving, or wriggling, or squirming upon the slab of the table. It shone like a glowworm. Unconsciously, I grasped the poker that stood at hand. But bethinking me how absurd to attack a glowworm with a poker, I put it down. How long I sat spellbound and staring there, with my body presented one way and my face another, I cannot say; but at length I rose, and, buttoning my coat up and down, made a sudden intrepid forced march full upon the table. And there, near the centre of the slab, as I live, I saw an irregular little hole, or, rather, a short nibbled sort of crack, from which (like a butterfly escaping its chrysalis) the sparkling object, whatever it might be, was struggling. Its motion was the motion of life. I stood becharmed. Are there, indeed, spirits, thought I; and is this one? No; I must be dreaming. I turned my glance off to the red fire on the hearth, then back to the pale lustre on the table. What I saw was no optical illusion, but a real marvel. The tremor was increasing, when, once again, Democritus befriended me. Supernatural coruscation as it appeared, I strove to look at the strange object in a purely scientific way. Thus viewed, it appeared some new sort of small shining beetle or bug, and, I thought, not without something of a hum to it, too.

I still watched it, and with still increasing self-possession. Sparkling and wriggling, it still continued its throes. In another moment it was just on the point of escaping its prison. A thought struck me. Running for a tumbler, I clapped it over the insect just in time to secure it.

After watching it a while longer under the tumbler, I left all as it was, and, tolerably composed, retired.

Now, for the soul of me, I could not, at that time, comprehend the phenomenon. A live bug come out of a dead table? A firefly bug come out of a piece of ancient lumber, for one knows not how many years stored away in an old garret? Was ever such a thing heard of, or even dreamed of? How got the bug there? Never mind. I bethought me of Democritus, and resolved to keep cool. At all events, the mystery of the ticking was explained. It was simply the sound of the gnawing and filing and tapping of the bug, in eating its way out. It was satisfactory to think that there was an end forever to the ticking. I resolved not to let the occasion pass without reaping some credit from it.

'Wife,' said I, next morning, 'you will not be troubled with any more ticking in our table. I have put a stop to all that.'

'Indeed, husband,' said she, with some incredulity.

'Yes, wife,' returned I, perhaps a little vaingloriously. 'I have put a quietus upon that ticking. Depend upon it, the ticking will trouble you no more.'

In vain she besought me to explain myself. I would not gratify her; being willing to balance any previous trepidation I might have betrayed, by leaving room now for the imputation of some heroic feat whereby I had silenced the ticking. It was a sort of innocent deceit by implication, quite harmless, and, I thought, of utility.

But when I went to breakfast, I saw my wife kneeling at the table again, and my girls looking ten times more frightened than ever.

'Why did you tell me that boastful tale?' said my wife indignantly. 'You might have known how easily it would be found out. See this crack, too; and here is the ticking again, plainer than ever.'

'Impossible,' I exclaimed; but upon applying my ear sure enough, tick! tick! tick! The ticking was there.

Recovering myself the best way I might, I demanded the bug.

'Bug?' screamed Julia. 'Good heavens, papa!'

'I hope, sir, you have been bringing no bugs into this house,' said my wife, severely.

'The bug, the bug!' I cried; 'the bug under the tumbler.'

'Bugs in tumblers!' cried the girls; 'not our tumblers, papa? You have not been putting bugs into our tumblers? Oh, what does – what *does* it all mean?'

'Do you see this hole, this crack here?' said I, putting my finger on the spot.

'That I do,' said my wife, with high displeasure. 'And how did it come there? What have you been doing to the table?'

'Do you see this crack?' repeated I, intensely.

'Yes, yes,' said Julia; 'that was what frightened me so; it looks so like witch-work.'

'Spirits! spirits!' cried Anna.

'Silence!' said my wife. 'Go on, sir, and tell us what you know of the crack.'

'Wife and daughters,' said I, solemnly, 'out of that crack, or hole, while I was sitting all alone here last night, a wonderful – '

Here, involuntarily, I paused, fascinated by the expectant attitudes and bursting eyes of Julia and Anna.

'What, what?' cried Julia.

'A bug, Julia.'

'A bug?' cried my wife. 'A bug come out of this table? And what did you do with it?'

'Clapped it under a tumbler.'

'Biddy! Biddy!' cried my wife, going to the door. 'Did you see a tumbler here on this table when you swept the room?'

'Sure I did, marm, and a 'bomnable bug under it.'

'And what did you do with it?' demanded I.

'Put the bug in the fire, sir, and rinsed out the tumbler ever so many times, marm.'

'Where is that tumbler?' cried Anna. 'I hope you scratched it – marked it some way. I'll never drink out of that tumbler; never put it before me, Biddy. A bug – a bug! Oh, Julia! Oh, mamma! I feel it crawling all over me, even now. Haunted table!'

'Spirits! spirits!' cried Julia.

'My daughters,' said their mother, with authority in her eyes, 'go to your chamber till you can behave more like reasonable creatures. Is it a bug – a bug that can frighten you out of what little wits you ever had? Leave the room. I am astonished. I am pained by such childish conduct.'

'Now tell me,' said she, addressing me, as soon as they had withdrawn, 'now tell me truly, did a bug really come out of this crack in the table?'

'Wife, it is even so.'

'Did you see it come out?'

'I did.'

She looked earnestly at the crack, leaning over it.

'Are you sure?' said she, looking up, but still bent over.

'Sure, sure.'

She was silent. I began to think that the mystery of the thing began to tell even upon her. Yes, thought I, I shall presently see my wife shaking and shuddering, and, who knows, calling in some old dominie to exorcise the table, and drive out the spirits.

'I'll tell you what we'll do,' said she suddenly, and not without excitement.

'What, wife?' said I, all eagerness, expecting some mystical proposition; 'what, wife?'

'We will rub this table all over with that celebrated roach powder I've heard of.'

'Good gracious! Then you don't think it's spirits?'

'Spirits?'

The emphasis of scornful incredulity was worthy of Democritus himself.

'But this ticking – this ticking?' said I.

'I'll whip that out of it.'

'Come, come, wife,' said I, 'you are going too far the other way, now. Neither roach powder nor whipping will cure this table. It's a queer table, wife; there's no blinking it.'

'I'll have it rubbed, though,' she replied, 'well rubbed;' and calling Biddy, she bade her get wax and brush, and give the table a vigorous manipulation. That done, the cloth was again laid, and we sat down to our morning meal; but my daughters did not make their appearance. Julia and Anna took no breakfast that day.

When the cloth was removed, in a businesslike way my wife went to work with a dark-coloured cement and hermetically closed the little hole in the table.

My daughters looking pale, I insisted upon taking them out for a walk that morning, when the following conversation ensued.

'My worst presentiments about that table are being verified, papa,' said Julia; 'not for nothing was that intimation of the cloven foot on my shoulder.'

'Nonsense,' said I. 'Let us go into Mrs Brown's, and have an ice-cream.'

The spirit of Democritus was stronger on me now. By a curious coincidence, it strengthened with the strength of the sunlight.

'But is it not miraculous,' said Anna, 'how a bug should come out of a table?'

'Not at all, my daughter. It is a very common thing for bugs to come out of wood. You yourself must have seen them coming out of the ends of the billets on the hearth.'

'Ah, but that wood is almost fresh from the woodland. But the table is at least a hundred years old.'

'What of that?' said I, gaily. 'Have not live toads been found in the hearts of dead rocks, as old as creation?'

'Say what you will, papa, I feel it is spirits,' said Julia. 'Do, do now, my dear papa, have that haunted table removed from the house.'

'Nonsense,' said I.

By another curious coincidence, the more they felt frightened, the more I felt brave.

Evening came.

'This ticking,' said my wife; 'do you think that another bug will come of this continued ticking?'

Curiously enough, that had not occurred to me before. I had not thought of there being twins of bugs. But now, who knew – there might be even triplets.

I resolved to take precautions and, if there was to be a second bug, infallibly secure it. During the evening, the ticking was again heard. About ten o'clock I clapped a tumbler over the spot, as near as I could judge of it by my ear. Then we all retired, and locking the door of the cedar-parlour, I put the key in my pocket.

In the morning, nothing was to be seen, but the ticking was heard. The trepidation of my daughters returned. They wanted to call in the neighbours. But to this my wife was vigorously opposed. We should be the laughing-stock of the whole town. So it was agreed that nothing should be disclosed. Biddy received strict charges; and, to make sure, was not allowed that week to go to confession, lest she should tell the priest.

I stayed home all that day, every hour or two bending over the table, both eye and ear. Towards night, I thought the ticking grew more distinct, and seemed divided from my ear by a thinner and thinner partition of the wood. I thought, too, that I perceived a faint heaving up, or bulging of the wood, in the place where I had placed the tumbler. To put an end to the suspense, my wife proposed taking a knife and cutting into the wood there; but I had a less impatient plan; namely, that she and I should sit up with the table that night, as, from present symptoms the bug would probably make its appearance before morning. For myself, I was curious to see the first advent of the thing – the first dazzle of the chick as it chipped the shell.

The idea struck my wife not unfavourably. She insisted that both Julia and Anna should be of the party, in order that the evidence of their senses should disabuse their minds of all nursery nonsense. For that spirits should tick, and that spirits should take unto themselves the form of bugs, was, to my wife, the most foolish of all foolish imaginations. True, she could not account for the thing; but she had all confidence that it could be, and would yet be, somehow explained, and that to her entire satisfaction. Without knowing it herself, my wife was a female Democritus. For my own part, my present feelings were of a mixed sort. In a strange and not unpleasing way, I gently oscillated between Democritus and Cotton Mather. But to my wife and daughters I assumed to be pure Democritus – a jeerer at all tea-table spirits whatever.

So, laying in a good supply of candles and crackers, all four of us sat up with the table, and at the same time sat round it. For a while my wife and I carried on an animated conversation. But my daughters were silent. Then my wife and I would have had a rubber of whist, but my daughters could not be prevailed upon to join. So we played whist with two dummies, literally; my wife won the rubber, and, fatigued with victory, put away the cards.

Half-past eleven o'clock. No sign of the bug. The candles began to burn dim. My wife was just in the act of snuffing them when a sudden, violent, hollow, resounding, rumbling thumping was heard.

Julia and Anna sprang to their feet.

'All well!' cried a voice from the street. It was the watchman, first ringing down his club on the pavement, and then following it up with this highly satisfactory verbal announcement.

'All well! Do you hear that, my girls?' said I, gaily.

Indeed it was astonishing how brave as Bruce I felt in company with three women, and two of them half frightened out of their wits.

I rose for my pipe, and took a philosophic smoke.

Democritus forever, thought I.

In profound silence, I sat smoking, when lo! – pop! pop! pop! – right under the table, a terrible popping.

This time we all four sprang up, and my pipe was broken.

'Good heavens! what's that?'

'Spirits! spirits!' cried Julia.

'Oh, oh, oh!' cried Anna.

'Shame,' said my wife, 'it's that new bottled cider, in the cellar, going off. I told Biddy to wire the bottles today.'

I shall here transcribe from memoranda kept during part of the night:

> One o'clock. No sign of the bug. Ticking continues. Wife getting sleepy.
>
> Two o'clock. No sign of the bug. Ticking intermittent. Wife fast asleep.
>
> Three o'clock. No sign of the bug. Ticking pretty steady. Julia and Anna getting sleepy.
>
> Four o'clock. No sign of the bug. Ticking regular, but not spirited. Wife, Julia and Anna, all fast asleep in their chairs.
>
> Five o'clock. No sign of the bug. Ticking faint. Myself feeling drowsy. The rest still asleep.

So far the journal.

– Rap! rap! rap!

A terrific, portentous rapping against a door.

Startled from our dreams, we started to our feet.

Rap! rap! rap!

Julia and Anna shrieked.

I cowered in the corner.

'You fools!' cried my wife, 'it's the baker with the bread.'

Six o'clock.

She went to throw back the shutters, but ere it was done, a cry came from Julia. There, half in and half out its crack, there wriggled the bug, flashing in the room's general dimness like a fiery opal.

Had this bug had a tiny sword by its side – a Damascus sword – and a tiny necklace round its neck – a diamond necklace – and a tiny gun in its claw – a brass gun – and a tiny manuscript in its mouth – a

Chaldee manuscript – Julia and Anna could not have stood more charmed.

In truth, it was a beautiful bug – a Jew jeweller's bug – a bug like a sparkle of a glorious sunset.

Julia and Anna had never dreamed of such a bug. To them, bug had been a word synonymous with hideousness. But this was a seraphical bug; or, rather, all it had of the bug was the B, for it was beautiful as a butterfly.

Julia and Anna gazed and gazed. They were no more alarmed. They were delighted.

'But how got this strange, pretty creature into the table?' cried Julia.

'Spirits can get anywhere,' replied Anna.

'Pshaw!' said my wife.

'Do you hear any more ticking?' said I.

They all applied their ears, but heard nothing.

'Well, then, wife and daughters, now that it is all over, this very morning I will go and make enquiries about it.'

'Oh, do, papa,' cried Julia, 'do go and consult Madame Pazzi, the conjuress.'

'Better go and consult Professor Johnson, the naturalist,' said my wife.

'Bravo, Mrs Democritus!' said I. 'Professor Johnson is the man.'

By good fortune I found the professor in. Informed briefly of the incident, he manifested a cool, collected sort of interest, and gravely accompanied me home. The table was produced, the two openings pointed out, the bug displayed, and the details of the affair set forth; my wife and daughters being present.

'And now, professor,' said I, 'what do you think of it?'

Putting on his spectacles, the learned professor looked hard at the table, and gently scraped with his penknife into the holes, but said nothing.

'Is it not an unusual thing, this?' anxiously asked Anna.

'Very unusual, miss.'

At which Julia and Anna exchanged significant glances.

'But is it not wonderful, very wonderful?' demanded Julia.

'Very wonderful, miss.'

My daughters exchanged still more significant glances, and Julia, emboldened, again spoke.

'And must you not admit, sir, that it is the work of – of – sp – ?'

'Spirits? No,' was the crusty rejoinder.

'My daughters,' said I, mildly, 'you should remember that this is not Madame Pazzi, the conjuress, you put your questions to, but the eminent naturalist, Professor Johnson. And now, professor,' I added, 'be pleased to explain. Enlighten our ignorance.'

Without repeating all that the learned gentleman said for, indeed, though lucid, he was a little prosy – let the following summary of his explication suffice.

The incident was not wholly without example. The wood of the table was apple-tree, a sort of tree much fancied by various insects. The bugs had come from eggs laid inside the bark of the living tree in the orchard. By careful examination of the position of the hole from which the last bug had emerged, in relation to the cortical layers of the slab, and then allowing for the inch and a half along the grain, ere the bug had eaten its way entirely out, and then computing the whole number of cortical layers in the slab, with a reasonable conjecture for the number cut off from the outside, it appeared that the egg must have been laid in the tree some ninety years, more or less, before the tree could have been felled. But between the felling of the tree and the present time, how long might that be? It was a very old-fashioned table. Allow eighty years for the age of the table, which would make one hundred and seventy years that the bug had lain in the egg. Such, at least, was Professor Johnson's computation.

'Now, Julia,' said I, 'after that scientific statement of the case (though, I confess, I don't exactly understand it), where are your spirits? It is very wonderful as it is, but where are your spirits?'

'Where, indeed?' said my wife.

'Why, now, she did not *really* associate this purely natural phenomenon with any crude spiritual hypothesis did she?' observed the learned professor, with a slight sneer.

'Say what you will,' said Julia, holding up, in the covered tumbler, the glorious, lustrous, flashing live opal, 'say what you will, if this beauteous creature be not a spirit, it yet teaches a spiritual lesson. For if, after one hundred and seventy years' entombment, a mere insect comes forth at last into light, itself an effulgence, shall there be no glorified resurrection for the spirit of man? Spirits! spirits!' she exclaimed, with rapture, 'I still believe in spirits, only now I believe in them with delight, when before I but thought of them with terror.'

The mysterious insect did not long enjoy its radiant life; it expired the next day. But my girls have preserved it. Embalmed in a silver vinaigrette, it lies on the little apple-tree table in the pier of the cedar-parlour.

And whatever lady doubts this story, my daughters will be happy to show her both the bug and the table, and point out to her, in the repaired slab of the latter, the two sealing-wax drops designating the exact place of the two holes made by the two bugs, something in the same way in which are marked the spots where the cannon balls struck Brattle Street Church.

THE PIAZZA

With fairest flowers,
Whilst summer lasts, and I live here, Fidele –

WHEN I REMOVED into the country it was to occupy an old-fashioned farmhouse, which had no piazza – a deficiency the more regretted, because not only did I like piazzas, as somehow combining the cosiness of indoors with the freedom of outdoors, and it is so pleasant to inspect your thermometer there, but the country round about was such a picture that in berry time no boy climbs hill or crosses vale without coming upon easels planted in every nook, and sunburnt painters painting there. A very paradise of painters. The circle of the stars cut by the circle of the mountains. At least, so looks it from the house; though, once upon the mountains, no circle of them can you see. Had the site been chosen five rods off, this charmed ring would not have been.

The house is old. Seventy years since, from the heart of the Hearth Stone Hills, they quarried the Kaaba, or Holy Stone, to which, each Thanksgiving, the social pilgrims used to come. So long ago, that, in digging for the foundation, the workmen used both spade and axe, fighting the troglodytes of those subterranean parts – sturdy roots of a sturdy wood, encamped upon what is now a long landslide of sleeping meadow, sloping away off from my poppy-bed. Of that knit wood, but one survivor stands – an elm, lonely through steadfastness.

Whoever built the house, he builded better than he knew; or else Orion in the zenith flashed down his Damocles' sword to him some starry night, and said, 'Build there.' For how, otherwise, could it have entered the builder's mind that, upon the clearing being made, such a purple prospect would be his? – nothing less than Greylock, with all his hills about him, like Charlemagne among his peers.

Now, for a house, so situated in such a country, to have no piazza for the convenience of those who might desire to feast upon the view, and take their time and ease about it, seemed as much of an omission as if a picture-gallery should have no bench; for what but picture-galleries are the marble halls of these same limestone hills? – galleries hung, month after month anew, with pictures ever fading into pictures ever fresh. And beauty is like piety – you cannot run and read it; tranquillity and constancy, with, nowadays, an easy chair, are needed. For though, of old, when reverence was in vogue, and indolence was not, the devotees of nature, doubtless, used to stand and adore – just as, in the cathedrals of those ages, the worshippers of a higher power did – yet, in these times of failing faith and feeble knees, we have the piazza and the pew.

During the first years of my residence, the more leisurely to witness the coronation of Charlemagne (weather permitting, they crown him every sunrise and sunset), I chose me, on the hillside bank near by, a royal lounge of turf – a green velvet lounge, with long, moss-padded back; while at the head, strangely enough, there grew (but, I suppose, for heraldry) three tufts of blue violets in a field-argent of wild strawberries; and a trellis, with honeysuckle, I set for canopy. Very majestical lounge, indeed. So much so, that here, as with the reclining majesty of Denmark in his orchard, a sly earache invaded me. But, if damps abound at times in Westminster Abbey, because it is so old, why not within this monastery of mountains, which is older?

A piazza must be had.

The house was wide – my fortune narrow; so that to build a panoramic piazza, one round and round, it could not be – although, indeed, considering the matter by rule and square, the carpenters, in the kindest way, were anxious to gratify my furthest wishes, at I've forgotten how much a foot.

Upon but one of the four sides would prudence grant me what I wanted. Now, which side?

To the east, that long camp of the Hearth Stone Hills, fading far away towards Quito; and every fall, a small white flake of something peering suddenly, of a coolish morning, from the topmost cliff – the season's new-dropped lamb, its earliest fleece; and then the Christmas dawn, draping those dun highlands with redbarred plaids and tartans – goodly sight from your piazza, that. Good sight; but, to the north is Charlemagne – can't have the Hearth Stone Hills with Charlemagne.

Well, the south side. Apple-trees are there. Pleasant, of a balmy morning, in the month of May, to sit and see that orchard, white-budded, as for a bridal; and, in October, one green arsenal yard: such piles of ruddy shot. Very fine, I grant; but, to the north is Charlemagne.

The west side, look. An upland pasture, alleying away into a maple wood at top. Sweet, in opening spring, to trace upon the hill-side, otherwise grey and bare – to trace, I say, the oldest paths by their streaks of earliest green. Sweet, indeed, I can't deny; but, to the north is Charlemagne.

So Charlemagne, he carried it. It was not long after 1848; and, somehow, about that time, all round the world, these kings, they had the casting vote, and voted for themselves.

No sooner was ground broken, than all the neighbourhood (neighbour Dives, in particular) broke, too – into a laugh. Piazza to the north! Winter piazza! Wants, of winter midnights, to watch the aurora borealis, I suppose; hope he's laid in good store of polar muffs and mittens.

That was in the lion month of March. Not forgotten are the blue noses of the carpenters, and how they scouted at the greenness of the cit, who would build his sole piazza to the north. But March don't last forever; patience, and August comes. And then, in the cool elysium of my northern bower, I, Lazarus in Abraham's bosom, cast down the hill a pitying glance on poor old Dives, tormented in the purgatory of his piazza to the south.

But, even in December, this northern piazza does not repel – nipping cold and gusty though it be, and the north wind, like any miller, bolting by the snow, in finest flour – for then, once more, with frosted beard, I pace the sleety deck, weathering Cape Horn.

In summer, too, Canute-like; sitting here, one is often reminded of the sea. For not only do long ground-swells roll the slanting grain, and little wavelets of the grass ripple over upon the low piazza, as their beach, and the blown down of dandelions is wafted like the spray, and the purple of the mountains is just the purple of the billows, and a still August noon broods upon the deep meadows, as a calm upon the Line; but the vastness and the lonesomeness are so oceanic, and the silence and the sameness, too, that the first peep of a strange house, rising beyond the trees, is for all the world like spying, on the Barbary coast, an unknown sail.

And this recalls my inland voyage to fairyland. A true voyage; but, take it all in all, interesting as if invented.

From the piazza, some uncertain object I had caught, mysteriously snugged away, to all appearance, in a sort of p... breast-pocket, high up in a hopper-like hollow, or s..., be- among the northwestern mountains – yet, wheth... a blue summit, a mountainside or a mountain-top could... as it were, talk to you over cause, though, viewed from favo... peering up away behind the...

their heads, and plainly tell you that, though he (the blue summit) seems among them, he is not of them (God forbid!), and, indeed, would have you know that he considers himself – as, to say truth, he has good right – by several cubits their superior, nevertheless, certain ranges, here and there double-filed, as in platoons, so shoulder and follow up upon one another, with their irregular shapes and heights, that, from the piazza, a nigher and lower mountain will, in most states of the atmosphere, effacingly shade itself away into a higher and further one; that an object, bleak on the former's crest, will, for all that, appear nested in the latter's flank. These mountains, somehow, they play at hide-and-seek, and all before one's eyes.

But, be that as it may, the spot in question was, at all events, so situated as to be only visible, and then but vaguely, under certain witching conditions of light and shadow.

Indeed, for a year or more, I knew not there was such a spot, and might, perhaps, have never known, had it not been for a wizard afternoon in autumn – late in autumn – a mad poet's afternoon; when the turned maple woods in the broad basin below me, having lost their first vermilion tint, dully smoked, like smouldering towns, when flames expire upon their prey; and rumour had it, that this smokiness in the general air was not all Indian summer – which was not used to be so sick a thing, however mild – but, in great part, was blown from far-off forests, for weeks on fire, in Vermont; so that no wonder the sky was ominous as Hecate's cauldron – and two sportsmen, crossing a red stubble buckwheat field, seemed guilty Macbeth and foreboding Banquo; and the hermit-sun, hutted in an Adullam cave, well towards the south, according to his season, did little else but, by indirect reflection of narrow rays shot down a Simplon Pass among the clouds, just steadily paint one small, round, strawberry mole upon the wan cheek of northwestern hills. Signal as a candle. One spot of radiance, where all else was shade.

Fairies there, thought I; some haunted ring where fairies dance.

Time passed; and the following May, after a gentle shower upon the mountains – a little shower islanded in misty seas of sunshine; such a distant shower – and sometimes two, and three, and four of them, all visible together in different parts – as I love to watch from the piazza, instead of thunderstorms, as I used to, which wrap old marked the like a Sinai, till one thinks swart Moses must be climbing the hemlocks there; after, I say, that gentle shower, I further end just where, in autumn, I had thought I; remembering that rainbows bring out the blooms, and that if one can but get to the rainbow's end, one's fortune is made in a bag of gold. Yon rainbow's end, would I were there, thought I. And none the less I wished it, for now first noticing what seemed some sort of glen, or grotto, in the mountainside; at least, whatever it was, viewed through the rainbow's medium, it glowed like the Potosi mine. But a work-a-day neighbour said no doubt it was but some old barn – an abandoned one, its broadside beaten in, the acclivity its background. But I, though I had never been there, I knew better.

A few days after, a cheery sunrise kindled a golden sparkle in the same spot as before. The sparkle was of that vividness, it seemed as if it could only come from glass. The building, then – if building, after all, it was – could, at least, not be a barn, much less an abandoned one; stale hay ten years musting in it. No; if aught built by mortal, it must be a cottage; perhaps long vacant and dismantled, but this very spring magically fitted up and glazed.

Again, one noon, in the same direction, I marked, over dimmed tops of terraced foliage, a broader gleam, as of a silver buckler, held sunwards over some croucher's head; which gleam, experience in like cases taught, must come from a roof newly shingled. This, to me, made pretty sure the recent occupancy of that far cot in fairyland.

Day after day, now, full of interest in my discovery, what time I could spare from reading the *Midsummer Night's Dream*, and all about Titania, wishfully I gazed off towards the hills: but in vain. Either troops of shadows, an imperial guard, with slow pace and solemn, defiled along the steeps; or, routed by pursuing light, fled broadcast from east to west – old wars of Lucifer and Michael; or the mountains, though unvexed by these mirrored sham fights in the sky, had an atmosphere otherwise unfavourable for fairy views. I was sorry; the more so, because I had to keep to my chamber for some time after – which chamber did not face those hills.

At length, when pretty well again, and sitting out, in the September morning, upon the piazza, and thinking to myself, when, just after a little flock of sheep, the farmer's banded children passed, a-nutting, and said, 'How sweet a day' – it was, after all, but what their fathers call a weather-breeder – and, indeed, was become so sensitive through my illness as that I could not bear to look upon a Chinese creeper of my adoption, and which, to my delight, climbing a post of the piazza, had burst out in starry bloom, but now, if you removed the leaves a little, showed millions of strange, cankerous worms, which feeding upon those blossoms, so shared their blessed hue, as to make it unblessed evermore – worms, whose germs had doubtless lurked in the very bulb which, so hopefully, I had planted: in this ingrate peevishness of my weary convalescence, was I sitting there; when, suddenly looking off, I saw the golden mountain window, dazzling like a deep-sea dolphin. Fairies there, thought I, once more; the queen of fairies at her fairy window; at any rate, some glad mountain-girl; it will do me good, it will cure this weariness, to look on her. No more; I'll launch my yawl – ho, cheerly, heart! and push away for fairyland – for rainbow's end, in fairyland.

How to get to fairyland, by what road, I did not know – nor could anyone inform me; not even one Edmund Spenser, who had been there – so he wrote me – further than that to reach fairyland it must be voyaged to, and with faith. I took the fairy mountain's bearings, and the first fine day, when strength permitted, got into my yawl – high-pommelled, leather one – cast off the fast, and away I sailed, free voyager as an autumn leaf. Early dawn; and, sallying westward, I sowed the morning before me.

Some miles brought me nigh the hills; but out of present sight of them. I was not lost; for roadside golden-rods, as guide-posts, pointed, I doubted not, the way to the golden window. Following them, I came to a lone and languid region, where the grassgrown ways were travelled but by drowsy cattle that, less waked than stirred by day, seemed to walk in sleep. Browse, they did not – the enchanted never eat. At least, so says Don Quixote, that sagest sage that ever lived.

On I went, and gained at last the fairy mountain's base, but saw yet no fairy ring. A pasture rose before me. Letting down five mouldering bars – so moistly green, they seemed fished up from some sunken wreck – a wigged old Aries, long-visaged, and with crumpled horn, came snuffing up; and then, retreating, decorously led on along a milky-way of white-weed, past dim-clustering Pleiades and Hyades, of small forget-me-nots; and would have led me further still his astral path, but for golden flights of yellow-birds – pilots, surely, to the golden window, to one side flying before me, from bush to bush, towards deep woods – which woods themselves were luring – and, somehow, lured, too, by their fence, banning a dark road, which, however dark, led up. I pushed through; when Aries, renouncing me now for some lost soul, wheeled, and went his wiser way. Forbidding and forbidden ground – to him.

A winter wood road, matted all along with winter-green. By the side of pebbly waters – waters the cheerier for their solitude; beneath swaying fir-boughs, petted by no season, but still green in all, on I journeyed – my horse and I; on, by an old saw-mill, bound down and hushed with vines, that his grating voice no more was heard; on, by a deep flume clove through snowy marble, vernal-tinted, where freshet eddies had, on each side, spun out empty chapels in the living rock; on, where Jacks-in-the-pulpit, like their Baptist namesake, preached but to the wilderness; on, where a huge, cross-grain block, fern-bedded, showed where, in forgotten times, man after man had tried to split it, but lost his wedges for his pains – which wedges yet rusted in their holes; on, where, ages past, in step-like ledges of a cascade, skull-hollow pots had been churned out by ceaseless whirling of a flintstone – ever wearing, but itself unworn; on, by wild rapids pouring into a secret pool, but soothed by circling there awhile, issued forth serenely; on, to less broken ground, and by a little ring, where, truly, fairies must have danced! or else some wheel-tyre been heated – for all was bare; still on, and up, and out into a hanging orchard, where maidenly looked down upon me a crescent moon, from morning.

My horse hitched low his head. Red apples rolled before him; Eve's apples; seek-no-furthers. He tasted one, I another; it tasted of the ground. Fairyland not yet, thought I, flinging my bridle to a humped old tree that crooked out an arm to catch it. For the way now lay where path was none, and none might go but by himself, and only go by daring. Through blackberry brakes that tried to pluck me back, though I but strained towards fruitless growths of mountain-laurel; up slippery steeps to barren heights, where stood none to welcome. Fairyland not yet, thought I, though the morning is here before me.

Footsore enough and weary, I gained not then my journey's end, but came ere long to a craggy pass, dipping towards growing regions still beyond. A zigzag road, half overgrown with blueberry bushes, here turned among the cliffs. A rent was in their ragged sides; through it a little track branched off, which, upwards threading that short defile, came breezily out above, to where the mountain-top, part sheltered northward by a taller brother, sloped gently off a space, ere darkly plunging; and here, among fantastic rocks, reposing in a herd, the foot-track wound, half beaten, up to a little, low-storeyed, greyish cottage, capped, nun-like, with a peaked roof.

On one slope, the roof was deeply weather-stained, and, nigh the turfy eaves-trough, all velvet-napped; no doubt the snail-monks founded mossy priories there. The other slope was newly shingled. On the north side, doorless and windowless, the clapboards, innocent of paint, were yet green as the north side of lichened pines, or copperless hulls of Japanese junks, becalmed. The whole base, like those of the neighbouring rocks, was rimmed about with shaded streaks of richest sod; for, with hearthstones in fairyland, the natural rock, though housed, preserves to the last, just as in open fields, its fertilising charm; only, by necessity, working now at a remove, to the sward without. So, at least, says Oberon, grave authority in fairy lore. Though setting Oberon aside, certain it is that, even in the common world, the soil, close up to farmhouses, as close up to pasture rocks, is, even though untended, ever richer than it is a few rods off – such gentle, nurturing heat is radiated there.

But with this cottage, the shaded streaks were richest in its front and about its entrance, where the ground-sill, and especially the door-sill had, through long eld, quietly settled down.

No fence was seen, no enclosure. Near by – ferns, ferns, ferns; further – woods, woods, woods; beyond – mountains, mountains, mountains; then – sky, sky, sky. Turned out in aerial commons, pasture for the mountain moon. Nature, and but nature, house and all; even a low cross-pile of silver birch, piled openly, to season; up among whose silvery sticks, as through the fencing of some sequestered grave, sprang vagrant raspberry bushes – wilful assertors of their right of way.

The foot-track, so dainty narrow, just like a sheep-track, led through long ferns that lodged. Fairyland at last, thought I; Una and her lamb dwell here. Truly, a small abode – mere palanquin, set down on the summit, in a pass between two worlds, participant of neither.

A sultry hour, and I wore a light hat, of yellow sinnet, with white duck trousers – both relics of my tropic sea-going. Clogged in the muffling ferns, I softly stumbled, staining the knees a sea-green.

Pausing at the threshold, or rather where threshold once had been, I saw, through the open doorway, a lonely girl, sewing at a lonely window. A pale-cheeked girl, and fly-specked window, with wasps about the mended upper panes. I spoke. She shyly started, like some Tahiti girl, secreted for a sacrifice, first catching sight, through palms, of Captain Cook. Recovering, she bade me enter; with her apron brushed off a stool; then silently resumed her own. With thanks I took the stool; but now, for a space, I, too, was mute. This, then, is the fairy-mountain house, and here, the fairy queen sitting at her fairy window.

I went up to it. Downwards, directed by the tunnelled pass, as through a levelled telescope, I caught sight of a far-off, soft, azure world. I hardly knew it, though I came from it.

'You must find this view very pleasant,' said I, at last.

'Oh, sir,' tears starting in her eyes, 'the first time I looked out of this window, I said, "Never, never shall I weary of this." '

'And what wearies you of it now?'

'I don't know,' while a tear fell; 'but it is not the view, it is Marianna.'

Some months back, her brother, only seventeen, had come hither, a long way from the other side, to cut wood and burn coal, and she, elder sister, had accompanied him. Long had they been orphans, and now, sole inhabitants of the sole house upon the mountain. No guest came, no traveller passed. The zigzag perilous road was only used at seasons by the coal wagons. The brother was absent the entire day, sometimes the entire night. When at evening, fagged out, he did come home, he soon left his bench, poor fellow, for his bed; just as one, at last, wearily quits that, too, for still deeper rest. The bench, the bed, the grave.

Silent I stood by the fairy window, while these things were being told.

'Do you know,' said she at last, as stealing from her story, 'do you know who lives yonder? – I have never been down into that country – away off there, I mean; that house, that marble one,' pointing far across the lower landscape; 'have you not caught it? there, on the long hillside: the field before, the woods behind; the white shines out against their blue; don't you mark it? the only house in sight.'

I looked; and after a time, to my surprise, recognised, more by its position than its aspect, or Marianna's description, my own abode, glimmering much like this mountain one from the piazza. The mirage haze made it appear less a farmhouse than King Charming's palace.

'I have often wondered who lives there; but it must be some happy one; again this morning was I thinking so.'

'Some happy one,' returned I, starting; 'and why do you think that? You judge some rich one lives there?'

'Rich or not, I never thought; but it looks so happy, I can't tell how; and it is so far away. Sometimes I think I do but dream it is there. You should see it in a sunset.'

'No doubt the sunset gilds it finely; but not more than the sunrise does this house, perhaps.'

'This house? The sun is a good sun, but it never gilds this house.

Why should it? This old house is rotting. That makes it so mossy.
In the morning, the sun comes in at this old window, to be sure –
boarded up, when first we came; a window I can't keep clean, do
what I may – and half burns, and nearly blinds me at my sewing,
besides setting the flies and wasps astir – such flies and wasps as only
lone mountain houses know. See, here is the curtain – this apron – I
try to shut it out with then. It fades it, you see. Sun gild this house?
not that ever Marianna saw.'

'Because when this roof is gilded most, then you stay here within.'

'The hottest, weariest hour of day, you mean? Sir, the sun gilds
not this roof. It leaked so, brother newly shingled all one side. Did
you not see it? The north side, where the sun strikes most on what
the rain has wetted. The sun is a good sun; but this roof, it first
scorches, and then rots. An old house. They went West, and are
long dead, they say, who built it. A mountain house. In winter no
fox could den in it. That chimney-place has been blocked up with
snow, just like a hollow stump.'

'Yours are strange fancies, Marianna.'

'They but reflect the things.'

'Then I should have said, "These are strange things," rather than,
"Yours are strange fancies." '

'As you will,' and took up her sewing.

Something in those quiet words, or in that quiet act, it made me
mute again; while, noting, through the fairy window, a broad
shadow stealing on, as cast by some gigantic condor, floating at
brooding poise on outstretched wings, I marked how, by its deeper
and inclusive dusk, it wiped away into itself all lesser shades of rock
or fern.

'You watch the cloud,' said Marianna.

'No, a shadow; a cloud's, no doubt – though that I cannot see.
How did you know it? Your eyes are on your work.'

'It dusked my work. There, now the cloud is gone, Tray comes
back.'

'How?'

'The dog, the shaggy dog. At noon, he steals off, of himself, to
change his shape – returns, and lies down awhile, nigh the door.
Don't you see him? His head is turned round at you; though, when
you came, he looked before him.'

'Your eyes rest but on your work; what do you speak of?'

'By the window, crossing.'

'You mean this shaggy shadow – the nigh one? And, yes, now that
I mark it, it is not unlike a large, black Newfoundland dog. The

invading shadow gone, the invaded one returns. But I do not see what casts it.'

'For that, you must go without.'

'One of those grassy rocks, no doubt.'

'You see his head, his face?'

'The shadow's? You speak as if you saw it, and all the time your eyes are on your work.'

'Tray looks at you,' still without glancing up; 'this is his hour; I see him.'

'Have you, then, so long sat at this mountain-window, where but clouds and vapours pass, that, to you, shadows are as things, though you speak of them as of phantoms; that, by familiar knowledge, working like a second sight, you can, without looking for them, tell just where they are, though, as having mice-like feet, they creep about, and come and go; that, to you, these lifeless shadows are as living friends, who, though out of sight, are not out of mind, even in their faces – is it so?'

'That way I never thought of it. But the friendliest one, that used to soothe my weariness so much, coolly quivering on the ferns, it was taken from me, never to return, as Tray did just now. The shadow of a birch. The tree was struck by lightning, and brother cut it up. You saw the cross-pile outdoors – the buried root lies under it; but not the shadow. That is flown, and never will come back, nor ever anywhere stir again.'

Another cloud here stole along, once more blotting out the dog, and blackening all the mountain; while the stillness was so still, deafness might have forgot itself, or else believed that noiseless shadow spoke.

'Birds, Marianna, singing-birds, I hear none; I hear nothing. Boys and bob-o-links, do they never come a-berrying up here?'

'Birds, I seldom hear; boys, never. The berries mostly ripe and fall – few, but me, the wiser.'

'But yellow-birds showed me the way – part way, at least.'

'And then flew back. I guess they play about the mountainside, but don't make the top their home. And no doubt you think that, living so lonesome here, knowing nothing, hearing nothing – little, at least, but sound of thunder and the fall of trees – never reading, seldom speaking, yet ever wakeful, this is what gives me my strange thoughts – for so you call them – this weariness and wakefulness together. Brother, who stands and works in open air, would I could rest like him; but mine is mostly but dull woman's work – sitting, sitting, restless sitting.'

'But, do you not go walk at times? These woods are wide.'

'And lonesome; lonesome, because so wide. Sometimes, 'tis true, of afternoons, I go a little way; but soon come back again. Better feel lone by hearth, than rock. The shadows hereabouts I know – those in the woods are strangers.'

'But the night?'

'Just like the day. Thinking, thinking – a wheel I cannot stop; pure want of sleep it is that turns it.'

'I have heard that, for this wakeful weariness, to say one's prayers, and then lay one's head upon a fresh hop pillow – '

'Look!'

Through the fairy window, she pointed down the steep to a small garden patch near by – mere pot of rifled loam, half rounded in by sheltering rocks – where, side by side, some feet apart, nipped and puny, two hop-vines climbed two poles, and, gaining their tip-ends, would have then joined over in an upward clasp, but the baffled shoots, groping awhile in empty air, trailed back whence they sprang.

'You have tried the pillow, then?'

'Yes.'

'And prayer?'

'Prayer and pillow.'

'Is there no other cure, or charm?'

'Oh, if I could but once get to yonder house, and but look upon whoever the happy being is that lives there! A foolish thought: why do I think it? Is it that I live so lonesome, and know nothing?'

'I, too, know nothing; and, therefore, cannot answer; but, for your sake, Marianna, well could wish that I were that happy one of the happy house you dream you see; for then you would behold him now, and, as you say, this weariness might leave you.'

– Enough. Launching my yawl no more for fairyland, I stick to the piazza. It is my box-royal; and this amphitheatre, my theatre of San Carlo. Yes, the scenery is magical – the illusion so complete. And Madam Meadow Lark, my prima donna, plays her grand engagement here; and, drinking in her sunrise note, which, Memnon-like, seems struck from the golden window, how far from me the weary face behind it.

But, every night, when the curtain falls, truth comes in with darkness. No light shows from the mountain. To and fro I walk the piazza-deck haunted by Marianna's face, and many as real a story.

BILLY BUDD, FORETOPMAN

Preface

The year 1797, the year of this narrative, belongs to a period which, as every thinker now feels, involved a crisis for Christendom, not exceeded in its undetermined momentousness at the time by any other era whereof there is record. The opening proposition made by the spirit of that age* involved a rectification of the Old World's hereditary wrongs. In France, to some extent, this was bloodily effected. But what then? Straightway the revolution itself became a wrongdoer, one more oppressive than the kings. Under Napoleon it enthroned upstart kings, and initiated that prolonged agony of continual war whose final throe was Waterloo. During those years not the wisest could have foreseen that the outcome of all would be what to some thinkers apparently it has since turned out to be, a political advance along nearly the whole line for Europeans.

Now, as elsewhere hinted, it was something caught from the revolutionary spirit that at Spithead emboldened the man-of-war's men to rise against real abuses, long-standing ones, and afterwards at the Nore to make inordinate and aggressive demands, successful resistance to which was confirmed only when the ringleaders were hung for an admonitory spectacle to the anchored fleet. Yet in a way analogous to the operation of the revolution at large, the Great Mutiny, though by Englishmen naturally deemed monstrous at the time, doubtless gave the first latent prompting to most important reforms in the British navy.

---

* Crossed out:
> Even the dry tinder of Wordsworth took fire.
> Was one hailed by the noblest men of it.

An inside narrative

IN THE TIME BEFORE STEAMSHIPS, or then more frequently than now, a stroller along the docks of any considerable seaport would occasionally have his attention arrested by a group of bronzed marines, man-of-war's men or merchant sailors in holiday attire ashore on liberty. In certain instances they would flank, or, like a bodyguard, quite surround some superior figure of their own class, moving along with them like Aldebaran amongst the lesser lights of his constellation. That signal object was the Handsome Sailor of the less prosaic time alike of the military and merchant navies. With no perceptible trace of the vainglorious about him, rather with the offhand unaffectedness of natural regality, he seemed to accept the spontaneous homage of his shipmates. A somewhat remarkable instance recurs to me. In Liverpool, now half a century ago, I saw under the shadow of the great dingy street-wall of Prince's Dock (an obstruction long since removed) a common sailor, so intensely black that he must needs have been a native African of the unadulterate blood of Ham. A symmetric figure much above the average height. The two ends of a gay silk handkerchief thrown loose about the neck danced upon the displayed ebony of his chest; in his ears were big hoops of gold, and a Scotch Highland bonnet with a tartan band set off his shapely head.

It was a hot noon in July; and his face, lustrous with perspiration, beamed with barbaric good-humour. In jovial sallies right and left, his white teeth flashing into view, he rollicked along, the centre of a company of his shipmates. These were made up of such an assortment of tribes and complexions as would have well fitted them to be marched up by Anacharsis Cloots before the bar of the first French Assembly as representatives of the human race. At each spontaneous tribute rendered by the wayfarers to this black pagod of a fellow – the tribute of a pause and stare, and less frequent, an exclamation – the motley retinue showed that they took that sort of pride in the evoker of it which the Assyrian priests doubtless showed for their grand sculptured bull when the faithful prostrated themselves. To return –

If in some cases a bit of a nautical Murat in setting forth his person ashore, the Handsome Sailor of the period in question evinced nothing of the dandified Billy-be-Damn, an amusing character all but extinct now, but occasionally to be encountered, and in a form yet more amusing than the original, at the tiller of the boats on the tempestuous Erie Canal or, more likely, vapouring in the groggeries along the towpath. Invariably a proficient in his perilous calling, he was also more or less of a mighty boxer or wrestler. He was strength and beauty. Tales of his prowess were recited. Ashore he was the champion, afloat the spokesman; on every suitable occasion always foremost. Close-reefing topsails in a gale, there he was, astride the weather yard-arm-end, foot in 'stirrup', both hands tugging at the 'earring' as at a bridle, in very much the attitude of young Alexander curbing the fiery Bucephalus. A superb figure, tossed up as by the horns of Taurus against the thunderous sky, cheerily ballooning to the strenuous file along the spar.

The moral nature was seldom out of keeping with the physical make. Indeed, except as toned by the former, the comeliness and power, always attractive in masculine conjunction, hardly could have drawn the sort of homage the Handsome Sailor in some examples received from his less gifted associates.

Such a cynosure, at least in aspect, and something such too in nature, though with important variations made apparent as the story proceeds, was welkin-eyed Billy Budd – or Baby Budd, as more familiarly, under circumstances hereafter to be given, he at last came to be called – aged twenty-one, a foretopman of the fleet towards the close of the last decade of the eighteenth century. It was not very long prior to the time of the narration that follows that he had entered the king's service, having been impressed on the narrow seas from a homeward-bound English merchantman into a seventy-four outward-bound, HMS *Indomitable*; which ship, as was not unusual in those hurried days, had been obliged to put to sea short of her proper complement of men. Plump upon Billy at first sight in the gangway the boarding-officer, Lieutenant Ratcliffe, pounced, even before the merchantman's crew formally was mustered on the quarter-deck for his deliberate inspection. And him only he selected. For whether it was because the other men when ranged before him showed to ill advantage after Billy, or whether he had some scruples in view of the merchantman being rather short-handed, however it might be, the officer contented himself with his first spontaneous choice. To the surprise of the ship's company, though much to the lieutenant's satisfaction, Billy made no demur. But indeed any demur would have been as idle as the protest of a goldfinch popped into a cage.

Noting this uncomplaining acquiescence, all but cheerful one might say, the shipmates turned a surprised glance of silent reproach at the sailor. The shipmaster was one of those worthy mortals found in every vocation, even the humbler ones – the sort of person whom everybody agrees in calling 'a respectable man'. And – nor so strange to report as it may appear to be – though a ploughman of the troubled waters, life-long contending with the intractable elements, there was nothing this honest soul at heart loved better than simple peace and quiet. For the rest, he was fifty or thereabouts, a little inclined to corpulence, a prepossessing face, unwhiskered, and of an agreeable colour, a rather full face, humanely intelligent in expression. On a fair day with a fair wind and all going well, a certain musical chime in his voice seemed to be the veritable unobstructed outcome of the innermost man. He had much prudence, much conscientiousness, and there were occasions when these virtues were the cause of overmuch disquietude in him. On a passage, so long as his craft was in any proximity to land, no sleep for Captain Graveling. He took to heart those serious responsibilities not so heavily borne by some shipmasters.

Now while Billy Budd was down in the forecastle getting his kit together, the *Indomitable*'s lieutenant, burly and bluff, nowise disconcerted by Captain Graveling's omitting to proffer the customary hospitalities on an occasion so unwelcome to him, an omission simply caused by preoccupation of thought, unceremoniously invited himself into the cabin, and also to a flask from the spirit locker, a receptacle which his experienced eye instantly discovered. In fact, he was one of those sea-dogs in whom all the hardship and peril of naval life in the great prolonged wars of his time never impaired the natural instinct for sensuous enjoyment. His duty he always faithfully did; but duty is sometimes a dry obligation, and he was for irrigating its aridity whensover possible with a fertilising decoction of strong waters. For the cabin's proprietor there was nothing left but to play the part of the enforced host with whatever grace and alacrity were practicable. As necessary adjuncts to the flask, he silently placed tumbler and water-jug before the irrepressible guest. But excusing himself from partaking just then, dismally watched the unembarrassed officer deliberately diluting his grog a little, then tossing it off in three swallows, pushing the empty tumbler away, yet not so far as to be beyond easy reach, at the same time settling himself in his seat, and smacking his lips with high satisfaction, looking straight at the host.

These proceedings over, the master broke the silence and there lurked a rueful reproach in the tone of his voice: 'Lieutenant, you are going to take my best man from me, the jewel of 'em.'

'Yes, I know,' rejoined the other, immediately drawing back the tumbler, preliminary to a replenishing; 'yes, I know. Sorry.'

'Beg pardon, but you don't understand, lieutenant. See here now. Before I shipped that young fellow, my forecastle was a rat-pit of quarrels. It was black times, I tell you, aboard the *Rights* here. I was worried to that degree my pipe had no comfort for me. But Billy came; and it was like a Catholic priest striking peace in an Irish shindy. Not that he preached to them or said or did anything in particular; but a virtue went out of him sugaring the sour ones. They took to him like hornets to treacle, all but the bluffer of the gang, the big, shaggy chap with the fire-red whiskers. He indeed, out of envy, perhaps, of the newcomer, and thinking such a "sweet and pleasant fellow", as he mockingly designated him to the others, could hardly have the spirit of a game-cock, must needs bestir himself in trying to get up an ugly row with him. Billy forbore with him, and reassured with him in a pleasant way – he is something like myself, lieutenant, to whom aught like a quarrel is hateful – but nothing served. So, in the second dog-watch one day the Red Whiskers, in presence of the others, under pretence of showing Billy just whence a sirloin steak was cut – for the fellow had once been a butcher – insultingly gave him a dig under the ribs. Quick as lightning Billy let fly his arm. I dare say he never meant to do quite as much as he did, but anyhow he gave the burly fool a terrible drubbing. It took about half a minute, I should think. And, Lord bless you, the lubber was astonished at the celerity. And will you believe it, lieutenant, the Red Whiskers now really loves Billy – loves him, or is the biggest hypocrite that ever I heard of. But they all love him. Some of 'em do his washing, darn old trousers for him; the carpenter is at odd times making a pretty little chest of drawers for him. Anybody will do anything for Billy Budd; and it's the happy family here. Now, lieutenant, if that young fellow goes, I know how it will be aboard the *Rights*. Not again very soon shall I, coming up from dinner, lean over the capstan smoking a quiet pipe – no, not very soon again, I think. Aye, lieutenant, you are going to take away the jewel of 'em; you are going to take away my peacemaker.' And with that the good soul had really some ado in checking a rising sob.

'Well,' said the lieutenant, who had listened with amused interest to all this, and now waxing merry with his tipple, 'well, blessed are the peacemakers, especially the fighting peacemakers! And such are the seventy-four beauties, some of which you see poking their noses out of the port-holes of yonder warship lying-to for me,' pointing through the cabin windows at the *Indomitable*. 'But courage! don't look so downhearted, man. Why, I pledge you in advance the royal approbation. Rest assured that His Majesty will be delighted to know that in time when his hardtack is not sought for by sailors with such avidity as should be; a time also when some shipmasters privily resent the borrowing from them of a tar or two for the service; His Majesty, I say, will be delighted to learn that *one* shipmaster at least cheerfully surrenders to the king the flower of his flock, a sailor who with equal loyalty makes no dissent. But where's my beauty? Ah,' looking through the cabin's open door, 'here he comes; and, by Jove! lugging along his chest – Apollo with his portmanteau! My man,' stepping out to him, 'you can't take that big box aboard a warship. The boxes there are mostly shot-boxes. Put your duds in a bag, lad. Boot and saddle for the cavalryman, bag and hammock for the man-of-war's man.'

The transfer from chest to bag was made. And, after seeing his man into the cutter, and then following him down, the lieutenant pushed off from the *Rights of Man*. That was the merchant ship's name; though by her master and crew abbreviated in sailor fashion into the *Rights*. The hard-headed Dundee owner was a staunch admirer of Thomas Paine, whose book in rejoinder to Burke's arraignment of the French Revolution had then been published for some time, and had gone everywhere. In christening his vessel after the title of Paine's volume, the man of Dundee was something like his contemporary shipowner, Stephen Girard of Philadelphia, whose sympathies alike with his native land and its liberal philosophies he evinced by naming his ships after Voltaire, Diderot, and so forth.

But now when the boat swept under the merchantman's stern, and officer and oarsmen were noting, some bitterly and others with a grin, the name emblazoned there; just then it was that the new recruit jumped up from the bow where the coxswain had directed him to sit, and, waving his hat to his silent shipmates sorrowfully looking over at him from the taffrail, bade the lads a genial good-bye. Then making a salutation as to the ship herself, 'And goodbye to you too, old *Rights-of-Man*!'

'Down, sir,' roared the lieutenant, instantly assuming all the rigour of his rank, though with difficulty repressing a smile.

To be sure, Billy's action was a terrible breach of naval decorum. But in that decorum he had never been instructed; in consideration of which the lieutenant would hardly have been so energetic in reproof but for the concluding farewell to the ship. This he rather took as meant to convey a covert sally on the new recruit's part, a sly slur at impressment in general, and that of himself in especial. And yet, more likely, if satire it was in effect, it was hardly so by intention, for Billy, though happily endowed with the gaiety of high health, youth and a free heart, was yet by no means of a satirical turn. The will to it and the sinister dexterity were alike wanting. To deal in double meaning and insinuations of any sort was quite foreign to his nature.

As to his enforced enlistment, that he seemed to take pretty much as he was wont to take any vicissitudes of weather. Like the animals, though no philosopher he was, without knowing it, practically a fatalist. And it may be that he rather liked this adventurous turn in his affairs which promised an opening into novel scenes and martial excitements.

Aboard the *Indomitable* our merchant-sailor was forthwith rated as an able seaman, and assigned to the starboard watch of the foretop. He was soon at home in the service, not at all disliked for his unpretentious good looks, and a sort of genial happy-go-lucky air. No merrier man in his mess; in marked contrast to certain other individuals included like himself among the impressed portion of the ship's company; for these when not actively employed were sometimes, and more particularly in the last dog-watch, when the drawing near of twilight induced reverie, apt to fall into a saddish mood which in some partook of sullenness. But they were not so young as our foretopman, and no few of them must have known a hearth of some sort, others may have had wives and children left, too probably, in uncertain circumstances, and hardly any but must have acknowledged kith and kin; while for Billy, as will shortly be seen, his entire family was practically invested in himself.

2

Though our new-made foretopman was well received in the top and on the gun-decks, hardly here was he that cynosure he had previously been among those minor ships' companies of the merchant marine, with which companies only had he hitherto consorted.

He was young; and despite his all but fully developed frame, in aspect looked even younger than he really was. This was owing to a lingering adolescent expression in the as yet smooth face, all but feminine in purity of natural complexion, but where, thanks to his sea-going, the lily was quite suppressed and the rose had some ado visibly to flush through the tan.

To one essentially such a novice in the complexities of factitious life, the abrupt transition from his former and simpler sphere to the ampler and more knowing world of a great warship – this might well have abashed him had there been any conceit or vanity in his composition. Among her miscellaneous multitude, the *Indomitable* mustered several individuals who, however inferior in grade, were of no common natural stamp sailors more signally; susceptive of that air which continuous martial discipline and repeated presence in battle can in some degree impart even to the average man. As the Handsome Sailor, Billy Budd's position aboard the seventy-four was something analogous to that of a rustic beauty transplanted from the provinces and brought into competition with the high-born dames of the court. But this change of circumstances he scarce noted. As little did he observe that something about him provoked an ambiguous smile in one or two harder faces among the bluejackets. Nor less unaware was he of the peculiar favourable effect his person and demeanour had upon the more intelligent gentlemen of the quarter-deck. Nor could this well have been otherwise. Cast in a mould peculiar to the finest physical examples of those Englishmen in whom the Saxon strain would seem not at all to partake of any Norman or other admixture, he showed in face that humane look of reposeful good-nature which the Greek sculptor in some instances gave to his heroic strong man, Hercules. But this again was subtly modified by another and pervasive quality. The ear, small and shapely, the arch of the foot, the curve in mouth and nostril, even the indurated hand dyed to the orange-tawny of the toucan's bill, a hand telling of the halyards and tar-buckets; but, above all, something in the mobile expression, and every chance attitude and movement, something suggestive of a mother eminently favoured by Love and the Graces; all this strangely indicated a lineage in direct contradiction to his lot. The mysteriousness here, became less mysterious through a matter of fact elicited when Billy at the capstan was being formally mustered into the service. Asked by the officer, a small, brisk little gentleman as it chanced, among other questions, his place of birth, he replied, 'Please, sir, I don't know.'

'Don't you know where you were born? Who was your father?'

'God knows, sir.'

Struck by the straightforward simplicity of these replies, the officer next asked, 'Do you know anything about your beginning?'

'No, sir. But I have heard that I was found in a pretty silk-lined basket hanging one morning from the knocker of a good man's door in Bristol.'

'*Found*, say you? Well,' throwing back his head, and looking up and down the raw recruit – 'well, it turns out to have been a pretty good find. Hope they'll find some more like you, my man; the fleet sadly needs them.'

Yes, Billy Budd was a foundling, a presumable by-blow, and, evidently, no ignoble one. Noble descent was as evident in him as in a blood horse.

For the rest, with little or no sharpness of faculty or any trace of the wisdom of the serpent, nor yet quite a dove, he possessed a certain degree of intelligence along with the unconventional rectitude of a sound human creature – one to whom not yet has been proffered the questionable apple of knowledge. He was illiterate; he could not read, but he could sing, and like the illiterate nightingale was sometimes the composer of his own song.

Of self-consciousness he seemed to have little or none, or about as much as we may reasonably impute to a dog of St Bernard's breed.

Habitually being with the elements and knowing little more of the land than as a beach, or, rather, that portion of the terraqueous globe providentially set apart for dance-houses, doxies and tapsters, in short, what sailors call a 'fiddlers' green', his simple nature remained unsophisticated by those moral obliquities which are not in every case incomparable with that manufacturable thing known as respectability. But are sailor frequenters of fiddlers' greens without vices? No; but less often than with landsmen do their vices, so-called, partake of crookedness of heart, seeming less to proceed from viciousness than exuberance of vitality after long restraint, frank manifestations in accordance with natural law. By his original constitution, aided by the cooperating influences of his lot, Billy in many respects was little more than a sort of upright barbarian, much such perhaps as Adam presumably might have been ere the urbane serpent wriggled himself into his company.

And here be it submitted that, apparently going to corroborate the doctrine of man's fall (a doctrine now popularly ignored), it is observable that where certain virtues pristine and unadulterate peculiarly characterise anybody in the external uniform of civilisation, they will upon scrutiny seem not to be derived from custom or convention but rather to be out of keeping with these, as if indeed exceptionally transmitted from a period prior to Cain's city and citified man. The character marked by such qualities has to an unvitiated taste an untampered-with flavour like that of berries, while the man thoroughly civilised, even in a fair specimen of the breed, has to the same moral palate a questionable smack as of a compounded wine. To any stray inheritor of these primitive qualities found, like Caspar Hauser, wandering dazed in any Christian capital of our time, the poet's famous invocation, near two thousand years ago, of the good rustic out of his latitude in the Rome of the Caesars, still appropriately holds:

> Faithful in word and thought,
> What has thee, Fabian, to the city brought?

Though our Handsome Sailor had as much of masculine beauty as one can expect anywhere to see; nevertheless, like the beautiful woman in one of Hawthorne's minor tales, there was just one thing amiss in him. No visible blemish, indeed, as with the lady; no, but an occasional liability to a vocal defect. Though in the hour of elemental uproar or peril, he was everything that a sailor should be, yet under sudden provocation of strong heartfeeling his voice, otherwise singularly musical, as if expressive of the harmony within, was apt to develop an organic hesitancy – in fact, more or less of a stutter or even worse. In this particular Billy was a striking instance that the arch-interpreter, the envious marplot of Eden, still has more or less to do with every human consignment to this planet of earth. In every case, one way or another, he is sure to slip in his little card, as much as to remind us – I too have a hand here.

The avowal of such an imperfection in the Handsome Sailor should be evidence not alone that he is not presented as a conventional hero, but also that the story in which he is the main figure is no romance.

3

At the time of Billy Budd's arbitrary enlistment into the *Indomitable* that ship was on her way to join the Mediterranean fleet. No long time elapsed before the junction was effected. As one of that fleet, the seventy-four participated in its movements, though at times, on account of her superior sailing qualities, in the absence of frigates, dispatched on separate duty as a scout, and at times on less temporary service. But with all this the story has little concernment, restricted as it is to the inner life of one particular ship and the career of an individual sailor.

It was the summer of 1797. In the April of that year had occurred the commotion at Spithead, followed in May by a second and yet more serious outbreak in the fleet at the Nore. The latter is known, and without exaggeration in the epithet, as the Great Mutiny. It was indeed a demonstration more menacing to England than the contemporary manifestos and conquering and proselytising armies of the French Directory.

To the Empire, the Nore mutiny was what a strike in the fire brigade would be to London threatened by general arson. In a crisis when the kingdom might well have anticipated the famous signal that some years later published along the naval line of battle what it was that upon occasion England expected of Englishmen; *that* was the time when at the mastheads of the three-deckers and seventy-fours moored in her own roadstead – a fleet, the right arm of a power then all but the sole free conservative one of the Old World, the bluejackets, to be numbered by thousands, ran up with hurrahs the British colours with the union and cross wiped out; by that cancellation transmuting the flag of founded law and freedom defined, into the enemy's red meteor of unbridled and unbounded revolt. Reasonable discontent growing out of practical grievances in the fleet had been ignited into irrational combustion as by live cinders blown across the Channel from France in flames.

The event converted into irony for a time those spirited strains of Dibdin – as a song-writer no mean auxiliary to the English government – at this European conjuncture, strains celebrating, among other things, the patriotic devotion of the British tar –

And as for my life, 'tis the King's!

Such an episode in the island's grand naval story her naval historians naturally abridge; one of them (G. P. R. James) candidly acknowledging that fain would he pass it over did not 'impartiality forbid fastidiousness'. And yet his mention is less a narration than a reference, having to do hardly at all with details. Nor are these readily to be found in the libraries. Like some other events in every age befalling states everywhere, including America, the Great Mutiny was of such character that national pride along with views of policy would fain shade it off into the historical background. Such events cannot be ignored, but there is a considerate way of historically treating them. If a well-constituted individual refrains from blazoning aught amiss or calamitous in his family, a nation in the like circumstances may without reproach be equally discreet.

Though after parleyings between government and the ringleaders, and concessions by the former as to some glaring abuses, the first uprising – that at Spithead – with difficulty was put down, or matters for a time pacified; yet at the Nore the unforeseen renewal of insurrection on a yet larger scale, and emphasised in the conferences that ensued by demands deemed by the authorities not only inadmissible but aggressively insolent, indicated, if the red flag did not sufficiently do so, what was the spirit animating the men. Final suppression, however, there was; but only made possible perhaps by the unswerving loyalty of the marine corps, and a voluntary resumption of loyalty among influential sections of the crews. To some extent the Nore mutiny may be regarded as analogous to the distempering irruption of contagious fever in a frame constitutionally sound, and which anon throws it off.

At all events, among these thousands of mutineers were some of the tars who not so very long afterwards – whether wholly prompted thereto by patriotism, or pugnacious instinct, or by both – helped to win a coronet for Nelson at the Nile, and the naval crown of crowns for him at Trafalgar. To the mutineer those battles, and especially Trafalgar, were a plenary absolution, and a grand one; for that which goes to make up scenic naval display is heroic magnificence in arms. Those battles, especially Trafalgar, stand unmatched in human annals.

4

The greatest sailor since the world began.

TENNYSON

In this matter of writing, resolve as one may to keep to the main road, some bypaths have an enticement not readily to be withstood. Beckoned by the genius of Nelson I am going to err into such a by-path. If the reader will keep me company I shall be glad. At the least we can promise ourselves that pleasure which is wickedly said to be in sinning, for a literary sin the divergence will be.

Very likely it is no new remark that the inventions of our time have at last brought about a change in sea warfare in degree corresponding to the revolution in all warfare effected by the original introduction from China into Europe of gunpowder. The first European firearm, a clumsy contrivance, was, as is well known, scouted by no few of the knights as a base implement, good enough peradventure for weavers too craven to stand up crossing steel with steel in frank fight But as ashore knightly valour, though shorn of its blazonry, did not cease with the knights, neither on the seas, though nowadays in encounters there a certain kind of displayed gallantry be fallen out of date as hardly applicable under changed circumstances, did the nobler qualities of such naval magnates as Don John of Austria, Doria, Van Tromp, Jean Bart, the long line of British admirals and the American Decaturs of 1812 become obsolete with their wooden walls.

Nevertheless, to anybody who can hold the present at its worth without being inappreciative of the past, it may be forgiven if to such a one the solitary old hulk at Portsmouth, Nelson's *Victory*, seems to float there, not alone as the decaying monument of a fame incorruptible, but also as a poetic reproach, softened by its picturesqueness, to the *Monitors* and yet mightier hulls of the European ironclads. And this not altogether because such craft are unsightly, unavoidably lacking the symmetry and grand lines of the old battleships, but equally for other reasons.

There are some, perhaps, who while not altogether inaccessible to that poetic reproach just alluded to, may yet on behalf of the new order be disposed to parry it; and this to the extent of iconoclasm, if need be. For example, prompted by the sight of the star inserted in the *Victory's* deck designating the spot where the great sailor fell, these martial utilitarians may suggest considerations implying that Nelson's ornate publication of his person in battle was not only unnecessary, but not military, nay, savoured of foolhardiness and vanity. They may add, too, that at Trafalgar it was in effect nothing less than a challenge to death; and death came; and that but for his bravado the victorious admiral might possibly have survived the battle, and so, instead of having his sagacious dying injunctions overruled by his immediate successor in command, he himself when the contest was decided might have brought his shattered fleet to anchor, a proceeding which might have averted the deplorable loss of life by shipwreck in the elemental tempest that followed the martial one.

Well, should we set aside the more than disputable point whether for various reasons it was possible to anchor the fleet, then plausibly enough the Benthamites of war may urge the above.

But he *might have been* is but boggy ground to build on. And certainly in foresight as to the larger issue of an encounter, and anxious preparations for it – buoying the deadly way and mapping it out, as at Copenhagen – few commanders have been so painstakingly circumspect as this reckless declarer of his person in fight.

Personal prudence, even when dictated by quite other than selfish considerations, is surely no special virtue in a military man; while an excessive love of glory, exercising to the uttermost the honest heartfelt sense of duty, is the first. If the name Wellington is not so much of a trumpet to the blood as the simpler name Nelson, the reason for this may perhaps be inferred from the above. Alfred in his funeral ode on the victor of Waterloo ventures not to call him the greatest soldier of all time, though in the same ode he invokes Nelson as 'the greatest sailor since the world began'.

At Trafalgar Nelson, on the brink of opening the fight, sat down and wrote his last brief will and testament. If under the presentiment of the most magnificent of all victories, to be crowned by his own glorious death, a sort of priestly motive led him to dress his person in the jewelled vouchers of his own shining deeds; if thus to have adorned himself for the altar and the sacrifice were indeed vainglory, then affectation and fustian is each truly heroic line in the great epics and dramas, since in such lines the poet but embodies in verse those exaltations of sentiment that a nature like Nelson, the opportunity being given, vitalises into acts.

5

The outbreak at the Nore was put down. But not every grievance was redressed. If the contractors, for example, were no longer permitted to ply some practices peculiar to their tribe everywhere, such as providing shoddy cloth, rations not sound or false in the measure, not the less impressment, for one thing, went on. By custom sanctioned for centuries, and judicially maintained by a lord chancellor as late as Mansfield, that mode of manning the fleet, a mode now fallen into a sort of abeyance but never formally renounced, it was not practicable to give up in those years. Its abrogation would have crippled the indispensable fleet, one wholly under canvas, no steam-power, its innumerable sails and thousands of cannon, everything in short, worked by muscle alone; a fleet the more insatiate in demand for men, because then multiplying its ships of all grades against contingencies present and to come of the convulsed continent.

Discontent foreran the two mutinies, and more or less it lurkingly survived them. Hence it was not unreasonable to apprehend some return of trouble sporadic or general. One instance of such apprehensions: In the same year with this story, Nelson, then Vice-Admiral Sir Horatio, being with the fleet off the Spanish coast, was directed by the admiral in command to shift his pennant from the *Captain* to the *Theseus*; and for this reason: that the latter ship having newly arrived in the station from home where it had taken part in the Great Mutiny, danger was apprehended from the temper of the men; and it was thought that an officer like Nelson was the one, not indeed to terrorise the crew into base subjection, but to win them by force of his mere presence back to an allegiance, if not as enthusiastic as his own, yet as true. So it was that for a time on more than one quarter-deck anxiety did exist. At sea precautionary vigilance was strained against relapse. At short notice an engagement might come on. When it did, the lieutenants assigned to batteries felt it incumbent on them in some instances to stand with drawn swords behind the men working the guns.

But on board the seventy-four in which Billy now swung his hammock, very little in the manner of the men and nothing obvious in the demeanour of the officers would have suggested to an ordinary observer that the Great Mutiny was a recent event. In their general bearing and conduct the commissioned officers of a warship naturally take their tone from the commander, that is if he have that ascendancy of character that ought to be his.

Captain the Honourable Edward Fairfax Vere, to give him his full title, was a bachelor of forty or thereabouts, a sailor of distinction, even in a time prolific of renowned seamen. Though allied to the higher nobility, his advancement had not been altogether owing to influences connected with that circumstance. He had seen much service, been in various engagements, always acquitting himself as an officer mindful of the welfare of his men, but never tolerating an infraction of discipline; thoroughly versed in the science of his profession, and intrepid to the verge of temerity, though never injudiciously so. For his gallantry in the West Indian waters as flag-lieutenant under Rodney in that admiral's crowning victory over de Grasse, he was made a post-captain.

Ashore in the garb of a civilian, scarce anyone would have taken him for a sailor, more especially that he never garnished unprofessional talk with nautical terms, and grave in his bearing, evinced little appreciation of mere humour. It was not out of keeping with these traits that on a passage when nothing demanded his paramount action, he was the most undemonstrative of men. Any landsman observing this gentleman, not conspicuous by his stature and wearing no pronounced insignia, emerging from his retreat to the open deck, and noting the silent deference of the officers retiring to leeward, might have taken him for the king's guest, a civilian aboard the king's ship, some highly honourable discreet envoy on his way to an important post. But, in fact, this unobtrusiveness of demeanour may have proceeded from a certain unaffected modesty of manhood sometimes accompanying a resolute nature, a modesty evinced at all times not calling for pronounced action, and which shown in any rank of life suggests a virtue aristocratic in kind.

As with some others engaged in various departments of the world's more heroic activities, Captain Vere, though practical enough upon occasion, would at times betray a certain dreaminess of mood. Standing alone on the weather-side of the greater-deck, one hand holding by the rigging, he would absently gaze off at the black sea. At the presentation to him of some minor matter interrupting the current of his thoughts, he would show more or less irascibility; but instantly he would control it.

In the navy he was popularly known by the appellation Starry Vere. How such a designation happened to fall upon one who, whatever his sturdy qualities, was without any brilliant ones, was in this wise: a favourite kinsman, Lord Denton, a free-handed fellow, had been the first to meet and congratulate him upon his return to England from the West Indian cruise; and but the day previous turning over a copy of Andrew Marvell's poems had lighted, not for the first time however, upon the lines entitled 'Appleton House', the name of one of the seats of their common ancestor, a hero in the German wars of the seventeenth century, in which poem occur the lines,

> This 'tis to have been from the first
> In a domestic heaven nursed,
> Under the discipline severe
> Of Fairfax and the starry Vere.

And so, upon embracing his cousin fresh from Rodney's victory, wherein he had played so gallant a part, brimming over with just family pride in the sailor of their house, he exuberantly exclaimed, 'Give ye joy, Ed; give ye joy, my starry Vere!' This got currency, and the novel prefix serving in familiar parlance readily to distinguish the *Indomitable*'s captain from another Vere, his senior, a distant relative, an officer of like rank in the navy, it remained permanently attached to the surname.

6

In view of the part that the commander of the *Indomitable* plays in scenes shortly to follow, it may be well to fill out that sketch of him outlined in the previous chapter. Aside from his qualities as a sea-officer Captain Vere was an exceptional character. Unlike no few of England's renowned sailors, long and arduous service with signal devotion to it had not resulted in absorbing and *salting* the entire man. He had a marked leading towards everything intellectual. He loved books, never going to sea without a newly replenished library, compact but of the best. The isolated leisure, in some cases so wearisome, falling at intervals to commanders even during a war-cruise, never was tedious to Captain Vere. With nothing of that literary taste which less heeds the thing conveyed than the vehicle, his bias was towards those books to which every serious mind of superior order, occupying any active post of authority in the world, naturally inclines; books treating of actual men and events, no matter of what era – history, biography, and unconventional writers who, free from cant and convention, like Montaigne, honestly, and in the spirit of common sense, philosophise upon realities.

In this love of reading he found confirmation of his own more reserved thoughts – confirmation which he had vainly sought in social converse, so that as touching most fundamental topics, there had got to be established in him some positive convictions which he felt would abide in him essentially unmodified so long as his intelligent part remained unimpaired. In view of the humbled period in which his lot was cast, this was well for him. His settled convictions were as a dyke against those invading waters of novel opinion, social, political, and otherwise, which carried away as in a torrent no few minds in those days, minds by nature not inferior to his own. While other members of that aristocracy to which by birth he belonged were incensed at the innovators mainly because their theories were inimical to the privileged classes, Captain Vere disinterestedly opposed them not alone because they seemed to him incapable of embodiment in lasting institutions, but at war with the world and the peace of mankind.

With minds less stored than his and less earnest, some officers of his rank, with whom at times he would necessarily consort, found him lacking in the companionable quality, a dry and bookish gentleman as they deemed. Upon any chance withdrawal from their company one would be apt to say to another something like this: 'Vere is a noble fellow, "Starry Vere". 'Spite the gazettes, Sir Horatio is at bottom scarce a better seaman or fighter. But between you and me now, don't you think there is a queer streak of the pedantic running through him? Yes, like the king's yarn in a coil of navy-rope.'

Some apparent ground there was for this sort of confidential criticism, since not only did the captain's discourse never fall into the jocosely familiar, but in illustrating any point touching the stirring personages and events of the time, he would cite some historical character or incident of antiquity with the same easy air that he would cite from the moderns. He seemed unmindful of the circumstance that to his bluff company such allusions, however pertinent they might really be, were altogether alien to men whose reading was mainly confined to the journals. But considerateness in such matters is not easy in natures constituted like Captain Vere's. Their honesty prescribes to them directness, sometimes far-reaching like that of a migratory fowl that in its flight never heeds when it crosses a frontier.

7

The lieutenants and other commissioned gentlemen forming
Captain Vere's staff it is not necessary here to particularise, nor
needs it to make mention of any of the warrant-officers. But among
the petty officers was one who, having much to do with the story,
may as well be forthwith introduced. This portrait I essay, but shall
never hit it.

This was John Claggart, the master-at-arms. But that sea-title
may to landsmen seem somewhat equivocal. Originally, doubtless,
that petty officer's function was the instruction of the men in the
use of arms, sword or cutlass. But very long ago, owing to the
advance in gunnery, making hand-to-hand encounters less frequent,
and giving to nitre and sulphur the pre-eminence over steel, that
function ceased; the master-at-arms of a great warship becoming a
sort of chief of police charged among other matters with the duty of
preserving order on the populous lower gun-decks.

Claggart was a man of about five-and-thirty, somewhat spare and
tall, yet of no ill figure upon the whole. His hand was too small and
shapely to have been accustomed to hard toil. The face was a notable
one; the features, all except the chin, cleanly cut as those on a Greek
medallion; yet the chin, beardless as Tecumseh's, had something of
the strange protuberant heaviness in its make that recalled the prints
of the Revd Dr Titus Oates, the historical deponent with the clerical
drawl in the time of Charles II, and the fraud of the alleged Popish
Plot. It served Claggart in his office that his eye could cast a tutoring
glance. His brow was of the sort phrenologically associated with
more than average intellect; silken jet curls, partly clustering over it,
making a foil to the pallor below, a pallor tinged with a faint shade
of amber akin to the hue of time-tinted marbles of old.

This complexion singularly contrasting with the red or deeply
bronzed visages of the sailors, and in part the result of his official
seclusion from the sunlight, though it was not exactly displeasing,
nevertheless seemed to hint of something defective or abnormal in
the constitution and blood. But his general aspect and manner were
so suggestive of an education and career incongruous with his naval
function, that when not actively engaged in it he looked like a man
of high quality, social and moral, who for reasons of his own was
keeping incognito. Nothing was known of his former life. It might
be that he was an Englishman; and yet there lurked a bit of accent in
his speech suggesting that possibly he was not such by birth, but

through naturalisation in early childhood. Among certain grizzled sea-gossips of the gun-decks and forecastle went a rumour perdue that the master-at-arms was a chevalier who had volunteered into the king's navy by way of compounding for some mysterious swindle whereof he had been arraigned at the king's bench. The fact that nobody could substantiate this report was, of course, nothing against its secret currency. Such a rumour once started on the gun-decks in reference to almost anyone below the rank of a commissioned officer would, during the period assigned to this narrative, have seemed not altogether wanting in credibility to the tarry old wiseacres of a man-of-war crew. And indeed a man of Claggart's accomplishments, without prior nautical experience entering the navy at mature life, as he did, and necessarily allotted at the start to the lowest grade in it; a man, too, who never made allusion to his previous life ashore; these were circumstances which in the dearth of exact knowledge as to his true antecedents opened to the invidious a vague field for unfavourable surmise.

But the sailors' dog-watch gossip concerning him derived a vague plausibility from the fact that now for some period the British navy could so little afford to be squeamish in the matter of keeping up the muster-rolls, that not only were press-gangs notoriously abroad both afloat and ashore, but there was little or no secret about another matter, namely, that the London police were at liberty to capture any able-bodied suspect, and any questionable fellow at large, and summarily ship him to the dockyard or fleet. Furthermore, even among voluntary enlistments, there were instances where the motive thereto partook neither of patriotic impulse nor yet of a random desire to experience a bit of sea-life and martial adventure. Insolvent debtors of minor grade, together with the promiscuous lame ducks of morality, found in the navy a convenient and secure refuge. Secure, because once enlisted aboard a king's ship, they were as much in sanctuary as the transgressor of the Middle Ages harbouring himself under the shadow of the altar. Such sanctioned irregularities, which for obvious reasons the government would hardly think to parade at the time, and which consequently, and as affecting the least influential class of mankind, have all but dropped into oblivion, lend colour to something for the truth whereof I do not vouch, and hence have some scruple in stating; something I remember having seen in print, though the book I cannot recall; but the same thing was personally communicated to me now more than forty years ago by an old pensioner in a cocked hat, with whom I had a most interesting talk on the terrace at Greenwich – a Baltimore negro, a Trafalgar man. It was to this effect: In the case of a warship short of hands, whose speedy sailing was imperative, the deficient quota, in lack of any other way of making it good, would be eked out by drafts called direct from the jails. For reasons previously suggested it would not perhaps be easy at the present day directly to prove or disprove the allegation. But allowed as a verity, how significant would it be of England's straits at the time, confronted by these wars which like a flight of harpies rose shrieking from the din and dust of the fallen Bastille. That era appears measurably clear to us who look back at it, and but read of it. But to the grandfathers of us greybeards, the thoughtful of them, the genius of it presented an aspect like that of Camoens' 'Spirit of the Cape', an eclipsing menace mysterious and prodigious. Not America was exempt from apprehension. At the height of Napoleon's unexampled conquests, there were Americans who had fought at Bunker Hill who looked forward to the possibility that the Atlantic might prove no barrier against the ultimate schemes of this portentous upstart from the revolutionary chaos, who seemed in act of fulfilling judgment prefigured in the Apocalypse.

But the less credence was to be given to the gun-deck talk touching Claggart, seeing that no man holding his office in a man-of-war can ever hope to be popular with the crew. Besides, in derogatory comments upon one against whom they have a grudge, or for any reason or no reason mislike, sailors are much like landsmen, they are apt to exaggerate or romance.

About as much was really known to the *Indomitable*'s tars of the master-at-arms' career before entering the service as an astronomer knows about a comet's travels prior to its first observable appearance in the sky. The verdict of the sea-quidnuncs has been cited only by way of showing what sort of moral impression the man made upon rude uncultivated natures, whose conceptions of human wickedness were necessarily of the narrowest, limited to ideas of vulgar rascality – a thief among the swinging hammocks during a night-watch, or the man-brokers and land-sharks of the seaports.

It was no gossip, however, but fact, that though, as before hinted, Claggart upon his entrance into the navy was, as a novice, assigned to the least honourable section of a man-of-war's crew, embracing the drudges, he did not long remain there.

The superior capacity he immediately evinced, his constitutional sobriety, ingratiating deference to superiors, together with a peculiar ferreting genius manifested on a singular occasion, all this capped by a certain austere patriotism, abruptly advanced him to the position of master-at-arms.

Of this maritime chief of police the ship's corporals, so called, were the immediate subordinates, and compliant ones; and this, as is to be noted in some business departments ashore, almost to a degree inconsistent with entire moral volition. His place put various converging wires of underground influence under the chief's control, capable when astutely worked through his understrappers of operating to the mysterious discomfort, if nothing worse, of any of the sea-commonalty.

8

Life in the foretop well agreed with Billy Budd. There, when not actually engaged on the yards yet higher aloft, the topmen, who as such had been picked out for youth and activity, constituted an aerial club, lounging at ease against the smaller stun'-sails rolled up into cushions, spinning yarns like the lazy gods and frequently amused with what was going on in the busy world of the decks below. No wonder then that a young fellow of Billy's disposition was well content in such society. Giving no cause of offence to anybody, he was always alert at a call. So in the merchant service it had been with him. But now such punctiliousness in duty was shown that his topmates would sometimes good-naturedly laugh at him for it. This heightened alacrity had its cause, namely: the impression made upon him by the first formal gangway-punishment he had ever witnessed, which befell the day following his impressment. It had been incurred by a little fellow, young, a novice, an after-guardsman absent from his assigned post when the ship was being put about, a dereliction resulting in a rather serious hitch to that manoeuvre, one demanding instantaneous promptitude in letting go and making fast. When Billy saw the culprit's naked back under the scourge gridironed with red welts, and worse; when he marked the dire expression in the liberated man's face, as with his woollen shirt flung over him by the executioner he rushed forward from the spot to bury himself in the crowd, Billy was horrified. He resolved that never through remissness would he make himself liable to such a visitation, or do or omit aught that might merit even verbal reproof. What then was his surprise and concern when ultimately he found himself getting into petty trouble occasionally about such matters as the stowage of his bag, or something amiss in his hammock, matters under the police oversight of the ship's corporals of the lower decks, and which brought down on him a vague threat from one of them.

So heedful in all things as he was, how could this be? He could not understand it, and it more than vexed him. When he spoke to his young topmates about it, they were either lightly incredulous, or found something comical in his unconcealed anxiety. 'Is it your bag, Billy?' said one; 'well, sew yourself up in it, Billy boy, and then you'll be sure to know if anybody meddles with it.'

Now there was a veteran aboard who, because his years began to disqualify him from more active work, had been recently assigned duty as mainmast-man in his watch, looking to the gear belayed at the rail round about that great spar near the deck. At off-times the foretopman had picked up some acquaintance with him, and now in his trouble it occurred to him that he might be the sort of person to go to for wise counsel. He was an old Dansker long anglicised in the service, of few words, many wrinkles and some honourable scars. His wizened face, time-tinted and weather-stormed to the complexion of an antique parchment, was here and there peppered blue by the chance explosion of a gun-carriage in action. He was an *Agamemnon* man; some two years prior to the time of this story having served under Nelson, when but Sir Horatio, in that ship immortal in naval memory, and which, dismantled and in parts broken up to her bare ribs, is seen a grand skeleton in Haydon's etching. As one of a boarding-party from the *Agamemnon* he had received a cut slantwise along one temple and cheek, leaving a long pale scar like a streak of dawn's light falling athwart the dark visage. It was on account of that scar and the affair in which it was known that he had received it, as well as from his blue-peppered complexion, that the Dansker went among the *Indomitable*'s crew by the name of 'Board-her-in-the-smoke'.

Now the first time that his small weasel eyes happened to light on Billy Budd, a certain grim internal merriment set all his ancient wrinkles into antic play. Was it that his eccentric unsentimental old sapience, primitive in its kind, saw, or thought it saw, something which in contrast with the warship's environment looked oddly incongruous in the Handsome Sailor? But after slyly studying him at intervals, the old Merlin's equivocal merriment was modified by now. For now when the twain would meet, it would start in his face a quizzing sort of look, but it would be but momentary and sometimes replaced by an expression of speculative query as to what might eventually befall a nature like that, dropped into a world not without some mantraps and against whose subtleties simple courage, lacking experience and address and without any touch of defensive ugliness, is of little avail; and where such innocence as man is capable of does yet in a moral emergency not always sharpen the faculties or enlighten the will.

However it was, the Dansker in his ascetic way rather took to Billy. Nor was this only because of a certain philosophic interest in such a character. There was another cause. While the old man's eccentricities, sometimes bordering on the ursine, repelled the juniors, Billy, undeterred thereby, would make advances, never passing the old *Agamemnon* man without a salutation marked by that respect which is seldom lost on the aged, however crabbed at times, or whatever their station in life. There was a vein of dry humour, or what not, in the mastman; and whether in freak of patriarchal irony touching Billy's youth and athletic frame, or for some other and more recondite reason, from the first in addressing him he always substituted Baby for Billy. The Dansker, in fact, being the originator of the name by which the foretopman eventually became known aboard ship.

Well then, in his mysterious little difficulty going in quest of the wrinkled one, Billy found him off duty in a dog-watch ruminating by himself, seated on a shot-box of the upper gun-deck, now and then surveying with a somewhat cynical regard certain of the more swaggering promenaders there. Billy recounted his trouble, again wondering how it all happened. The salt seer attentively listened, accompanying the foretopman's recitals with queer twitchings of his wrinkles and problematical little sparkles of his small ferret eyes. Making an end of his story, the foretopman asked, 'And now, Dansker, do tell me what you think of it.' The old man, shoving up the front of his tarpaulin and deliberately rubbing the long slant scar at the point where it entered the thin hair, laconically said, 'Baby Budd, Jemmy Legs' (meaning the master-at-arms) 'is down on you.'

'Jemmy Legs!' ejaculated Billy, his welkin eyes expanding; 'what for? Why, he calls me *the sweet and pleasant young fellow*, they tell me.'

'Does he so?' grinned the grizzled one; then said, 'Aye, Baby lad, a sweet voice has Jemmy Legs.'

'No, not always. But to me he has. I seldom pass him but there comes a pleasant word.'

'And that's because he's down upon you, Baby Budd.'

Such reiteration, along with the manner of it, incomprehensible to a novice, disturbed Billy almost as much as the mystery for which he had sought explanation. Something less unpleasingly oracular he tried to extract; but the old sea-Chiron, thinking perhaps that for the nonce he had sufficiently instructed his young Achilles, pursed his lips, gathered all his wrinkles together, and would commit himself to nothing further.

Years, and those experiences which befall certain shrewder men subordinated lifelong to the will of superiors, all this had developed in the Dansker the pithy guarded cynicism that was his leading characteristic.

9

The next day an incident served to confirm Billy Budd in his incredulity as to the Dansker's strange summing-up of the case submitted.

The ship at noon going large before the wind was rolling on her course, and he, below at dinner and engaged in some sportful talk with the members of his mess, chanced in a sudden lurch to spill the entire contents of his soup-pan upon the new-scrubbed deck. Claggart, the master-at-arms, official rattan in hand, happened to be passing along the battery in a bay of which the mess was lodged, and the greasy liquid streamed just across his path. Stepping over it, he was proceeding on his way without comment, since the matter was nothing to take notice of under the circumstances, when he happened to observe who it was that had done the spilling. His countenance changed. Pausing, he was about to ejaculate something hasty at the sailor, but checked himself, and pointing down to the streaming soup, playfully tapped him from behind with his rattan, saying, in a low musical voice, peculiar to him at times, 'Handsomely done, my lad! And handsome is as handsome did it, too!' and with that passed on. Not noted by Billy as not coming within his view was the involuntary smile, or rather grimace, that accompanied Claggart's equivocal words. Aridly it drew down the thin corners of his shapely mouth. But everybody taking his remark as meant for humorous, and at which therefore as coming from a superior they were bound to laugh, 'with counterfeited glee', acted accordingly; and Billy, tickled, it may be, by the allusion to his being the Handsome Sailor, merrily joined in; then addressing his messmates exclaimed, 'There, now, who says that Jemmy Legs is down on me!'

'And who said he was, Beauty?' demanded one Donald with some surprise. Whereat the foretopman looked a little foolish, recalling that it was only one person, Board-her-in-the-smoke, who had suggested what to him was the smoky idea that this pleasant master-at-arms was in any peculiar way hostile to him. Meantime that functionary resuming his path must have momentarily worn some expression less guarded than that of the bitter smile and, usurping the face from the heart, some distorting expression perhaps, for a drummer-boy, heedlessly frolicking along from the opposite direction, and chancing to come into light collision with his person, was strangely disconcerted by his aspect. Nor was the impression lessened when the official, impulsively giving him a sharp cut with the rattan, vehemently exclaimed, 'Look where you go!'

10

What was the matter with the master-at-arms? And be the matter what it might, how could it have direct relation to Billy Budd, with whom prior to the affair of the spilled soup he had never come into any special contact, official or otherwise? What indeed could the trouble have to do with one so little inclined to give offence as the merchant ship's peacemaker, even him who in Claggart's own phrase was 'the sweet and pleasant young fellow'? Yes, why should Jemmy Legs, to borrow the Dansker's expression, be *down* on the Handsome Sailor?

But, at heart and not for nothing, as the late chance encounter may indicate to the discerning, down on him, secretly down on him, he assuredly was.

Now to invent something touching the more private career of Claggart, something involving Billy Budd, of which something the latter should be wholly ignorant, some romantic incident implying that Claggart's knowledge of the young bluejacket began at some period anterior to catching sight of him on board the seventy-four – all this, not so difficult to do, might avail in a way more or less interesting to account for whatever enigma may appear to lurk in the case. But, in fact, there was nothing of the sort. And yet the cause, necessarily to be assumed as the sole one assignable, is in its very realism as much charged with that prime element of Radcliffian romance, the mysterious, as any that the ingenuity of the author of the *Mysteries of Udolpho* could devise. For what can more partake of the mysterious than an antipathy spontaneous and profound such as is evoked in certain exceptional mortals by the mere aspect of some

other mortal, however harmless he may be? – if not called forth by
that very harmlessness itself.

Now there can exist no irritating juxtaposition of dissimilar
personalities comparable to that which is possible aboard a great
warship fully manned and at sea. There, every day, among all ranks,
almost every man comes into more or less of contact with almost
every other man. Wholly there to avoid even the sight of an
aggravating object one must needs give it Jonah's toss, or jump
overboard himself. Imagine how all this might eventually operate
on some peculiar human creature the direct reverse of a saint?

But for the adequate comprehending of Claggart by a normal
nature these hints are insufficient. To pass from a normal nature to
him one must cross 'the deadly space between', and this is best done
by indirection.

Long ago an honest scholar, my senior, said to me in reference to
one who like himself is now no more, a man so unimpeachably
respectable that against him nothing was ever openly said, though
among the few something was whispered, 'Yes, X is a nut not to be
cracked by the tap of a lady's fan. You are aware that I am the
adherent of no organised religion, much less of any philosophy built
into a system. Well, for all that, I think that to try and get into X,
enter his labyrinth, and get out again, without a clue derived from
some source other than what is known as *knowledge of the world*, that
were hardly possible, at least for me.'

'Why,' said I, 'X, however singular a study to some, is yet human,
and knowledge of the world assuredly implies the knowledge of
human nature, and in most of its varieties.'

'Yes, but a superficial knowledge of it, serving ordinary purposes.
But for anything deeper I am not certain whether to know the world
and to know human nature be not two distinct branches of knowledge, which while they may coexist in the same heart, yet either
may exist with little or nothing of the other. Nay, in an average man
of the world, his constant rubbing with it blunts that fine spiritual
insight indispensable to the understanding of the essential in certain
exceptional characters, whether evil ones or good. In a matter of
some importance I have seen a girl wind an old lawyer about her
little finger. Nor was it dotage or senile love. Nothing of the sort.
But he knew law better than he knew the girl's heart. Coke and
Blackstone hardly shed so much light into obscure spiritual places as
the Hebrew prophets. And who were they? Mostly recluses.'

At the time my inexperience was such that I did not quite see the
drift of all this. It may be that I see it now. And, indeed, if that

lexicon which is based on holy writ were any longer popular, one might with less difficulty define and denominate certain phenomenal men. As it is, one must turn to some authority not liable to the charge of being tinctured with the biblical element.

In a list of definitions included in the authentic translation of Plato, a list attributed to him, occurs this: *natural depravity* – a depravity according to nature. A definition which, though savouring of Calvinism, by no means involves Calvin's dogma as to total mankind. Evidently its intent makes it applicable but to individuals. Not many are the examples of this depravity which the gallows and jail supply. At any rate, for notable instances – since these have no vulgar alloy of the brute in them, but invariably are dominated by intellectuality – one must go elsewhere. Civilisation, especially if of the austerer sort, is auspicious to it. It folds itself in the mantle of respectability. It has its certain negative virtues serving as silent auxiliaries. It is not going too far to say that it is without vices or small sins. There is a phenomenal pride in it that excludes them from anything – never mercenary or avaricious. In short, the depravity here meant partakes nothing of the sordid or sensual. It is serious, but free from acerbity. Though no flatterer of mankind, it never speaks ill of it.

But the thing which in eminent instances signalises so exceptional a nature is this: though the man's even temper and discreet bearing would seem to intimate a mind peculiarly subject to the law of reason, not the less in his soul's recesses he would seem to riot in complete exemption from that law, having apparently little to do with reason further than to employ it as an ambidexter implement for effecting the irrational. That is to say: towards the accomplishment of an aim which in wantonness of malignity would seem to partake of the insane, he will direct a cool judgement, sagacious and sound.

These men are true madmen, and of the most dangerous sort, for their lunacy is not continuous, but occasional, evoked by some special object; it is secretive and self-contained, so that when most active it is to the average mind not distinguished from sanity, and for the reason above suggested that whatever its aim may be, and the aim is never disclosed, the method and the outward proceeding is always perfectly rational.

Now something such was Claggart, in whom was the mania of an evil nature, not engendered by vicious training or corrupting books or licentious living, but born with him and innate, in short, 'a depravity according to nature'.

Can it be this phenomenon, disowned or not acknowledged, that in some criminal cases puzzles the courts? For this cause have our juries at times not only to endure the prolonged contentions of lawyers with their fees, but also the yet more perplexing strife of the medical experts with theirs? But why leave it to them? Why not subpoena as well the clerical proficients? Their vocation bringing them into peculiar contact with so many human beings, and sometimes in their least guarded hour, in interviews very much more confidential than those of physician and patient; this would seem to qualify them to know something about those intricacies involved in the question of moral responsibility; whether in a given case, say, the crime proceeded from mania in the brain or rabies of the heart. As to any differences among themselves these clerical proficients might develop on the stand, these could hardly be greater than the direct contradictions exchanged between the remunerated medical experts.

Dark sayings are these, some will say. But why? It is because they somewhat savour of holy writ in its phrase 'mysteries of iniquity'.

The point of the story turning on the hidden nature of the master-at-arms has necessitated this chapter. With an added hint or two in connection with the accident of the mess, the resumed narrative must be left to vindicate as it may its own credibility.

11

Pale ire, envy and despair

That Claggart's figure was not amiss, and his face, save the chin, well moulded, has already been said. Of these favourable points he seemed not insensible, for he was not only neat but careful in his dress. But the form of Billy Budd was heroic; and if his face was without the intellectual look of the pallid Claggart's, not the less was it lit, like his, from within, though from a different source. The bonfire in his heart made luminous the rose-tan in his cheek.

In view of the marked contrast between the persons of the twain, it is more than probable that when the master-at-arms in the scene last given applied to the sailor the proverb *Handsome is as handsome does*, he there let escape an ironic inkling, not caught by the young sailors who heard it, as to what it was that had first moved him against Billy, namely, his significant personal beauty.

Now envy and antipathy, passions irreconcilable in reason,

nevertheless in fact may spring conjoined like Chang and Eng in one birth. Is envy then such a monster? Well, though many an arraigned mortal has in hopes of mitigated penalty pleaded guilty to horrible actions, did ever anybody seriously confess to envy? Something there is in it universally felt to be more shameful than even felonious crime. And not only does everybody disown it, but the better sort are inclined to incredulity when it is in earnest imputed to an intelligent man. But since its lodgement is in the heart, not the brain, no degree of intellect supplies a guarantee against it. But Claggart's was no vulgar form of the passion. Nor, as directed towards Billy Budd, did it partake of that streak of apprehensive jealousy that marred Saul's visage perturbedly brooding on the comely young David. Claggart's envy struck deeper. If askance he eyed the good looks, cheery health, and frank enjoyment of young life in Billy Budd, it was because these happened to go along with a nature that, as Claggart magnetically felt, had in its simplicity never willed malice, or experienced the reactionary bite of that serpent. To him, the spirit lodged within Billy and looking out from his welkin eyes as from windows, that ineffability which made the dimple in his dyed cheek, suppled his joints and danced in his yellow curls, made him pre-eminently the Handsome Sailor. One person excepted, the master-at-arms was perhaps the only man in the ship intellectually capable of adequately appreciating the moral phenomenon presented in Billy Budd, and the insight but intensified his passion, which assuming various secret forms within him, at times assumed that of cynic disdain – disdain of innocence. To be nothing more than innocent! Yet in an aesthetic way he saw the charm of it, the courageous free-and-easy temper of it, and fain would have shared it, but he despaired of it.

With no power to annul the elemental evil in himself, though he could hide it readily enough; apprehending the good, but powerless to be it; what recourse is left to a nature like Claggart's, surcharged with energy as such natures almost invariably are, but to recoil upon itself, and, like the scorpion for which the Creator alone is responsible, act out to the end its allotted part?

Passion, and passion in its profoundest, is not a thing demanding a palatial stage whereon to play its part. Down among the groundlings, among the beggars and rakers of the garbage, profound passion is enacted. And the circumstances that provoke it, however trivial or mean, are no measure of its power. In the present instance the stage is a scrubbed gun-deck, and one of the external provocations a man-of-war's man's spilled soup.

Now when the master-at-arms noticed whence came that greasy fluid streaming before his feet, he must have taken it – to some extent wilfully perhaps – not for the mere accident it assuredly was, but for the sly escape of a spontaneous feeling on Billy's part more or less answering to the antipathy on his own. In effect a foolish demonstration he must have thought, and very harmless, like the futile kick of a heifer, which yet, were the heifer a shod stallion, would not be so harmless. Even so was it that into the gall of envy Claggart infused the vitriol of his contempt. But the incident confirmed to him certain tell-tale reports purveyed to his ear by Squeak, one of his more cunning corporals, a grizzled little man, so nicknamed by the sailors on account of his squeaky voice and sharp visage ferreting about the dark corners of the lower decks after interlopers, satirically suggesting to them the idea of a rat in a cellar.

Now his chief's employing him as an implicit tool in laying little traps for the worriment of the foretopman – for it was from the master-at-arms that the petty persecutions heretofore adverted to had proceeded – the corporal, having naturally enough concluded that his master could have no love for the sailor, made it his business, faithful understrapper that he was, to ferment the ill blood by perverting to his chief certain innocent frolics of the good-natured foretopman, besides inventing for his mouth sundry contumelious epithets he claimed to have overheard him let fall. The master-at-arms never suspected the veracity of these reports, more especially as to the epithets, for he well knew how secretly unpopular may become a master-at-arms – at least, a master-at-arms in those days, zealous in his function – and how the bluejackets shoot at him in private their raillery and wit; the nickname by which he goes among them (Jemmy Legs) implying under the form of merriment their cherished disrespect and dislike.

In view of the greediness of hate for provocation, it hardly needed a purveyor to feed Claggart's passion. An uncommon prudence is habitual with the subtler depravity, for it has everything to hide. And in case of any merely suspected injury, its secretiveness voluntarily cuts it off from enlightenment or disillusion; and not unreluctantly, action is taken upon surmise as upon certainty. And the retaliation is apt to be in monstrous disproportion to the supposed offence; for when in anybody was revenge in its exactions aught else but an inordinate usurer? But how with Claggart's conscience? For though consciences are unlike as foreheads, every intelligence, not excluding the scriptural devils who 'believe and tremble', has one. But Claggart's conscience, being but the lawyer to his will, made ogres of trifles, probably arguing that the motive imputed to Billy in spilling the soup just when he did, together with the epithets alleged, these, if nothing more, made a strong case against him; nay, justified animosity into a sort of retributive righteousness. The Pharisee is the Guy Fawkes prowling in the hid chambers underlying some natures like Claggart's. And they can really form no conception of an unreciprocated malice. Probably, the master-at-arms' clandestine persecution of Billy was started to try the temper of the man; but it had not developed any quality in him that enmity could make official use of, or ever pervert into even plausible self-justification; so that the occurrence at the mess, petty if it were, was a welcome one to that peculiar conscience assigned to be the private mentor of Claggart; and for the rest, not improbably, it put him upon new experiments.

12

Not many days after the last incident narrated, something befell Billy Budd that more gravelled him than aught that had previously occurred.

It was a warm night for the latitude; and the foretopman whose watch at the time was properly below, was dozing on the uppermost deck whither he had ascended from his hot hammock – one of hundreds suspended so closely wedged together over a lower gun-deck that there was little or no swing to them. He lay as in the shadow of a hillside stretched under the lee of the booms, a piled ridge of spare spars among which the ship's largest boat, the launch, was stowed. Alongside of three other slumberers from below, he lay near one end of the booms which approached from the foremast; his station aloft on duty as a foretopman being just over the deck station of the forecastleman, entitling him according to usage to make himself more or less at home in that neighbourhood.

Presently he was stirred into semi-consciousness by somebody, who must have previously sounded the sleep of the others, touching his shoulder, and then, as the foretopman raised his head, breathing into his ear in a quick whisper, 'Slip into the lee fore-chains, Billy; there is something in the wind. Don't speak. Quick. I will meet you there;' and who then disappeared.

Now Billy, like sundry other essentially good-natured ones, had some of the weaknesses inseparable from essential good nature; and among these was a reluctance, almost an incapacity, of plumply saying no to an abrupt proposition not obviously absurd on the face of it, nor obviously unfriendly, nor iniquitous. And being of warm blood he had not the phlegm to negate any proposition by unresponsive inaction. Like his sense of fear, his apprehension as to aught outside of the honest and natural was seldom very quick. Besides, upon the present occasion, the drowse from his sleep still hung upon him.

However it was, he mechanically rose, and sleepily wondering what could be 'in the wind', betook himself to the designated place – a narrow platform, one of six, outside of the high bulwarks, and screened by the great dead-eyes and multiple columned lanyards of the shrouds and back-stays; and, in a great warship of that time, of dimensions commensurate to the ample hull's magnitude; a tarry balcony, in short, overhanging the sea, and so secluded that one mariner of the *Indomitable*, a nonconformist old tar of a serious turn, made it even in daytime his private oratory.

In this retired nook the stranger soon joined Billy Budd. There was no moon as yet; a haze obscured the starlight. He could not distinctly see the stranger's face. Yet from something in the outline and carriage, Billy took him to be, and correctly, one of the afterguard.

'Hist, Billy!' said the man, in the same quick, cautionary whisper as before; 'you were impressed, weren't you? Well, so was I . . . ' and he paused, as to mark the effect. But Billy, not knowing exactly what to make of this, said nothing. Then the other: 'We are not the only impressed ones, Billy. There's a gang of us. Couldn't you – help – at a pinch?'

'What do you mean?' demanded Billy, here shaking off his drowse.

'Hist, hist!' the hurried whisper now growing husky; 'see here,' and the man held up two small objects faintly twinkling in the night light; 'see, they are yours, Billy, if you'll only – '

But Billy broke in, and in his resentful eagerness to deliver himself, his vocal infirmity somewhat intruded. 'D–d–damme, I don't know what you are d–driving at, or what you mean, but you had better g–g–go where you belong!' For the moment the fellow, as confounded, did not stir; and Billy, springing to his feet, said, 'If you d–don't start, I'll t–t–t–oss you back over the r–rail!' There was no mistaking this, and the mysterious emissary decamped, disappearing in the direction of the mainmast in the shadow of the booms.

'Hallo, what's the matter?' here came growling from a forecastleman awakened from his deck-doze by Billy's raised voice. And as the foretopman reappeared, and was recognised by him, 'Ah,

Beauty, is it you? Well, something must have been the matter, for you st–st–stuttered.'

'Oh,' rejoined Billy, now mastering the impediment; 'I found an afterguardsman in our part of the ship here, and I bid him be off where he belongs.'

'And is that all you did about it, foretopman?' gruffly demanded another, an irascible old fellow of brick-coloured visage and hair, and who was known to his associate forecastlemen as Red Pepper. 'Such sneaks I should like to marry to the gunner's daughter!' by that expression meaning that he would like to subject them to disciplinary castigation over a gun.

However, Billy's rendering of the matter satisfactorily accounted to these enquirers for the brief commotion, since of all the sections of a ship's company the forecastlemen, veterans for the most part, and bigoted in their sea-prejudices, are the most jealous in resenting territorial encroachments, especially on the part of any of the afterguard, of whom they have but a sorry opinion, chiefly lands-men, never going aloft except to reef or furl the mainsail, and in no wise competent to handle a marling-spike or turn in a dead-eye, say.

13

This incident sorely puzzled Billy Budd. It was an entirely new experience; the first time in his life that he had ever been personally approached in underhand intriguing fashion. Prior to this encounter he had known nothing of the afterguardsman, the two men being stationed wide apart, one forward and aloft during his watch, the other on deck and aft.

What could it mean? And could they really be guineas, those two glittering objects the interloper had held up to his (Billy's) eyes? Where could the fellow get guineas? Why, even buttons, spare buttons, are not so plentiful at sea. The more he turned the matter over, the more he was nonplussed, and made uneasy and discomforted. In his disgustful recoil from an overture which though he but ill comprehended he instinctively knew must involve evil of some sort, Billy Budd was like a young horse fresh from the pasture suddenly inhaling a vile whiff from some chemical factory, and by repeated snortings trying to get it out of his nostrils and lungs. This frame of mind barred all desire of holding further parley with the fellow, even were it but for the purpose of gaining some enlightenment as to his design in approaching him. And yet he was not without natural curiosity to see how such a visitor in the dark would look in broad day.

He espied him the following afternoon in his first dog-watch below, one of the smokers on that forward part of the upper gun-deck allotted to the pipe. He recognised him by his general cut and build, more than by his round freckled face and glassy eyes of pale blue veiled with lashes all but white. And yet Billy was a bit uncertain whether indeed it were he – yonder chap about his own age, chatting and laughing in free-hearted way, leaning against a gun; a genial young fellow enough to look at, and something of a rattle-brain, to all appearance. Rather chubby, too, for a sailor, even an afterguardsman. In short, the last man in the world, one would think, to be overburthened with thoughts, especially those perilous thoughts that must needs belong to a conspirator in any serious project, or even to the underling of such a conspirator.

Although Billy was not aware of it, the fellow with a sidelong watchful glance had perceived Billy first, and then noting that Billy was looking at him, thereupon nodded a familiar sort of friendly recognition as to an old acquaintance, without interrupting the talk he was engaged in with the group of smokers. A day or two afterwards, chancing in the evening promenade on a gun-deck to pass Billy, he offered a flying word of good-fellowship, as it were, which by its unexpectedness, and equivocalness under the circumstances, so embarrassed Billy that he knew not how to respond to it, and let it go unnoticed.

Billy was now left more at a loss than before. The ineffectual speculations into which he was led were so disturbingly alien to him, that he did his best to smother them. It never entered his mind that here was a matter which, from its extreme questionableness, it was his duty as a loyal bluejacket to report in the proper quarter. And, probably, had such a step been suggested to him, he would have been deterred from taking it by the thought, one of novice-magnanimity, that it would savour overmuch of the dirty work of a tell-tale. He kept the thing to himself. Yet upon one occasion he could not forbear a little disburthening himself to the old Dansker, tempted thereto perhaps by the influence of a balmy night when the ship lay becalmed; the twain, silent for the most part, sitting together on deck, their heads propped against the bulwarks. But it was only a partial and anonymous account that Billy gave, the unfounded scruples above referred to preventing full disclosure to anybody. Upon hearing Billy's version, the sage Dansker seemed to divine more than he was told; and after a little meditation, during which his wrinkles were pursed as into a point, quite effacing for the time that quizzing expression his face sometimes wore – 'Didn't I say so, Baby Budd?'

'Say what?' demanded Billy.

'Why, Jemmy Legs is *down* on you.'

'And what,' rejoined Billy in amazement, 'has Jemmy Legs to do with that cracked afterguardsman?'

'Ho, it was an afterguardsman, then. A cat's-paw, a cat's-paw!' And with that exclamation, which, whether it had reference to a light puff of air just then coming over the calm sea, or subtler relation to the afterguardsman, there is no telling. The old Merlin gave a twisting wrench with his black teeth at his plug of tobacco, vouchsafing no reply to Billy's impetuous question. For it was his wont to relapse into grim silence when interrogated in sceptical sort as to any of his sententious oracles, not always very clear ones, rather partaking of that obscurity which invests most Delphic deliverances from any quarter.

14

Long experience had very likely brought this old man to that bitter prudence which never interferes in aught, and never gives advice.

Yet, despite the Dansker's pithy insistence as to the master-at-arms being at the bottom of these strange experiences of Billy on board the *Indomitable*, the young sailor was ready to ascribe them to almost anybody but the man who, to use Billy's own expression, 'always had a pleasant word for him'. This is to be wondered at. Yet not so much to be wondered at. In certain matters some sailors even in mature life remain unsophisticated enough. But a young seafarer of the disposition of our athletic foretopman is much of a child-man. And yet a child's utter innocence is but its blank ignorance, and the innocence more or less wanes as intelligence waxes. But in Billy Budd intelligence, such as it was, had advanced, while yet his simple-mindedness remained for the most part unaffected. Experience is a teacher indeed; yet did Billy's years make his experience small. Besides, he had none of that intuitive knowledge of the bad which in natures not good or incompletely so, foreruns experience, and therefore may pertain, as in some instances it too clearly does pertain, even to youth.

And what could Billy know of man except of man as a mere sailor? And the old-fashioned sailor, the veritable man-before-the-mast, the sailor from boyhood up, he, though indeed of the same species as a landsman, is in some respects singularly distinct from him. The sailor is frankness, the landsman is finesse. Life us not a game with the sailor, demanding the long head; no intricate game of chess where few moves are made in straightforwardness, but ends are attained by indirection; an oblique, tedious, barren game, hardly worth that poor candle burnt out in playing it.

Yes, as a class, sailors are in character a juvenile race. Even their deviations are marked by juvenility. And this more especially held true with the sailors of Billy's time. Then, too, certain things which apply to all sailors do more pointedly operate here and there upon the junior one. Every sailor, too, is accustomed to obey orders without debating them; his life afloat is externally ruled for him; he is not brought into that promiscuous commerce with mankind where unobstructed free agency on equal terms – equal superficially, at least – soon teaches one that unless upon occasion he exercises a distrust keen in proportion to the fairness of the appearance, some foul turn may be served him. A ruled, undemonstrative distrustfulness is so habitual, not with businessmen so much as with men who know their kind in less shallow relations than business, namely certain men of the world, that they come at last to employ it all but unconsciously; and some of them would very likely feel real surprise at being charged with it as one of their general characteristics.

15

But after the little matter at the mess Billy Budd no more found himself in strange trouble at times about his hammock or his clothes-bag, or what not. While, as to that smile that occasionally sunned him, and the pleasant passing word, these were, if not more frequent, yet if anything more pronounced than before.

But for all that, there were certain other demonstrations now. When Claggart's unobserved glance happened to light on belted Billy rolling along the upper gun-deck in the leisure of the second dog-watch, exchanging passing broadsides of fun with other young promenaders in the crowd, that glance would follow the cheerful sea-Hyperion with a settled meditative and melancholy expression, his eyes strangely suffused with incipient feverish tears. Then would

Claggart look like the man of sorrows. Yes, and sometimes the melancholy expression would have in it a touch of soft yearning, as if Claggart could even have loved Billy but for fate and ban. But this was an evanescence, and quickly repented of, as it were, by an immitigable look, pinching and shrivelling the visage into the momentary semblance of a wrinkled walnut. But sometimes catching sight in advance of the foretopman coming in his direction, he would, upon their nearing, step aside a little to let him pass, dwelling upon Billy for the moment with the glittering dental satire of a guise. But upon any abrupt unforeseen encounter a red light would flash forth from his eye, like a spark from an anvil in a dusk smithy. That quick fierce light was a strange one, darted from orbs which in repose were of a colour nearest approaching a deeper violet, the softest of shades.

Though some of these caprices of the pit could not but be observed by their object, yet were they beyond the construing of such a nature. And the thews of Billy were hardly comparable with that sort of sensitive spiritual organisation which in some cases instinctively conveys to ignorant innocence an admonition of the proximity of the malign. He thought the master-at-arms acted in a manner rather queer at times. That was all. But the occasional frank air and pleasant word went for what they purported to be, the young sailor never having heard as yet of the 'too fair-spoken man'.

Had the foretopman been conscious of having done or said anything to provoke the ill-will of the official, it would have been different with him, and his sight might have been purged if not sharpened.

So was it with him in yet another matter. Two minor officers, the armourer and captain of the hold, with whom he had never exchanged a word, his position on the ship not bringing him into contact with them; these men now for the first time began to cast upon Billy, when they chanced to encounter him, that peculiar glance which evidences that the man from whom it comes has been some way tampered with, and to the prejudice of him upon whom the glance lights. Never did it occur to Billy as a thing to be noted, or a thing suspicious, though he well knew the fact that the armourer and captain of the hold, with the ship's yeoman, apothecary and others of that grade, were, by naval usage, messmates of the master-at-arms, men with ears convenient to his confidential tongue.

Our Handsome Sailor's manly forwardness upon occasion, and irresistible good-nature, indicating no mental superiority tending to excite an invidious feeling, bred general popularity, and this good-will on the part of most of his shipmates made him the less apt to concern himself about such mute aspects towards him as those whereto allusion has just been made.

As to the afterguardsman, though Billy for reasons already given necessarily saw little of him, yet when the two did happen to meet, invariably came the fellow's off-hand cheerful recognition, some-times accompanied by a passing pleasant word or two. Whatever that equivocal young person's original design may really have been, or the design of which he might have been the deputy, certain it was from his manner upon these occasions that he had wholly dropped it.

It was as if his precocity of crookedness (and every vulgar villain is precocious) had for once deceived him, and the man he had sought to entrap as a simpleton had, through his very simplicity, baffled him.

But shrewd ones may opine that it was hardly possible for Billy to refrain from going up to the afterguardsman and bluntly demanding to know his purpose in the initial interview, so abruptly closed in the fore-chains. Shrewd ones may also think it but natural in Billy to set about sounding some of the other impressed men of the ship in order to discover what basis, if any, there was for the emissary's obscure suggestions as to plotting disaffection aboard. Yes, the shrewd may so think. But something more, or rather, something else than mere shrewdness is perhaps needful for the due under-standing of such a character as Billy Budd's.

As to Claggart, the monomania in the man – if that indeed it were – as involuntarily disclosed by starts in the manifestations detailed, yet in general covered over by his self-contained and rational demeanour; this, like a subterranean fire, was eating its way deeper and deeper in him. Something decisive must come of it.

16

After the mysterious interview in the fore-chains, the one so abruptly ended there by Billy, nothing especially germane to the story occurred until the events now about to be narrated.

Elsewhere it has been said that owing to the lack of frigates (of course, better sailers than line-of-battle ships) in the English squadron up the Straits at that period, the *Indomitable* seventy-four was occasionally employed not only as an available substitute for a scout, but at times on detached service of more important kind. This was not alone because of her sailing qualities, not common in a ship of her rate, but quite as much, probably, that the character of her commander, it was thought, specially adapted him for any duty where under unforeseen difficulties a prompt initiative might have to be taken in some matter demanding knowledge and ability in addition to those qualities employed in good seamanship. It was on an expedition of the latter sort, a somewhat distant one, and when the *Indomitable* was almost at her furthest remove from the fleet, that in the latter part of an afternoon-watch she unexpectedly came in sight of a ship of the enemy. It proved to be a frigate. The latter, perceiving through the glass that the weight of men and metal would be heavily against her, invoking her light heels, crowded sail to get away. After a chase urged almost against hope, and lasting until about the middle of the first dog-watch, she signally succeeded in effecting her escape.

Not long after the pursuit had been given up, and ere the excitement incident thereto had altogether waned away, the master-at-arms, ascending from his cavernous sphere, made his appearance cap in hand by the main-mast, respectfully waiting the notice of Captain Vere, then solitarily walking the weather-side of the quarter-deck, doubtless somewhat chafed at the failure of the pursuit. The spot where Claggart stood was the place allotted to men of lesser grades seeking some more particular interview either with the officer of the deck or the captain himself. But from the latter it was not open that a sailor or petty officer of those days would seek a hearing; only some exceptional cause would, according to established custom, have warranted that.

Presently, just as the commander, absorbed in his reflections was on the point of turning aft in his promenade, he became sensible of Claggart's presence, and saw the doffed cap held in deferential expectancy. Here be it said that Captain Vere's personal knowledge of this petty officer had only begun at the time of the ship's last sailing from home, Claggart then for the first time, in transfer from a ship detained for repairs, supplying on board the *Indomitable* the place of a previous master-at-arms disabled and ashore.

No sooner did the commander observe who it was that now so deferentially stood awaiting his notice, than a peculiar expression came over his face. It was not unlike that which uncontrollably will flit across the countenance of one at unawares encountering a person who though known to him indeed has hardly been long enough known for thorough knowledge, but something in whose aspect nevertheless now for the first provokes a vaguely repellent distaste. But coming to a stand, and resuming much of his wonted official manner, save that a sort of impatience lurked in the intonation of the opening word, he said, 'Well, what is it, master-at-arms?'

With the air of a subordinate grieved at the necessity of being messenger of ill-tidings, and while conscientiously determined to be frank, yet equally resolved upon shunning overstatement, Claggart at this invitation, or rather summons to disburthen, spoke up. What he said, conveyed in the language of no uneducated man, was to the effect following, if not altogether in these words, namely: That during the chase and preparations for the possible encounter he had seen enough to convince him that at least one sailor aboard was a dangerous character in a ship mustering some who not only had taken a guilty part in the late serious trouble, but others also who, like the man in question, had entered His Majesty's service under another form than enlistment.

At this point Captain Vere with some impatience interrupted him. 'Be direct, man; say impressed men.'

Claggart made a gesture of subservience and proceeded. Quite lately he (Claggart) had begun to suspect that some sort of movement prompted by the sailor in question was covertly going on, but he had not thought himself warranted in reporting the suspicion so long as it remained indistinct. But from what he had that afternoon observed in the man referred to, the suspicion of something clandestine going on had advanced to a point less removed from certainty. He deeply felt, he added, the serious responsibility assumed in making a report involving such possible consequences to the individual mainly concerned, besides tending to augment those natural anxieties which every naval commander must feel in view of extraordinary outbreaks so recent as those which, he sorrowfully said it, it needed not to name.

Now at the first broaching of the matter Captain Vere, taken by surprise, could not wholly dissemble his disquietude, but as Claggart went on, the former's aspect changed into restiveness under something in the testifier's manner in giving his testimony. However, he refrained from interrupting him. And Claggart, continuing, concluded with this, 'God forbid, your honour, that the *Indomitable*'s should be the experience of the – '

'Never mind that!' here peremptorily broke in the superior, his face altering with anger instantly, divining the ship that the other was about to name, one in which the Nore mutiny had assumed a singularly tragical character that for a time jeopardised the life of its commander. Under the circumstances he was indignant at the purposed allusion. When the commissioned officers themselves were on all occasions very heedful how they referred to the recent event, for a petty officer unnecessarily to allude to it in the presence of his captain, this struck him as a most immodest presumption. Besides, to his quick sense of self-respect, it even looked under the circumstances something like an attempt to alarm him. Nor at that was he without some surprise that one who, so far as he had hitherto come under his notice, had shown considerable tact in his function, should in this particular evince such lack of it.

But these thoughts and kindred dubious ones flitting across his mind were suddenly replaced by an intuitional surmise, which though as yet obscure in form, served practically to affect his reception of the ill tidings. Certain it is that, long versed in everything pertaining to the complicated gun-deck life, which like every other form of life has its secret mines and dubious side, the side popularly disclaimed, Captain Vere did not permit himself to be unduly disturbed by the general tenor of his subordinate's report. Furthermore, if in view of recent events prompt action should be taken at the first palpable sign of recurring insubordination, for all that, not judicious would it be, he thought, to keep the idea of lingering disaffection alive by undue forwardness in crediting an informer, even if his own subordinate and charged among other honours with police surveillance of the crew. This feeling would not perhaps have so prevailed with him were it not that upon a prior occasion the patriotic zeal officially evinced by Claggart had somewhat irritated him as appearing rather super-sensitive and strained. Furthermore, something even in the official's self-possessed and somewhat ostentatious manner in making his specifications strangely reminded him of a bandsman, a perjured witness in a capital case before a court-martial ashore of which when a lieutenant he, Captain Vere, had been a member.

Now the peremptory check given to Claggart in the matter of the arrested allusion was quickly followed up by this: 'You say that there is at least one dangerous man aboard. Name him.'

'William Budd, a foretopman, your honour.'

'William Budd!'repeated Captain Vere with unfeigned astonishment; 'and mean you the man that Lieutenant Ratcliffe took from the merchantman not very long ago – the young fellow who seems to be so popular with the men – Billy, the Handsome Sailor, as they call him?'

'The same, your honour; but for all his youth and good looks, a deep one. Not for nothing does he insinuate himself into the good-will of his shipmates, since at the least they will at a pinch say a good word for him at all hazards. Did Lieutenant Ratcliffe happen to tell your honour of that adroit fling of Budd's jumping up in the cutter's bow under the merchantman's stern when he was being taken off? That sort of good-humoured air even masks that at heart he resents his impressment. You have but noted his fair cheek. A mantrap may be under his ruddy-tipped daisies.'

Now the Handsome Sailor as a signal figure among the crew had naturally enough attracted the captain's attention from the first. Though in general not very demonstrative to his officers, he had congratulated Lieutenant Ratcliffe upon his good fortune in lighting on such a fine specimen of the *genus homo*, who in the nude might have passed for a statue of young Adam before the Fall.

As to Billy's adieu to the ship *Rights-of-Man*, which the boarding lieutenant, in a deferential way, had indeed reported to him, Captain Vere, more as a good story than aught else (having mistakenly understood it as a satiric sally), had but thought so much the better of the impressed man for it; as a military sailor, admiring the spirit that could take an arbitrary enlistment so merrily and sensibly. The foretopman's conduct, too, so far as it had fallen under the captain's notice, had confirmed the first happy augury, while the new recruit's qualities as a sailor-man seemed to be such that he had thought of recommending him to the executive officer for promotion to a place that would more frequently bring him under his own observation, namely, the captaincy of the mizzen-top, replacing there in the starboard-watch a man not so young whom partly for that reason he deemed less fitted for the post. Be it parenthesised here that since the mizzen-topmen have not to handle such breadths of heavy canvas as the lower sails on the mainmast and foremast, a young man if of the right stuff not only seems best adapted to duty there, but, in fact, is generally selected for the captaincy of that top, and the company under him are light hands, and often but striplings. In sum, Captain Vere had from the beginning deemed Billy Budd to be what in the naval parlance of the time was called a 'king's bargain', that is to say, for His Britannic Majesty's navy a capital investment at small outlay or none at all.

After a brief pause, during which the reminiscences above mentioned passed vividly through his mind, he weighed the import of Claggart's last suggestion conveyed in the phrase 'a mantrap under his ruddy-tipped daisies', and the more he weighed it the less reliance he felt in the informer's good faith. Suddenly he turned upon him: 'Do you come to me, master-at-arms, with so foggy a tale? As to Budd, cite me an act or spoken word of his confirmatory of what you in general charge against him. Stay,' drawing nearer to him, 'heed what you speak. Just now and in a case like this, there is a yard-arm-end for the false witness.'

'Ah, your honour!' sighed Claggart, mildly shaking his shapely head as in sad deprecation of such unmerited severity of tone. Then bridling, erecting himself as in virtuous self-assertion, he circumstantially alleged certain words and acts which collectively, if credited, led to presumptions mortally inculpating Budd, and for some of these averments, he added, substantiating proof was not far.

With grey eyes impatient and distrustful, essaying to fathom to the bottom Claggart's calm violet ones, Captain Vere again heard him out, then for the moment stood ruminating. Claggart – himself for the time liberated from the other's scrutiny – steadily regarded Captain Vere with a look difficult to render – a look curious of the operation of his tactics, a look such as might have been that of the spokesman of the envious children of Jacob deceptively imposing upon the troubled patriarch the blood-dyed coat of young Joseph.

Though something exceptional in the moral quality of Captain Vere made him, in earnest encounter with a fellow man, a veritable touchstone of that man's essential nature, yet now as to Claggart and what was really going on in him, his feeling partook less of intuitional conviction than of strong suspicion clogged by strange dubieties. The perplexity he evinced proceeded less from aught touching the man informed against – as Claggart doubtless opined – than from considerations how best to act in regard to the informer. At first, indeed, he was naturally for summoning that substantiation of his allegations which Claggart said was at hand. But such a proceeding would result in the matter at once getting abroad, which in the present stage of it, he thought, might undesirably affect the ship's company. If Claggart was a false witness–that closed the affair. And therefore, before trying the accusation, he would first practically test the accuser; and he thought this could be done in a quiet undemonstrative way.

The measure he determined upon involved a shifting of the scene, a transfer to a place less exposed to observation than the broad quarter-deck. For although the few gunroom officers there at the time had, in due observance of naval etiquette, withdrawn to leeward the moment Captain Vere had begun his promenade on the deck's weather-side; and though during the colloquy with Claggart they of course ventured not to diminish the distance; and though throughout the interview Captain Vere's voice was far from high, and Claggart's silvery and low; and though the wind in the cordage and the wash of the sea helped the more to put them beyond earshot; nevertheless, the interviewer's continuance already had attracted observation from some topmen aloft, and other sailors in the waist or farther forward.

Having determined upon his measures, Captain Vere forthwith took action. Abruptly turning to Claggart he asked, 'Master-at-arms, is it now Budd's watch aloft?'

'No, your honour.'

Whereupon, 'Mr Wilkes,' summoning the nearest midshipman, 'tell Albert to come to me.' Albert was the captain's hammock-boy, a sort of sea-valet, in whose discretion and fidelity his master had much confidence. The lad appeared. 'You know Budd, the foretopman?'

'I do, sir.'

'Go find him. It is his watch off. Manage to tell him out of earshot that he is wanted aft. Contrive it that he speaks to nobody. Keep him in talk yourself. And not till you get well aft here, not till then, let him know that the place where he is wanted is my cabin. You understand? Go. Master-at-arms, show yourself on the decks below, and when you think it time for Albert to be coming with his man, stand by quietly to follow the sailor in.'

17

Now when the foretopman found himself closeted, as it were, in the cabin with the captain and Claggart, he was surprised enough. But it was a surprise unaccompanied by apprehension or distrust. To an immature nature, essentially honest and humane, forewarning intimations of subtler danger from one's kind came tardily, if at all. The only thing that took shape in the young sailor's mind was this: 'Yes, the captain, I have always thought, looks kindly upon me. Wonder if he's going to make me his coxswain. I should like that. And maybe now he is going to ask the master-at-arms about me.'

'Shut the door there, sentry,' said the commander. 'Stand without and let nobody come in. Now, master-at-arms, tell this man to his face what you told of him to me' – and stood prepared to scrutinise the mutually confronting visages.

With the measured step and calm collected air of an asylum physician approaching in the public hall some patient beginning to show indications of a coming paroxysm, Claggart deliberately advanced within short range of Billy, and mesmerically looking him in the eye, briefly recapitulated the accusation.

Not at first did Billy take it in. When he did the rose-tan of his cheek looked struck as by white leprosy. He stood like one impaled and gagged. Meanwhile the accuser's eyes, removing not as yet from the blue, dilated ones, underwent a phenomenal change, their wonted rich violet colour blurring into a muddy purple. Those lights of human intelligence, losing human expression, gelidly protruded like the alien eyes of certain uncatalogued creatures of the deep. The first mesmeric glance was one of surprised fascination; the last was as the hungry lurch of the torpedo-fish.

'Speak, man!' said Captain Vere to the transfixed one, struck by his aspect even more than by Claggart's. 'Speak! defend yourself.' Which appeal caused but a strange, dumb gesturing and gurgling in Billy, amazement at such an accusation so suddenly sprung on inexperienced nonage; this, and it may be horror at the accuser, served to bring out his lurking defect, and in this instance for the time intensified it into a convulsed tongue-tie; while the intent head and entire form, straining forward in an agony of ineffectual eagerness to obey the injunction to speak and defend himself, gave an expression to the face like that of a condemned vestal priestess in the moment of being buried alive, and in the first struggle against suffocation.

Though at the time Captain Vere was quite ignorant of Billy's liability to vocal impediment, he now immediately divined it, since vividly Billy's aspect recalled to him that of a bright young schoolmate of his whom he had seen struck by much the same startling impotence in the act of eagerly rising in the class to be foremost in response to a testing question put to it by the master. Going close up to the young sailor, and laying a soothing hand on his shoulder, he said, 'There is no hurry, my boy. Take your time, take your time.' Contrary to the effect intended, these words, so fatherly in tone, doubtless touching Billy's heart to the quick, prompted yet more violent efforts at utterance – efforts soon ending for the time in confirming the paralysis, and bringing to the face an expression which was as a crucifixion to behold. The next instant, quick as the flame from a discharged cannon at night, his right arm shot out, and Claggart dropped to the deck. Whether intentionally, or but owing to the young athlete's superior height, the blow had taken effect full upon the forehead, so shapely and intellectual-looking a feature in the master-at-arms; so that the body fell over lengthwise, like a heavy plank tilted from erectness. A gasp or two, and he lay motionless.

'Fated boy,' breathed Captain Vere, in tone so low as to be almost a whisper, 'what have you done! But here, help me.'

The twain raised the felled one from the loins up into a sitting position. The spare form flexibly acquiesced, but inertly. It was like handling a dead snake. They lowered it back. Regaining erectness, Captain Vere with one hand covering his face stood to all appearance as impassive as the object at his feet. Was he absorbed in taking in all the bearings of the event, and what was best not only now at once to be done, but also in the sequel? Slowly he uncovered his face; and the effect was as if the moon emerging from eclipse should reappear with quite another aspect than that which had gone into hiding. The father in him, manifested towards Billy thus far in the scene, was replaced by the military disciplinarian. In his official tone he bade the foretopman retire to a stateroom aft (pointing it out), and there remain till thence summoned. This order Billy in silence mechanically obeyed. Then going to the cabin door where it opened on the quarter-deck, Captain Vere said to the sentry without, 'Tell somebody to send Albert here.' When the lad appeared, his master so contrived it that he should not catch sight of the prone one. 'Albert,' he said to him, 'tell the surgeon I wish to see him. You need not come back till called.'

When the surgeon entered – a self-poised character of that grave sense and experience that hardly anything could take him aback – Captain Vere advanced to meet him, thus unconsciously interrupting his view of Claggart, and interrupting the other's wonted unceremonious salutation said, 'Nay, tell me how it is with yonder man,' directing his attention to the prostrate one.

The surgeon looked, and for all his self-command, somewhat startled at the abrupt revelation. On Claggart's always pallid complexion thick black blood was now oozing from mouth and ear. To the gazer's professional eyes it was unmistakably no living man that he saw.

'Is it so, then?' said Captain Vere, intently watching him. 'I thought it. But verify it.' Whereupon the customary tests confirmed the surgeon's first glance, who now looking up in unfeigned concern, cast a look of intense inquisitiveness upon his superior. But Captain Vere, with one hand to his brow, was standing motionless. Suddenly, catching the surgeon's arm convulsively, he exclaimed, pointing down to the body, 'It is the divine judgment of Ananias! Look!'

Disturbed by the excited manner he had never before observed in the *Indomitable*'s captain, and as yet wholly ignorant of the affair, the prudent surgeon nevertheless held his peace, only again looking an earnest interrogation as to what it was that had resulted in such a tragedy.

But Captain Vere was now again motionless, standing absorbed in thought. But again starting, he vehemently exclaimed, 'Struck dead by an angel of God. Yet the angel must hang!'

At these interjections, incoherences to the listener as yet unapprised of the antecedent events, the surgeon was profoundly discomforted. But now, as recollecting himself, Captain Vere in less harsh tone briefly related the circumstances leading up to the event.

'But come; we must dispatch,' he added; 'help me to remove him' (meaning the body) 'to yonder compartment' designating one opposite where the foretopman remained immured. Anew disturbed by a request that, as implying a desire for secrecy, seemed unaccountably strange to him, there was nothing for the subordinate to do but comply.

'Go now,' said Captain Vere, with something of his wonted manner, 'go now. I shall presently call a drumhead court. Tell the lieutenants what has happened, and tell Mr Morton' – meaning the captain of marines. 'And charge them to keep the matter to themselves.'

Full of disquietude and misgivings, the surgeon left the cabin. Was Captain Vere suddenly affected in his mind, or was it but a transient excitement brought about by so strange and extraordinary a happening? As to the drumhead court, it struck the surgeon as impolitic, if nothing more. The thing to do, he thought, was to place Billy Budd in confinement, and in a way dictated by usage, and postpone further action in so extraordinary a case to such time as they should again join the squadron, and then transfer it to the admiral. He recalled the unwonted agitation of Captain Vere and his excited exclamations, so at variance with his normal manner. Was he unhinged? But assuming that he was, it were not so susceptible of proof. What then could he do? No more trying situation is conceivable than that of an officer subordinated under a captain whom he suspects to be, not mad indeed, but yet not quite unaffected in his intellect. To argue his order to him would be insolence. To resist him would be mutiny. In obedience to Captain Vere he communicated to the lieutenants and captain of marines what had happened, saying nothing more as to the captain's state. They stared at him in surprise and concern. Like him, they seemed to think that such a matter should be reported to the admiral.

Who in the rainbow can draw the line where the violet tint ends and the orange tint begins? Distinctly we see the difference of the colour, but where exactly does the first one visibly enter into the other? So with sanity and insanity. In pronounced cases there is no question about them. But in some cases, in various degrees supposedly less pronounced, to draw the line of demarcation few will undertake, though for a fee some professional experts will. There is nothing nameable but that some men will undertake to do for pay. In other words, there are instances where it is next to impossible to determine whether a man is sane or beginning to be otherwise.

Whether Captain Vere, as the surgeon professionally surmised, was really the sudden victim of any degree of aberration, one must determine for himself by such light as this narrative may afford.

18

The unhappy event which has been narrated could not have happened at a worse juncture. For it was close on the heel of the suppressed insurrections, an after-time very critical to naval authority, demanding from every English sea-commander two qualities not readily interfusable – prudence and rigour. Moreover, there was something crucial in the case.

In the jugglery of circumstances preceding and attending the event on board the *Indomitable*, and in the light of that martial code whereby it was formally to be judged, innocence and guilt, personified in Claggart and Budd, in effect changed places.

In the legal view, the apparent victim of the tragedy was he who had sought to victimise a man blameless; and the indisputable deed of the latter, navally regarded, constituted the most heinous of military crimes. Yet more. The essential right and wrong involved in the matter, the clearer that might be, so much the worse for the responsibility of a loyal sea-commander, inasmuch as he was authorised to determine the matter on that primitive legal basis.

Small wonder then that the *Indomitable*'s captain, though in general a man of rigid decision, felt that circumspectness not less than promptitude was necessary. Until he could decide upon his course, and in each detail, and not only so, but until the concluding measure was upon the point of being enacted, he deemed it advisable, in view of all the circumstances, to guard as much as possible against publicity. Here he may or may not have erred. Certain it is, however, that subsequently in the confidential talk of more than one or two gunrooms and cabins he was not a little criticised by some officers, a fact imputed by his friends, and vehemently by his cousin Jack Denton, to professional jealousy of Starry Vere. Some imaginative ground for invidious comment there was. The maintenance of secrecy in the matter, the confining all knowledge of it for a time to the place where the homicide occurred – the quarter-deck cabin; in these particulars lurked some resemblance to the policy adopted in those tragedies of the palace which have occurred more than once in the capital founded by Peter the Barbarian, great chiefly by his crimes.

The case was such that fain would the *Indomitable*'s captain have deferred taking any action whatever respecting it further than to keep the foretopman a close prisoner till the ship rejoined the squadron, and then submitting the matter to the judgment of his admiral.

But a true military officer is in one particular like a true monk. Not with more of self-abnegation will the latter keep his vows of monastic obedience than the former his vows of allegiance to martial duty.

Feeling that unless quick action was taken on it, the deed of the foretopman, as soon as it should be known on the gun-decks, would tend to awaken any slumbering embers of the Nore among the crew, a sense of the urgency of the case overruled in Captain Vere every other consideration. But though a conscientious disciplinarian he was no lover of authority for mere authority's sake. Very far was he from embracing opportunities for monopolising to himself the perils of moral responsibility, none at least that could properly be referred to an official superior, or shared with him by his official equals, or even subordinates. So thinking, he was glad it would not be at variance with usage to turn the matter over to a summary court of his own officers, reserving to himself, as the one on whom the ultimate accountability would rest, the right of maintaining a supervision of it, or formally or informally interposing at need. Accordingly a drumhead court was summarily convened, he electing the individuals composing it – the first lieutenant, the captain of marines and the sailing-master.

In associating an officer of marines with the sea-lieutenant in a case having to do with a sailor, the commander perhaps deviated from general custom. He was prompted thereto by the circumstances that he took that soldier to be a judicious person, thoughtful and not altogether incapable of grappling with a difficult case unprecedented in his prior experience. Yet even as to him he was not without some latent misgiving, for withal he was an extremely good-natured man, an enjoyer of his dinner, a sound sleeper and inclined to obesity. The sort of man who, though he would always maintain his manhood in battle, might not prove altogether reliable in a moral dilemma involving aught of the tragic. As to the first lieutenant and the sailing-master, Captain Vere could not but be aware that though honest natures of approved gallantry upon occasion, their intelligence was mostly confined to the matter of active seamanship, and the fighting demands of their profession. The court was held in the same cabin where the unfortunate affair had taken place. This cabin, the commander's, embraced the entire area under the poop-deck. Aft, and on either side, was a small stateroom – the one room temporarily a jail, and the other a dead-house – and a yet smaller compartment leaving a space between, expanding forward into a goodly oblong of length coinciding with the ship's beam. A skylight of moderate dimensions was overhead, and at each end of the oblong space were two sashed port-hole windows easily convertible back into embrasures for short carronades.

All being quickly in readiness, Billy Budd was arraigned, Captain Vere necessarily appearing as the sole witness in the case, and as such temporarily sinking his rank, though singularly maintaining it in a matter apparently trivial, namely, that he testified from the ship's weather-side, with that object having caused the court to sit on the leeside. Concisely he narrated all that had led up to the catastrophe, omitting nothing in Claggart's accusation, and deposing as to the manner in which the prisoner had received it. At this testimony the three officers glanced with no little surprise at Billy Budd, the last man they would have suspected, either of mutinous design alleged by Claggart, or of the undeniable deed he himself had done. The first lieutenant taking judicial primary, and turning towards the prisoner, said, 'Captain Vere has spoken. Is it or is it not as Captain Vere says?' In response came syllables not so much impeded in the utterances as might have been anticipated. They were these: 'Captain Vere tells the truth. It is just as Captain Vere says, but it is not as the master-at-arms said. I have eaten the king's bread, and I am true to the king.'

'I believe you, my man,' said the witness, his voice indicating a suppressed emotion not otherwise betrayed.

'God will bless you for that, your honour!' not without stammering, said Billy, and all but broke down. But immediately was recalled to self-control by another question, to which with the same emotional difficulty of utterance he said, 'No, there was no malice

between us. I never bore malice against the master-at-arms. I am
sorry that he is dead. I did not mean to kill him. Could I have used
my tongue I would not have struck him. But he foully lied to my
face, and in the presence of my captain, and I had to say something,
and I could only say it with a blow. God help me!'

In the impulsive above-board manner of the frank one the court
saw confirmed all that was implied in words that just previously had
perplexed them, coming as they did from the testifier to the
tragedy, and promptly following Billy's impassioned disclaimer of
mutinous intent – Captain Vere's words, 'I believe you, my man.'

Next, it was asked of him whether he knew of or suspected aught
savouring of incipient trouble (meaning mutiny, though the explicit
term was avoided) going on in any section of the ship's company.

The reply lingered. This was naturally imputed by the court to
the same vocal embarrassment which had retarded or obstructed
previous answers. But in main it was otherwise here, the question
immediately recalling to Billy's mind the interview with the
afterguardsman in the fore-chains. But an innate repugnance to
playing a part at all approaching that of an informer against one's
own shipmates – the same erring sense of uninstructed honour
which had stood in the way of his reporting the matter at the time,
though as a loyal man-of-war's man it was incumbent on him, and
failure so to do it, charged against him and proven, would have
subjected him to the heaviest of penalties. This, with the blind
feeling now his, that nothing really was being hatched, prevailed
with him. When the answer came it was a negative.

'One question more,' said the officer of marines now first speaking, and with a troubled earnestness. 'You tell us that what the
master-at-arms said against you was a lie. Now why should he have
so lied, so maliciously lied, since you declare there was no malice
between you?'

At that question, unintentionally touching on a spiritual sphere,
wholly obscure to Billy's thoughts, he was nonplussed, evincing a
confusion indeed that some observers, such as can be imagined,
would have construed into involuntary evidence of hidden guilt.
Nevertheless he strove some way to answer, but all at once relin-
quished the vain endeavour, at the same time turning an appealing
glance towards Captain Vere, as deeming him his best helper and
friend. Captain Vere, who had been seated for a time, rose to his feet,
addressing the interrogator 'The question you put to him comes
naturally enough. But how can he rightly answer it, or anybody else?
unless indeed it be he who lies within there,' designating the

compartment where lay the corpse. 'But the prone one there will not rise to our summons. In effect though, as it seems to me, the point you make is hardly material. Quite aside from any conceivable motive actuating the master-at-arms, and irrespective of the provocation of the blow, a martial court must needs in the present case confine its attention to the blow's consequence which consequence is to be deemed not otherwise than as the striker's deed!'

This utterance, the full significance of which it was not at all likely that Billy took in, nevertheless caused him to turn a wistful, interrogative look towards the speaker, a look in its dumb expressiveness not unlike that which a dog of generous breed might turn upon his master, seeking in his face some elucidation of a previous gesture ambiguous to the canine intelligence. Nor was the same utterance without marked effect upon the three officers, more especially the soldier. Couched in it seemed to them a meaning unanticipated, involving a prejudgment on the speaker's part. It served to augment a mental disturbance previously evident enough.

The soldier once more spoke, in a tone of suggestive dubiety addressing at once his associates and Captain Vere: 'Nobody is present – none of the ship's company, I mean, who might shed lateral light, if any is to be had, upon what remains mysterious in this matter.'

'That is thoughtfully put,' said Captain Vere, 'I see your drift. Aye, there is a mystery; but to use a scriptural phrase, it is "a mystery of iniquity", a matter for psychological theologians to discuss. But what has a military court to do with it? Not to add that, for us, any possible investigation of it is cut off by the lasting tongue-tie – him – in yonder,' again designating the mortuary stateroom. 'The prisoner's deed. With that alone we have to do.'

To this, and particularly the closing reiteration, the marine soldier, knowing not how aptly to reply, sadly abstained from saying aught. The first lieutenant, who at the outset had not unnaturally assumed primacy in the court, now over-rulingly instructed by a glance from Captain Vere, a glance more effective than words, resumed that primacy. Turning to the prisoner: 'Budd,' he said, and scarce in equable tones, 'Budd, if you have aught further to say for yourself, say it now.'

Upon this the young sailor turned another quick glance towards Captain Vere; then, as taking a hint from that aspect, a hint confirming his own instinct that silence was now best, replied to the lieutenant, 'I have said all, sir.'

The marine – the same who had been the sentinel without the

cabin-door at the time that the foretopman, followed by the master-at-arms, entered it – he, standing by the sailor throughout their judicial proceedings, was now directed to take him back to the after-compartment originally assigned to the prisoner and his custodian. As the twain disappeared from view, the three officers, as partially liberated from some inward constraint associated with Billy's mere presence, simultaneously stirred in their seats. They exchanged looks of troubled indecision, yet feeling that decide they must and without long delay, for Captain Vere was for the time sitting unconsciously with his back towards them, apparently in one of his absent fits, gazing out from a sashed port-hole to windward upon the monotonous blank of the twilight sea. But the court's silence continuing, broken only at moments by brief consultations in low, earnest tones, this seemed to assure him and encourage him. Turning, he to and fro paced the cabin athwart; in the returning ascent to windward, climbing the slant deck in the ship's lee roll; without knowing it symbolising thus in his action a mind resolute to surmount difficulties even if against primitive instincts strong as the wind and the sea. Presently he came to a stand before the three. After scanning their faces he stood less as mustering his thoughts for expression, than as one only deliberating how best to put them to well-meaning men not intellectually mature, men with whom it was necessary to demonstrate certain principles that were axioms to himself. Similar impatience as to talking is perhaps one reason that deters some minds from addressing any popular assemblies; under which head is to be classed most legislatures in a democracy.

When speak he did, something both in the substance of what he said and his manner of saying it showed the influence of unshared studies modifying and tempering the practical training of an active career. This, along with his phraseology now and then, was sugges-tive of the grounds whereon rested that imputation of a certain pedantry socially alleged against him by certain naval men of wholly practical cast, captains who nevertheless would frankly concede that His Majesty's navy mustered no more efficient officers of their grade than Starry Vere.

What he said was to this effect: 'Hitherto I have been but the witness, little more; and I should hardly think now to take another tone, that of your coadjutor, for the time, did I not perceive in you – at the crisis too – a troubled hesitancy, proceeding, I doubt not, from the clashing of military duty with moral scruple – scruple vitalised by compassion. For the compassion, how can I otherwise but share it? But mindful of paramount obligation, I strive against scruples that may tend to enervate decision. Not, gentlemen, that I hide from myself that the case is an exceptional one. Speculatively regarded, it well might be referred to a jury of casuists. But for us here, acting not as casuists or moralists, it is a case practical and under martial law practically to be dealt with.

'But your scruples! Do they move as in a dusk? Challenge them. Make them advance and declare themselves. Come now: do they impart something like this: If, mindless of palliating circumstances, we are bound to regard the death of the master-at-arms as the prisoner's deed, then does that deed constitute a capital crime whereof the penalty is a mortal one? But in natural justice is nothing but the prisoner's overt act to be considered? Now can we adjudge to summary and shameful death a fellow-creature innocent before God, and whom we feel to be so? – Does that state it aright? You sign sad assent. Well, I too feel that, the full force of that. It is nature. But do these buttons that we wear attest that our allegiance is to nature? No, to the king. Though the ocean, which is inviolate nature primeval, though this be the element where we move and have our being as sailors, yet as the king's officers lies our duty in a sphere correspondingly natural? So little is that true, that in receiving our commissions we in the most important regards ceased to be natural free agents. When war is declared, are we the commissioned fighters previously consulted? We fight at command. If our judgements approve the war, that is but coincidence. So in other particulars. So now, would it be so much we ourselves that would condemn as it would be martial law operating through us? For that law, and the rigour of it, we are not responsible. Our vowed responsibility is in this: that however pitilessly that law may operate, we nevertheless adhere to it and administer it.

'But the exceptional in the matter moves the heart within you. Even so, too, is mine moved. But let not warm hearts betray heads that should be cool. Ashore in a criminal case will an upright judge allow himself off the bench to be waylaid by some tender kinswoman of the accused seeking to touch him with her tearful plea? Well, the heart here is as that piteous woman. The heart is the feminine in man, and hard though it be, she must here be ruled out.'

He paused, earnestly studying them for a moment; then resumed. 'But something in your aspect seems to urge that it is not solely that heart that moves in you, but also the conscience, the private conscience. But tell me whether or not, occupying the position we do, private conscience should not yield to that imperial one formulated in the code under which alone we officially proceed?'

Here the three men moved in their seats, less convinced than agitated by the course of an argument troubling but the more the spontaneous conflict within. Perceiving which, the speaker paused for a moment; then abruptly changing his tone, went on. 'To steady us a bit, let us recur to the facts. In wartime at sea a man-of-war's man strikes his superior in grade, and the blow kills. Apart from its effect, the blow itself is, according to the Articles of War, a capital crime. Furthermore – '

'Aye, sir,' emotionally broke in the officer of marines, 'in one sense it was. But surely Budd purposed neither mutiny nor homicide?'

'Surely not, my good man. And before a court less arbitrary and more merciful than a martial one that plea would largely extenuate. At the Last Assizes it shall acquit. But how here? We proceed under the law of the Mutiny Act. In feature no child can resemble his father more than that act resembles in spirit the thing from which it derives – war. In His Majesty's service – in this ship indeed – there are Englishmen forced to fight for the king against their will. Against their conscience, for aught we know. Though as their fellow-creatures some of us may appreciate their position, yet as navy officers, what reck we of it? Still less recks the enemy. Our impressed men he would fain cut down in the same swath with our volunteers. As regards the enemy's naval conscripts, some of whom may even share our own abhorrence of the regicidal French Directory, it is the same on our side, war looks but to the frontage, the appearance. And the Mutiny Act, war's child, takes after the father. Budd's intent or non-intent is nothing to the purpose.

'But while, put to it by those anxieties in you which I cannot but respect, I only repeat myself – while thus strangely we prolong proceedings that should be summary, the enemy may be sighted and an engagement result. We must do; and one of two things must we do – condemn or let go.'

'Can we not convict and yet mitigate the penalty?' asked the junior lieutenant, here speaking, and falteringly, for the first.

'Lieutenant, were that clearly lawful for us under the circumstances, consider the consequences of such clemency. The people' (meaning the ship's company) 'have native sense; most of them are familiar with our naval usage and tradition; and how would they take it? Even could you explain to them – which our official position forbids – they, long moulded by arbitrary discipline, have not that kind of intelligent responsiveness that might qualify them to comprehend and discriminate. No, to the people the foretopman's deed, however it be worded in the announcement, will be plain homicide committed in a flagrant act of mutiny. What penalty for that should follow, they know. But it does not follow. *Why?* they will ruminate. You know what sailors are. Will they not revert to the recent outbreak at the Nore? Aye, they know the well-founded alarm – the panic it struck throughout England. Your clement sentence they would account pusillanimous. They would think that we flinch, that we are afraid of them – afraid of practising a lawful rigour singularly demanded at this juncture lest it should provoke new troubles. What shame to us such a conjecture on their part, and how deadly to discipline. You see then whither, prompted by duty and the law, I steadfastly drive. But I beseech you, my friends, do not take me amiss. I feel as you do for this unfortunate boy. But did he know our hearts, I take him to be of that generous nature that he would feel even for us on whom in this military necessity so heavy a compulsion is laid.'

With that, crossing the deck, he resumed his place by the sashed port-hole, tacitly leaving the three to come to a decision. On the cabin's opposite side the troubled court sat silent. Loyal lieges, plain and practical, though at bottom they dissented from some points Captain Vere had put to them, they were without the faculty, hardly had the inclination to gainsay one whom they felt to be an earnest man, one, too, not less their superior in mind than in naval rank. But it is not improbable that even such of his words as were not without influence over them, came home to them less than his closing appeal to their instinct as sea-officers. He forecasted the practical consequences to discipline (considering the unconfirmed tone of the fleet at the time), if violent killing at sea by a man-of-war's man of a superior in grade were allowed to pass for aught else than a capital crime, and one demanding prompt infliction of the penalty.

Not unlikely they were brought to something more or less akin to that harassed frame of mind which in the year 1842 actuated the commander of the US brig-of-war *Somers* to resolve – under the so-called Articles of War, articles modelled upon the English Mutiny Act – upon the execution at sea of a midshipman and two petty officers as mutineers designing the seizure of the brig. This resolution was carried out, though in a time of peace and within not many days' sail of home, and vindicated by a naval court of inquiry subsequently convened ashore. History, and here cited without comment. True, the circumstances on board the *Somers* were different from those on board the *Indomitable*. But the urgency felt, well warranted or otherwise, was much the same.

Says a writer whom few know, 'Forty years after a battle it is easy for a noncombatant to reason about how it ought to have been fought. It is another thing personally and under fire to direct the fighting while involved in the obscuring smoke of it. Much so with respect to other emergencies involving considerations both practical and moral, and when it is imperative promptly to act. The greater the fog the more it imperils the steamer, and speed is put on though at the hazard of running somebody down. Little ween the snug card-players in the cabin of the responsibilities of the sleepless man on the bridge.'

In brief, Billy Budd was formally convicted and sentenced to be hung at the yard-arm in the early morning-watch, it being now night. Otherwise, as is customary in such cases, the sentence would forthwith have been carried out. In wartime on the field or in the fleet, a mortal punishment decreed by a drumhead court – on the field sometimes decreed by but a nod from the general – follows without delay on the heel of conviction without appeal.

19

It was Captain Vere himself who of his own motion communicated the finding of the court to the prisoner; for that purpose going to the compartment where he was in custody, and bidding the marine there to withdraw for the time.

Beyond the communication of the sentence what took place at this interview was never known. But, in view of the character of the twain briefly closeted in that stateroom, each radically sharing in the rarer qualities of one nature – so rare, indeed, as to be all but incredible to average minds, however much cultivated – some conjectures may be ventured.

It would have been in consonance with the spirit of Captain Vere should he on this occasion have concealed nothing from the condemned one; should he indeed have frankly disclosed to him the part he himself had played in bringing about the decision, at the same time revealing his actuated motives. On Billy's side it is not improbable that such a confession would have been received in much the same spirit that prompted it. Not without a sort of joy indeed he might have appreciated the brave opinion of him implied in his captain making such a confidant of him. Nor as to the sentence itself

could he have been insensible that it was imparted to him as to one
not afraid to die. Even more may have been. Captain Vere in the end
may have developed the passion sometimes latent under an exterior
stoical or indifferent. He was old enough to have been Billy's father.
The austere devotee of military duty, letting himself melt back into
what remains primeval in our formalised humanity, may in the end
have caught Billy to his heart, even as Abraham may have caught
young Isaac on the brink of resolutely offering him up in obedience
to the exacting behest. But there is no telling the sacrament – seldom
if in any case revealed to the gadding world wherever, under
circumstances at all akin to those here attempted to be set forth, two
of great nature's nobler order embrace. There is privacy at the time,
inviolable to the survivor, and holy oblivion, the sequel to each
diviner magnanimity, providentially covers all at last.

The first to encounter Captain Vere in the act of leaving the
compartment was the senior lieutenant. The face he beheld, for the
moment one expressive of the agony of the strong, was to that
officer, though a man of fifty, a startling revelation. That the
condemned one suffered less than he who mainly had effected the
condemnation was apparently indicated by the former's exclamation
in the scene soon perforce to be touched upon.

Of a series of incidents within a brief term rapidly following each
other the adequate narration may take up a term less brief, especially if explanation or comment here and there seem requisite to
the better understanding of such incidents. Between the entrance
into the cabin of him who never left it alive, and him who when he
did leave it left it as one condemned to die; between this and the
closeted interview just given, less than an hour and a half had
elapsed. It was an interval long enough, however, to awaken
speculations among no few of the ship's company as to what it was
that could be detaining in the cabin the master-at-arms and the
sailor, for it was rumoured that both of them had been seen to enter
it, and neither of them had been seen to emerge. This rumour had
got abroad upon the gun-decks and in the tops; the people of a great
warship being in one respect like villagers, taking microscopic note
of every untoward movement or non-movement going on. When
therefore in weather not at all tempestuous all hands were called in
the second dog-watch, a summons under such circumstances not
usual in those hours, the crew were not wholly unprepared for some
announcement extraordinary, one having connection, too, with the
continued absence of the two men from their wonted haunts.

There was a moderate sea at the time; and the moon newly risen, and near to being at its full, silvered the white spar-deck wherever not blotted by the clear-cut shadows horizontally thrown of fixtures and moving men. On either side the quarter-deck the marine guard under arms was drawn up; and Captain Vere, standing in his place surrounded by all the wardroom officers, addressed his men. In so doing his manner showed neither more nor less than that properly pertaining to his supreme position aboard his own ship. In clear terms and concise he told them what had taken place in the cabin; that the master-at-arms was dead; that he who had killed him had been already tried by a summary court and condemned to death; and that the execution would take place in the early morning watch. The word *mutiny* was not named in what he said. He refrained, too, from making the occasion an opportunity for any preachment as to the maintenance of discipline, thinking, perhaps, that under existing circumstances in the navy, the consequence of violating discipline should be made to speak for itself.

Their captain's announcement was listened to by the throng of standing sailors in a dumbness like that of a seated congregation of believers in hell listening to their clergyman's announcement of his Calvinistic text *

At the close, however, a confused murmur went up. It began to wax all but instantly, then at a sign, was pierced and suppressed by shrill whistles of the boatswain and his mates piping, 'Down one watch.'†

To be prepared for burial Claggart's body was delivered to certain petty officers of his mess. And here, not to clog the sequel with lateral matters, it may be added that at a suitable hour, the master-at-arms was committed to the sea with every funeral honour properly belonging to his naval grade.

In this proceeding, as in every public one growing out of the tragedy, strict adherence to usage was observed. Nor in any point could it have been at all deviated from, either with respect to Claggart or Billy Budd, without begetting undesirable speculations in the ship's company, sailors, and more particularly man-of-war's men, being of all men the greatest sticklers for usage.

For similar cause all communication between Captain Vere and

---

* Melville's manuscript contains at this point the words 'Jonathan Edwards' in brackets. Clearly Melville had in mind the great New England Calvinist preacher and theologian when he was writing this sentence.

† There is an author's note in the margin of the manuscript reading: *Another order to be given here in place of this one.*

the condemned one ended with the closeted interview already given, the latter being now surrendered to the ordinary routine preliminary to the end. This transfer under guard from the captain's quarters was effected without unusual precautions – at least no visible ones.

If possible, not to let the men so much as surmise that their officers anticipate aught amiss from them, is the tacit rule in a military ship. And the more that some sort of trouble should really be apprehended, the more do the officers keep that apprehension to themselves; though not the less unostentatious vigilance may be augmented.

In the present instance the sentry placed over the prisoner had strict orders to let no one have communication with him but the chaplain. And certain unobtrusive measures were taken absolutely to ensure this point.

20

In a seventy-four of the old order the deck known as the upper gun-deck was the one covered over by the spar-deck, which last, though not without its armament, was for the most part exposed to the weather. In general it was at all hours free from hammocks; those of the crew swinging on the lower gun-deck and berth-deck, the latter being not only a dormitory but also the place for the stowing of the sailors' bags, and on both sides lined with the large chests or movable pantries of the many messes of the men.

On the starboard side of the *Indomitable*'s upper gun-deck, behold Billy Budd under sentry lying prone in irons in one of the bays formed by the regular spacing of the guns comprising the batteries on either side. All these pieces were of the heavier calibre of that period. Mounted on lumbering wooden carriages, they were hampered with cumbersome harness of breeching and strong side-tackles for running them out. Guns and carriages, together with the long rammers and shorter lintstocks lodged in loops overhead – all these, as customary, were painted black; and the heavy hempen breechings tarred to the same tint, wore the like livery of the undertaker. In contrast with the funereal tone of these surroundings the prone sailor's exterior apparel, white jumper and white duck trousers, each more or less soiled, dimly glimmered in the obscure light of the bay like a patch of discoloured snow in early April lingering at some upland cave's black mouth. In effect he is already in his shroud or the garments that shall serve him in lieu of one. Over him, but scarce illuminating him, two battle-lanterns swing from two massive beams of the deck above. Fed with the oil supplied by the war-contractors (whose gains, honest or otherwise, are in every land an anticipated portion of the harvest of death), with flickering splashes of dirty yellow light they pollute the pale moonshine all but ineffectually struggling in obstructed flecks through the open ports from which the tompioned cannon protrude. Other lanterns at intervals serve but to bring out somewhat the obscurer bays which, like small confessionals or side-chapels in a cathedral, branch from the long, dim-vista'd, broad aisle, between the two batteries of that covered tier.

Such was the deck where now lay the Handsome Sailor. Through the rose-tan of his complexion, no pallor could have shown. It would have taken days of sequestration from the winds and the sun to have brought about the effacement of that. But the skeleton in the cheek-bone at the point of its angle was just beginning delicately to be defined under the warm-tinted skin. In fervid hearts self-contained some brief experiences devour our human tissue as secret fire in a ship's hold consumes cotton in the bale.

But now, lying between the two guns, as nipped in the vice of fate, Billy's agony, mainly proceeding from a generous young heart's virgin experience of the diabolical incarnate and effective in some men – the tension of that agony was over now. It survived not the something healing in the closeted interview with Captain Vere. Without movement he lay as in a trance, that adolescent expression, previously noted as his, taking on something akin to the look of a slumbering child in the cradle when the warm hearth-glow of the still chamber of night plays on the dimples that at whiles mysteriously form in the cheek, silently coming and going there. For now and then in the gyved one's trance, a serene happy light born of some wandering reminiscence or dream would diffuse itself over his face, and then wane away only anew to return.

The chaplain coming to see him and finding him thus, and perceiving no sign that he was conscious of his presence, attentively regarded him for a space, then slipping aside, withdrew for the time, peradventure feeling that even he, the minister of Christ, though receiving his stipend from wars, had no consolation to proffer which could result in a peace transcending that which he beheld. But in the small hours he came again. And the prisoner, now awake to his surroundings, noticed his approach, and civilly, all but cheerfully, welcomed him. But it was to little purpose that in the interview following the good man sought to bring Billy Budd to some godly understanding that he must die, and at dawn. True, Billy himself freely referred to his death as a thing close at hand; but it was something in the way that children will refer to death in general, who yet among their other sports will play a funeral with hearse and mourners. Not that like children Billy was incapable of conceiving what death really is. No, but he was wholly without irrational fear of it, a fear more prevalent in highly civilised communities than those so-called barbarous ones which in all respects stand nearer to unadulterate nature. And, as elsewhere said, a barbarian Billy radically was; quite as much so (for all the costume) as his countrymen the British captives, living trophies made to march in the Roman triumph of Germanicus. Quite as much so as those later barbarians, young men probably, and picked specimens among the earlier British converts to Christianity, at least nominally such, and taken to Rome (as today converts from lesser isles of the sea may be taken to London), of whom the pope of that time, admiring the strangeness of their personal beauty, so unlike the Italian stamp, their clear, ruddy complexions and curled flaxen locks, exclaimed, 'Angles' (meaning *English*, the modern derivative), 'Angles do you call them? And is it because they look so like Angels?' Had it been later in time one would think that the pope had in mind Fra Angelico's seraphs, some of whom, plucking apples in gardens of Hesperides, have the faint rosebud complexion of the more beautiful English girls.

21

If in vain the good chaplain sought to impress the young barbarian with ideas of death akin to those conveyed in the skull, dial and crossbones on old tombstones; equally futile to all appearance were his efforts to bring home to him the thought of salvation and a Saviour. Billy listened, but less out of awe or reverence, perhaps, than from a certain natural politeness; doubtless at bottom regarding all that in much the same way that most mariners of his class take any discourse, abstract or out of the common tone of the workaday world. And this sailor way of taking clerical discourse is not wholly unlike the way in which the pioneer of Christianity, full of transcendent miracles, was received long ago on tropic isles by any superior 'savage' so called – a Tahitian, say, of Captain Cook's time or shortly after that time. Out of natural courtesy he received but did not appreciate. It was like a gift placed in the palm of an outstretched hand upon which the fingers do not close.

But the *Indomitable*'s chaplain was a discreet man possessing the good sense of a good heart. So he insisted not on his vocation here. At the instance of Captain Vere, a lieutenant had apprised him of pretty much everything as to Billy; and since he felt that innocence was even a better thing than religion wherewith to go to judgment, he reluctantly withdrew; but in his emotion not without first performing an act strange enough in an Englishman, and under the circumstances yet more so in any regular priest. Stooping over, he kissed on the fair cheek his fellow-man, a felon in martial law, one who, though in the confines of death, he felt he could never convert to a dogma; nor for all that did he fear for his future.

Marvel not that having been made acquainted with the young sailor's essential innocence, the worthy man lifted not a finger to avert the doom of such a martyr to martial discipline. So to do would not only have been as idle as invoking the desert, but would also have been an audacious transgression of the bounds of his function, one as exactly prescribed to him by military law as that of the boatswain or any other naval officer. Bluntly put, a chaplain is the minister of the Prince of Peace serving in the host of the god of war – Mars. As such, he is as incongruous as a musket would be on the altar at Christmas. Why, then, is he there? Because he indirectly subserves the purpose attested by the cannon; because, too, he lends the sanction of the religion of the meek to that which practically is the abrogation of everything but force.*

22

The night so luminous on the spar-deck (otherwise on the cavernous ones below – levels so like the tiered galleries in a coal-mine) passed away. Like the prophet in the chariot disappearing in heaven and dropping his mantle to Elisha, the withdrawing night transferred its pale robe to the peeping day. A meek, shy light appeared in the east, where stretched a diaphanous fleece of white furrowed vapour. That light slowly waxed. Suddenly one bell was

* There is an author's note in the margin of the manuscript reading: 'An irruption of heretic thought hard to suppress.'

struck aft, responded to by one louder metallic stroke from forward. It was four o'clock in the morning. Instantly the silver whistles were heard summoning all hands to witness punishment. Up through the great hatchway, rimmed with racks of heavy shot, the watch-below came pouring, overspreading with the watch already on deck the space between the mainmast and foremast, including that occupied by the capacious launch and the black booms tiered on either side of it, boat and booms making a summit of observation for the powder-boys and younger tars. A different group comprising one watch of topmen leaned over the side of the rail of that sea-balcony, no small one in a seventy-four, looking down on the crowd below. Man or boy, none spake but in whispers, and few spake at all. Captain Vere – as before, the central figure among the assembled commissioned officers – stood nigh the break of the poop-deck, facing forward. Just below him on the quarter-deck the marines in full equipment were drawn up much as at the scene of the promulgated sentence.

At sea in the old time, the execution by halter of a military sailor was generally from the fore-yard. In the present instance, for special reasons, the main-yard was assigned. Under an arm of that yard the prisoner was presently brought up, the chaplain attending him. It was noted at the time, and remarked upon afterwards, that in this final scene the good man evinced little or nothing of the perfunctory. Brief speech indeed he had with the condemned one, but the genuine Gospel was less on his tongue than in his aspect and manner towards him. The final preparations personal to the latter being speedily brought to an end by two boatswain's-mates, the consummation impended. Billy stood facing aft. At the penultimate moment, his words, his only ones, words wholly unobstructed in the utterance, were these – 'God bless Captain Vere!' Syllables so unanticipated coming from one with the ignominious hemp about his neck – a conventional felon's benediction directed aft towards the quarters of honour; syllables which, delivered in the clear melody of a singing-bird on the point of launching from the twig, had a phenomenal effect, not unenhanced by the rare personal beauty of the young sailor, spiritualised now through late experiences so poignantly profound.

Without volition, as it were, as if indeed the ship's populace were the vehicles of some vocal current-electric, with one voice, from alow and aloft, came a resonant echo – 'God bless Captain Vere!' And yet at that instant Billy alone must have been in their hearts, even as he was in their eyes.

At the pronounced words and the spontaneous echo that voluminously resounded them, Captain Vere, either through stoic self-control or a sort of momentary paralysis induced by emotional shock, stood erectly rigid as a musket in the ship-armourer's rack.

The hill, deliberately recovering from the periodic roll to leeward, was just regaining an even keel, when the last signal, the preconcerted dumb one, was given. At the same moment it chanced that the vapoury fleece hanging low in the east was shot through with a soft glory as of the fleece of the Lamb of God seen in mystical vision, and simultaneously therewith, watched by the wedged mass of upturned faces, Billy ascended; and ascending, took the full rose of the dawn.

In the pinioned figure, arrived at the yard-end, to the wonder of all, no motion was apparent save that created by the slow roll of the hull, in moderate weather so majestic in a great ship heavy-cannoned.

A digression

When some days afterwards in reference to the singularity just mentioned, the purser, a rather ruddy, rotund person, more accurate as an accountant than profound as a philosopher, said at mess to the surgeon, 'What testimony to the force lodged in will-power,' the latter, spare and tall, one in whom a discreet causticity went along with a manner less genial than polite, replied, 'Your pardon, Mr Purser. In a hanging scientifically conducted – and under special orders I myself directed how Budd's was to be effected – any movement following the completed suspension and originating in the body suspended, such movement indicates mechanical spasm in the muscular system. Hence the absence of that is no more attributable to will-power, as you call it, than to horse-power – begging your pardon.'

'But this muscular spasm you speak of, is not that in a degree more or less invariable in these cases?'

'Assuredly so, Mr Purser.'

'How then, my good sir, do you account for its absence in this instance?'

'Mr Purser, it is clear that your sense of the singularity in this matter equals not mine. You account for it by what you call will-power, a term not yet included in the lexicon of science. For me I do not with my present knowledge pretend to account for it at all. Even should one assume the hypothesis that at the first touch of the halyards the action of Budd's heart, intensified by extraordinary emotion at its climax, abruptly stopped – much like a watch when in carelessly winding it up you strain at the finish, thus snapping the chain – even under that hypothesis how account for the phenomenon that followed?'

'You admit, then, that the absence of spasmodic movement was phenomenal?'

'It was phenomenal, Mr Purser, in the sense that it was an appearance, the cause of which is not immediately to be assigned.'

'But tell me, my dear sir,' pertinaciously continued the other, 'was the man's death effected by the halter, or was it a species of euthanasia?'

'Euthanasia, Mr Purser, is something like your will-power; I doubt its authenticity as a scientific term – begging your pardon again. It is at once imaginative and metaphysical – in short, Greek. But,' abruptly changing his tone, 'there is a case in the sick-bay that I do not care to leave to my assistants. Beg your pardon, but excuse me.' And rising from the mess he formally withdrew.

23

The silence at the moment of execution, and for a moment or two continuing thereafter, but emphasised by the regular wash of the sea against the hull, or the flutter of a sail caused by the helmsman's eyes being tempted astray, this emphasised silence was gradually disturbed by a sound not easily to be verbally rendered. Whoever has heard the freshet-wave of a torrent suddenly swelled by pouring showers in tropical mountains, showers not shared by the plain; whoever has heard the first muffled murmur of its sloping advance through precipitous woods, may form some conception of the sound now heard. The seeming remoteness of its source was because of its murmurous indistinctness, since it came from close by, even from the men massed on the ship's open deck. Being inarticulate, it was dubious in significance further than it seemed to indicate some capricious revulsion of thought or feeling such as mobs ashore are liable to, in the present instance possibly implying a sullen revocation on the men's part of their involuntary echoing of Billy's benediction. But ere the murmur had time to wax into clamour it was met by a strategic command, the more telling that it came with abrupt unexpectedness.

'Pipe down the starboard watch, boatswain, and see that they go.'

Shrill as the shriek of the sea-hawk the whistles of the boatswain and his mates pierced that ominous low sound, dissipating it; and yielding to the mechanism of discipline the throng was thinned by one half. For the remainder, most of them were set to temporary employments connected with trimming the yards and so forth, business readily to be found upon occasion by any officer-of-the-deck.

Now each proceeding that follows a mortal sentence pronounced at sea by a drumhead court is characterised by promptitude not perceptibly merging into hurry, though bordering that. The hammock, the one which had been Billy's bed when alive, having already been ballasted with shot, and otherwise prepared to serve for his canvas coffin, the last office of the sea-undertakers, the sailmaker's mates, was now speedily completed. When everything was in readiness a second call for all hands, made necessary by the strategic movement before mentioned, was sounded, and now to witness burial.

The details of this closing formality it needs not to give. But when the tilted plank let slide its freight into the sea, a second strange human murmur was heard, blended now with another inarticulate sound proceeding from certain larger sea-fowl, who, their attention having been attracted by the peculiar commotion in the water resulting from the heavy sloped dive of the shotted hammock into the sea, flew screaming to the spot. So near the hull did they come that the stridor or bony creak of their gaunt double-jointed pinions was audible. As the ship under light airs passed on, leaving the burial spot astern, they still kept circling it low down with the moving shadow of their outstretched wings and the croaked requiem of their cries.

Upon sailors as superstitious as those of the age preceding ours, man-of-war's men, too, who had just beheld the prodigy of repose in the form suspended in air and now floundering in the deeps; to such mariners the action of the sea-fowl, though dictated by mere animal greed for prey, was big with no prosaic significance. An uncertain movement began among them, in which some encroachment was made. It was tolerated but for a moment. For suddenly the drum beat to quarters, which familiar sound happening at least twice every day, had upon the present occasion a signal peremptoriness in it. True martial discipline long continued superinduces in the average man a sort of impulse of docility whose operation at the official tone of command much resembles in its promptitude the effect of an instinct.

The drumbeat dissolved the multitude, distributing most of them along the batteries of the two covered gun-decks. There, as wont, the gun crews stood by their respective cannon, erect and silent. In due course the first officer, sword under arm and standing in his place on the quarter-deck, formally received the successive reports of the sworded lieutenants commanding the sections of batteries below; the last of which reports being made, the summed report he delivered with the customary salute to the commander. All this occupied time, which in the present case was the object of beating to quarters at any hour prior to the customary one. That such variance from usage was authorised by an officer like Captain Vere, a martinet as some deemed him, was evidence of the necessity for unusual action implied in what he deemed to be temporarily the mood of his men. 'With mankind,' he would say, 'forms, measured forms, are everything; and that is the import couched in the story of Orpheus with his lyre spellbinding the wild denizens of the woods.' And this he once applied to the disruption of forms going on across the Channel and the consequences thereof.

At this unwonted muster at quarters all proceeded as at the regular hour. The band on the quarter-deck played a sacred air. After which the chaplain went through the customary morning service. That done, the drum beat the retreat, and toned by music and religious rites subserving the discipline and purpose of war, the men in their wonted orderly manner dispersed to the places allotted them when not at the guns.

And now it was full day. The fleece of low-hanging vapour had vanished, licked up by the sun that late had so glorified it. And the circumambient air in the clearness of its serenity was like smooth white marble in the polished block not yet removed from the marble-dealer's yard.

24

The symmetry of form attainable in pure fiction cannot so readily be achieved in a narration essentially having less to do with fable than with fact. Truth uncompromisingly told will always have its ragged edges; hence the conclusion of such a narration is apt to be less finished than an architectural finial.

How it fared with the Handsome Sailor during the year of the Great Mutiny has been faithfully given. But though properly the story ends with his life, something in way of sequel will not be amiss. Three brief chapters will suffice.

In the general re-christening under the Directory of the craft originally forming the navy of the French monarchy, the *St Louis* line-of-battle ship was named the *Athéiste*. Such a name, like some other substituted ones in the Revolutionary fleet, while proclaiming the infidel audacity of the ruling power, was yet, though not so intended to be, the aptest name, if one consider it, ever given to a warship; far more so indeed than the *Devastation*, the *Erebus* (the Hell) and similar names bestowed upon fighting-ships.

On the return passage to the English fleet from the detached cruise during which occurred the events already recorded, the *Indomitable* fell in with the *Athéiste*. An engagement ensued, during which Captain Vere, in the act of putting his ship alongside the enemy with a view of throwing his boarders across the bulwarks, was hit by a musket-ball from a port-hole of the enemy's main cabin. More than disabled, he dropped to the deck and was carried below to the same cock-pit where some of his men already lay. The senior lieutenant took command. Under him the enemy was finally captured, and though much crippled, was by rare good fortune successfully taken into Gibraltar, an English port not very distant from the scene of the fight. There Captain Vere with the rest of the wounded was put ashore. He lingered for some days, but the end came. Unhappily he was cut off too early for the Nile and Trafalgar. The spirit that despite its philosophic austerity may yet have indulged in the most secret of all passions, ambition, never attained to the fullness of fame.

Not long before death, while lying under the influence of that magical drug which, soothing the physical frame, mysteriously operates on the subtler element in man, he was heard to murmur words inexplicable to his attendant – 'Billy Budd, Billy Budd.' That these were not the accents of remorse would seem clear from what the attendant said to the *Indomitable*'s senior officer of marines, who, as the most reluctant to condemn of the members of the drumhead court, too well knew, though here he kept the knowledge to himself, who Billy Budd was.

25

Some few weeks after the execution, among other matters under the head of *News from the Mediterranean*, there appeared in a naval chronicle of the time, an authorised weekly publication, an account of the affair. It was doubtless for the most part written in good faith, though the medium, partly rumour, through which the facts must have reached the writer, served to deflect, and in part falsify them. Because it appeared in a publication now long ago superannuated and forgotten, and is all that hitherto has stood in human record to attest what manner of men respectively were John Claggart and Billy Budd, it is here reproduced.

On the tenth of the last month a deplorable occurrence took place on board HMS *Indomitable*. John Claggart, the ship's master-at-arms, discovering that some sort of plot was incipient among an inferior section of the ship's company, and that the ringleader was one William Budd, he, Claggart, in the act of arraigning the man before the captain was vindictively stabbed to the heart by the suddenly drawn sheath-knife of Budd.

The deed and the implement employed sufficiently suggest that though mustered into the service under an English name the assassin was no Englishman, but one of those aliens adopting an English cognomen whom the present extraordinary necessities of the service have caused to be admitted into it in considerable numbers.

The enormity of the crime and the extreme depravity of the criminal, appear the greater in view of the character of the victim, a middle-aged man, respectable and discreet, belonging to that minor official grade, the petty officers, upon whom, as none know better than the commissioned gentlemen, the efficiency of His Majesty's navy so largely depends. His function was a responsible one; at once onerous and thankless, and his fidelity in it the greater because of his strong patriotic impulse. In this instance, as in so many other instances in these days, the character of the unfortunate man signally refutes, if refutation were needed, that peevish saying attributed to Dr Johnson that patriotism is the last refuge of a scoundrel.

The criminal paid the penalty of his crime. The promptitude of the punishment has proved salutary. Nothing amiss is now apprehended aboard HMS *Indomitable*.*

---

* An author's note, crossed out, here appears in the original manuscript. It reads: 'Here ends a story not unwarranted by what happens in this incongruous world of ours – innocence and infirmity, spiritual depravity and fair respite.'

26

Everything is for a season remarkable in navies. Any tangible object associated with some striking incident of the service is converted into a monument. The spar from which the foretopman was suspended was for some few years kept trace of by the bluejackets. Then knowledge followed it from ship to dockyard and again from dockyard to ship, still pursuing it even when at last reduced to a mere dockyard boom. To them a chip of it was as a piece of the Cross. Ignorant though they were of the real facts of the happening and not thinking but that the penalty was unavoidably inflicted from the naval point of view, for all that they instinctively felt that Billy was a sort of man as incapable of mutiny as of wilful murder. They recalled the fresh young image of the Handsome Sailor, that face never deformed by a sneer or subtler vile freak of the heart within! This impression of him was doubtless deepened by the fact that he was gone and in a measure mysteriously gone. On the gun decks of the *Indomitable*, the general estimate of his nature and its unconscious simplicity eventually found rude utterance from another foretopman, one of his own watch, gifted, as some sailors are, with an artless poetic temperament. The tarry hands made some lines, which, after circulating among the shipboard crew for a while, finally got rudely printed at Portsmouth as a ballad. The title given to it was the sailor's.

Billy in the Darbies

Good of the chaplain to enter Lone Bay
And down on his marrow-bones here and pray
For the likes just o' me, Billy Budd. – But look:
Through the port comes the moonshine astray!
It tips the guard's cutlass and silvers this nook;
But 'twill die in the dawning of Billy's last day.
A jewel-block they'll make of me tomorrow,
Pendant pearl from the yard-arm-end,
Like the ear-drop I gave to Bristol Molly –
Oh, 'tis me, not the sentence, they'll suspend.
Aye, aye, all is up; and I must up, too,
Early in the morning, aloft from alow.
On an empty stomach, now, never it would do.
They'll give me a nibble – bit o' biscuit ere I go.

Sure, a messmate will reach me the last parting cup;
But turning heads away from the hoist and the belay,
Heaven knows who will have the running of me up!
No pipe to those halyards – but aren't it all sham?
A blur's in my eyes; it is dreaming that I am.
A hatchet to my panzer? all adrift to go?
The drumroll to grog, and Billy never know?
But Donald he has promised to stand by the plank;
So I'll shake a friendly hand ere I sink.
But – no! It is dead then I'll be, come to think.
I remember Taff the Welshman when he sank,
And his cheek it was like the budding pink.
But me, they'll lash me in a hammock, drop me deep
Fathoms down, fathoms down, how I'll dream fast asleep.
I feel it stealing now. Sentry, are you there?
Just ease these darbies at the wrist,
And roll me over fair.
I am sleepy, and the oozy weeds about me twist.

END OF BOOK

April 19, 1891